VANISHED

Dr. Ally Simbert

CONTENTS

CHAPTER 1: UNCOVERING THE TRUTH

Sitting at the breakfast table, Curtis Styles gazed at the front page of the local newspaper, his face etched with deep perplexity. "Another young woman vanishes without a trace," he replied to his wife, Katherine, who had inquired about his troubled expression. "That makes it the fourth disappearance in less than a year!"

"It's incredibly frightening," Katherine responded, her expression downcast. "Who is she?"

"They skip her name. Just that a local young woman left her house for a jog at four o'clock on Monday afternoon and hasn't been seen or heard from since. It's been nearly two days," he replied ruefully.

"They probably don't want to release personal details just yet, especially considering how recent it is. They're likely hoping she will turn up with a perfectly logical explanation for her absence. You know how the younger generation can be," Katherine stated thoughtfully.

"Damn irresponsible journalism, if you ask me," Curtis bluntly replied.

Observing Katherine's furrowed brows, Curtis recognized the telltale signs of her concern. It was no secret that she worried about him getting involved in these cases.

Having spent his entire career as an investigative journalist, Curtis would readily admit that he pursued leads with the abandonment of someone with no family responsibilities. At times, his recklessness almost had resulted in tragic consequences.

Although now retired, he was hard-wired not to ignore this situation, especially when it involved his community.

Gently, Katherine said, "The police will solve this. We just need to have faith that it will happen soon."

He looked at her with a determined expression. "I wish I could let it go, Katherine, but I feel compelled to do something."

"No!" She fired back at him. "Those days are behind you. Leave it to the professionals whose job it is to solve these cases."

"Four missing women, Katherine! When do we stop turning a blind eye and start taking action as a community?" Curtis argued, his agitation rising. "Maybe I can reach out to my old sources from my reporting days. Someone might know something."

"Curtis, have you considered that maybe the authorities don't want your help? We're all worried, but now is not the time for you to embark on a personal crusade," she said firmly, adding, "Don't say it because the answer is no."

With that, she turned on her heels and promptly left the room.

Glancing back at his newspaper, Curtis couldn't help but smile ruefully. Katherine, he knew, was not one to back down. She had been a strong parental figure to their two children, Parker and Jennifer.

Now in their late thirties, he was grateful that she had provided unwavering guidance while he had been so focused on building his career as a reporter.

"Oh well," he said aloud to himself, "I better get back to the gardening. Those hedges won't trim themselves."

Just as he was about to head out into the backyard, he heard the phone ring. Katherine answered it and suddenly exclaimed, "Oh, Jane, I'm so sorry! It's going to be alright. They will find her."

Frozen in place, a sense of foreboding washed over Curtis. He knew it was a harbinger of bad things to come.

He listened to the soothing tones of his wife's voice as she tried to comfort the person on the other end of the line. It must be Jane Thomas, he thought, as she was the only Jane he knew associated with Katherine.

He remembered Jane Thomas, twenty years younger than Katherine, who had been a loyal and supportive friend to his wife. Since meeting at a local book club a few years ago, Jane has been a pillar of strength whenever Katherine needs it.

As Katherine hurried back into the kitchen after ending the call, Curtis could immediately sense her distress. Her face had turned pale, and she looked visibly shaken. He approached her gently and pulled her into an embrace, concern etched across his face.

"What happened, Katherine?" Curtis inquired; his voice filled with worry.

Katherine met his gaze, her voice trembling with fear, as she revealed the unsettling news. "It's Jane's daughter, Chloe. She's the young woman who went missing on Monday night. Jane is completely distraught. Oh my God, Curtis!

Chloe has vanished!"

In the days that followed, Curtis and Katherine decided to take a break from their worries and embarked on a journey. The married couple set out on a road trip through the picturesque landscapes of Vermont. During the trip, they reminisced about their past, from their first encounter in London to their marriage and their move from South Africa to California. They also fondly recalled their discovery of Erinsdale in Vermont, a place they had envisioned as their retirement destination. However, their trip held a somber purpose: they were determined to investigate the disappearance of the young woman.

With determination, they diligently searched for their dream home in Vermont. By the time Curtis celebrated his sixtieth birthday, they had found and settled into their ideal property. Their new house afforded them daily views of the beauty of life in a charming community that spanned four interconnected towns, from Erinsdale to Stratford. Curtis considered this place their own paradise.

As the road trip came to an end, Katherine's voice broke the silence. "Curtis, we've arrived!" she exclaimed. Curtis refocused his attention and noticed their house's front door swinging open. A figure, consumed by fear, sprinted towards their car. Curtis realized that this was it—the nightmare was about to begin.

Jane Thomas, with a heavy heart, poured out her anguish at the dining room table. She shared the agonizing 48-hour journey from the moment she sensed something was amiss with her daughter to the torturous minutes she spent awaiting news about her.

Her voice trembled with sorrow as she uttered, "She shouldn't have been here, you know. It was her father's fiftieth birthday last Saturday. With looming exams, she had planned to stay at college and celebrate with us during her semester break, which was still a month away." Jane exhaled deeply, grappling with her overwhelming emotions.

Tears welled up in her eyes as she continued, "But out of the blue, on Friday, she surprised us by showing up, unable to resist being with her father on his special day. She had arranged for a ride back to college on Wednesday."

Overwhelmed, Jane's tears cascaded down her cheeks, seeking solace in her friend Katherine's comforting arm. "We'll find her, Jane. There must be a logical explanation," Katherine reassured, her voice gentle and consoling.

"Logical?" Jane's voice quivered with a mix of fear and frustration. "How

does someone vanish into thin air while jogging on a sunny afternoon in a supposedly safe neighborhood?"

Curtis, observing his wife's less-than-optimistic facade, couldn't help but
sense the weight of their shared concerns. But what more could be said in times
like these?

He spoke up, offering comfort, "Jane, I'm deeply sorry for what you're going through. The police are undoubtedly doing everything they can to locate
Chloe."

Jane turned her gaze toward Curtis, her eyes filled with desperation. "Are
they truly doing everything? And what about those other missing girls? Have
they made any progress?"

Her face tightened as she continued, her resolve intensifying, "I can't just
sit idly by, waiting for answers. This is my daughter, Curtis!"

Curtis attempted to pacify her, struggling to find the right words. "There
could be other reasons why she hasn't returned home yet. Until we know more,
we must try to hold onto optimism."

Jane's response was resolute, "Well, I can't just wait and hope. Curtis, will
you help me?"

Perplexed, Curtis confessed, "Me? I'm not a police officer or a private investigator. What could I possibly do?"

Jane pleaded earnestly, "You were a crime reporter once, Curtis. You must
have connections, people who might have information. Please, I don't know
where else to turn."

Curtis remembered Katherine's warning about staying away from the disappearances. He looked at his wife, expecting her to dissuade Jane.

To his surprise, she said, "Of course he will, Jane. Before you called, we
had been talking about these girls, and I had suggested he do some digging himself."

Sarcastically, Curtis thought to himself, that's exactly how it happened.
Aloud, he conceded, "I'll see what I can uncover. However, I advise considering
the possibility of hiring a private investigator if you're uncomfortable relying
solely on the police. I know someone who might be of assistance. But let me dig
deeper first."

"Even though the temptation is strong, we need to keep a clear perspective,"
he advised carefully. "It's been forty-eight hours since anyone saw her, and

leaping to conclusions too soon could prove risky. It's natural to be concerned, but let's also be cautious."

Jane clutched Curtis's hand firmly, her appreciation evident. "Thank you so, so much!"

Feeling uneasy with Jane's firm grip, Curtis studied her, sensing her strength despite her small, unassuming appearance. Grief had transformed her, revealing the power it could unearth in someone.

The journey back home was marked by a somber silence, contrasting the earlier effortless conversation. An air of solemnity hung in the car, affecting Curtis deeply.

He turned to Katherine, seeking reassurance amidst his doubts. "Are you sure you want me to get involved?" He questioned; his voice laden with caution.

"Absolutely," Katherine affirmed, her response unwavering. "Otherwise, I wouldn't have suggested it."

"You do realize the outcome might not be favorable?" Curtis pressed further, before admitting, "I wanted to delve into this earlier during our conversation, but now it's personal, especially for you. Once I start digging, it will be difficult to stop until we find answers."

Meeting his gaze head-on, Katherine's eyes held a resolute determination. "I know, and that's precisely why we must seek those answers. It's personal. Chloe is my best friend's daughter. It could have just as easily been our own."

Curtis acknowledged Katherine's determination and felt the weight of responsibility he had taken on. After their discussion with Jane, they couldn't shake the mystery of Chloe's disappearance. They were at the White Horse Inn, awaiting a rendezvous in their quest for answers.

Retired police chief Paul Harlow, formerly of the Montpelier Police Department, entered the cozy bar of the White Horse Inn with purpose. He spotted a familiar face in the far corner and greeted him warmly, exclaiming, "Styles, my friend! It's been far too long."

Curtis rose from his seat, offering a firm handshake. "Harlow, you're absolutely right. Time slips away."

Curtis marveled at Harlow's imposing stature and determination, which had earned him respect and a reputation for reverence.

Offering a drink, Curtis asked, "What can I get you, Harlow?" Harlow requested bourbon, emphasizing the importance of their discussion.

Returning with the drinks, Curtis mentioned his preference for whiskey, to which Harlow nodded approvingly. Curtis then got to the point, seeking Harlow's insight on the four missing young women.

Harlow, surprised, fixed his gaze on Curtis, his no-nonsense demeanor in place.

"I thought you were retired, Styles! Do you miss it so much that you've taken up freelance investigations?"

"No, I'm truly retired. But the latest missing girl, Chloe Thomas, happens to be the daughter of Katherine's closest friend. I made a promise to look into it," Curtis explained, his commitment evident. "I simply want to do what I can to assist."

Harlow held his gaze, pondering the situation. "You know, Styles, I knew it was a mistake to retire near you. I even told my wife," He chuckled. "Alright, let's be candid. The police are at a loss, as you've likely heard.

I won't delve into the specifics of each disappearance, assuming you've read up on them," Harlow continued, his voice laden with gravity. "They've involved the FBI, but it's been one dead end after another. Frustrating, to say the least."

"In my opinion," Harlow continued, "we're likely looking at human trafficking or a serial killer. And as for where they'll be found? Most likely buried deep in the woods. Look at the vast countryside. From here to Stratford, it's a sea of woodlands. Perfect for hiding the darkest secrets."

"I wish I had more to offer, my friend, but the accounts provide little to go on. Nevertheless, I'll give you something," Harlow added, his sincerity palpable. "There's a fellow named Tom Haddonfield, a private investigator who recently set up shop in Big Bear Falls. He's a city slicker type, hired by one of the victims' parents. If anyone has fresh leads, it'd be him. I can get you his contact information."

"Have you met him?" Curtis inquired. "Since he's in your area..."

"Briefly, at the Falls Hotel. Comes off rather pompous, if you ask me. The 'I' in 'PI' is there for a reason, after all," Harlow's voice dripped with disdain. "Glory hunters, the lot of them."

Curtis nodded, remembering Harlow's skepticism towards private investigators. "You've never been fond of them," Curtis replied. "But how did you come across this information? Your ear is always to the ground."

Harlow smirked a glint of mischief in his eyes. "My sources run deep, my friend."

Curtis raised an eyebrow, intrigued. "Surely there must be someone within the force who would be willing to share information with me instead."

Harlow's expression grew serious. "Styles, the police won't talk to you. They've developed a distrust for reporters, especially now that they find themselves facing a barrage of questions without answers," he explained. "But Haddonfield is your best shot at finding something. Just make sure you have a good reason to reach out to him, or he might see it as meddling in his affairs."

Harlow glanced at his watch, a reminder of his impending departure. "I need to go, Styles. Always a pleasure sharing a lunchtime drink with you. The wife is waiting at the shops across the road. No drinking and driving, as I always say. Are you being picked up?"

Curtis smiled up at his towering friend. "Indeed, the wife will be here shortly after I give her a call. Ever the law-abiding citizen."

With a final warm handshake, the two men bid each other farewell.

As Harlow turned to leave, he called back, his voice echoing in the bar, "I'll send you that number, Styles! Stay safe!"

On the short drive home, Curtis's mind whirled with the limited information Harlow had shared. Then, a spark of inspiration ignited within him.

Hastily exiting the car as Katherine pulled into the driveway, Curtis exclaimed, "I just need to do something in my study quickly, and then we can have lunch, honey."

Settling behind the desk in his study, Curtis retrieved a notepad and began to write:

Jemma Anderson, aged 23, employed as a beer representative, vanished following a night spent at The Stables Lodge in Stratford. She departed at approximately 2 a.m. with the intention of returning to her bed and breakfast, situated 1.5 miles away, on June 28, 2018.

Sophie Hunt, a 25-year-old woman employed, vanished after enjoying drinks with a friend at The White Horse Inn in Erinsdale. After escorting her friend safely home, she had only a short 300-yard journey left to reach her own house. Regrettably, she never arrived, and this occurred on September 15th, 2018.

Gabriella Atkins, an 18-year-old receptionist, went missing after

Having finished jotting down the notes, Curtis shut the notepad and placed it aside. He then reached for his mobile and scrolled through his contacts until he located the desired name. After pressing the dial button, he patiently waited for an answer.

"Hello, Richard Smith speaking," the voice from the other end of the line greeted.

"Richard, it's Curtis Styles. I have a proposition for you," Curtis began, his voice brimming with determination.

During their leisurely lunch, Curtis and Katherine chatted about Curtis's recent talks with Paul Harlow and Richard Smith. Katherine, with a touch of worry in her voice, asked, "Are you sure it's a good idea to take on that freelance writing gig? It sounds risky!"

Curtis leaned in, explaining, "I needed a legitimate excuse to meet Haddonfield. He's a private investigator who will scrutinize every detail. Richard Smith's platform is highly respected and can get Haddonfield's attention. Harlow thinks the police won't cooperate, so this might be our best shot at making progress on these cases."

Curtis received a message on his phone and shared with Katherine that Harlow had sent him Haddonfield's contact number.

After lunch, Curtis dialed the number and patiently waited as it rang. Just when he feared it would go to voicemail, a voice answered, "Hello, Haddonfield speaking."

"Hello, is this Tom Haddonfield?" Curtis asked.

"The one and only, pal! How can I help you?"

Haddonfield replied. "I'm Curtis Styles from Erinsdale. I have information about the missing women that might interest you. Could we meet up?" Curtis proposed.

"Hmm... How did you get my number, and why do you think I'd be interested?" Haddonfield questioned; his voice laced with suspicion.

"I recently discussed the case with my friend, Paul Harlow. He's a retired police officer and mentioned your name in connection with the investigation. As a concerned citizen, I feel obligated to help.

I've stumbled upon something that could be significant or nothing at all, but I believe it's my duty to share," Curtis explained.

Haddonfield seemed satisfied, his voice softer, "Look, I don't know this Harlow character, but let's meet and see if your information holds any weight. Are you familiar with The Falls Hotel in Big Bear?"

"I know it well," Curtis replied.

"Is one o'clock tomorrow convenient for you?" Haddonfield asked. "That would be perfect!" Curtis confirmed.

"See you tomorrow then," Haddonfield replied, and the call ended.

Curtis gazed at himself in the hallway mirror, uttering softly, "This man exudes an enormous ego. I just need to stroke it, old boy!"

Glancing at his wristwatch, Curtis noted the time—twelve forty-five PM. "Excellent, I'll be there in less than ten minutes," he muttered aloud.

Entering the bar of The Falls Hotel, Curtis admired the rich, mahogany interior. Scanning the room, his eyes settled on a man seated at a table, dressed in a bright yellow floral shirt and sporting a black flat cap. Curtis also noticed the man's eye-catching red and navy checked pants.

"That must be him," Curtis thought, unable to resist a mental quip, *"Only a guy with a massive ego would go into public dressed like a clown!"*

Approaching the table, Curtis asked, "Tom Haddonfield?"

"In the flesh, pal. Curtis Styles, I presume?"

Following a brief exchange of pleasantries, Curtis requested a soft drink and settled into his seat. Haddonfield arched an eyebrow, inquiring if Curtis abstained from alcohol, to which Curtis responded that he preferred to stay sober for driving.

Haddonfield, curious, inquired about the information Curtis mentioned earlier. Curtis clarified that it was more of a proposal, and Haddonfield leaned forward, asking about the nature of the proposal.

Curtis clarified that he had a feeling Haddonfield might require some information before agreeing to meet with him. Haddonfield expressed frustration, emphasizing that time was money and that their meeting so far had been a waste.

Curtis earnestly requested ten minutes of Haddonfield's time and promised that if what he shared didn't pique Haddonfield's interest, he would never contact him again.

After pondering briefly, Haddonfield reluctantly agreed to hear Curtis out. Curtis then began explaining his plan to write an opinion piece from a private investigator's perspective, inspired by Paul Harlow's suggestion.

Haddonfield raised concerns about potential damage to his reputation, considering the ongoing unsolved cases. Curtis argued that the risk was worth taking, given the national attention the cases were receiving, and added, "They say there's no such thing as bad publicity."

"That's fine. Before we conclude, I want to emphasize that this is a promising opportunity for you, Tom," Curtis stated, pulling out a pen and notebook from his jacket pocket. After jotting something down, he tore out the page and handed it to Tom Haddonfield. "My number, in case you haven't saved it on your phone."

With that, the meeting seemed to end, and the two parted ways with a brief handshake. Climbing back into his car, Curtis switched on the engine, wearing a satisfied, wry smile. The bait has been cast! He thought to himself. And with that, he headed home.

As days turned into a week since Curtis and Tom Haddonfield's first meeting, the initial anticipation had given way to a sense of disappointment. Curtis, feeling a growing impatience and frustration at the lack of contact from Haddonfield, turned to Katherine and shared his thoughts, "I thought offering him free publicity would reel him in. Looks like I'll have to tackle this on my own. Oh well, you know what they say about trying..."

Katherine, perceptive as ever, observed Curtis's unease and offered her support as they discussed their next steps. Just as Curtis was about to complete the cliché, the doorbell rang, interrupting him. Katherine rose from her chair and went to answer it.

Opening the door, she politely asked, "Hello, can I help you?"

A voice replied, "Hi, I'm Tom Haddonfield. I hope I've got the right address. Does Curtis Styles live here?"

Thinking quickly, Curtis picked up a magazine and pretended to read, silently urging himself, "Stay calm, Curtis! Don't appear too eager."

As Tom Haddonfield entered the room, Curtis placed the magazine back on the table and appraised the figure before him. Mid-forties, around six foot four, with a charming boyish face, athletic build, and tousled blond hair. He seemed like someone who belonged on a beach with a surfboard under his arm.

What struck Curtis most was Haddonfield's transformation. Gone were the ridiculous pants and overly bright top, replaced by a crisp white collared shirt, trendy waistcoat, and expensive jeans. His black leather shoes spoke of refined tastes.

A man of many faces, Curtis stood up extended a hand, and greeted. "Hello, Tom!"

After shaking hands, Haddonfield joked, "I told you not to waste your time waiting for the phone to ring."

Curtis replied somewhat sarcastically, "Indeed you did!"

Haddonfield politely asked, "Is there somewhere we can talk privately?"

"Sure, we can go to my study," Curtis responded, turning to Katherine. "You don't mind, do you, honey? It won't take long."

"Take all the time you need," Katherine sweetly replied.

Seated on opposite sides of the desk in Curtis's study, Haddonfield spoke first, "As I'm about to say this, I know I'll regret it, but let's give this 'partnership' a trial run. I have conditions, though."

With his earlier thoughts in mind, Curtis asked in a measured tone, "Okay, what are your conditions?"

"Firstly, we'll give it a week or two, and if it's not working, we call it quits. Secondly, I'm the professional investigator here, so I lead all the interviews. Can we agree on that?"

"Agreed!" Curtis promptly replied.

"I have some personal matters to attend to today, but we can meet at my place tomorrow to discuss the way forward. I'll text you the directions later."

"That works," Curtis acknowledged.

"Until tomorrow, then," said Tom Haddonfield.

As Curtis walked him to the door, he said with optimism, "I have a good feeling about this."

Haddonfield responded, "For the sake of these missing women, I hope you're right, pal!"

Returning to the living room, Curtis chuckled to see Katherine had promptly returned.

"Curiosity and women, inseparable. Like two peas in a pod," he thought to

himself. "I'm just going to make myself a cup of coffee, love. Would you like one?"

"No, you don't, Curtis Styles! You sit down and fill me in on your conversation," Katherine insisted.

With a wide grin on his face, Curtis shared, "I'm going to work with him. We'll see how it goes for a week, but it's just a formality, in my opinion. All I need to do is stroke his ego enough."

"That's fantastic news, honey. Funny thing is, he didn't come across as particularly egotistical to me. And he was well-dressed too, nothing like how you described him," Katherine remarked.

"Funny indeed," replied Curtis. "He was almost like a completely different person."

"Don't overthink it," she advised. "He probably put on a confident façade when he thought you were just an information source. Now that you're supposedly turning him into a 'national star,' you're seeing another side of him."

"You're right, but still, the sudden change of character caught me off guard," Curtis reflected. "I think I'll keep a close eye on him."

CHAPTER 2: A PLAN OF INVESTIGATION

C urtis made a quick stop at a corner store, grabbed the local morning newspaper, and stumbled upon a small article on page five reporting a dead-end in the investigation into Chloe Thomas's disappearance.

"This feels like déjà vu," Curtis muttered to himself.

As Curtis turned left into the driveway of Haddonfield's tranquil residence, he couldn't help but notice the contrasting atmosphere of serenity and the grave matter he was about to discuss. Parking his car in a small clearing near the top of the drive, Curtis stepped out and saw Haddonfield approaching him.

"Good morning, pal! I'm glad you found the place without any issues," greeted Haddonfield cheerfully.

"Thankfully, your directions were spot on. It's a beautiful place. Is it yours?" Curtis inquired.

"No, it belongs to my girlfriend. It's a great escape from the bustling city lights," Haddonfield responded appreciatively.

"Oh! I assumed you were new to the area," Curtis replied.

"I moved here recently, but my girlfriend has been here for two years. Her family is from this region. When her father had a stroke, she returned to help with the family business. They operate a trading store up in Ashbury," explained Haddonfield.

Curtis couldn't help but notice that Haddonfield maintained the same professional demeanor he had displayed during their unexpected meeting the previous day.

"Shall we go inside and get started?" Haddonfield suggested.

"Lead the way," Curtis replied.

They entered a spacious hallway and opened the door to Haddonfield's cluttered temporary office, featuring a desk, laptop, files, a bookcase filled with relevant books, scattered beanbags, and a detailed whiteboard summarizing information on the missing women.

"Looks pretty organized to me," Curtis remarked.

Tom Haddonfield replied with pride, "One does one's best!"

"If you don't mind me asking," Curtis inquired, "Why the beanbags?"

Haddonfield replied, "Sometimes a case can become too overwhelming and intense. So, if I feel myself getting caught up in that mindset, I take a break and relax on one of the beanbags. It allows me to let the information settle in. It may sound odd, but I suppose it's a remnant from my advertising days!"

"That sounds reasonable," Curtis replied. "I had no idea you had a background in advertising."

"I used to work as a copywriter and later as a creative director at an agency in Los Angeles. It feels like a lifetime ago. Sorry, I just need to make a few phone calls before we begin—just tying up loose ends on another case. Meanwhile, feel free to review the details on the whiteboard. It summarizes the facts I've gathered on the current case," Haddonfield said pleasantly. "Please take a seat behind the desk. I believe it will be more comfortable than the beanbags. By the way, would you like something to drink before I go?"

"I would kill for a cup of coffee," replied Curtis longingly.

Seated comfortably behind the desk, with his much-needed coffee in hand, Curtis felt prepared to delve into the notes scattered across the whiteboard before him.

Taking out a small notebook and pen from his jacket pocket, he carefully placed them on one side of the desk. With a determined gaze, he began to scrutinize the written points on the whiteboard:

Jemma Anderson:
- *Age: 23*
- *Occupation: Beer representative for Lockhart Breweries in Montpelier.*
- *Marital status: Single, residing with her parents.*
- *Physical description: 6 feet tall, slim build, blonde hair, blue eyes.*
- *Limited local contacts, primarily restaurant and bar staff.*
- *She had been on the job for just six months, focusing on this*

area for only two months before her disappearance.

Sophie Hunt:

- *Age: 25*
- *Occupation: "Working girl."*
- *Marital status: Single.*
- *Physical description: 5 feet 10 inches tall, medium build, black hair, brown eyes.*
- *History of substance addiction.*
- *Plans to return to rehab and enroll in college.*
- *Her last known whereabouts were leaving a bar with a friend named Paula Johns on the evening of September 15, 2018. Although she was supposed to walk home alone that night, Sophie never made it back, leaving her whereabouts unknown.*

Gabriella Atkins:

- *Age: 18*
- *Occupation: Receptionist at JB Plumbing.*
- *Marital status: Single.*
- *Physical description: 5 feet 10 inches tall, medium build, black hair, brown eyes.*
- *Recently out of high school, planning a gap year.*
- *Gabriella's last known plans were to meet a friend for coffee at a place referred to as the Pirates, although specific details about this location were not provided. Her disappearance remains a mystery, with no further information on her whereabouts available.*

Chloe Thomas:

- *Age: 20*
- *Occupation: She was a college student in New York, studying marketing and business management.*
- *Marital status: Single, lived in a sorority house.*
- *Physical description: 5 feet 9 inches.*
- *Visiting home for her father's 50th birthday.*
- *Went for a jog around the neighborhood and disappeared*

- *They first thought Chloe's phone had died, but by 9 PM, with no return, they called the police. All her friends were questioned and ruled out as suspects, including the unidentified person she was supposed to meet. There's speculation she met someone online, but no leads have emerged.*

After finishing the reading, Curtis reached for his notebook and began scribbling down notes. He had been engrossed in this activity for a few minutes when Tom Haddonfield returned.

"Anything catches your attention, buddy?" Haddonfield inquired.

Curtis responded with enthusiasm, "Oh, quite fascinating! Truly captivating!"

As Curtis examined the details, pondering the perplexing nature of the cases, he suddenly felt Tom Haddonfield's inquisitive gaze upon him.

"What do you find interesting?" Tom Haddonfield inquired.

"The absence of a clear pattern," Curtis frankly replied.

"Aside from the women falling within the eighteen to twenty-five age group, I struggle to find any other common thread. In a serial killer scenario, you would expect some sort of connection, be it physical attributes or a particular modus operandi. But it's a mishmash of sizes and shapes."

Curtis continued; his disappointment palpable. "Even their occupations vary: a university student, a sales rep, and a prostitute. And their disappearances occurred in different ways. One on her way to coffee, another out for a jog. No glaring clues jump out at me."

Haddonfield paused; his gaze fixed intently on Curtis. After a brief moment, he resumed speaking. "Hold on, let's backtrack a bit. We need to establish some ground rules for our working relationship."

"Apologies," Curtis responded, "I tend to get carried away when discussing topics, I'm passionate about. You're right, though. We do need to clarify our approach." Curtis continued, "The immediate challenge lies in the fact that your focus is on finding out what happened to Gabriella Atkins specifically, while my article needs to cover the investigation of all four women."

Haddonfield asserted, "My main focus is Gabriella, but I must explore the other cases since their disappearances are likely interconnected. It's a challenge we can overcome."

Curtis felt a surge of excitement. He sensed that Haddonfield had fully embraced the idea of working together. The time had come to seal the deal.

"If you don't mind my asking," Curtis inquired, "How long have you been working on this investigation?"

"A relatively short period. I arrived just a few weeks ago. I decided to move to the countryside, as my partner resides here, and I don't mind commuting to work. It was during a night out at The Falls Hotel that I met Gabriella's father. We got talking, and soon after, he contacted me, eager to have me on board. I did mention that I needed to wrap up another case first before fully committing. He was agreeable to that. Not to boast, but I have built a solid reputation," Haddonfield proudly explained.

"Oh, I see! The way Paul Harlow spoke, I got the impression you had been on the case for a while," Curtis said earnestly.

A faint smirk appeared on Haddonfield's face. "The local police intelligence seems lacking. Frankly, I pay little attention to them. You've joined the investigation at an early stage. Good timing on your part, I must say."

Curtis pressed on, seeking more details. "So, most of your work so far has involved preliminary background research?"

"You got it, mate!" Haddonfield replied nonchalantly.

"Alright, then! You mentioned earlier that you'll be leading the way. How do you envision our progress?" Curtis asked directly, noticing Haddonfield's posture straightening and chest puffing out—an unmistakable display of leadership mode.

"Firstly, I don't want you interfering with my investigation. However, I understand you have a story to write. I'll arrange interviews with key witnesses for all four cases, and you can accompany me for some," Haddonfield stated firmly. "How does that sound?"

"Perfect to me," Curtis affirmed. "Just let me know when and where, and I'll be there. I assume we'll start with Jemma Anderson..."

"Being methodical is always a good policy—starting from the very beginning and working our way forward," Haddonfield interjected.

"Sensible approach," Curtis agreed. "Although time seems to be of the Haddonfield's gaze bore into Curtis, a silent reprimand for his impulsive remark. Sensing his misstep, Curtis quickly added, "I apologize. Let's focus on the present, as you rightly pointed out."

Haddonfield appeared satisfied with the explanation. "Besides, it seems the perpetrator strikes at approximately three-month intervals, if we're dealing with a single individual."

"True," Curtis concurred. "Let's hope this person is apprehended before inflicting any more sorrow."

"I'll set up the interviews and be in touch," Haddonfield concluded.

"Thanks," Curtis replied.

Returning home, he ventured to the backyard, where Katherine immersed herself in gardening.

"How did it go, love?" she inquired.

"As well as could be expected," Curtis responded. "I genuinely believe our friend Tom Haddonfield is warming up to me."

That night, Curtis settled into his study, perched behind the desk, engrossed in an email recently received from Haddonfield. Jotting down notes on his trusty notepad, he meticulously planned his agenda for the following day:

"10 am tomorrow – Pick up TH and drive to The Stables Lodge in Stratford.

Speak with the proprietor, NB, to gather names and contact details of individuals who may have been present on the night Jemma Anderson disappeared.

*Proceed to The Hamlet Bed and Breakfast for a chat with the owner. ** It's crucial to thoroughly survey the area between The Stables and The Hamlet, exploring all potential routes she might have taken that fateful night.*

Additionally, we might visit local coffee shops to engage in conversations with the townsfolk, as small-town gossip can sometimes unveil unexpected leads. I'll discuss this idea with Haddonfield. If he opposes it, Katherine and I can explore it later."

Curtis snapped shut his notebook, glancing at the time displayed on his laptop—9:23 PM. With a sense of satisfaction, he swiftly responded to Tom Haddonfield's email, confirming his approval of the plans for the upcoming day. The living room beckoned, and Curtis succumbed, pouring himself a glass of whiskey to unwind.

Katherine sat engrossed in a television program; her attention fixed on the screen. Curtis, aware of her propensity for digressions, chose not to inquire about the show. Maintaining focus on the tasks ahead, he asked, "Would you like something to drink, dear?"

"For now, I'm fine, thanks," came Katherine's unswerving response. "I'll take my whiskey to bed then. I feel like indulging in some pre-slumber reading," Curtis announced.

"Alright, honey. I'll join you once this program concludes," she murmured, her gaze never wavering from the television screen.

Settling into bed, Curtis reached for the book resting on his bedside table. "Why Didn't They Ask Evans?" He read aloud, the title reigniting memories of his fervent love for Agatha Christie's mysteries during his youth. A startling realization struck him—four decades had elapsed since he last immersed himself in such a gripping tale. The transient nature of passion unsettled him, a disquieting notion indeed.

Suddenly, a voice pierced through the haze of slumber, calling out his name. Curtis blinked, rousing himself from a deep sleep. Orienting himself, he discovered Katherine sitting upright beside him, genuine concern etched across her features. Beads of sweat dotted his forehead.

Taking deep breaths to compose himself, Curtis responded, "What's the matter, honey?"

"You were restless in your sleep, tossing and turning. Must have been a bad dream," she tenderly remarked.

"A dream, yes..." Curtis trailed off, piecing together his scattered thoughts. "I recall now. I was reading for one moment, then dozed off. It involved a woman—stranger to me—perched on a precarious ledge, with sheer cliffs below. She implored me to save her, reaching out as I strained to reach down. Alas, my arms fell short, unable to bridge the gap."

"Bizarre indeed," Katherine responded. "But it was only a dream, my love. Would you like some water?"

"No, thanks. I'll be alright. What time is it?" Curtis inquired; his mind still somewhat muddled.

"It's three-thirty in the morning," Katherine answered gently.

With a yawn, Curtis responded, "Okay, I'll attempt to go back to sleep. Tomorrow is a big day with Haddonfield. Goodnight."

"Goodnight, honey," Katherine whispered softly, leaning over to switch off the bedside lamp, enveloping the room in darkness.

Lying there, shrouded in the stillness of the night, Curtis couldn't shake off the persistent replay of his dream in his mind. It gnawed at him, leaving him contemplating whether it stemmed from the book he had been reading or if it held a deeper meaning, a foreboding glimpse into what lay ahead.

"What if..." Curtis's thoughts spiraled, gripping him with a sense of unease. "What if this dream is a premonition? A glimpse into the path that awaits us." A chill crept up his spine, casting shadows of doubt across his thoughts.

Curtis made a conscious effort to dismiss unsettling thoughts and relax, seeking solace in sleep. The weight of tomorrow's investigation blurred reality and dreams.

In the silent room, he surrendered to slumber, his mind filled with mysteries, secrets, and the echoing plea of an enigmatic woman. The deep abyss of sleep promised a chance to unlock the enigma of the waking world.

As Curtis and Haddonfield delved deeper into their investigation, the haunting dream that had unsettled Curtis the previous night lingered like a shadow, casting an eerie foreboding over their quest for answers.

Katherine sat at the breakfast table, lost in thought about her husband's recent unsettling dream. Curtis, standing tall at six feet with a striking face and captivating blue eyes, intrigued her. His unwavering courage, despite his smaller stature, charmed her most.

Just as the morning light cascaded through the doorway, Curtis walked in, wearing a gentle smile. "I'm all set to begin," he announced, his words filled with determination.

Katherine reassured him, her voice laced with confidence, "If there's anyone capable of bringing justice to these cases, it's you."

After Curtis picked up his companion, Haddonfield, the two embarked on a serene journey along the country roads to Stratford. Conversation flowed easily, centered around sports, as they made their way to their destination. Eventually, they arrived at The Stables Lodge, a picturesque place nestled amidst nature's embrace. Curtis marveled at the scenic beauty that surrounded him—a grand driveway flanked by majestic trees led them to what appeared more like a small hotel than a mere lodge.

They stepped into the foyer, a spacious entrance that welcomed them with open arms. Approaching the oak reception desk, they were met with the warm smile of Nikita, a petite blonde in her mid-twenties. "Good morning, gentlemen. How can I help you today?" She greeted them cheerfully.

"We're looking for Jim Richardson. Is he available this morning?" Haddonfield inquired.

Nikita's expression turned inquisitive. "Do you have an appointment to meet with him?"

Curtis, glancing at her name badge, replied, "Unfortunately, we don't, Nikita. We happened to be in the area and thought we'd take a chance to see if he was available. We're investigating the Jemma Anderson disappearance."

A flicker of alarm danced across Nikita's face. "Police?" she asked, her voice tinged with concern.

"No, we're private investigators," Haddonfield clarified promptly.

Nikita offered her assistance, her voice filled with helpfulness. "He's typically swamped in the mornings but let me check if he's available to speak with you," she said.

Shortly after, she returned and gestured, saying, "Please, come with me, gentlemen."

Haddonfield spoke up, his tone calm and professional. "We've been assigned to investigate the cases of the four missing women in this area over the past year. We were hoping to gather some information about the night Jemma Anderson disappeared."

Jim Richardson, the owner of The Stables Lodge, greeted them warmly from behind his desk. After exchanging introductions, they settled into a comfortable discussion. Jim expressed his willingness to cooperate and revealed that he had already shared all relevant information with the police. "I'm more than happy to share it with you, gentlemen, if it could be of any assistance," Jim nodded earnestly.

A flicker of thought passed through Curtis's mind. *People can be very trusting. Jim hadn't asked for any proof of identification or who had hired us.*

Curtis chimed in, expressing gratitude. "We really appreciate your co-operation. Please tell us everything you can recall; it would be immensely helpful."

Haddonfield interjected, seeking some background information. "Could you give us a brief overview of this place?"

Jim complied. "Certainly. I've owned this lodge for the past three years, but I don't live on the premises. My wife and I have a house in town. The lodge itself has ten guest rooms, a restaurant, a bar, and a leisure area. Outside, we offer various activities like a tennis court and a mini-golf course. Most people come here for peace, quiet time, and to explore the local surroundings."

Curtis followed up with a question. "How many staff members do you have?"

"We have three full-time receptionists working in twelve-hour shifts, two bar and restaurant managers, and I often help out with shifts in the bar and restaurant to ease the workload. We also have part-time and outsourced staff for cleaning, bar services, and the restaurant," Jim responded.

Haddonfield inquired about Jemma Anderson. "How long had you known her?"

Jim reflected for a moment. "She had only been coming here for a few months. I used to deal with someone else from Lockhart Breweries before that."

Curiosity sparked, Haddonfield asked directly, "What was your impression of her?"

Jim responded with a tinge of sadness. "She was a very nice young lady. Always helpful if I needed anything. I still can't believe she's missing."

Curtis sought clarity. "She was here for a competition, right?"

Jim nodded. "Yes, we were having an eighties fancy dress night, and Jemma had asked the brewery to sponsor some prizes. She came through for me, providing five generous prizes. I convinced her to stay the night instead of driving back to Montpelier alone in the dark. It's not safe for a young woman to drive on these roads at night."

Haddonfield probed further. "Did she not want to stay here?"

Jim explained, "I offered her a free room since we only had five rooms booked for the night, but she insisted on booking a bed and breakfast. She said it's not a good idea to sleep where you work."

Curiosity piqued; Haddonfield delved into the night in question. "Tell us about that night and the people present."

Jim recalled, "It was a fantastic night overall. We had about a hundred guests, most of them in fancy dress. There were no issues throughout the evening. We had a local DJ, and everyone seemed to be in good spirits. Jemma appeared to be enjoying herself, mingling and having a great time from what I could tell."

Haddonfield focused on the crucial moment. "Who was present when Jemma left for the bed and breakfast?"

Jim recounted, "After the party wound down around one, only a few of us stayed back for a celebratory drink. Jemma, myself, Matt, the bar manager, Sergio Lassiter, the DJ, and his friend Sebastian McIntyre. Sergio and Sebastian live together in an apartment nearby, so Sebastian was waiting for Sergio to pack up before they left together."

"What about the security and lodge personnel?" Curtis inquired.

"The night receptionist was present, and we had a doorman until around one-thirty. We also employed a security guard from six in the evening until six in the morning. Apart from them, there were the guests in the five booked rooms," responded Jim.

Haddonfield pondered further. "Did anyone leave at the same time as Jemma?"

Jim shared what he knew. "According to Matt, I left about fifteen minutes before Jemma. He did a quick stock take and then left with Sebastian and Sergio at around three am. The security guard mentioned that Jemma left alone around two am."

Curtis, in a polite manner, asked an additional question. "Do any of the staff members stay on the premises?"

Jim clarified, "The reception staff does. We've converted the old stables at the back into cottages for the staff."

Curtis expressed gratitude and added, "Thank you. One last thing, could you kindly provide us with the names of the guests who were booked for that night?"

"No problem, Nikita will be able to give you those on your way out," Jim replied. "Anything else you need to know, gentlemen?"

"That wraps it up for me, although I'm curious if you could tell me the most direct route to The Hamlet Bed and Breakfast?" Curtis inquired.

"That's easy. There's only one route. Just head straight out the gates at the bottom of the driveway, take a left, and follow the road for about two miles. You won't miss it on your right. The place is well signposted," Jim explained genially.

"That's all for me," said Curtis. "Thanks for all your help."

Haddonfield turned to Curtis and said, "I just need to use the restroom before we leave. You can gather the guests' details while I do that."

After exchanging thanks and farewells, Curtis and Haddonfield went their separate ways. Nikita, as accommodating as before, provided the guest registry to Curtis. He diligently noted down the names in his notebook:

Room 1 - Mr. and Mrs. Bob Bradshow
Room 2 - Jinty Jones
Room 6 - Mr. and Mrs. Mason Homan
Room 8 - John Myers

Curtis made additional notes on the guests' contact information and then proceeded to wait outside by the car for Haddonfield. Time seemed to drag on, and after what felt like half an hour, Haddonfield finally reappeared.

"I was starting to think I'd have to send out a search party!" Curtis exclaimed.

"I just took a quick look around the lodge," replied Haddonfield. "Did you find anything?"

"No, but the fire exit at the back could be a place where someone could slip away unnoticed."

Curtis speculated, "So, you think it could have been a guest?"

"Not necessarily. It's just a convenient escape route into the night," Haddonfield cryptically remarked.

CHAPTER 3: A BODY DISCOVERED

At the end of the driveway, Curtis made a left turn, embarking on a short two-mile journey to the Hamlet Bed and Breakfast. The first mile was lined with two bars, numerous houses, and a gas station on either side of the road.

Observing their surroundings, Haddonfield remarked, "If she had stopped along here, there would have been plenty of places to seek help. Although that would depend on whether she was taken by surprise."

Curtis pondered, "You think she stopped along this route?"

Haddonfield responded with conviction, "I don't see any other plausible explanation."

Curtis, considering alternative possibilities, suggested, "On the surface, it seems likely, but what if she turned right at the bottom of the drive instead of left?"

Haddonfield appeared slightly annoyed by the question. "Why on earth would she do that at two o'clock in the morning?"

Curtis remained calm, explaining his reasoning. "I'm just exploring all angles, covering every possibility."

Haddonfield, authoritatively dismissing the idea, retorted, "Bloody stupid suggestion if you ask me!"

As Curtis observed him intently, a thought crossed his mind: "As improbable as it may seem, he's simply furious that he didn't come up with it first."

Examining the landscape as they entered the second mile, they found themselves surrounded by farmland on both sides of the road.

Haddonfield's eyes twinkled with intrigue. "Now, this must be the area where she stopped. At two o'clock in the morning, there wouldn't be much activity here. Like a lamb to the slaughter if she was with the wrong person."

Curtis agreed, "It certainly seems like a plausible scenario. It must be pitch black out here at night. I don't see any streetlights."

Just as Haddonfield was about to respond, Curtis pointed out, "There's the Hamlet Bed and Breakfast."

They turned off the road onto a sandy driveway and approached a metal gate. Curtis leaned out of the car window and pressed an intercom button, waiting for a response.

After a few seconds, a voice came through, "Hello, can I help you?"

Curtis introduced himself, "Hi, my name is Curtis Styles. Is Mrs. Edna Braithwaite in?"

There was a brief pause, then the cautious voice replied, "I am Edna Braithwaite. Is there something I can do for you?"

Apologizing for the intrusion, Curtis explained, "I'm an investigative reporter working on an article about the Jemma Anderson disappearance. Would it be possible to come inside and have a brief chat with you?"

Edna Braithwaite expressed her skepticism, asking, "How do I know that you are who you say you are?"

Curtis offered proof, "I have a press card from a previous job. If needed, I can provide you with the name and number of my boss so you can verify my credentials."

Seemingly satisfied, Edna replied, "You sound trustworthy enough, Mr. Styles. I will open the gate now. Park at the top of the drive and come around to the cottage at the back of the house."

Curtis and Haddonfield introduced themselves to Edna Braithwaite and used a photographer's cover story. Edna invited them in for coffee, and Curtis noticed Haddonfield's discomfort. They discussed Jemma Anderson staying at Edna's place on the night she disappeared, and Edna mentioned she had a brief conversation with her, claiming to be good at judging people's character, which Curtis found dubious.

Curious, Curtis asked, "Is there anything you can tell us that hasn't been reported so far?"

After pondering for a moment, Edna replied, "Actually, come to think of it, there is something."

Curtis and Haddonfield became alert, sitting up straight.

Edna continued, "I recall reading the reports about her disappearance, and they never mentioned the fellow she was supposed to return with."

Curtis and Haddonfield exchanged excited glances.

Curtis pressed for more information, "What fellow? There was no mention of anyone. Wasn't she staying here alone?"

Edna clarified, "No, it wasn't like that. There was a booking made by a man named Barrington Jones for that same night. When Jemma left, she mentioned she would be back later with that gentleman. I assumed he was her boyfriend, but she said he was just a work colleague coming to help with the raffle. He had paid a deposit for a separate room, so I didn't ask further questions."

Curtis took a deep breath, "And he never arrived?"

Edna stated plainly, "No, he didn't."

"And you informed the police about this?" Haddonfield chimed in, finding his voice.

She stared at him incredulously. "Of course, I bloody well did!"

"Do you have a contact number for this Barrington Jones?" Curtis asked eagerly.

"Well, here's the strange thing. We have a lady who handles reception during the day, and she takes most of the bookings. When I gave the number to the police, it turned out to be the exact same number as Jemma Anderson's. I don't think she noticed because Jemma had made her booking a few days before Barrington," Edna explained defensively.

"Do you have any idea what happened with that lead?" Haddonfield pressed.

"How would I know that?" Edna responded sharply.

Sensing her irritation, Curtis interjected calmly, "Thank you, Mrs. Braithwaite. That's quite fascinating. Is there anything else you can recall about that day?"

She pondered for a while before apologetically responding, "Nothing comes to mind at the moment."

Having gathered all available information, Curtis stood up and thanked Edna sincerely. She smiled with pride, saying, "Glad I could help." Haddonfield followed Curtis as they left.

At the car, they exchanged farewells with waves. Settling inside, Haddonfield couldn't hide his excitement. He turned to Curtis; eyes gleaming with anticipation. "Dude, I think we've hit the jackpot! This could be the break-through we've been waiting for!"

As Curtis drove home, he looked forward to his upcoming conversation with Tom Haddonfield. He had chosen to skip his usual coffee shop visits, suspecting that Haddonfield might be displeased with him taking the lead with Edna Braithwaite.

"It wouldn't be wise to bring that up now," Curtis thought to himself. "He probably already thinks I'm trying to take over the investigation."

To his surprise, Haddonfield turned to him and commended, "Well done, Curtis! Great thinking back there with the reporter/photographer angle."

Caught off guard, Curtis took a moment to collect himself. "Thanks. Just so you know, I'm not trying to step on your toes. It just felt like the right approach at the time."

"Gut instinct, pal! Trust it because, more often than not, it won't let you down."

Curious about their findings, Curtis asked, "What did you make of what we learned today?"

"Jim seems genuine enough. However, he left fifteen minutes before Jemma. That would have been enough time for him to stage a breakdown on the side of the road. She would have stopped to help," Haddonfield stated.

"Agreed," Curtis responded, pondering the situation. "But a couple of things puzzle me. Firstly, if she stopped to assist someone, it's likely that the staged breakdown would have occurred in a desolate area surrounded by farmland. That means two cars stuck on a desolate road. However, her car has never been found. It would be difficult for one person to dispose of both vehicles without being seen. This suggests the involvement of two people. So, wouldn't it have been easier to stage a scene on foot? For instance, someone running in the road to flag down help. It would look odd for Jim to be alone on a desolate road with no visible vehicle, having driven off earlier."

Continuing his thoughts, Curtis added, "Secondly, while we assume she stopped to assist someone if it was a random attack, the predator would be waiting to flag down someone who might never come. In those early morning hours, long stretches could pass without a single car passing by. Would a predator be willing to flag down just anyone? They could potentially encounter someone dangerous. It all seems too well planned for a random attack."

"I understand your point, but at the same time, we're assuming Jim drove himself home. He never explicitly said that; he only mentioned leaving before Jemma," Haddonfield remarked.

Curtis agreed, "True."

Haddonfield continued, "I do like the angle of the predator being on foot. However, I'm not ruling out the possibility of two people. Perhaps someone else arrived later to assist Jim. What we don't know is who Jemma spoke to that evening and what she told them. She could have mentioned her whereabouts to anyone during the '80s night. And as I mentioned before, it would be easy for one of the guests to slip out unnoticed through the fire exit."

Curtis expressed his skepticism, "Call me crazy, but I don't think that's what happened. On one hand, it seems plausible, but on the other, it appears clumsy and poorly thought out. Whoever is behind this seems intelligent and skilled at covering their tracks and crimes. We don't even have any bodies to confirm that crimes have occurred."

Haddonfield sighed, placing his hands over his face. "As much as I hate to admit it, you may have a point there."

Shifting the conversation, Haddonfield asked about the Barrington Jones revelation. Curtis responded, mentioning Edna Braithwaite's claim and the doubts about whether she had informed the police.

Haddonfield's initial excitement waned, leading him to suggest splitting up tasks. Curtis and Haddonfield deliberated on their respective assignments, deciding that Haddonfield would head to Montpelier to investigate Barrington Jones while Curtis would focus on researching the guests at the Stables Lodge. They also made arrangements to conduct interviews with key individuals upon Haddonfield's return.

Curtis and Katherine embarked on their day trip, with Katherine proposing that they initiate casual conversations with locals to gather information. They playfully compared themselves to Holmes and Watson as they made their way to Roxy's Coffee Bar to kick off their investigative journey.

Upon arriving, they secured a nearby table, and Linda, a friendly, plump blonde waitress in her thirties, came over to greet them. Linda handed them menus and cheerfully stated, "I'll return in a few moments to take your order."

"She seems nice and approachable," Katherine commented as Linda walked away. "Why don't we strike up a conversation with her and see if she knows anything? She seems like someone who might enjoy a bit of local gossip."

Curtis agreed, "I'll let you take the lead on this one."

A few minutes later, Linda returned to their table. "Have you folks decided what you'd like to have?" She asked.

"Just two regular filter coffees, please," Katherine replied.

Linda couldn't help but recommend something. "Nothing to eat? You've got to try the Death by Chocolate cake. It's absolutely to die for! The slices are big, but I can cut one in half for you to share. It's only eleven, so you'll still have room for lunch."

"You've convinced us," Katherine said with a smile. She turned to Curtis, who agreed, "Sounds great, dear."

During their cake outing, Katherine and Curtis subtly brought up the topic of the missing women with their acquaintance Linda. Linda mentioned that she knew two of the missing women, Chloe Thomas and Gabriella Atkins, and Curtis couldn't hide his surprise upon hearing Gabriella's name. Linda revealed that Gabriella might have been pregnant at the time of her disappearance, causing Curtis to exclaim with astonishment. Katherine intervened, explaining Curtis's enthusiasm as he had a friend hired by the Atkins family to investigate Gabriella's case. Linda, visibly nervous, asked them not to mention her suspicion about Gabriella's pregnancy to anyone, and Katherine emphasized the need for discretion, sensing Linda's unease.

Message received, Curtis thought. I should keep quiet about it.

Katherine reassured Linda, saying, "None of us will say anything. Don't worry."

Feeling more at ease, Linda sighed and responded, "Thank you. I appreciate it. As for why I thought she might be pregnant..."

Linda proceeded to recount her recent encounter with Gabriella at the pharmacy. She had observed Gabriella appearing distressed and clutching a pamphlet on teenage pregnancy, despite Gabriella's attempts to conceal it. When asked about the pamphlet, Gabriella denied any pregnancy suspicions and mentioned it was a friend who had raised the concern. Abruptly,

Gabriella excused herself, citing an urgent appointment.

Katherine asked softly, "Do you think she was lying?"

Linda paused, considering her words. "I can't say for sure, but her reaction seemed too personal like there was something more going on. It's just a hunch, nothing concrete, you understand. I'm sorry, I need to attend to other customers. It was nice chatting with you. Let me know if you need anything else."

Curtis remarked, "What other customers? There are only two other occupied tables, and there's another waitress on duty."

Curtis and Katherine concluded their coffee shop visits in Stratford and ventured to The Green Lantern. Curtis hoped for a more fruitful discussion without relying on a talkative waitress.

Upon entering, they both appreciated the cozy atmosphere as they settled at a table. Curtis expressed his wish for another talkative waitress, but Katherine had a surprise for him. She revealed that Jenny Lassiter, the cafe's owner and a member of her book club, had been invited to join them after Curtis mentioned their visit. Their discussion touched on Sergio, Jenny's son, and the DJ at The Stables on the night Jemma Anderson went missing. Curtis commended Katherine for her foresight, and soon, Jenny joined them.

After placing their orders, they delved into the investigation. Curtis explained his role in the recent disappearances of young women in the area and sought Jenny's insights.

Curtis pondered aloud, "A mysterious boyfriend or lover seems to be surfacing in these cases. It makes you wonder if the supposed serial murderer targeting random females is not the case at all."

Surprised, Jenny exclaimed, "Oh!" Realizing he may have revealed too much, Curtis quickly shifted the focus. "By the way, before I forget, you mentioned your son is a mechanic?"

The diversion seemed to work, and Jenny responded, "Sergio? Yes, he is. He and his friend Sebastian have a small shop. Why do you ask?"

Explaining their situation, Katherine said, "Our car needs servicing, but our usual mechanic recently retired and moved away. We prefer going to someone we know or who comes recommended."

Proudly, Jenny assured them, "I may be biased, but most people around here swear by their work."

Katherine asked, "Could we have his contact details so Curtis can book the car?"

"Absolutely. I have his business card in my bag," Jenny said, reaching into her handbag and handing Curtis the card.

"Thank you so much. You're a real lifesaver," Curtis expressed his gratitude.

Forty-five minutes later, Katherine and Curtis were on their way back home.

"Bloody hell, Katherine, now I have to get the car serviced. We just had it done a few weeks ago," Curtis exclaimed incredulously.

Katherine responded, "I guess we do. I had to think quickly before you made things worse. At least now you have Sergio's contact details, and it gives us another reason to visit him."

Curtis admitted, "I guess you're right."

Curious, Katherine asked, "So, what did you make of today?"

Curtis reflected, "You know, the more we dig into this, the more small things come to light. You'd think the police would have conducted a thorough investigation, so it makes you wonder if these details are significant. But I can't help but feel that in this case, the devil really is in the details."

Curtis proposed inviting Paul and Judy Harlow over for a barbecue. Katherine suspected there might be an ulterior motive but agreed, suggesting that they briefly discuss the case and then enjoy the day.

Curtis, teasingly, said, "Aye, aye, captain! Should I give him a quick call?"

In the late afternoon, at approximately four o'clock, the Harlows made their entrance. Curtis offered them a warm greeting, and after exchanging pleasantries, he guided Paul to his study to chat about a recent purchase, allowing Judy and Katherine to reconnect.

As they entered the study, Paul Harlow asked, "Now, old boy, what did you want to show me?"

Curtis admitted sheepishly, "There's nothing to show. I just wanted to chat with you for a few minutes about the case. I called Haddonfield, as you suggested, and things have taken an interesting turn since then." He proceeded to fill Harlow in on the recent events, saying, "So, what do you make of all this?"

"Interesting, but most of that is already known to the police. The potential pregnancy is news to me, though," Harlow responded.

Curtis implored, "Just be honest with me, Harlow. I know you're retired from the force, but are you involved in this case in any way?"

Paul Harlow took a deep breath before answering, "It depends on what you mean by 'involved.' I'm not directly involved in the day-to-day investigations. They formed a task force a few months ago, and they asked me to be a part of it. It's more of a behind-the-scenes role, you know."

Curtis understood and pressed further, "So, you have access to all the information on the case?"

"I do, but I can't disclose anything that isn't public knowledge. You should know that by now, Styles," Harlow replied.

Aware of Harlow's hidden agenda, Curtis asked knowingly, "But when you suggested I contact Haddonfield, was that just a helpful tip, or did you have something else in mind, Mr. Harlow?"

Harlow burst into laughter. "Your instincts are still sharp, Styles," he said. "The idea came to me when we were chatting the other day. I could tell you were determined to get involved in this investigation, so I thought nudging you in Haddonfield's direction might be useful. If you two teamed up, I could keep an eye on both of you. Haddonfield probably wouldn't pay attention to me, but you, Styles, we go way back."

Curtis laughed as well. "I was like a horse to water, wasn't I? Am I meant to be your inside man with Haddonfield now?"

Harlow clarified, "Nothing like that, Styles. But you know how it works. We scratch each other's backs."

"Fair enough," Curtis acknowledged. "Now that I've filled you in on everything we've been doing, what can you share with me?"

"There are two things I can tell you," Harlow said. "Firstly, you were right about the Barrington Jones lead. He was Jemma Anderson's coworker at the brewery, as you know. The company preferred having a male escort accompany female staff for evening work functions out of town. It's a safety precaution. On the day of the event, Jones claimed to have stomach trouble, and Jemma agreed to go alone. She suggested they keep it a secret from their superiors to avoid canceling her trip."

Curtis interjected, "But from her conversation with Edna Braithwaite, it seemed like he was coming."

Harlow clarified, "She probably wanted to keep up appearances. We've already ruled out the roommate as a suspect, so there's no need to involve the press. Interestingly, Barrington Jones has roots in this area, with a family farm in Ashbury. Surprisingly, though, he hasn't worked in this region before, despite his local knowledge and connections. Our initial inquiries didn't uncover any issues with his reputation here."

Curtis inquired further, "You mentioned two things." Harlow proceeded, "What do you know about Haddonfield?"

Curtis confessed, "Not much, aside from him having a local girlfriend and being hired by the Atkins family for their daughter's case."

Harlow revealed, "Here's the deal. Haddonfield used to be a creative genius at a top Los Angeles ad agency, but he suddenly switched to being a private investigator, teaming up with his cop friend, Lyndon Whiteford. Lyndon eventually left, leaving Haddonfield in charge."

Curtis questioned, "Do you think this relates to the case?"

Harlow replied, "Doubt it, but it's good to know. Haddonfield's unconventional background might explain his approach."

Curtis nodded, "That makes sense, given my impression of him."

"Clothing?" Harlow asked, puzzled.

Curtis explained, "It's nothing significant. I just found his style of dress a bit flashy when I first met him."

Harlow chuckled. "Oh, I see. Well, what's next?" Curtis asked, "What do you mean?"

Harlow clarified, "I feel like I'm working with Haddonfield indirectly through you."

Laughing, Harlow said, "Don't overthink it, Styles. You continue doing what you're doing, and we can touch base now and then."

Curtis concluded, "Alright then. Now, I think there's a steak waiting for me with my name on it."

"And two women who are surely looking forward to our company," Harlow retorted playfully.

Sitting face-to-face in Curtis's study, he had just finished updating Haddonfield on his conversation with Paul Harlow. However, Curtis chose not to disclose the information he received about Haddonfield or their occasional note exchanges.

"Jones turned out to be a dead end," Haddonfield remarked. "Seems like we hit a wall there."

Curtis pondered, unable to find any reason for Jones's avoidance of the area.

Haddonfield clarified, "Jones is from here and initially wanted to work in this area. The brewery suggested he gain experience in different regions, and the timing didn't align."

Curtis sighed, feeling stuck.

Haddonfield's excitement returned. "But there's a lead. I talked to Jemma's coworker, Crystal Jennings. She mentioned a mysterious married man in Jem-ma's life, someone hesitant to leave his wife, and Jemma confided in Crystal."

Curtis chimed in, connecting the dots. "They rarely do! Now it makes sense. Here's something interesting: I was out in Stratford with my wife recently, having lunch at The Green Lantern. It's a place owned by one of Katherine's friends who joined us. During our conversation, she mentioned that Jemma was there that day and had a heated argument with someone. It seemed like a lover's quarrel, probably with a man."

Haddonfield's excitement grew. "That's fascinating! So, if I'm thinking what you're thinking, it wasn't Jones she was expecting at the bed and breakfast that night, but this mystery man!"

"Exactly!" Curtis confirmed. "She convinced Jones to keep quiet, not because she was worried about the trip being canceled, but because it presented the perfect opportunity to meet up with this guy."

Haddonfield contemplated the possibilities. "That would explain why she told Edna Braithwaite that her colleague would join her later. Edna wouldn't know who he is, so there would be no harm done."

Curtis voiced another worry. "The issue is, based on what Katherine's friend mentioned, it appeared that the guy was canceling their plans for the evening."

Haddonfield posed a question. "But what if he didn't? What if he changed his mind later? She would likely have agreed to see him."

"You're right," Curtis responded, his mood shifting to a more optimistic one. "If that's the case, there wouldn't be a need for staged breakdowns or elaborate schemes. She would have welcomed seeing him."

Haddonfield, sensing progress, said, "We're onto something here."

Curtis inquired about their next course of action. Haddonfield outlined the plan, saying "Our next step should involve returning to Stratford for interviews. We'll need to speak with the DJ, his friend, the security guard, and the bar manager. I'll arrange those meetings and keep you informed. Also, see if Harlow can get Jemma's phone records; I have a contact who might help speed things up."

Curtis expressed doubt. "I can give it a try, though I'm not sure we'll get anywhere with that request."

"Use your charm, my friend. We can't afford to lose momentum now that we finally have something to work with," Haddonfield encouraged, standing up to leave. "By the way, have you managed to gather any information about the guests who stayed at The Stables the night she disappeared?"

Curtis admitted sheepishly, "Sorry, I haven't gotten around to it yet. It's high on my to-do list."

Haddonfield summarized their tasks. "So, two things to do. I'll see myself out. Good luck!" With those words, Haddonfield exited the room.

Curtis hesitated, uncertain if reaching out to Harlow would violate department protocol. However, on a whim, he dialed Harlow's number, and Harlow picked up.

"Hi, Harlow, it's Curtis here," he said matter-of-factly. "I was wondering if you could help me with something."

"Why do I get the feeling I won't like this?" Harlow responded.

Curtis chuckled. "You're probably right. I thought I'd ask anyway. Can you get me a copy of Jemma Anderson's mobile records from the night she disappeared?"

"Have you completely lost your mind, Styles? You know that goes against department protocol," Harlow barked back.

"That's what I thought, but I had to try," Curtis said, feeling slightly embarrassed.

"Do you have a pen and paper with you?" asked Harlow.

Surprised by the sudden turn, Curtis replied, "Yes, I do."

"Write down this number," Harlow instructed.

Curtis quickly jotted down the number and asked, "Thank you so much. By the way, whose number is this?"

"Never mention that I gave it to you. Not even to your wife. Goodbye, Styles," Harlow said firmly, and the line went dead.

Staring at the number, Curtis wondered whether he should attempt to trace it or take a chance and dial it. It was clear to him that the number held some importance, or Harlow wouldn't have given it to him.

Speaking aloud to himself, he pondered, "I might as well call it. In any case, I probably won't recognize the person. I'll try to get a name and explain it away as a wrong number."

Curtis dialed the number, waiting patiently. After a few rings, a voice answered, "Hello, Nikita speaking!"

Curtis stood frozen for a moment, his mind racing as he recognized the voice on the other end of the line. Collecting himself, he regained composure and said, "Hello, Nikita. It's Curtis Styles speaking."

"You're one of the gentlemen who were here the other day, investigating the missing women," Nikita responded.

"That's correct," Curtis confirmed. "I was wondering if you could assist us. We're following up with people who were at The Stables on the night Jemma disappeared, and I wanted to find out who was working reception that night. We forgot to ask when we were there."

"Oh, that would be me," she replied.

Taken aback by Nikita's admission, Curtis questioned why Jim had not mentioned her. He inquired if she could recall anything unusual from the night of Jemma's disappearance, but Nikita struggled to remember anything significant. Curtis offered his mobile number, which Nikita already had, and reassured her that she should call if anything came to mind. Nikita explained that she had asked Jim to remove their contact information from the lodge's website as a precaution.

Following the call, Curtis felt frustrated by what appeared to be an unproductive conversation. However, Nikita phoned back, expressing a desire to meet in person to discuss something that had been weighing on her mind. They agreed to meet the next morning at Ashbury Park.

Curtis then spoke to Katherine about his morning and asked if she had seen Haddonfield leave before inquiring about her day. He proceeded to fill her in on all the details, including the conversations with Paul Harlow and Nikita, and then asked, "Do you think this is another dead end? She doesn't seem like a significant figure."

Taking a brief pause, Katherine responded, "You know, I think it might not be. Think about it. Nikita was working that night, so she would likely have observed people coming and going, and possibly even overheard some conversations. She could have valuable insights."

"If that were the case, wouldn't she have already shared that information with the police?" Curtis pondered.

"Not necessarily," Katherine explained. "People are often wary of getting involved with the police and may choose to say as little as possible. They might think it's not relevant or prefer to stay out of it."

"Is that why Harlow gave me her number?" Curtis mused.

"Exactly! She may be more willing to share things with you that she wouldn't tell the police," Katherine suggested.

"I suppose that makes sense," Curtis conceded.

"By the way, what did Tom think of the news about Gabriella Atkins potentially being pregnant?" Katherine asked.

"I didn't tell him," Curtis admitted. "We don't know if it's true. I think Linda, our 'friend,' enjoys spreading gossip and baseless speculation."

"Maybe... Although there could be some truth to it. I would tell Tom and let him decide what he wants to do with the information," Katherine advised thoughtfully. "Are you taking Tom with you to the meeting tomorrow?"

Curtis chuckled nervously. "Harlow told me not to tell anyone that he gave me Nikita's number. I wasn't even supposed to tell you."

She responded with laughter. "Just wait till I run into that man again!"

Approaching the Ashbury turnoff, Curtis's thoughts began to drift, likely influenced by the recent revelations. Despite his reservations about the meeting's significance, Katherine's words about Nikita continued to occupy his mind.

He parked his car near the park, muttering, "This has to be the spot," and glanced at his watch—11:02.

As he waited, he observed the serene surroundings, a park nestled at the hill's base. Not a soul in sight, only the beauty of nature. Nevertheless, he couldn't shake the feeling that such an idyllic place was now tied to a troubling story.

Time seemed to stretch endlessly until he checked his watch again. It now reads 11:18. "Her timekeeping is certainly shambolic for someone in the hospitality industry," he mused, frustration creeping in.

Pulling out his mobile, Curtis decided to call Nikita. Dialing her number from his call list, he was met with voicemail. Nothing to do but wait. He hesitated to contact anyone at The Stables for her number, respecting her desire for privacy.

Noon approached, and Curtis felt it was time to depart. "Could there possibly be another park?" He questioned aloud, doubting it. Nevertheless, he walked a short distance to JB Trading.

Upon arriving at the park, Curtis sought help from an employee to locate his meeting spot. The woman recognized him as Curtis Styles, Tom Haddonfield's acquaintance. They exchanged pleasantries, and Curtis explained his situation, waiting for someone who had yet to arrive. The woman offered assistance but had no additional information to provide.

Curtis returned to the park, finding Nikita still absent. Frustration crept in, and he eventually decided to head home. Back at home, he shared the disappointing outcome with Katherine, who consoled him, acknowledging that they had at least tried to gather information from Nikita.

"You don't understand," Curtis replied cautiously, "She didn't show up at all."

"What! Did you try calling her?"

"I did, but it went straight to voicemail."

Katherine suggested kindly, "Well, let's have lunch first, and then maybe you can try calling her again later. There could be a reasonable explanation for her absence."

The following morning, Curtis awoke still grappling with the events of the previous day. Lost in thought, he muttered, "Her phone must be on by now."

Picking up his mobile, he dialed Nikita's number once more, only to reach her voicemail again. He showered, dressed, grabbed his car keys, and headed out to buy the morning paper and some milk. Just as he stepped out of his front door, he noticed Tom Haddonfield approaching.

Excitedly pointing at a newspaper, Haddonfield exclaimed, "Have you seen this?"

"I was just about to get the newspaper when you arrived," Curtis replied.

Haddonfield handed him the paper, his face reflecting shock. Curtis unfolded it, and the front-page headline hit him like a ton of bricks:

"FEARS GROW FOR THE SAFETY OF ANOTHER MISSING WOMAN"

A sudden chill ran down his spine as he stared at the accompanying photograph. It was Nikita Marsh, the receptionist from The Stables Lodge.

CHAPTER 4: THE BROWN PACKAGE

Curtis, overwhelmed by the article about Nikita Marsh's disappearance, expressed disbelief to Tom Haddonfield. Haddonfield, remaining hopeful, suggested that they shouldn't immediately assume a connection to other disappearances, as Nikita's case had some differences, such as her car being found. Curtis, while acknowledging these differences, highlighted the unsettling similarities that couldn't be overlooked.

"Let me summarize the facts. Nikita finished work at two in the morning. Her car was later found near Highgate Bridge, abandoned with the driver's side door open and the park lights on. A passing motorist discovered it and alerted the authorities."

Haddonfield concisely confirmed, "That's correct so far."

Curtis pondered aloud; his voice laced with curiosity. "Highgate Bridge, on the outskirts of Stratford, crosses the Salem River. It's a desolate place, especially in the early hours. What could she have been doing there? Unless it was on her way home."

Haddonfield corrected him, recalling their previous conversation. "She actually lives on the premises, as Jim informed us."

Realizing the discrepancy, Curtis raised an important question. "That's right. So why would she be heading to such an isolated spot at that time? The only plausible explanation would be if she encountered car trouble while en route to another destination."

Haddonfield countered with a grim possibility. "Or perhaps she took her own life, and her body hasn't been found yet."

After perusing the article, Katherine glanced up and remarked, "You made it here quite early, Tom."

Both men turned to her, surprised by her remark. Haddonfield was puzzled. "I'm not sure I understand."

Katherine clarified her statement. "It's only eight-thirty in the morning. I was just wondering why you're in our area at this time."

Haddonfield explained, "I was on my way to a cash and carry in

Montpelier. Penny asked if I could go today because her delivery got delayed until Friday. She really needs the stock before then. I stopped at the shop here to grab a coffee and saw the newspaper headline. Naturally, I rushed over here after reading the story."

Understanding his reasons, Katherine remarked, "Your girlfriend is lucky to have such a thoughtful boyfriend."

Confused by the exchange, Curtis interjected, "There's something you should know, Tom. Yesterday morning, I was supposed to meet Nikita in Ashbury."

Realizing who Curtis was referring to, Haddonfield responded, "So, that's who you were meeting. Penny mentioned you coming into the store yesterday and mentioned meeting someone."

Curtis explained his reasoning, apologizing for not sharing earlier. "I didn't mention it because she called and asked for a private meeting. She claimed to have some useful information. I wasn't sure if it was worth pursuing, so I didn't want to waste your time. If it had turned out to be significant, we could have investigated further."

Haddonfield understood and reassured him, "No need to apologize. It's completely understandable."

Curtis turned his attention to the ongoing search. "The newspaper mentioned that a search team has been called in. I assume they'll scour the surrounding woods and the river."

Haddonfield inquired about their last conversation. "How did she sound when you spoke to her?"

Curtis replied, "She seemed fine to me. I didn't know her well, but she didn't sound distressed. You mentioned the possibility of suicide earlier. Do you really think that's a possibility?"

Haddonfield shook his head, acknowledging the uncertainty. "You never know. As you said, we didn't know her personally. It often comes as a shock when those closest to a person are unaware of their inner struggles."

Curtis accepted the uncertainty, agreeing with Haddonfield's observation. "That's true."

Haddonfield proposed a plan, appealing to Curtis for assistance. "I think one of us should go to the search area and see what's happening. I'm not sure if the police will allow us to close, though. I hate to ask, but I really need to collect the delivery in Montpelier. Could you go there, Curtis?"

Curtis readily agreed, offering his support. "No problem. Harlow is likely to be there, so maybe I'll have better luck getting close to the scene. I'll grab a quick bite and head out. It might be a long day. If I hear anything, I'll give you a call."

After Haddonfield left, Curtis turned to Katherine with a somber expression. "Bloody hell! What just happened here?"

Katherine shook her head, still in disbelief.

Curtis's frustration grew, and anger tinged his voice. "This is Harlow's fault! He gave me a cryptic number without explanation, and now a girl is missing, possibly dead!"

Katherine urged him to calm down and wait for more information. "Take a breath, Curtis, and let's not jump to conclusions. We need to let the facts come to light."

Curtis, burdened by guilt, admitted, "I have a sick feeling in the pit of my stomach. I might indirectly be responsible for her death."

After breakfast, Curtis asked Katherine about her interrogation of Haddonfield earlier.

Katherine chuckled and responded, "That? Honestly, I'm not sure why I said all that. I suppose this entire situation is making me quite skeptical."

A concerned look crossed Curtis' face as he asked, "You don't think Haddonfield could be involved in this, do you?"

Katherine reassured him, "No, not at all. It just struck me as odd that he arrived here so early, that's all."

Curtis nodded and said, "Seemed like a reasonable explanation to me." Katherine smiled and agreed, "Can't argue with that."

While driving to Stratford, Curtis couldn't shake the feeling that he had missed something in his phone calls with Nikita Marsh. Suddenly, he realized that when he made the first call, Nikita couldn't speak due to people at the reception desk. He pulled over and exclaimed, "That's it! Someone from that party must have overheard her second call to me."

The possibility sent shivers down his spine. If his hunch was correct, it meant that the person who overheard the call might have something to do with Jemma's disappearance.

A little while later, Curtis parked his car on a grassy verge a few hundred yards away from Highgate Bridge, where Nikita's vehicle had been found abandoned. The area buzzed with police activity.

Deciding to keep a reasonable distance for the time being, Curtis stood by his car, patiently observing. There was no sign of Paul Harlow, whom he hoped to spot as a signal to take action. Forty-five minutes passed, and Curtis continued to scan the surroundings, but there was no sight of Harlow.

Suddenly, a voice startled him, "What are you doing here, Styles?"

Curtis spun around and found Paul Harlow standing behind him. Curtis quickly came up with an explanation, "I was on my way to see my mechanic in Stratford when I noticed all the activity by the bridge. I decided to stop and see what was going on."

Harlow wasn't convinced and replied bluntly, "Cut the bull, Styles! You've read the morning paper, and you know there's a search happening here."

Taking a moment to gather his thoughts, Curtis retorted, "Talking about bull, you gave me a mysterious number and the next day the person disappeared. This is not the time to take the high ground."

Caught off guard, Harlow softened his tone, "Fair point, Styles. Alright, what is it you want?"

Sensing an opportunity, Curtis jumped in, "I want to know what the hell is going on here. You could have simply told me you couldn't help with the phone records, but instead, you led me on a wild goose chase that brought us here."

Trying to placate Curtis, Harlow said, "Calm down, mate. I would never have given you that number if I knew something like this would happen."

Curtis raised his voice, "I don't want to calm down! This is not a game, Harlow!"

Harlow took a more earnest approach, "Listen carefully, Styles. There's nothing you can do here. The police won't let you near the possible crime scene. But there is something you can do for me."

"Why should I do anything for you?" Curtis shot back.

Harlow explained, "Let me finish, and I'll explain. I'll give you an address in Ashbury, on the Ashbury turnoff. Go there and tell them Paul Harlow sent you. There's a package waiting for me. I'd do it myself, Styles, but as you can see, I may not be leaving here anytime soon."

Curtis remained skeptical, "This better not be drugs or anything illegal."

"Don't be daft, man! Just pick it up and take it back home with you. I'll come by later this evening or tomorrow morning to collect it. I promise to answer all your questions then, with complete honesty," Harlow assured him.

Reluctantly, Curtis agreed, "Okay, against my better judgment, I'll do it. But remember, Harlow, if you're not completely forth-coming with me tomorrow, you'll have to find someone else to help you."

"You've got a deal, my friend. And, Styles, for what it's worth, I genuinely didn't expect any of this to happen," Harlow admitted.

As Curtis made his way to Ashbury, a surge of pride welled up within him. Throughout his interactions with Harlow, he had always found himself at a disadvantage. But this time, witnessing Harlow's unexpected retreat, Curtis felt a newfound sense of triumph.

Glancing at the address Harlow had provided, Curtis soon found himself navigating a familiar street. Scanning the surroundings for the specified location, he soon stood face to face with what he was looking for.

There it was, a signboard that bore a familiar name: JB Trading. A jolt of surprise shot through him. How could he have forgotten this place? It had only been forty-eight hours since he last set foot here.

"The eyes see what they want to," Curtis mused, realizing the power of selective memory. Yet, conflicting thoughts clouded his mind. Part of him questioned whether this address could truly be the right one. However, throwing caution to the wind, Curtis decided to take the plunge and entered the store.

Penny greeted him in a friendly manner, saying, "Hello, Curtis. Back again so soon. What brings you here?"

"Hello, Penny." Curtis explained the morning's events and added, "A friend asked me to come and collect a package for him."

Penny inquired, "And who would that friend be?" "Paul Harlow," Curtis replied.

Penny disappeared into the back and returned shortly with a brown package in a box. Handing it to Curtis, she said, "Here you go. I'm usually strict about package collection, but I'll make an exception. Just know that I'll track you down if it goes missing." She chuckled heartily.

Thanking her, Curtis said, "Thanks very much. By the way, do you happen to know when Tom will be back from Montpelier?"

"He should be back later this afternoon," Penny replied. "He went to collect a delivery for me. Is there a reason you're asking?"

Curtis pondered for a moment and replied, "Not specifically. I was just wondering whether I should call him today or tomorrow. There's something I forgot to discuss with him this morning, and I'd prefer to do it in person. It can wait until tomorrow morning. Let him know I'll give him a call then to set up a meeting."

"I'll let him know," Penny assured him.

Sitting in his car, Curtis examined the brown package, determined to end the cat-and-mouse games with Paul Harlow. He muttered to himself, "Alright, Mr. Paul Harlow, the cat-and-mouse games end here."

The next morning, Katherine informed Curtis that Harlow had arrived. Curtis inquired about the search's progress.

Paul replied, "We haven't found anything yet, Curtis. The search continues today."

After closing the study door, Curtis got straight to the point. "Tell me what's really happening here."

Paul admitted, "Nothing much until Nikita Marsh went miss-ing." He expressed his disappointment, admitting that he initially intended to gather information but didn't anticipate the complexity of the case.

"What in the world just happened here?" Curtis exclaimed, his frustration boiling over as he slammed his fist onto the desk. "Let's say I believe your explanation! You handed me a contact number, and before long, the person associated with that very phone went missing. That's far from a mere search for information, don't you think?"

Paul tried to explain, "It was just a hunch, Styles. I couldn't give you access to the phone records, but I thought the night receptionist might have known something without realizing it. I had faith that your reporter's instinct would kick in, and you would pursue it. I never thought it would be this significant."

"Thanks a lot," Curtis replied bluntly. "So now, I'm only good enough for dead-end leads?" Paul threw his hands up in resignation. "There's nothing I can say to make this better, Styles."

"Trust me, it definitely won't," Curtis affirmed earnestly.

"Can we put all of this behind us and begin anew?" Harlow proposed, a glimmer of hope in his eyes. "I might just have a proposition for you."

"Go ahead," Curtis urged, his tone demanding, "I hope you have something truly significant to share."

Haddonfield took a deep breath, his eyes reflecting the gravity of the situation. "What has transpired here is a complete game-changer. Although we haven't located her yet, that phone call is undoubtedly at the core of it all. I'm willing to stake my reputation on that," he began, his voice filled with conviction. "Unbeknownst to you, Styles, your actions have disturbed a hornet's nest. Yesterday, I spoke with Kent Devonshire, the head of this investigation. I inquired if there was a way to involve you more directly. And guess what? He's agreed to meet with you once the search operation concludes."

Curtis shook his head, torn. "I don't know, Paul. I got involved to help, not to put people in danger."

Paul urged him, "All I ask is that you hear Devonshire out. We can decide our next steps after the meeting. If we don't agree, we go our separate ways."

"Alright," Curtis agreed reluctantly. "I'll meet with him, and my decision afterward will be final. But what about Haddonfield? What happens with him?"

Paul assured him, "Nothing changes with Haddonfield. You can continue working with him as before."

Curtis pressed further, "I don't want to work both ends unless there's complete transparency. We've seen where the secrecy has led us."

"Speak with Devonshire first, and then we can work out the rest," Paul responded.

Feeling some of the tension dissipate, Curtis spoke up. "By the way, what's in that brown package you had me collect?"

Paul laughed and clarified, "It's a gift for Judy, but there's something in there for you too."

Observing Curtis's perplexed expression, Harlow quickly interjected, "Hold on, before your imagination runs wild with theories, let me clarify that I simply asked you to pick up the package because you were there yesterday. There's no hidden agenda or ulterior motive, I assure you!"

Curtis looked puzzled. "Why would there be something for me?" Paul asked, "Where's the package now?"

Curtis replied, "It's in a drawer in the living room." "Get it, and I'll show you," Paul instructed.

Curtis retrieved the package and handed it to Paul. As he unwrapped it, Paul revealed a scrapbook and handed it to Curtis.

Confused, Curtis asked, "What's this?"

"After the barbecue the other night, I thought about how I could assist you without interfering with the official investigation," Paul explained. "Believe it or not, I felt guilty about dragging you into this with Haddonfield. So, I reached out to a friend of mine in New York, an enthusiastic amateur sleuth. He's been closely following the missing women cases and has compiled a scrapbook with newspaper cuttings and internet research. I convinced him to send it to me. Of course, I left your name out of it."

Curtis stared at Paul, contemplating the unexpected gift. "What am I supposed to do with it?"

"Stop being stubborn, Styles! As a reporter, I assume you're used to conducting research. Consider it as me doing the ground-work for you," Paul said, a hint of sincerity in his voice. "Trust me, it's likely to be thorough. The guy is an ex-college professor, one of those meticulous academic types."

After a brief hesitation, Curtis conceded, "I suppose it can't hurt."

"I have no doubt you'll enlighten me with the gems you uncover," Harlow remarked, a wide grin spreading across his face. "Remember what I said at the barbecue? We're in this together, my friend. Consider this my way of lending a hand."

Curtis pondered for a moment, weighing his options. "Well, I guess it couldn't hurt," he conceded, acknowledging Harlow's offer.

Paul smiled broadly. "I really need to get to the search site now, Styles. I'll call you once I have a date and time for the meeting with Devonshire."

Left alone in the room, Curtis picked up the scrapbook and began flipping through its pages. An article caught his eye—a piece from the Ashbury Herald about Tom Haddonfield and his involvement in the Gabriela Atkins case. Curtis read the names of the individuals in the accompanying photograph: Mr. Tom Haddonfield, his partner, Miss Penny Jones, and her brother, Mr. Barrington Jones.

In stunned silence, Curtis absorbed the unexpected revelation, his mind swirling with newfound possibilities and connections.

While driving to Stratford, Curtis voiced his surprise, "I thought you would have called a day or two before the meetings were scheduled to take place."

"I apologize for that. I had initially set up the meetings for next week, but when Sergio called this morning and asked if I could come today, I thought it would be best to strike while the iron is hot," replied Haddonfield. "I did confirm with the lodge that Matthew Hargreaves, the bar manager, is working today. Unfortunately, the security guard from that night, Max Smith, isn't. We can try to obtain his address while we're there and pay him an impromptu visit afterward."

Curtis resigned to the situation and said, "I suppose there's not much we can do about it." Then he added with a mischievous grin, attempting to catch Haddonfield off guard, "Oh, by the way, you never mentioned that Barrington Jones is your girlfriend's brother!"

Haddonfield looked puzzled and asked, "Where did you learn that?"

Curtis explained, "I've been diligently researching these cases since the outset, and I stumbled upon an article in the Ashbury Herald detailing your involvement in the Atkins case. There was a photograph featuring the three of you."

"Ah, that darn article! Alright, you caught me, pal. Yes, he is Penny's brother. When Edna mentioned his name, I went up to Montpelier to verify the facts. When that turned out to be a dead end, I thought it would be better to let sleeping dogs lie," Haddonfield admitted.

"Tom, going forward, we need to be completely upfront with each other. Keeping things from one another will only hinder our progress," Curtis insisted.

"Agreed," Haddonfield concurred. "From now on, we'll practice complete openness."

As they drove past The Stables Lodge, they approached a T-junction and noticed a sign for SS Motors about a hundred yards ahead.

Haddonfield pointed and said, "This is the place."

Upon entering the reception area, they explained their purpose to the receptionist and were directed to wait in Sergio's office. Before long, a tall man in his mid-twenties with sandy brown hair walked in.

"Hello," he introduced himself. "I'm Sergio Lassiter. And you are?"

Haddonfield extended his hand and replied, "I'm Tom Haddonfield. We spoke this morning. This is my colleague, Curtis Styles."

After they all took their seats, Haddonfield began, "We're investigating the missing women cases. Any information about that night would be appreciated."

Sergio responded, "I'll be glad to help, although I hardly knew her."

Haddonfield inquired further, "What do you mean by hardly knew her?"

Sergio clarified, "I had met her and Jim a couple of times to discuss the event, but that's about it."

"Did anything unusual happen that night?" Haddonfield asked. "In general?" Sergio questioned.

"Yes," Haddonfield confirmed.

"Not really. I was DJing, so I wasn't mingling. There weren't any fights or disturbances if that's what you're getting at," Sergio replied.

"You said 'not really.' Does that mean something did happen?" Haddonfield pressed.

"Well... There was something. I did notice some guy trying to dance with her, but she seemed to be avoiding him. He left after a while, so it didn't seem like a big deal. Sebastian might know more since he spent some time chatting and drinking with her," Sergio revealed.

"Interesting," Haddonfield remarked. "Is there anything else, even if it seems trivial?"

Sergio shrugged. "Not that I can remember. As I said, I don't think I'll be of much help."

Curtis interjected, "Did you leave before or after Jemma?"

"It must have been at least thirty minutes after. I had to pack up my DJing gear. Sebastian helped me, and then we went home," Sergio replied.

"Thank you for your assistance. Could we have a quick chat with Sebastian if he's here?" Haddonfield requested.

"Sure, I'll call him for you. He's in the workshop," Sergio offered.

As Sergio left the room, Curtis couldn't resist making a light-hearted comment, "By the way, doesn't your girlfriend get jealous? You know what they say about ladies loving DJs."

Initially taken aback, Sergio chuckled, "No, don't believe what they tell you. She knows she's the only one for me. Two years together and stronger than ever. Let me go and get Sebastian. Sorry, I couldn't be more helpful."

Sergio exited the room, and shortly after, a stocky, bald man around the same age entered. Curtis couldn't warm up to his boyish face, sensing something was amiss.

Haddonfield introduced themselves, saying, "Hi, Sebastian. I'm Tom Haddonfield, and this is Curtis Styles. We're conducting an investigating into the missing women cases and would like to ask you a few questions about the night Jemma was last seen, if that's alright."

Sebastian, appearing wary, asked, "Are you police detectives?" Haddonfield clarified, "No, we're private investigators."

Sebastian agreed, saying, "Alright, no problem. I'm not sure how much I can tell you but go ahead with the questions."

Haddonfield started, "How well did you know Jemma Anderson?" Sebastian replied curtly, "I didn't know her."

Curtis interrupted, saying, "That's odd. Sergio mentioned that you spent some time with her that night. He must have been mistaken."

Sebastian shifted uncomfortably in his chair. "What I meant was, I didn't know her well. I met her for the first time that night. Jim introduced us, and we chatted for a while. That was all."

"Apparently, she had some trouble on the dance floor. Is that true?" Haddonfield inquired.

Sebastian recounted an incident involving a persistent individual who wanted to dance with Jemma but left after her refusal. Curtis probed for any other noteworthy occurrences that evening, but Sebastian couldn't recall any. They also discussed their departure times from the club, during which Curtis clumsily inquired about Sebastian's relationship, mistakenly assuming he had a jealous girlfriend. Sebastian clarified his single status and left the room in annoyance. Haddonfield chided Curtis for his communication approach, but Curtis defended his curiosity.

Upon arriving at The Stables Lodge, Curtis expressed unease about their joint investigation, mentioning Nikita Marsh's disappearance. Haddonfield suggested a more casual approach for their next visit to the bar. Inside the nearly empty bar, they encountered Matt, the bartender, who noted the unusual quietness for lunchtime. After delving into Nikita's disappearance and their roles as private investigators, the conversation shifted to the night Jemma went missing. Matt recalled an altercation on the dance floor involving Johnny Dawson and mentioned the turbulent relationship between Sebastian McIntyre and Belinda.

Matt offered to introduce them to Fred Smith, the security guard, seated at the other end of the bar. Haddonfield accepted, and Matt made a call to summon Fred over. "Sorry to disturb you, Fred. We were wondering if you remember anything unusual from the night Jemma disappeared."

Fred seemed shy but answered, "There was no trouble that night, just an argument between Sergio and Sebastian before they left. I told them to keep it down and leave before they woke up the guests."

Curtis asked kindly, "Do you happen to know what the argument was about?"

Fred's memory kicked in. "They were arguing about some girl, but I didn't catch the whole conversation."

Haddonfield inquired about whether Fred had informed the police, and Fred responded, "I told Mr. Jim about it, and he said to keep it quiet. He would handle it and speak to them. Those two are always arguing."

Curtis wanted to dig deeper. "Did you happen to catch the girl's name?" Fred seemed disappointed. "Sorry, I didn't."

Thanking Fred, Curtis offered to buy him a beer. After Fred returned to his seat, Curtis turned to Haddonfield, a sense of suspicion creeping in. "Sergio and Sebastian haven't been completely honest with us. I wonder what else they could be hiding."

Haddonfield cautioned against jumping to conclusions. "Let's not let our imagination run wild, pal. People may have their fair share of secrets and cover-ups, but that doesn't automatically make them murderers."

Just then, Curtis received a call on his mobile. After a brief conversation, he ended the call and turned to Haddonfield with a somber expression. "That was Paul Harlow. They found a body, and they thought it was Nikita Marsh. He wants us to stay put. He's on his way here and wants to talk to us."

A heavy silence pervaded the room as they grasped the seriousness of the situation. Curtis and Haddonfield occupied a secluded table, patiently awaiting the arrival of Paul Harlow, who eventually joined them after a forty-five-minute delay. Curtis introduced Haddonfield to Harlow, and they proceeded to order beverages.

The conversation shifted towards the discovery of the body, with Harlow delivering the information matter-of-factly, "She was recovered from the river, approximately two miles downstream from the bridge. Although we strongly suspect it's Nikita Marsh, official identification is still pending."

Haddonfield inquired about the cause of death.

Harlow replied, "We're not sure at this point. Once the autopsy is conducted and the coroner compiles the report, we'll have a better understanding."

Curtis, wanting to know the reason for Harlow's urgency, asked, "So why did you need to speak with us so urgently, Paul?"

Harlow explained, "I wanted to touch base with both of you. I know you're working together on these cases. If you have any information that we may not be aware of, it's crucial that you share it with us. We don't want any more bodies turning up in the river."

Curtis began to respond, but Harlow interrupted. "Nobody is pointing fingers at you two, but this is an official police investigation, and we would greatly appreciate your cooperation."

Curtis felt a surge of anger, his eyes burning with intensity. He carefully chose his words, stating, "If we had any vital information, we would naturally pass it on to the police, wouldn't we, Haddonfield?"

Haddonfield obstinately replied, "Not if they're going to start making baseless accusations."

Intently, he observed as Harlow shifted his gaze towards Haddonfield, a menacing expression etched on his face. "I strongly advise you to consider the consequences of aligning yourself with the wrong person," Harlow warned, his tone dripping with a palpable threat.

Tension filled the room, escalating rapidly. Curtis sensed an impending conflict. He raised his hands, pleading, "Stop! This is absurd! Ultimately, we're all on the same side here."

A sudden silence fell upon them. Haddonfield spoke defiantly, "If you want our cooperation, treat us with respect. We're not a couple of bumbling fools. The pot calling the kettle black comes to mind."

Before Harlow could respond, Curtis interjected, "I believe we've said all that needs to be said. I thought this would be a productive meeting." He added, "Paul, I think it's best if you leave before things are said that can't be taken back. If we come across any information, we'll pass it on."

Harlow simply said, "Good to hear," and without saying goodbye, he got up and left.

Haddonfield turned to Curtis, inquiring, "What was that all about?"

Curtis replied, "I honestly couldn't tell you."

Haddonfield expressed his opinion, "Sorry to say this, but your friend isn't the most likable character."

Curtis agreed, saying, "This time, I have to agree with you. The pressure must be getting to him."

In the afternoon, Curtis and Katherine sat on the porch, discussing Nikita Marsh's tragic situation. Katherine offered comfort to Curtis about Paul's surprising behavior. Curtis outlined their plan: he would investigate the guest list, Tom would inquire further, and they would meet later to decide what to do next.

The following morning, Curtis decided to concentrate on examining the guest list. His phone rang, and it was Paul Harlow, who requested a meeting at his residence at noon.

Curtis apprised Katherine of the upcoming meeting, to which she suggested, "Maybe he intends to offer an apology for his behavior."

Amused, Curtis responded, "I guess I should go and listen to what he has to say."

At noon, Curtis reached Paul's residence, and Judy informed him that Paul was presently in the cottage at the far end of the garden, which had been transformed into his private workspace.

As Curtis approached the cottage, curiosity gnawed at him. The door was shut, so he knocked, and Harlow's voice invited him in, saying, "Enter!"

Upon entering, Curtis was taken aback. Seated around the table in the center of the room were Paul Harlow, Tom Haddonfield, Richard Smith, and a middle-aged man with graying black hair. Curtis couldn't help but exclaim, "What's happening here?"

Harlow burst into laughter, his jovial voice filling the room. "Take it easy, Styles. Come and have a seat, and all will be explained," he said, gesturing for Curtis to join them. "But first, let me introduce you to Kent Devonshire. You already know the rest of the crew."

Kent Devonshire, a tall and athletic figure, stood up and extended his hand toward Curtis. As they shook hands, Curtis was immediately captivated by Devonshire's angular face and calm, intelligent eyes. "Pleased to meet you," Curtis greeted him.

Devonshire smiled and replied, "Good to meet you too. Paul has spoken highly of you."

As everyone settled into their seats, Harlow proceeded with the introductions, highlighting Devonshire as the lead investigator for the missing women cases.

Cutting to the chase, Devonshire began, "Gentlemen, I've recently taken charge of this investigation. In just two months, we've had one woman go missing and another found dead. To be frank, it's been frustrating."

Curtis couldn't help but respect Devonshire's authoritative demeanor as he continued, "I have a strong aversion to failure. In my twenty-five years on the force, I've only had one unsolved case. But we can save that story for another time. I'm resolute in not allowing this figure to double."

Intrigued, Haddonfield inquired, "So, what's your proposal? If you're suggesting a reduction in our investigation efforts, we should address that right away."

Tension gripped the room as they anxiously awaited Devonshire's response.

Devonshire remained composed and replied, "Tom, quite the opposite. Before I continue, let me explain my philosophy. I don't believe that the police always know best and that everyone else should step aside. I strongly believe that different parties can all contribute to solving crimes. It's the result that matters, nothing more."

He paused and then added, "That being said, people need to understand their roles and fulfill them diligently. Stepping on each other's toes won't lead us anywhere."

Haddonfield shifted in his chair, clearly intrigued. "Very interesting. You have my full attention."

Devonshire continued, "As you all know, we have a police task force for these cases, which I chair. What I propose here is something similar. We are all involved in these cases, but we represent different groups. If you gentlemen agree, we can meet weekly, unless there's an urgent need for a meeting."

Haddonfield, with a hint of skepticism, questioned, "If we agree to this, would you be the chairperson as well?"

Devonshire remained unfazed. "Not necessarily." "We'll democratically elect a chairperson."

Curtis shot Haddonfield a sharp glance, sensing his resistance. He already admired Devonshire but couldn't help but feel that Haddonfield was being disruptive.

Curtis spoke up, "I think it's a great idea, and if we move forward with this, Devonshire should be the chairperson. I believe Paul and Devonshire can contribute to both groups, but I worry that it might put the rest of us at a disadvantage."

"I don't quite follow, Curtis," Devonshire responded. "Do you think we're here just to gather information from you and use it for the police investigation?" Curtis looked ashamed but admitted, "Pretty much, yes."

Devonshire clarified, "Here's how I see it. We are all following our own paths in these investigations. Just as you and Tom will collaborate, Paul, myself, and the task team will do the same. We're simply bringing these groups together and pooling our information."

Curtis nodded and said, "I'm happy with that. Count me in."

Haddonfield reluctantly agreed, "Alright, count me in too. But what role does Richard play in all of this?"

Devonshire explained, "Richard represents the media. He heads up LSB Online, the digital news publication. I thought it was important to have him on board to advise us on how we can make the best use of digital media to advance these investigations."

Curtis noticed a glint in Haddonfield's eye at the mention of the media.

Richard Smith, a small bespectacled man, spoke up, "Devonshire and I have been friends for years. When he approached me with this idea, I couldn't pass up the opportunity. Being in the media, it's frustrating to always comment from the sidelines."

Curtis agreed, "That's a fair point. I've often felt that we could play a more active and productive role in crime solving."

Devonshire interjected, "Now, gentlemen, are we in agreement to move forward?"

The group nodded in unison.

"Richard will be staying with me until Monday when he flies back to Los Angeles. I suggest we have our first official meeting this weekend for a case review," Devonshire proposed.

After some discussion, they agreed to meet on Sunday afternoon at Kent Devonshire's house. Devonshire added, "We can have a barbecue and enjoy a few beers afterward, so wives and girlfriends are welcome."

As they left the cottage, Haddonfield turned to Curtis and said, "You can be the hunted, or you can be the hunter."

Confused, Curtis asked, "What do you mean by that?"

Haddonfield replied cryptically, "Just an observation, nothing more."

"Katherine, how about inviting Richard and Kent Devonshire over for dinner?" Curtis suggested. "After all, Richard helped me with a cover story when I first met Haddonfield."

Katherine smiled and agreed, "That's a fantastic idea! It'll also give me a chance to get to know Devonshire better."

Curtis chuckled and added, "Strike while the iron is hot, as they say."

After ending the phone call, Curtis turned to Katherine and informed her, "They'll be here at six. I wasn't sure if Devonshire was married, so I extended the invitation to his significant other. Turns out he is married, but they have a child recovering from the flu, so it will only be Devonshire and Richard."

"I need to get ready and go to the shops," Katherine said earnestly. Curtis looked at the clock and remarked, "It's only nine in the morning. Why the rush?"

"Oh, Curtis! How many times have I told you not to procrastinate when you can act now?" she said.

He burst out laughing. "Touché, my dear."

Sitting alone in his study, Curtis picked up his mobile and dialed a number.

"Hello, Dad!" came a familiar voice.

"How are you, Parker? Hope Los Angeles is treating you well," Curtis said.

"All going well on this side. How are you and Mom?"

"We are well, son. Listen, I wanted to ask you something."

"Dad, what are you up to?"

Curtis laughed. "Why would I be up to something? It's just that I met this fellow the other day, and he said he used to be in advertising in Los Angeles. Same game as you, so I thought you might know him."

"Do you know how many advertising agencies there are in LA?" asked Parker. "Give me a name, and I can ask around. Why are you so interested in this fellow?"

"You know I'm curious by nature. Can't help myself," responded Curtis. "I still think you're up to something. Maybe I should call Mom and find out what's going on," said Parker mischievously.

Curtis chuckled. "No need to do that." "Alright, whose trail am I hot on?" "The name is Tom Haddonfield."

"Tom Haddonfield? Now why does that name sound familiar?" Stated Parker quizzically. "I've heard that name somewhere, but for the life of me, I can't remember where. Let me ask around, and I'll get back to you, Dad."

"Thanks, son, and we'll chat soon." Curtis hung up the phone.

After a few minutes of contemplation, Curtis dialed another number. "Hello, Sarah speaking," came the voice on the other end of the line.

"Sarah, Curtis Styles speaking. How are you?"

"My word, Curtis, I'm well. And how are you enjoying your retirement?"

"I'm starting to feel really old," he said. "I just got off the phone with my son, and he asked me the exact same thing."

She laughed heartily. "What can I do for you?" "Why would you think I wanted something?"

"We were colleagues for years, my dear. I know how your mind works."

"You got me," he said resignedly. "I'm trying to find some information on someone."

"So, you're not retired then?" She said good-humoredly.

"Let's call it helping a friend," he said. "I know you have some contacts in New York. Could you see if you can find out anything about a guy named Lyndon Whiteford?"

"Alright, do you have any specifics for me?"

"He was a private investigator; I'm guessing in his forties. Unfortunately, that's all I have. I say 'was' because the last I heard; he had quit. He owned his agency at one time," said Curtis.

"No promises, but I'll see what I can do. Is he missing?" asked Sarah.

"Nothing like that. From what I've been told, he decided to go backpacking across Europe," stated Curtis.

"Mid-life crisis come early, then." "Something like that!"

"I'll see what I can do."

"You're a darling, Sarah Bowen, thank you," said Curtis gratefully.

She chuckled. "You better not let your wife hear you talking to other women like that!"

Getting up from his desk, Curtis entered the living room and turned on the local news channel. A press conference was about to start.

Sitting back, he was stunned to see Kent Devonshire walking up onto the stage. After the introductions were made, Devonshire began his address:

"It is with great sadness that we can reveal that the body discovered in the Salem River two days ago was Nikita Marsh. We delayed this press conference to alert the next of kin and make an official identification. Until we have the autopsy report, we have no further details to provide at this point. I do understand the frustration of the community surrounding not only this tragic event but also all of the missing women cases. I can promise you that I will not rest until the perpetrators have been brought to justice. I thank you for your time."

As Devonshire left the podium, a cacophony erupted from the assembled press.

A young woman stepped up to the microphone and announced, "That concludes today's press conference. We will not be taking any questions at this time."

Curtis sat glued to the television set. "Perpetrators plural," he said out loud. "Very interesting!"

"I must say, Katherine, that was an exquisite meal," complimented Devonshire as the small group reconvened in the living room.

"It was my pleasure," replied Katherine, visibly pleased by the praise. After Curtis had refilled everyone's drinks, a brief silence enveloped the room.

Breaking the quietude, Curtis addressed Devonshire. "I watched your press conference today, Devonshire, and something puzzled me. You mentioned perpetrators. Does that mean you suspect multiple killers are at large?"

Devonshire responded, "Not necessarily. It's more of a hunch, but I can't shake the feeling that not all the disappearances are connected to the same person. I believe there might be a copycat killer involved."

Curtis found it intriguing. "Interesting. Is it possible that we don't have a murderer at all?"

"Do you mean that these women vanished willingly or are being held against their will somewhere?" Devonshire asked, contemplating the idea.

"Exactly," Curtis confirmed.

"It is a possibility. In fact, it would be the best outcome, as it means there's a chance of finding them alive. However, if you ask me, the most likely scenario is that we are dealing with bodies," responded Devonshire gravely.

Curtis, intrigued, sought more information. "If I may ask, could you tell us about the unsolved case you mentioned?"

"Now, Curtis, our guests didn't come here for an interrogation," scolded Katherine sternly.

Devonshire, with a good-natured tone, reassured her. "It's alright, Katherine. I'm used to being bombarded with questions from the press. A nosy bunch they are!" Then his expression turned somber. "It's not something I usually discuss, but I suppose I can share it with you."

"Fifteen years ago, when I was a homicide detective in Stratford, there was a case. A young eighteen-year-old girl named Jessica Stones was murdered. Her throat was slit, and her body was left in a public park. I vividly remember promising her parents that I would bring them justice. Justice that I never achieved," Devonshire revealed, clearly distressed by the memories. "I'm sorry," he continued, "Talking about it stirs up unpleasant emotions. Would you mind if I stepped outside for some fresh air? Rick can fill you in on the details."

"Of course," replied Katherine kindly. "Please forgive my husband. He sometimes forgets his manners."

As Devonshire left the room, Curtis turned to Richard. "Wow! I didn't think anything could shake that man."

"Despite his composed exterior, that particular case hit him hard," explained Richard. "I've known Devonshire for a long time, and for some reason, this one really got under his skin."

"I suppose it's because it's the only case he never solved. It's understandable," remarked Curtis.

"You know, I've always felt it was more than that," Richard added.

"In any case, would you mind sharing more details about Jessica Stones' case?" Curtis inquired.

"Devonshire believed the murderer struck while Jessica was out with her roommates at a nightclub," Richard explained. "They returned, she got a text, left briefly, but never came back. The next morning, they found her bed untouched, and her body was found in a park nearby, brutally assaulted."

"That's horrifying," Curtis reacted.

"It was a case that haunted Devonshire; he invested everything in it, but it remains unsolved," Richard added.

"He seems deeply affected," Curtis noted.

"A year later, he transferred to Montpelier, possibly to distance himself from it," Richard speculated. "I think he regrets not staying to fight for justice."

Curtis had a thought, "What if the same person from that case is behind these recent crimes? A returning serial killer?"

Katherine interjected, "Curtis, drop it. It upsets him."

"Agreed, let's focus on the current investigation," Richard advised. "The cases aren't likely connected; Jessica was found in a park, unlike the recent disappearances."

Curtis paused, lost in contemplation as his mind ventured into its own realm of thought. "However," he interjected, his voice filled with intrigue, "we must also consider that a serial killer can evolve and change their patterns over time."

Curtis, momentarily snapped out of his thoughts by Katherine's stern glare, concurred. "You're both right. Let's leave it be."

Secretly, however, Curtis knew he couldn't let go of this line of inquiry.

The next morning, after a refreshing shower, Curtis spotted a missed call from his son on his phone. He promptly dialed back and was met with Parker's cheerful tone. "Hey, Dad. I've got some info on Tom Haddonfield for you."

"Wow, that was fast," Curtis remarked.

"I discussed Haddonfield with my boss," Parker revealed. "Surprisingly, Haddonfield had a successful career in advertising before transitioning to a private investigator."

"That must have been a significant change," Curtis replied.

"I don't really know him well," Curtis admitted. "We're only collaborating on a project."

"I hope you're not getting mixed up in anything troublesome," Parker teased.

Curtis decided to call Sarah next. "Do you have any information?"

"Lyndon spent a year backpacking and then relocated to Vermont," Sarah replied. "I'm not sure exactly where, but I'll keep searching."

"Thanks," Curtis responded. "This morning is becoming increasingly unusual."

Later, Curtis found Katherine in the garden and joined her. "Every day seems to bring unexpected surprises," he commented.

During their conversation, Curtis made an effort to repair their strained relationship, acknowledging his need for more tact. He also shared the surprising details he had uncovered about Haddonfield's divorce and Lyndon Whiteford's potential whereabouts in Vermont. While Katherine acknowledged his points, she urged caution and reminded him of the limitations of the information available.

Despite their conversation, an uneasy feeling continued to bother Curtis. He decided to search "Lyndon Whiteford private investigator" on Google, intensifying his intrigue and suspicion. As he scanned the search results, one headline caught his attention:

*"Private Investigator Lyndon Whiteford Probed
in Human Trafficking Case."*

Entering the kitchen, Katherine couldn't help but notice the puzzled expression on Curtis's face.

"What's on your mind?" she inquired.

Curtis let out a sigh and replied, "I just finished reading an article about Lyndon Whiteford. You know, the guy who was suspected of human trafficking a few years back."

Intrigued, Katherine leaned in and asked, "What happened with that?"

"He was eventually cleared of any wrongdoing, but you know the old saying, 'where there's smoke, there's fire,'" Curtis explained. Curious for more details, Katherine pressed, "Can you tell me how it all unfolded?"

Curtis summarized, "Well, he was initially hired to investigate cases of infidelity, but somehow, he ended up getting tangled in a human trafficking case."

"Guilty by association," Katherine noted.

"Exactly," Curtis agreed. "Maybe that's why he eventually left the private investigator business. Sometimes, it feels like I'm chasing illusions, you know? The truth might be simpler."

Katherine nodded knowingly and offered her perspective, saying, "That often happens. When you stumble upon something new, it's easy to get sidetracked. Perhaps you need a more focused approach, one that's independent of others' expectations."

Curtis nodded in appreciation, thankful for her insight.

Curtis realized the truth in her words. "You're absolutely right. I don't have a set method, and I've been going in circles. That needs to change, starting now."

Later, in his study, Curtis sat down and pulled out a piece of paper from his notepad. He began writing:

Victim: Jemma Anderson/Nikita Marsh.
Location: Last seen at the Stables Lodge.
Possible Suspects: Jim Richardson, Sergio Lassiter, Sebastian McIntyre, Barrington Jones, Matt Hargreaves, Mr. X

Curtis paced the room, deep in thought. "Think outside the box," he muttered. "Maybe it had nothing to do with Jemma Anderson."

Leaving, he grabbed his car keys. "Katherine, I need to go out for a bit."

"Sure, see you later," she replied.

At the Stables Lodge, Curtis asked the receptionist, "I'm investigating Nikita Marsh's death. Do you know who she was close to here at work?"

She didn't question him and said, "Frankie Walsh. They were close."

"Thanks. Anyone else?" Curtis pressed.

"Sorry, I'm new here. Just Frankie," she admitted.

Curtis thanked her and asked, "Did Frankie live with Nikita?"

"Yes, but she's out with her boyfriend this morning. She should return around noon," the receptionist informed him.

Curtis checked his watch. "That's in roughly ninety minutes. I'll think of how to pass the time. I'll be back then. Thanks again for your assistance."

Exiting the lodge, Curtis drove to Ashbury while contemplating his approach to the upcoming conversation. He parked and entered the store, greeted by Penny.

"Good morning, Curtis," Penny greeted him with a warm smile. "What can I do for you today?"

Curtis proceeded to explain, "I'm here to conduct an interview for a story on Nikita Marsh. My editor is really pushing for this piece. Additionally, I'd like to pick your brain about the local history, given that you grew up here."

Penny graciously offered her assistance, and Curtis continued, "I'm well aware of the recent cases involving missing women, including Nikita Marsh. What I'm trying to uncover is if any similar incidents occurred between Jessica Stones' tragic murder about fifteen years ago and these recent events. I believe your insights could be invaluable for my research."

Suddenly, Penny's complexion paled. Concerned, Curtis inquired, "Is everything okay?"

Her voice trembling, she revealed a deeply personal connection, "Jessica Stones was my roommate when she was murdered."

Curtis was stunned, "I had no idea. I apologize if I upset you."

Penny regained her composure and responded, "It's not your fault. You couldn't have known. It was just such a horrifying experience at the time that I tried my best to forget about it."

Empathetically, Curtis responded, "It's completely understandable to suppress such traumatic events as a coping mechanism."

A silence settled between them, and eventually, Penny was the one to break it, saying, "I've been away for years, and there haven't been any cases like this."

Curtis concurred, "It's hard to believe, especially in such a peaceful countryside."

Following their brief conversation, Curtis decided to take his leave. "Penny, I should get going. I'm sorry if this conversation brought back any distressing memories."

Penny reassured him, "No problem at all. See you on Sunday."

After the somewhat awkward exchange with Penny, Curtis returned to The Stables, feeling a sense of relief. He was eager about his recent discovery and hoped that Frankie Walsh might provide answers regarding her enigmatic phone call. Upon reaching the lodge, the receptionist informed him that Frankie had returned and was expecting him. Curtis followed the directions and introduced himself to Frankie on her porch, mentioning that Janet had informed her of his visit.

After a brief explanation of his involvement in the case, Curtis opened up about his guilt. "The thing is, I feel incredibly guilty. Nikita called me the day before she disappeared and said she had something important to tell me. I can't shake the feeling that whatever she wanted to say is connected to what happened to her."

He noticed Frankie's eyes welling up with tears.

Once again, Curtis found himself at a loss for words. "If now is a bad time, I can always come back later."

After taking a moment to compose herself, Frankie responded, "I'll be okay. It's just really hard knowing that someone you're so close to is never coming back."

"I understand," Curtis said, realizing he had been saying that a lot that day.

"Come inside," she suggested. "It's more comfortable than standing out here."

After they were seated, she asked, "How can I help you?"

"I was wondering if Nikita mentioned anything to you about these missing women cases. Something that might indicate she knew something." "No, not at all. She was naturally upset about what happened to those girls, but I never got the sense that she knew anything," Frankie replied.

"I figured it was a long shot," Curtis said in a resigned tone. "My wife always says I act before I think."

A sheepish look appeared on Frankie's face.

"Did you remember something?" Curtis inquired.

"No," she replied, "It's just that..."

Curtis inquired, "Frankie, if there's anything, no matter how minor, please don't hesitate to tell me."

Frankie hesitated briefly, then confessed, "I did something I shouldn't have. Nikita asked me to destroy her diary if something happened to her, but I didn't. I kept it in my work locker."

Curtis probed further, "Why did you decide to do that? Do you think it's connected to the missing women?"

Frankie appeared taken aback. "Oh, nothing like that! Nikita asked me this a long time ago. I just don't think she wanted her parents to find it."

Curtis, with curiosity, asked, "Have you read it?"

She explained, "I intended to destroy it, but I became worried that the police might search her belongings, and they knew she had a diary. If they couldn't find it, they might suspect me since we live together."

Curtis inquired, "What did you mean earlier when you said, 'if anything ever happened to her'?"

Frankie clarified, "Like a sudden accident, you know how life can change in an instant."

She turned to Curtis. "Do you think I should take it to the police?"

"Why don't you allow me to handle it? I have connections with the commissioner in charge. I'll request a private review, and if there's nothing of evidentiary significance, he'll return it to you," Curtis kindly suggested.

Frankie agreed, wiping her tears away, and they headed back to the lodge. Curtis hoped for a breakthrough. When he finally returned home, Katherine expressed her frustration over his extended absence.

"I apologize," Curtis said, showing her the diary. "But guess what I found?"

Katherine sighed and relented, "Go ahead, tell me."

"This is Nikita Marsh's diary," Curtis revealed.

Katherine raised ethical concerns about invading the deceased girl's privacy and suggested handing it over to the police, specifically Kent Devonshire. Curtis, feeling torn, acknowledged the logic in her argument.

Katherine pointed out, "You were supposed to collaborate on these cases, right?”

“That's what they said, but I'm still not entirely sure I trust it,” Curtis responded cynically.

Katherine suggested, “Leave the diary on the table and go for a walk in the garden.”

Curtis looked puzzled. “What's the point?” Katherine replied with a mischievous twinkle, “I'll 'accidentally' find it and satisfy my curiosity. It's just a simple notebook.”

Curtis chuckled. “So, you can read it but not me?”

Katherine clarified, “I'd prefer it that way. Once I've looked, I'll share what's relevant.”

Curtis agreed to go for a walk to give Katherine time to read the diary. Upon his return, Katherine informed him that most of it contained day-to-day entries, but she had marked two pages that might be of interest to him. Taking it in his hands, Curtis turned to the first marked page and began reading aloud:

“Dear Diary,

Two gentlemen came to see Jim today, inquiring about Jemma Anderson's disappearance. It was only after they left that I had this nagging feeling that I recognized the younger one. I can't quite put my finger on where, though. Ugh, my memory can be so frustratingly unreliable! But I'm sure it'll come back to me. Later, I went out for sushi with Frankie. I keep trying to convince her that Sergio will never leave his girlfriend, but she just won't listen. It's only a matter of time before the truth comes out.”

Yours in mystery,
Niki

Turning to the next entry, Curtis delved deeper into the diary's revelations:

“Dear Diary,

I finally remembered! The Bradshaws called today and

booked a two-night stay for next month. They were guests on the same night Jemma disappeared, and that triggered my memory. Another guest from that night checked in under the name Steven Somers. But here's the twist – that's not his real name. How do I know? When those two gentlemen came to see Jim about the missing women cases, one of them seemed so familiar. I couldn't shake it off. It has been bothering me ever since. So, being the curious person I am, I went through my stack of old magazines during lunchtime (call it a hunch). And there it was! His name is Tom Haddonfield. But wait, it gets stranger. In the photograph, he was standing alongside his business partner – Steven Somers, a.k.a. Lyndon Whiteford. That's when it clicked. I remember overhearing Jemma on her phone one evening when she disappeared, saying, 'Lyndon, I thought you were meant to be a big shot private investigator...' She caught me eavesdropping and we locked eyes briefly before I had to step away. I didn't think much of it then. But now, connecting all these puzzle pieces, I'm convinced this can't be a mere coincidence. They must be the same person! I've always longed to be part of a mystery. Now, I just need to figure out a way to reach that old detective guy."

Yours in mystery,
Niki

Curtis expressed his surprise, saying, "I never saw that coming!"

Deep in thought, Katherine shared her concerns, remarking, "The final entry is unsettling. It confirms her deep longing for significance."

Curtis nodded in agreement, commenting, "The idea of Lyndon Whiteford being Steven Somers seems plausible."

Pondering the situation, Katherine mused, "Perhaps she stumbled upon something she wasn't aware of."

Curtis drew a literary reference, stating, "It reminds me of Agatha Christie's books."

With a playful tone, Katherine teased, "Ah, your Agatha Christie obsession again."

Katherine contemplated the possibility of Nikita's other diaries. Curtis offered a suggestion, saying, "Maybe she stores them away each year." Katherine inquired about his next steps. Curtis responded, "I'll discuss it with Devonshire privately. But it always feels like someone is lurking when I investigate these cases."

The next day, Katherine approached Curtis with a question. "Did you manage to set up a meeting with Devonshire to discuss the diary?"

Curtis nodded and smiled. "Yes, honey. We're scheduled to meet before the group meeting tomorrow morning."

Curious about his plans for the day, Katherine asked, "And what do you have in mind for today?"

Curtis replied, "I thought I would dedicate the morning to researching the Jessica Stones murder. Afterward, how about I take my lovely wife out for lunch?"

Katherine agreed, albeit with a condition. "That sounds nice, as long as it has nothing to do with these cases."

Curtis grinned mischievously. "I promise, we won't talk about the cases at all."

Intrigued, Katherine asked, "Do you believe Jessica's murder is connected to our investigation?"

Curtis considered her question. "Honestly, I don't think so. But it's always helpful to be well-informed."

As Curtis delved into his research on the Jessica Stones case, he stumbled upon an article that caught his attention. It was an opinion piece that provided an overview of the case. After a quick skim, he decided to take a break and make himself a cup of coffee before delving deeper into the article.

Returning to his laptop, Curtis immersed himself in the article, reading every word with great attention. The headline captured his focus:

*Community on High Alert Following Brutal Killing of Young
Woman
By Matt Jeffrey*

The local community has been shaken to its core by the recent murder of Jessica Stones. The brutal and audacious nature of the attack has left residents feeling vulnerable and fearful. Gone are the days when doors could be left unlocked, or individuals could walk alone at night without a second thought.

As I delve into the details, it is important to present the facts.

Jessica Stones, a promising eighteen-year-old, had her entire future ahead of her. After a night of revelry at a club, she returned home with friends around 1 a.m. They gathered, enjoying a cup of coffee while reflecting on their evening. Jessica received a text message, informing her companions that she would step out briefly. Tragically, the next morning, she was discovered in the nearby park, having suffered a brutal sexual assault that claimed her life, her throat savagely slit. A young life abruptly extinguished before it had a chance to blossom.

Now, let us return to my initial hypothesis. Why do I believe this could be the prelude to something greater? A glance at recent crime statistics provides a clue. Gender-based violence in the extended community, spanning from Erinsdale to Stratford, has seen a disturbing 20% year-on-year increase. It was only a matter of time before such violence escalated to fatalities.

That time has arrived. It is evident that our police force has struggled to contain this disconcerting trend. Suddenly expecting them to rectify the situation seems far-fetched. The question looms: How long until we mourn another tragic loss?

Unless a swift resolution is achieved, I fear the emergence of vigilante justice within our community. A terror-stricken population teetering on the edge, abandoning the principle of "innocent until proven guilty" in a moment of desperation.

To avert such a scenario, I see only one viable path: collaboration between the police force and the local community. Working hand in hand, they must strive to enhance the safety of all citizens. This is a time that calls for unity and level-headedness in the face of adversity.

After reading an intriguing article, Curtis engaged in a conversation with Katherine to discuss its relevance. Surprisingly, the article penned fifteen years ago, had foreseen a trend that had only recently become evident following Jemma Anderson's disappearance. Curtis expressed his keen interest in contacting the article's author, Matt Jeffrey, to gain insight into his thought process at that time. Katherine cautioned him about potential ethical considerations but ultimately supported his decision.

When Curtis reached out to the author, he introduced himself, saying, "Mr. Jeffrey, my name is Curtis Styles. I was hoping to have a brief conversation with you regarding the Jessica Stones murder." To which came the reply, "Ah, Curtis Styles, your call was anticipated."

Curtis was taken by surprise. "You were?" He exclaimed.

The voice on the other end of the line started laughing.

"Not as sinister as it sounds," said Matt Jeffery. "I heard through the grapevine that you were involved in investigating these cases. As an ex-journalist myself, I figured you'd want to tap into any past cases in the area."

Curtis responded, "Very perceptive. But why did you think I would get in touch with you specifically?"

Matt Jeffrey, a seasoned crime reporter, couldn't help but feel a bit slighted when Curtis initially overlooked the opportunity to speak with local crime journalists. Curtis swiftly steered the conversation toward Matt's opinion piece, where he had predicted a surge in violence following Jessica Stones' murder. Matt clarified that it was more of an intuition, driven by the escalating issue of gender-based violence during that period.

Curtis expressed frustration at the delayed realization of those predictions, and Matt sympathized, acknowledging the tragic consequences. When Curtis inquired about the possibility of a single perpetrator being responsible for both cases, Matt expressed doubt, underscoring his earlier assertion regarding multiple potential incidents, thankfully unfulfilled at that time.

Curtis said, "From what I understand, the police never got close to charging anyone for that crime. Were there no suspects at the top of their list?"

Matt shared his perspective, "In my view, the police bungled that investigation, and by the time they assigned new officers to the case, there was very little to go on."

Curtis asked, "You mean Kent Devonshire?"

"He was one, and for the life of me, I can't remember his partner's name," replied Matt.

Curtis staunchly defended Devonshire's reputation, but Matt proposed that Devonshire's emotional involvement in the case might be clouded by a personal connection. When Curtis sought further details, Matt disclosed unsettling rumors suggesting that Devonshire could potentially be Jessica's father from a previous relationship with her mother.

Curtis was taken aback and inquired whether Matt had confronted

Devonshire and Jessica about these allegations. Matt had indeed approached them privately, only to have both parties vehemently deny any such relationship. Curtis then questioned the credibility of the source, but Matt adamantly refused to divulge it, stressing the immediate importance of focusing on securing justice for Jessica.

Reluctantly, Curtis concurred, recognizing the urgency of the situation. Matt then sought clarification on Curtis's final statement.

Curtis clarified, "It's nothing really. I had a conversation with Devonshire the other night, and when he talked about the case, he became very emotional. At the time, it seemed excessive to me, but maybe this is why."

Matt concluded, "This is one to leave in the past. Dredging it up won't do any good. The focus needs to be on finding out what has happened to these missing women now."

Curtis ruefully agreed, "You're probably right. By the way, do you have any thoughts on these cases?"

Matt replied, "Nothing specific, but I wouldn't be surprised if the culprit is someone lurking right under our noses."

After hanging up the phone, Curtis went for a stroll outside to clear his mind. Instead, he found himself consumed by thoughts of what lay ahead tomorrow and a sudden sense of dread. Matt Jeffery's parting words had struck a nerve.

"What if," he thought to himself, "Am I about to have a meeting and a barbecue with a killer?"

His imagination spiraled, envisioning the seemingly pleasant gathering taking a sinister turn.

"Katherine, are you ready to go?" Curtis called out.

"Just give me a moment, dear," she replied, before adding with a hint of perception, "I can't help but notice you're a tad on edge today."

"I am, and I know I shouldn't be." "I'm sure everything will be fine. Just don't overthink it."

An hour later, Curtis found himself seated in Kent Devonshire's private home office, accompanied by Richard Smith. They gathered around a circular table, where Curtis took out Nikita Marsh's diary from his briefcase and handed it to Devonshire, pointing out the marked pages. "I know I shouldn't have read it, but Katherine found it and..."

Devonshire interrupted, "No need to explain, Curtis. Let's focus on the important information contained in this diary."

After carefully studying the marked pages, Devonshire passed the diary to Richard Smith. "See what you make of this, Rick."

Turning back to Curtis, Devonshire dropped a bombshell. "Well, this certainly complicates things. Did you know that Steven Somers is deceased?"

Curtis looked visibly shocked. "I had no idea whatsoever!"

Devonshire continued, "When I took over this investigation and reviewed the case notes, I was astounded to see that it took the assigned officers over a month to follow up on the guest list from that night. However, the Bradshaws and the Homans, both retired couples, had solid alibis. We also ruled out the young lady, Jinty Jones."

"Somers, on the other hand, presented a different story. By the time the officers interviewed him, he had passed away from a sudden heart attack. We spoke to his wife, who informed us that he hadn't gone away that weekend due to feeling unwell. As a financial adviser with clients all over the state, it was not uncommon for him to offer booked accommodations to friends or associates. It seems that's what happened in this case."

Curtis, still processing the new information, responded, "That's very interesting."

Devonshire added, "The puzzling part is that we could never determine who Somers had given that booking to. But it seems we've just found out."

Richard spoke up skeptically, "I'm not so sure about the conversation she claimed to have overheard. It sounds a bit far-fetched. Seeing Lyndon in the photograph and overhearing a conversation mentioning the name Lyndon."

Curtis chuckled, "You and my wife seem to be on the same page. She said the exact same thing."

Devonshire, in a serious tone, said, "I wouldn't be too quick to dismiss it."

Curtis questioned, "You don't think it's just an overactive imagination?"

"Maybe it is, maybe it isn't," responded Devonshire. "We need to find out the relationship between Lyndon and Somers and locate him."

Surprisingly, Devonshire commended Curtis. "Good work, Curtis."

"Thanks. I was worried I might have overstepped my bounds," Curtis replied, feeling a bit embarrassed.

"Did you come across any other noteworthy discoveries?" Devonshire inquired.

"Not exactly," Curtis hesitated.

"But there is something, isn't there?" Devonshire pressed on.

"Yes, but I must admit, I feel a bit uneasy about bringing it up," Curtis admitted reluctantly.

"Just spit it out!" Devonshire urged, eager to hear the revelation.

"When I went to interview Frankie about Nikita Marsh, things took an unexpected turn," Curtis began, recounting his spontaneous trip to see Penny Jones.

"That led me to dig deeper into the Jessica Stones murder, which eventually led me to a former reporter named Matt Jeffery."

Aware of the case's significance to Devonshire, Curtis looked to Richard for support.

"Typical reporter," Smith offered helpfully. "Once their nose catches a scent, their body follows."

Curtis locked eyes with Devonshire, seeking assurance. "You don't need to walk on eggshells, Curtis. It's only natural to be curious about the case," Devonshire reassured him.

Noting Devonshire's unfamiliarity with Matt Jeffery's name, Curtis decided to get straight to the point. "I stumbled upon an old article that vaguely predicted a series of murders. I reached out to the author, who admitted it was merely a hunch based on flimsy statistics."

Curtis paused briefly, then hastily added, "Jeffery also mentioned something about the possibility of you being Jessica Stones' father."

In a soft, confirming tone, Devonshire replied, "That's correct. I am her father."

With this revelation, Curtis confronted Devonshire about the article predicting recent murders and shared Matt Jeffrey's rumor regarding Devonshire's connection to Jessica Stones. Devonshire confirmed it, and Curtis pledged discretion before their extensive two-hour discussion on the missing women cases with Harlow and Haddonfield.

Finally, Devonshire spoke up, addressing the matter of Nikita Marsh's death. "We're expecting a comprehensive coroner's report soon, which will be made public. Until we have a clearer understanding of the situation, I suggest we hold off on pursuing that angle."

Everyone in the room agreed with this decision.

Devonshire continued, shifting the focus. "Now, let's decide on our next course of action. Harlow and I are bound by procedural constraints in our official police investigation. But the three of you have more flexibility."

Haddonfield interjected, voicing his concern. "This is what I feared. You and Harlow carry on with the usual protocol while we're sent on wild goose chases."

Devonshire clarified, his lips forming a sly smile. "That's not what I meant, Tom. I simply meant that you can leverage that flexibility to your advantage. Let me put it this way: where we may require a warrant to search a property, you may find alternative routes that don't break the law but allow for a bit more creativity."

Haddonfield reluctantly acknowledged, "Okay, I understand your point."

Harlow interjected, emphasizing the importance of collaboration. "The key to our collective efforts lies in the fact that each of us brings something unique to the table. Sometimes, a seemingly insignificant piece of information can hold the key to solving the puzzle, tying together threads that connect different cases. We all need to remain open to that possibility."

Haddonfield nodded, acknowledging the wisdom in Harlow's words. "I see your point."

Devonshire returned to his initial line of inquiry. "Regarding your investigation, Tom, and Curtis, it seems you've been working from scratch, starting with the Jemma Anderson case and tracing the timeline of events."

Haddonfield confirmed, his tone resolute. "That's correct."

Devonshire pressed further, questioning their approach. "Considering the police have already covered much of that ground, do you have a specific angle in mind?"

Haddonfield sought clarification. "What do you mean?"

Devonshire explained, "I understand that you and Curtis have extensively focused on the Jemma Anderson case thus far. The information we shared today covers the other three cases. So, is it worth revisiting old ground?"

Curtis chimed in, speaking up with conviction. All eyes turned to him. "I believe it is. Thank you for the information on the other cases. Tom and I will review it carefully. Reinterviewing people might reveal something that you and Harlow may have missed. More importantly, it could help us establish connections between the possible suspects we've identified in the Jemma Anderson case and the other three women."

Harlow concurred, and both Devonshire and Richard nodded in agreement.

"So, when you say suspects, you're referring to Jim, the two mechanics, the bar manager, and Jones," Devonshire clarified.

"Exactly!" Curtis affirmed.

Haddonfield, however, expressed frustration. "Hold on a minute! You can't seriously think Barrington has anything to do with this. He has an alibi."

Devonshire interjected, attempting to ease the tension. The group burst into laughter, finding his comment unexpected. "Keep calm, Tom. I didn't mean to offend. What Curtis is saying is that we shouldn't dismiss any potential suspects. It doesn't mean we consider Barrington guilty."

Haddonfield firmly defended Barrington's innocence. "Alright, but let me assure you all that if anyone doubts his innocence, Barrington has no involvement in any of this."

Devonshire decided to wrap up the discussion, suggesting they join their partners for a barbecue. "Gentlemen, unless anyone has anything else to add, let's conclude this meeting and join our partners for the barbecue."

Harlow enthusiastically agreed, craving a drink. "You don't have to convince me. I could really use a beer right now."

As the group rose from the table, Devonshire remembered something important. "By the way, Curtis, you missed a name on that list. Some of you may not know this, but there was a mysterious guest at The Stables on the night Jemma Anderson disappeared. It appears this person was acquainted with her. You should add Lyndon Whiteford to your list, Curtis."

Curtis glanced at Haddonfield, gauging his reaction, and observed a look of utter astonishment spreading across his face.

"Yesterday seemed to go smoothly, wouldn't you agree?" Katherine inquired of Curtis.

Lost in contemplation, Curtis responded, "I suppose so."

"I thought everyone got along splendidly at the barbecue," Katherine remarked cheerfully.

"It was nice," Curtis responded. "Sorry, I've been going over yesterday's meetings in my mind. There was a lot to take in, especially finding out that Devonshire is Jessica Stones' father."

"That is quite a shock," Katherine replied. "So, what are your plans for today?"

"Haddonfield will be here at ten, and we'll go over our progress on the cases," Curtis explained.

"Okay," she said. "I was thinking of visiting Jane Thomas. We saw her right after Chloe disappeared, but besides a few phone calls, I haven't been in touch. I haven't been the best friend lately."

Curtis acknowledged, "It's always difficult when someone's going through so much pain. You want to help, but when you see them, words fail you, so you end up keeping your distance."

"Well, that stops today!" Katherine declared. "By the way, I'll let her know how dedicated you are to these cases. Is there anything specific you want me to ask her about?"

Curtis paused and then said, "Could you find out if Chloe had any boyfriends around the time, she went missing or in the recent past? It could be a sensitive topic, but I trust your discretion."

Later, in his study, Curtis discussed Devonshire's suggestion about focusing on potential suspects from their investigation into Jemma's disappearance with Haddonfield.

Haddonfield acknowledged, "I think it's the right approach."

Curtis scrutinized him and said, "I agree with you, which leads us to the elephant in the room."

"You mean Lyndon," Haddonfield replied with understanding.

Curtis noticed Haddonfield's reaction and asked, "I noticed your reaction when Lyndon's name came up yesterday."

Haddonfield shifted uneasily. "I was shocked to hear that he was there the night she disappeared, but there's something else you need to know."

Curtis patiently waited for Haddonfield to continue.

Haddonfield began to share, "Back when I initially joined Lyndon's team, he was in a relationship with Penny. They were going through a tough time, and that's when Penny and I started getting closer. One thing led to another."

Curtis remained silent, allowing Haddonfield to continue.

With mixed emotions, Haddonfield recounted the events, saying, "When Lyndon eventually found out about us, there was a significant confrontation. I feared our friendship and working relationship were irreparably damaged. But oddly enough, two days later he came to me and said he thought it was better for Penny and I to be together. He encouraged us to put it all behind us and carry on as we did before."

Curtis asked, "Do you think he genuinely felt that way?"

Haddonfield replied, "Honestly, no. It just seemed too good to be true."

Curtis pressed on with his questions, asking, "What happened after that?"

Haddonfield continued, "It seemed fine, and Lyndon found a new girlfriend. One day, he came in, and you know the rest. They were planning to go backpacking across Europe."

Curtis considered, "So, perhaps he genuinely meant it when he said you should leave it all in the past."

"For a while, I thought the same. But I haven't heard a word from him since he left," Haddonfield revealed.

"People drift apart," Curtis offered. "I wouldn't read too much into it."

Haddonfield disagreed, "Not if you knew Lyndon. He always made an effort to stay in touch with those he was close to. I thought I fit into that category, but apparently not."

Curtis understood and said, "Well, at least it didn't end on bad terms."

Haddonfield replied, "I suppose, but I can't shake the feeling that it might have all been a ruse."

Curtis inquired, "Do you think he might be harboring some resentment?"

Haddonfield responded thoughtfully, "That's what I'm starting to believe."

Curtis considered it and then said, "That might be true, but I don't think it has anything to do with him being at The Stables the night Jemma disappeared. It seems like we're trying to find connections that aren't there."

Haddonfield mentioned something Penny told him, "On our way home last night, I was talking to Penny about Lyndon being at The Stables that night, and she mentioned something. When they broke up, he told her that she wouldn't get away with treating him like this."

Curtis was curious, "Why didn't she bring this up at the time?"

Haddonfield explained, "She thought everything was fine between Lyndon and me, so she didn't want to worry me or create more tension."

Curtis pointed out, "She could have told you after he left."

Haddonfield responded, "She believed it was better to let sleeping dogs lie."

Curtis emphasized, "I still think Lyndon's presence that night and his potential connection to Jemma don't involve you. We need to focus on why he was there and what his link to her was."

Haddonfield confessed, "I agree, but my concern isn't for myself. When he made that threat to her, he also warned her that she didn't know what he was capable of."

Curtis considered it and remarked, "A lot of people say things like that, mostly just empty threats."

Haddonfield surprised Curtis by revealing, "Don't be so sure. I know for a fact that Lyndon has killed someone!"

Curtis and Haddonfield engaged in a conversation about Lyndon's history, which included an incident of self-defense. This discussion raised concerns about Lyndon's potential involvement in recent cases of missing women. They decided to launch an investigation into Lyndon's activities. However, their hopes for gathering valuable information were dashed during a committee meeting focused on unrelated cases. Curtis acknowledged that the committee recognized flaws in their investigation but remained steadfast in their commitment to pressing forward.

Later, they encountered Lisa Hunter, who shared her account of Sophie's disappearance. Lisa and Sophie had shared drinks at The White Horse Inn, but Sophie opted to walk home alone despite Lisa's offer to accompany her.

Curtis, intrigued, asked a question. "You mentioned having a bad feeling. Did you usually take any other mode of transportation?"

Lisa clarified, "Neither Sophie nor I had a car. We usually walked home from the bar since it's close by. Despite the area's appearance, it's generally safe to walk around at night. But that particular night, something felt off."

Listening attentively, Curtis realized he wouldn't feel comfortable walking these streets at night, regardless of the assurances.

Haddonfield inquired, "Where exactly is Sophie's house in relation to this place?"

Lisa explained, "There's an alley directly across the street. You must have seen it when you arrived. Sophie would walk up that alley, which is only about a hundred yards long. Then she'd turn left onto the next street and walk about another two hundred yards to her home."

Curtis and Haddonfield spoke with Lisa about Sophie's disappearance. They discovered that Sophie hadn't made it home on the night she vanished. Curtis suggested the possibility that Sophie might have been involved in something beyond her usual activities, and Lisa found it strange, hinting that Sophie might have recognized her client from a prior encounter. They also talked about Sophie's phone call from the previous day and her potential involvement in additional activities for the client. Lisa disclosed Sophie's struggles with narcotics and her plan to return to rehab. Curtis then requested to speak with Sophie's sister, Shelley.

Afterward, Curtis and Haddonfield departed to meet with Shelley and discuss their suspicions regarding Lyndon's involvement in the case during the journey.

Soon after their arrival, Curtis and Haddonfield found themselves in Shelley Hawkins' vibrant living room. Shelley, a cheerful and hospitable hostess with a warm smile, harmonized with the lively decor of her room. Haddonfield delicately broached the sensitive topic, emphasizing their dedication to assisting families affected by the disappearances.

Shelley responded with determination, "I will do anything I can to help find out what has happened to her."

Curiosity led Curtis to ask, "Were you and Sophie close?"

Shelley nodded; her expression slightly troubled. "Very close. Although she wasn't always the easiest person to live with. I assume Lisa told you about her drug habit."

Both investigators nodded in unison, indicating their awareness. Haddonfield continued the conversation, "Did Sophie have any enemies? Anyone who might have wanted to harm her?"

Shelley pondered for a moment before earnestly answering, "Nothing major that I know of, although she did have some trouble with Sebastian McIntyre."

Haddonfield sought clarification, "The mechanic?"

Shelley confirmed, "Yes, the same one. He seemed infatuated with her. I suppose it comes with the territory. You sleep with someone, and then they won't leave you alone."

Curiosity piqued, Curtis asked, "Is that what happened between them?"

Shelley reflected and replied, "He was a client, but then he wanted to take her out. So, I guess you could say that. But Sophie wasn't interested, and he started pestering her with phone calls and even showed up at our house once."

Curtis inquired further, "How did she handle the situation?"

Shelley explained, "She threatened to get a restraining order. He had a girlfriend at the time so that put a stop to it. He didn't want his association with Sophie to get back to her."

Haddonfield listed several names and asked, "Lyndon Whiteford, Jim Richardson, Paul Hargreaves, Sergio Lassiter. Have you heard any of these names in connection with your sister?"

Shelley thought for a moment and responded, "She knew all of them except Lyndon Whiteford. I'm not familiar with that name, and Sophie never mentioned it. The four towns are close together, so people tend to know each other. If you're asking if any of them were clients, the only one I know is Jim Richardson."

Both investigators exchanged knowing looks, understanding the implications. Haddonfield remarked sardonically, "Jim Richardson is playing away from home, it seems."

Shelley looked uncomfortable, hesitant to create trouble. "I don't want to start any drama. As far as I knew from Sophie, he visited her a couple of times a few years ago."

Curtis reassured her, "Don't worry, we won't say anything."

Haddonfield delved further, "But the name Lyndon Whiteford doesn't ring a bell?"

Shelley shook her head. "None at all. Sophie didn't share details about her clients, and I didn't ask. I didn't really want to know who she was involved with. Names would come up from time to time, like with Sebastian showing up at the house, you know what I mean?"

Curtis empathized, "I understand."

Haddonfield inquired about a mystery client in Stratford. "Do you have any knowledge about a mystery client in Stratford? Lisa mentioned that Sophie usually worked in Erinsdale but recently started doing outcalls for this person."

Shelley looked puzzled. "I know nothing about that."

Curtis asked if there was anything else she remembered around the time of Sophie's disappearance that might be important.

Shelley replied, "Off the top of my head, I'd have to say no. Leave your number, and I'll contact you if something comes to mind."

Curtis took out his notebook, jotting down their numbers on a piece of paper and handing it to her. "You can call either of us if anything comes up."

After thanking Shelley and bidding farewell, Curtis and Haddonfield walked silently back to their car. As they reached the vehicle, Curtis suddenly realized his need to use the bathroom.

"I need to quickly dash back inside to use the bathroom. I thought I could hold it, but it can't wait," Curtis informed Haddonfield. He pivoted swiftly and strode up the driveway, arriving at the front door. Curtis knocked, patiently awaiting a response. As Shelley eventually opened the door, tears cascaded down her face. Without hesitation, he enveloped her in a comforting embrace.

After a while, Curtis stepped back and made a promise to Shelley, "I promise you, Shelley, I won't rest until I uncover the truth behind these disappearances." Once he saw her regain her composure, he asked, "Do you mind if I use the bathroom?"

Shelley directed him, saying, "Straight down the passage, second door on the right."

Upon returning from the bathroom, Curtis noticed that Shelley seemed more cheerful.

"Sorry, but talking about it just reminded me of how much I miss Sophie," she apologized.

Curtis reassured her, "You have nothing to apologize for."

Then he remembered something he forgot to ask earlier. "By the way, I forgot to ask you earlier. Does the name Barrington Jones mean anything to you?"

Shelley looked at him, recalling the name. "I know him well. He used to live in Ashbury."

Curtis responded, "Ah! Would you happen to know if he ever was a client of your sister's?"

She laughed, dismissing the idea. "I couldn't imagine Barrington hiring an escort."

Curtis agreed, "I didn't think so, but I wanted to ask just in case."

A solemnity etched across Shelley's face. "Regarding these men, you're inquiring about... Do you suspect any of them might be involved in Sophie's disappearance?"

Curtis replied honestly, "Not necessarily. We're just following leads and trying to find connections between them and the other missing girls. We came across their names during the Jemma Anderson disappearance investigation." However, he noticed that the mention of Jemma Anderson seemed to trigger some thoughts in Shelley's mind.

She suddenly recalled, "You know, that just reminded me. I saw Barrington the night Jemma Anderson disappeared."

Curtis inquired of Shelley whether she was certain that Jemma's disappearance coincided with her meeting Barrington at the White Horse. Shelley affirmed this, recalling their encounter around midnight. She hadn't disclosed this to the police as their questions had solely pertained to Sophie's case.

Shelley expressed apprehension about implicating Barrington, and Curtis enigmatically replied, "Associations have a tendency to linger."

Earlier, Curtis and Katherine had discussed Chloe's case and the pending autopsy results for Nikita Marsh. They delved into Curtis's suspicion regarding Lyndon Whiteford's involvement with Sophie Hawkins and the potential connection to all the disappearances due to Sophie's associations with other suspects. Curtis grappled with self-doubt about his analytical abilities, but Katherine reassured him, underscoring the necessity for unconventional thinking in resolving the cases—a sentiment with which Curtis concurred.

Curtis poked his head into the kitchen, asking," "Do I have time for a quick shower before breakfast? Haddonfield called and wants to visit me later this morning. I'd rather get ready now because he tends to show up unexpectedly."

Katherine chuckled. "Hurry then! I was about to start cooking bacon and eggs. I need to leave by nine-thirty for the book club tea."

Curtis smirked, "Seems like the ladies are living la dolce vita while the husbands work hard to make money."

She playfully warned him, "Don't be cheeky, or you'll be making your own breakfast."

As the cuckoo clock struck eleven, Curtis stood by the living room window, gazing at his front lawn. He spotted Haddonfield's car pulling into the driveway, and two figures emerged from it, walking up the path.

"Morning, Tom," Curtis greeted cheerfully.

"Morning," Haddonfield replied, introducing the other person. "This is Barrington Jones."

After shaking hands with the stranger, Curtis couldn't help but think, "He looks completely different from what I expected." Before him stood a tall, bespectacled young man in his mid-twenties with tousled brown hair.

Curtis sensed Jones' nervous energy and extended a friendly hand. "Pleased to finally meet you."

Jones replied apprehensively, "Good to meet you too. Tom has told me quite a lot about you."

Curtis and Haddonfield came across Barrington Jones, who admitted to being in Erinsdale on the night Jemma vanished. Barrington had previously provided inaccurate information about his location, fearing that his presence in the area could be connected to Jemma's disappearance.

During their conversation, Barrington disclosed that he had seen Shelley Hawkins that same night and was aware of Lyndon's presence at The Stables Lodge. Curtis and Haddonfield strongly advised Barrington to cooperate with the police, a suggestion to which he agreed. They also discussed Jemma's enigmatic association with an unidentified man, although Barrington had limited information about him. After Barrington departed, Curtis shared this newfound information with Katherine and expressed reservations about Barrington's candor.

Katherine expressed her concern, saying, "That doesn't sound promising."

Curtis chuckled wryly and responded, "Perhaps I'm being a touch melodramatic, but he's definitely withholding information."

After a moment of contemplation, Katherine asked, "Are you planning to discuss your suspicions with Tom?"

Curtis shook his head. "I don't think that would be wise. Tom seems very protective of Jones, which is understandable considering he's dating his sister."

Katherine interjected, "Apologies for changing the topic abruptly, but I have news. Paul Harlow called while you were away. He expressed a desire to visit you today, accompanied by Devonshire. Apparently, he had been trying to reach you, but your phone was on voicemail."

"Argh... I completely forgot to charge it with Haddonfield coming over. Did he mention what time he'll be here?" Curtis exclaimed, a hint of frustration in his voice.

"He said they would come around two. You should give him a call when your phone is charged to confirm," Katherine responded.

"Good idea," Curtis said, rising to return to the house.

Shortly before two o'clock, Devonshire and Harlow arrived, and Curtis welcomed them into his study. "Gentlemen, what brings you here?"

Harlow explained, "We have the preliminary results from Nikita Marsh's autopsy. Devonshire thought it would be best if we informed you in person before it reaches the press."

Curtis convenes a meeting with Devonshire and Harlow to review the autopsy results for Nikita Marsh. The findings indicate that her cause of death was drowning, accompanied by a significant presence of narcotics in her system. The circumstances surrounding whether this was accidental or intentional remain uncertain. During the meeting, Curtis is informed that Nikita's other diaries have been located, but there is a lack of information regarding external factors that might have influenced the autopsy's conclusion.

"We discovered that she had a private lock-up. With a search warrant, we found them all there," Harlow interjected.

Realizing they had read the diaries, Curtis asked, "I assume you've gone through them?"

"We've read the last few years," Devonshire replied.

"Did anything interesting come up?" Curtis inquired.

"We couldn't find anything concrete, but I did bring last year's diary for you to peruse," Devonshire explained. Reaching into his briefcase, he retrieved the diary and handed it over to Curtis.

"Why last year's?" Curtis questioned. "Do you think I might find something you missed?"

"Something like that," Harlow said. "We thought it wouldn't hurt for you to take a look. We also want you to revisit her roommate, Frankie."

Curtis was skeptical. "Why? Frankie seemed to have told me everything she knew when we last spoke."

"Sometimes people remember things they had forgotten over time. Plus, you seemed to have developed a good rapport with her," Devonshire explained.

Curtis hesitated and replied, "I'm not sure if I would call it that."

Devonshire reminded him, "She trusted you enough to give you the diary, the same one she didn't give to the police. That says something. So, when can you go see her?”

Curtis asked, “Before that, is there something else you want to discuss?”

Devonshire replied, “Actually, there is. It slipped my mind earlier, but I had a conversation with Rick Smith yesterday, and he's eager to share an idea with you.”

“He never contacted me about it,” Curtis noted.

“I asked him not to. I wanted to handle this debrief myself,” Devonshire admitted. “Rick discovered some interesting folklore surrounding The Stables Lodge.”

Harlow chimed in dismissively, “Sounds like a load of nonsense to me.” Devonshire nodded, undeterred.

“Regardless, it ties into Rick's idea. It appears that before the lodge was established, it used to be an old farmhouse. In the 1970s, a tragic event occurred when the farmer's daughter was murdered by her lover within its walls. I understand it sounds like something ripped from the pages of a cheap fiction novel. Nevertheless, Rick uncovered an article written shortly after the farmhouse’s transformation into a lodge. Apparently, guests started complaining about peculiar disturbances in Room 3. Objects would inexplicably go missing and move around mysteriously. This caused quite a stir within the local community, and I'm sure you can imagine how the story unfolds from there.”

Curtis burst out laughing, “Let me guess. That's supposedly the room where she was murdered, and it gained a haunted reputation. You've got to be kidding me!”

“Look, I know it sounds like rubbish, but hear me out,” Devonshire insisted. “Rick believes that writing an article about the case could generate national interest in our current investigation. Think about the young woman and the elevator video from The Cecil Hotel. Are you familiar with that case?”

Curtis replied with annoyance, “It sounds vaguely familiar.”

“If you have a chance, take a look at it online. It's genuinely creepy,” Devonshire urged. “The video went viral in no time. Rick believes that by resurrecting a similar story and finding a way to connect it with the current disappearances, we could generate a tremendous amount of intrigue and attention.”

Curtis sighed, accepting the task, “I suppose I'll be the one writing it.”

"That's the idea," Devonshire affirmed. "So, Rick has already contacted Jim about sending a reporter to cover the story."

"Apparently, Jim likes the idea. Any publicity is good publicity, I guess. While you're there, you can talk to Frankie as well," added Harlow.

Feeling skeptical, Curtis responded, "It seems like you guys have it all figured out. Let me speak to Richard and see what he thinks. I'm not sure if chasing an alleged ghost story makes any sense right now unless we're trying to sensationalize it."

Devonshire concluded, "I'll leave it in your capable hands, Curtis. Come on, Paul, let's go."

As Harlow and Devonshire exited the door, Harlow whispered to Curtis, "If I were you, I wouldn't waste my time chasing ghosts."

Curtis stood on the driveway, waving goodbye to his visitors, and thought to himself, *That's the problem. It feels like we're chasing after a ghost.*

Curtis expressed his bewilderment, "What's all this nonsense about me writing a story about a ghost?"

On the other end of the line, Smith chuckled briefly. "I got interrupted during my meeting with Devonshire yesterday, and it seems my shortened version of the idea was misinterpreted," Smith explained.

"It just sounds like nonsense to me," Curtis stated frankly.

Smith clarified his intentions, "The idea isn't solely about a ghost story. Think of it as a series of articles focusing on the missing women cases. I know there has been a lot written about it already, but I want to approach it from a different angle. Plus, it'll make for an intriguing feature to start with."

Resignedly, Curtis responded, "I suppose there are plenty of people out there who are interested in this sort of thing."

"I'm glad to see you warming up to the idea," Smith responded.

"Don't push it!" Curtis retorted, still clearly unhappy with the proposal. "Just to be clear, I'll be paying you for your work," Smith assured him.

"Well, if I refuse, you'll just find someone else to do it. Fine, I'll write it. Against my better judgment, mind you," Curtis conceded unhappily.

"I knew you'd come around," Smith replied. "Oh, one last thing. It would be a good idea for you to spend the night in Room 3."

"This just keeps getting better," Curtis muttered.

"It'll provide an authentic experience for the readers," Smith explained. "Whatever! When do you need it by?" Curtis asked impatiently.

"The sooner, the better. I've spoken to Jim, and they have the room available for the whole weekend. Bookings have been slow lately, so he's eager for publicity," Smith said. "Is tomorrow night suitable for you? Bring Katherine along."

"Tomorrow night should be fine. I'll ask her, but I highly doubt she'll be thrilled about playing Ghostbusters," Curtis sarcastically remarked.

Intrigued by his curiosity, Curtis couldn't resist the persistent urge and opted to conduct an online search for additional information. Within moments, his query led him to a 1972 article detailing a tragic event that transpired at a farmhouse in Stratford. As he delved into the article, one particular photograph seized his attention—the visage of the victim struck a peculiar chord, her countenance oddly familiar, radiating youthful vitality. With rapt attention, Curtis embarked on a thorough reading of the article:

Tragic Incident at Marshfield Farm: Local Woman
Fatally Assaulted
By Josephine Hicks, Staff Writer

In a horrifying incident that unfolded last Saturday, Christine Marsh, a beloved member of the community, was mercilessly beaten to death at Marshfield Farm. A confidential source, wishing to remain anonymous, revealed that a group of friends had congregated at a local dance when a heated altercation erupted between Christine and her partner. The exact cause of the dispute remains unclear at present.

Following the altercation, the couple promptly departed from the dance. Subsequently, after an evening spent visiting friends, Christine's lifeless body was discovered in her bedroom by her distraught parents and brother. The extent of the attack suggests a brutal and sustained act of violence.

In response to this heinous crime, the authorities have apprehended a suspect under suspicion of murder. Presently, the police are refraining from divulging the individual's identity or confirming whether he is indeed the victim's boyfriend. Further investigations are underway, and updates will be shared as the case unfolds.

Curtis searched for more information but found nothing about her death. He then attempted to search for "The Stables, Stratford ghost" and stumbled upon another intriguing article from August 1986.

The Ghost in Room Three
By Noreen Summers

Guests staying in Room 3 of The Stables Lodge, formerly known as Marshfield Farm in Stratford, have recently come forward with accounts of eerie incidents during their stays. Reports include missing belongings and unexplained movements of objects within the room. These occurrences have ignited speculation among locals, who believe that this room may be connected to the unsolved murder of teenager Christine Marsh, which transpired fourteen years ago.

The tragic murder of Christine Marsh continues to baffle investigators to this day. While her boyfriend at the time was initially arrested on suspicion of the crime, he was later acquitted. The local community has since speculated that these strange happenings could be the restless spirit of Christine herself, seeking resolution from beyond the grave. Miss Edna Braithwaite, a resident of the area, shared her thoughts, stating, "The case remains unsolved, and until justice is served, I believe Christine's spirit won't find peace."

In response to these rumors, the proprietor of The Stables Lodge, Mr. Harry Greenwood, promptly dismissed any connection between the reported incidents and the tragic past associated with Room 3. In our attempt to gather his comments, Mr. Greenwood stated, "While it is true that some valuables have gone missing from that room, it is purely coincidental. We are conducting an internal investigation, and we are confident that we have identified the responsible party. As for the claims of objects moving in the room, no guest has ever reported such phenomena during their stay here. It appears that someone has been spreading baseless rumors, and I want to reassure everyone that these allegations are unfounded."

When pressed for further clarification on the possibility of Room 3 being linked to the murder of Christine Marsh, Mr. Greenwood declined to provide additional comments.

The debate over the mysterious events in Room 3 continues to

After reading the article, Curtis immediately picked up his phone and dialed Richard Smith.

"You didn't waste any time, Curtis," Smith remarked as he answered the call.

"Answer me this," Curtis demanded forcefully, "Is Christine Marsh related to Nikita?"

"You got it," Richard exclaimed, his voice brimming with revelation. "Turns out Christine Marsh's brother is Nikita's grandfather."

Curtis's voice trembled with agitation as he demanded, "What exactly is happening here?"

Richard sighed audibly on the other end of the line. "Calm down, and I'll explain."

"After returning to Los Angeles, I delved into the area's history and stumbled upon an interesting piece of information. Naturally, I called Devonshire and shared my findings with him," Richard explained.

Interrupting, Curtis expressed his skepticism, "Sorry, Richard, but I fail to see the relevance of something that occurred nearly half a century ago to the current cases. Nikita's great-aunt's murder is just a coincidental fact."

"I understand your perspective, but hear me out," Richard patiently pleaded. "I told Devonshire that other publications might uncover this information, and we would have no control over what they choose to reveal to the public. I wanted to warn him because the last thing he needs is an influx of thrill-seekers muddying the waters of this already complicated case."

A brief silence hung in the air before Curtis replied, "Please, continue. I believe I'm beginning to see your point."

"The initial call was merely to give Devonshire a heads up," Smith continued. "He called me late yesterday and explained that he had received the preliminary autopsy report on Nikita Marsh. He had an idea he wanted to discuss with me."

"And this is where the paranormal angle comes in," Curtis concluded.

"Exactly!" Richard confirmed. "The idea is quite simple, really. Devonshire wants to downplay this whole ghost phenomenon. He doesn't want it to overshadow the current events. The problem is people tend to spout wild theories, and the last thing we need is a flood of leads about alien abductions of these women. You know as well as I do, Curtis, that not all reporters have the same journalistic integrity."

"I understand that, but why didn't Devonshire come to me and discuss it? We could have devised a plan together," Curtis responded with a hint of frustration.

"He should have, but I believe Harlow influenced him, making him think you were touchy on the subject. I know about the phone call and the missed meeting," Richard sympathized.

"So, if I understand correctly, I'm going to write a story not to generate interest but rather to minimize any potential hype," Curtis said, disbelief in his voice.

"In a way, yes. Essentially, we're getting the story out before anyone else can sensationalize it. But there's another reason behind this," Richard explained.

"There is?" Curtis inquired.

"This is where Devonshire's idea truly shines. He thought it could be the perfect undercover ruse. You'll go and spend the night there, under the guise of writing this article. It'll allow you to interact with the locals more easily, and if someone there is involved or has knowledge of these cases, it might lower their guard. People will perceive you as a ghost hunter rather than someone gathering information about the ongoing investigation. That's when people are most likely to slip up and reveal things," Richard revealed.

"Devonshire should have just come and explained this to me. There's no need for all this secrecy," Curtis remarked.

Smith chuckled loudly, mockingly saying, "I think people are a little wary of you, the unpredictable Curtis Styles!"

Curtis retorted, "You're still paying me for this, right?"

"I am, but goodness, when did you become so money-hungry?" Richard replied, slightly exasperated.

"Just want to make sure I receive what's due to me," Curtis responded flatly. "By the way, what about the other articles you mentioned?"

"We'll discuss those when you return. For now, I'll confirm your booking for tomorrow night at The Stables," Richard informed him.

With their conversation coming to an end, the two men bid farewell.

Stepping into the backyard, Curtis spotted Katherine hard at work in the garden. Approaching her, he said, "What an afternoon. I have a lot to tell you."

After recounting the events in detail, Curtis asked, "Are you up for a night at the stables?"

Katherine stared at him intently and replied, "I'll accompany you, but I must admit, call me superstitious or spiritual, I believe meddling with the dead can only bring trouble."

As her words faded into the distance, Curtis felt a chilling breeze brush past his face.

Jim Richardson warmly welcomed his guests into Room 3, ensuring their comfort with a friendly, "Please enjoy your stay, and don't hesitate to call reception if you need anything." The room exceeded Curtis's expectations with its luxurious features. It boasted generous space, a grand king-size four-poster bed, sophisticated furnishings, and a private en suite bathroom. The ambiance was one of tranquility, adorned in tasteful Sherwood Green and White decor.

Jokingly, Curtis remarked, "If I were a ghost, I would feel right at home here."

Katherine responded with an icy glare, cautioning, "Come on, Curtis! Let's show some respect."

After settling into their accommodations, Curtis proposed a visit to Frankie's place for a discussion about their upcoming interview. As they descended the hill toward her house, they were pleasantly surprised when Frankie herself appeared, expressing her excitement about the article Curtis was working on. This unexpected encounter led to an engaging and lively conversation among them.

Frankie invited them inside her living room. Curtis dove straight into the conversation. "Did Nikita know about her great aunt being murdered here?"

"She did, but it wasn't a topic she liked to discuss," Frankie revealed. "I think she found it too morbid. However, this haunting business is news to me. I've never heard anything about it."

"That's probably for the best," remarked Curtis. "It would have made her job here quite unpleasant."

Frankie pondered the matter. "She wouldn't have liked that, for sure."

Curtis, feeling embarrassed, gently continued, "Would you happen to know if Nikita used drugs?"

Momentarily caught off-guard, Frankie looked at him intently. "Are you asking if she was an addict?"

Curtis blushed and quickly clarified, "No, sorry, that's not what I meant.

I was just wondering if she occasionally dabbled."

Sensing his discomfort, Katherine chimed in with a soothing tone. "There's a theory circulating that drugs might have been involved."

"Like an overdose?" Frankie asked directly.

Curtis nodded. "Yes, something like that. You know how people like to gossip and speculate? It doesn't matter whose reputation they tarnish in the process. We thought it would be best for you to be aware of the rumors."

Curtis felt immediately grateful for Katherine's input. *She knows just what to say.*

Frankie and Katherine, though initially defensive, admitted to occasional recreational drug use among lodge staff due to their demanding work schedules, and Curtis mentioned the discovery of Nikita's other diaries, noticing Frankie's discomfort.

"Oh!" Frankie stammered; her voice shaky. "I... I just hope they handle it discreetly. It would be mortifying if people read my innermost thoughts while I'm unable to defend myself."

Curtis reassured her, "I'm sure they'll maintain absolute confidentiality. I hope I haven't upset you today. It wasn't my intention. You've been so helpful, and I wanted to keep you informed about the case. We all want to bring this matter to a close as much as you do."

Frankie managed a weak smile. "Thank you for thinking of me. I appreciate it. It's still very upsetting. I suppose that's to be expected."

"Before we go, is there anything else you've remembered since our last conversation that could help us solve this case? Even the tiniest detail could make a big difference," Curtis pleaded.

Frankie, unable to remember anything substantial, assured them that they would share any pertinent details as they recollected them. Curtis, in response, expressed his gratitude to Katherine for her assistance and conveyed his embarrassment about the interview.

There was a brief pause before Curtis inquired, "Katherine, are you listening to me?"

Startled, she apologized, "Oops, sorry. My mind wandered off."

Curiosity piqued, Curtis pressed further, "What had your thoughts captivated?"

Katherine hesitated for a moment before responding, "Well, when you mentioned the police discovering the diaries, she appeared quite uneasy."

A seed of suspicion germinated in Curtis' mind, compelling him to express his thoughts. "Could it be possible that she's aware of something significant in those diaries, something she desperately wants to conceal?" He mused.

Katherine responded with a firm tone, "I can't say for certain if she has read them or is aware of their contents, but there's an undeniable sense that she's guarding a secret."

Curtis's excitement grew. "Then we better read that diary as soon as we get back to our room."

"That was a complete waste of time," Curtis grumbled as he closed the diary, placing it on the bedside table.

Katherine nodded in agreement. "It certainly seems that way. But do we even know what we're looking for?"

Curtis looked at her with a puzzled expression, waiting for her to elaborate.

She continued, "We're only looking for things that are obvious to us. Familiar names and such. Maybe we should approach it with a more open mind when we review it tomorrow."

Curtis nodded in agreement. "I'm going to take a shower and change. After all this, I think a night out at the pub might do us some good."

After what felt like an eternity in the shower, Curtis and Katherine drove to the pub and ordered food and drinks. Curtis added with enthusiasm, raising his beer glass in the air, "Cheers! And the food here is surprisingly better than I expected."

Katherine chuckled. "First the room, now the food. It seems like this place is growing on you, Curtis Styles."

He chuckled. "I must admit, despite the dubious circumstances that brought us here, I'm starting to appreciate it. I feel more relaxed than I have in ages." Glancing around the busy pub, he added, "It's quite lively tonight."

"It's Friday night," Katherine replied. "Oh, look who just walked in." She pointed towards the bar.

Curtis followed her gaze and spotted Paul Harlow. "Paul!"

Harlow turned, waved, and made his way over, drink in hand. "Curtis and Katherine, what a pleasant surprise."

"Don't act like you didn't know we'd be here," Curtis said, teasingly. "The real question is, what are you doing here?"

Harlow shrugged. "Just finished a round of golf at the Stratford Country Club. Thought I'd stop by for a quick drink on my way home."

Curtis narrowed his eyes playfully. "So, you weren't here to spy on me?"

Harlow scoffed. "Don't flatter yourself, Styles. I have better things to do with my time than follow you around."

"Good to hear," Curtis replied with a smile.

Just then, Jim approached their table. "Good evening, everyone. Mind if I join you for a drink?"

"Please do," Katherine said graciously.

As they settled in, Jim asked, "So, how are you enjoying your stay so far?"

"It's been quite pleasant," Katherine replied. "Although I still feel a bit uneasy about sleeping in that room. The thought of someone being murdered there gives me chills."

"Now, Katherine, you don't seriously believe in all that haunted nonsense," Harlow interjected, mockingly.

Katherine shot him a firm look. "You shouldn't dismiss things you know nothing about."

Changing the subject, Curtis spoke up. "Speaking of unusual occurrences, Jemma mentioned a guest staying here the night she disappeared—Mr. Lyndon Whiteford."

Jim gave him a quizzical look. "Lyndon? He wasn't here that night." Curtis shifted uncomfortably. "But you do know him, right?"

Jim nodded. "Quite well, actually. Before I bought this place, I managed a hotel in New York. We had a series of robberies, and we brought him in to investigate. He quickly solved the case."

Harlow grunted disapprovingly.

Ignoring the reaction, Curtis continued, "Are you sure he wasn't here that night?"

"Positive," Jim replied firmly. "Why do you ask?"

Curtis hesitated. "Nikita mentioned recognizing him from a photograph in a magazine."

"She must have been mistaken," Jim said confidently. "I know for a fact he wasn't here that night."

Curtis pressed further. "But how can you be so sure? I know the room wasn't booked under his name, but—"

Interrupting, Jim explained, "He was in Los Angeles on business."

"I'm sorry, but now you've completely lost me," Curtis admitted, a hint of confusion evident in his voice.

Jim, looking somewhat uncomfortable, began, "I'd rather not delve into too much detail, but I engaged Lyndon to look into a private matter for me. That evening, he was out on business, and we even had a phone conversation. I have the name of the place where he was staying. I handled the booking and payment, so please feel free to verify their records if necessary."

Curtis sighed. "If you could give me the name and contact details, I'd appreciate it. I don't doubt your story, but it's always good to follow up."

Harlow stood up. "Alright, I better get going before my wife blows up my phone."

After exchanging goodbyes, Harlow left.

Jim commented, "He's a peculiar fellow. Sometimes he's friendly, and other times he acts like he doesn't know you from Adam."

Curtis replied, "Don't mind him. Paul may have his quirks, but he has a good heart. You just need to understand him."

"I'll take your word for it," Jim said.

Curtis refocused the conversation. "Back to Lyndon Whiteford if you don't mind. Do you happen to know where he is now?"

Jim shook his head. "I'm afraid not. We haven't had any contact since he finished that job."

Curtis persisted, "Would you have his mobile number by any chance?"

"Initially, I did have it," Jim explained. "But a few months ago, a friend suspected his wife of infidelity and asked for my advice. I recommended hiring Lyndon and gave him the number I had. The next day, the guy told me the number was no longer in use and asked if I had an alternative contact number, which I didn't."

Curtis took a deep breath. "As I said before, the guy is like a ghost."

CHAPTER 6: AN OMINOUS LETTER

After Jim departed from the table, Curtis kindly volunteered to fetch Katherine another glass of wine at the bar. She humorously mused about getting a bit tipsy before rejoining the crowd, which left Curtis feeling somewhat apprehensive about the upcoming gathering.

Katherine's expression turned serious. "Apologies, but I can't shake this feeling. The mere thought of sleeping in that room sends shivers down my spine."

After patiently waiting his turn to be served, Curtis finally said, "A double whisky and a glass of dry red wine, please, Matt."

"Coming right up," Matt Hargreaves responded, "It's great to see you again. How's everything been?"

"I wish I had better news regarding the missing women cases, but other than that, can't complain too much," replied Curtis.

Matt placed the drinks on the bar counter. "Let's hope it gets sorted out soon. People around here are getting increasingly edgy."

Returning to the table, Curtis found Katherine in conversation with an unfamiliar man.

"Curtis, this is Matt Jeffery. He mentioned speaking to you about an article he had written," Katherine introduced.

Recalling the telephone call, Curtis said, "Hello, I remember talking to you. How did you know it was me?"

"The internet is a goldmine of information. Granted, a lot of it is useless, but finding a photograph wasn't difficult," Matt replied.

"Oh!" Curtis felt a twinge of embarrassment. "I didn't realize I was worth researching."

"Your conversation resonated with me, and I wanted to put a face to the voice. When I spotted you here tonight, I thought I'd come over and introduce myself."

"I'm glad you did. Sorry it took a while, but it's really busy in here tonight. I also had a brief chat with the bartender, who coincidentally shares your name," Curtis explained.

"Oh! I don't usually come here, so I wouldn't be familiar with the staff names," replied Matt Jeffery. "Your wife mentioned you're writing an article on the Christine Marsh murder."

Curtis paused for a moment. "You've given me an idea. When I took on this assignment, I thought the focus would be on the possibly haunted room where she was murdered. But writing an article about the actual case might be a more intriguing angle."

Matt Jeffery looked at him intently. "If only the walls could talk. After our phone call, I couldn't stop thinking about it. I've started to wonder if the Jessica Stones murder could be connected to these recent cases. I initially dismissed it, but now I'm not so sure."

Intrigued, Curtis asked, "What makes you think that?"

"I can't quite put my finger on it. Your mention of my theory about more tragedy to come stuck with me. I based it on statistics, but perhaps I wasn't entirely wrong. The person could have moved away for some reason and returned now, using a more sophisticated modus operandi," explained Jeffery.

Curtis pondered for a moment and said, "It might be a long shot, but it's conceivable."

"Anyway, I've taken up enough of your time. I just wanted to come over and say hello," Jeffery said, getting up. "Enjoy the rest of your evening." With that, he left the table.

"Pals! What are you doing here?" A voice came from behind Curtis. Turning around, Curtis saw Tom Haddonfield, Penny, and Barrington Jones.

"I could ask you the same question," Curtis replied. "To answer it, though, I have a writing assignment that involves this lodge."

"Sounds intriguing," Haddonfield responded. "You'll have to tell me all about it sometime. We're actually here to meet some friends of Penny's. Before we look for a table, can I get either of you a drink?"

"Thank you, but we're alright for now," Katherine graciously replied. "Okay, then. Enjoy your evening, folks. We'll chat in the next few days," Haddonfield said, and the three of them headed further into the bar.

"There are a lot of familiar faces here tonight," Katherine observed.

"You're right," Curtis remarked just as his phone began to ring. "Sergio Lassiter and Sebastian McIntyre are on the other side."

Answering the call, Curtis said, "Hello, Curtis speaking!"

"Curtis, it's Devonshire here. Can we talk?"

"Give me a minute to go outside. It's so loud in here, I can hardly hear you." Curtis moved into the foyer, which was also crowded. "Devonshire, I'll call you back in a few minutes. I'm going to find somewhere completely quiet."

Curtis dialed Devonshire's number as he strolled along the path toward the hill and the staff quarters. However, before he could complete the call, a rustling sound from behind caught his attention. He swiftly turned around, glimpsed an approaching figure, and suddenly, darkness enveloped him.

"Curtis! Curtis! Can you hear me?" A voice called out from the foggy haze. He struggled to open his heavy eyelids, feeling a throbbing pain in his forehead. Slowly, he regained consciousness and noticed blurry figures surrounding him. "Where am I?"

"Thank goodness!" came a familiar voice, and as his sight cleared, he identified Katherine, Haddonfield, Frankie, and a cluster of people surrounding him.

Katherine held a glass and said, "Drink some water."

Curtis took the glass and sipped slowly, feeling a revitalizing effect.

Haddonfield asked, "What happened?"

Taking a moment to gather his thoughts, Curtis replied, "I went outside to make a call to Devonshire. It was too noisy inside the bar. I remember walking down this path, then I heard a noise behind me. When I turned around to see, something struck my head, and everything went black."

Haddonfield's face showed concern. "Sounds like someone attacked you."

Curtis groaned. "Could someone help me get inside?"

"You need to go to the hospital, love. We have to get you checked out," Katherine said, her voice filled with concern.

"I'll be fine," Curtis assured them. "I just need to rest for a while."

"Your wife is right, buddy. You seriously need to see a doctor. I'll drive you there," Haddonfield insisted, his concern evident in his voice.

Surrounded by a sea of worried faces, Curtis responded, his voice tired but determined, "Just let me rest tonight, and I promise I'll go first thing in the morning." However, at that very moment, Curtis became aware of approaching footsteps that grew louder by the second.

Suddenly, Jim's voice boomed out, filled with alarm, "What the hell happened?!"

"Somebody attacked Curtis on the footpath," Haddonfield informed him.

"What? Why in the world would someone do such a thing? And who is responsible for this madness?" Jim questioned; his voice filled with disbelief.

"I don't know, and I didn't see who it was," Curtis weakly replied.

"Please, honey, let's go to the hospital now," Katherine pleaded. "I guess arguing will be pointless," Curtis said. "I hate hospitals."

Curtis comes under attack while on a hill close to the staff quarters, and he experiences a brief loss of consciousness. Jim Richardson and Tom Haddonfield come to his aid, rushing him to a hospital where he receives a diagnosis of a mild concussion. Katherine contacts Frankie to provide an update on Curtis's condition and requests assistance from Tom in helping Curtis get to bed.

"You need to get some rest, buddy. It's been quite a night."

In the hallway, Katherine expressed her gratitude to Haddonfield for his assistance.

Curtis inquired about how they had located him.

Upon returning to the room, Katherine responded, saying, "You should take a pain reliever before resting. I'll go get it for you." She went on to explain that Frankie had contacted Devonshire, who couldn't get through to Curtis. Consequently, Frankie went outside and discovered you unconscious on the pathway.

Curtis pondered why Devonshire hadn't come personally, and Katherine clarified that he was currently out of town. She expressed her concern when she called him from the hospital.

Curtis took the painkiller and a glass of water from Katherine. "I didn't expect the outing to go like this."

"I told you that no good will come from messing with the afterlife," said Katherine sternly.

"The dead!" Curtis replied sarcastically. "They're hardly the problem. It's the living maniac who decided to use my head as a punching bag."

"This is not a joke, Curtis!" Katherine said firmly. "This situation is getting too dangerous. You need to tell Devonshire that you won't be involved anymore."

Before he could respond, Katherine added, "No, Curtis, this isn't up for discussion. You will tell him tomorrow."

Knowing it was futile to argue when Katherine was in this state, Curtis acquiesced, "I just need to try and get some sleep. We can talk about it in the morning."

"There's nothing to talk about. Now, try to rest. Wake me up if you need anything, though I doubt I'll get any sleep," she replied.

The next morning, Curtis woke up and was instantly reminded of the previous evening's events by the dull ache in his head. "Morning, love. Did you get any sleep?"

"Barely, but I managed a couple of hours. How are you feeling?" Katherine asked. "I have a headache, but otherwise, I'm alright. I think a shower will help freshen me up," Curtis replied, trying to sound upbeat.

"I think we should have breakfast before we leave. No point in staying any longer. We need to get you home and into bed," Katherine said matter-of-factly. "You also need to call Devonshire and let him know you won't be working on these cases anymore."

Curtis cautiously ate at the breakfast table when Frankie hurriedly entered the room. "Are you still working?"

"I finished a few hours ago. I wanted to make sure you were alright before going back to my place to get some sleep. A letter was just delivered for you." Frankie handed him a white envelope.

"Who would send me a letter here?" Curtis wondered aloud. He tore open the envelope and read the contents, his face turning pale.

"What is it?" Katherine asked, concerned. Handing her the letter, she read aloud:

Last night was just a warning!
IF YOU CONTINUE WITH THIS INVESTIGATION, YOU WON'T
WAKE UP NEXT TIME!

Frankie's sudden shriek startled the other guests in the dining room, prompting them to look in her direction with concern. She had just received a letter that sent her into a panic. However, Curtis quickly stepped in, reassuring everyone that it was nothing more than a tasteless prank. Frankie went on to describe the young man who had delivered the letter, and her unease about the safety of the lodge grew.

Katherine voiced her apprehensions regarding Curtis's decision to continue the investigation, expressing deep concern for his well-being. Curtis acknowledged her worries but remained resolute in his determination to press forward, despite the risks involved.

Curiosity tinged his voice as Curtis asked, "What exactly are you suggesting?"

Katherine continued with determination, "But here's what I want. Tell Devonshire that you're no longer working on the case. If you won't do that, then I'll have to accept it for now. Promise me, though, that you'll be honest with me at all times."

Curtis contemplated her words. "Alright, I promise." Katherine's tone softened slightly. "Good. And from now on, I want to be more involved. No more running off without me. I want to know where you're going at all times. I won't sit at home wondering what has happened to my husband."

Curtis replied, "Alright, but to be fair, it's only happened a couple of times."

"Well, it won't happen anymore," Katherine stated sternly. "By the way, Devonshire called while you were in the shower. He wants to see you when he gets back from his trip, but I told him you needed rest and suggested Monday instead."

Curtis replied sarcastically, "Yes, Mom. I'm not sure who I should be more afraid of, the bat-wielding maniac or you!"

Katherine allowed herself a brief chuckle. "It's definitely me, and don't you forget it!"

Sitting on his porch later, Curtis spoke to Devonshire. "You know, this weekend has made me reflect on how short life can be."

"I'm truly sorry for what you've been through. I never intended to put you in harm's way," Devonshire said earnestly.

"No need to apologize. It's made me think about my family—Katherine, the kids. It's surreal. But it's also made me more determined than ever to uncover the truth. I've definitely rattled someone's cage," Curtis replied.

"If you want to back out, just say the word. That letter is enough to scare anyone," Devonshire empathized.

Curtis shook his head. "Definitely not! I must continue, but I'll be more cautious. By the way, why did you call that night?"

Devonshire explained, "I was called to a meeting in Montpelier. My superiors found out about our secret committee and gave me a hard time. They weren't happy about involving you and Haddonfield in the investigation. Rick, they understood due to the media angle."

Curtis covered his mouth, rubbing his lips. "They haven't shut us down then?"

"Not yet. I convinced them it was just an information exchange. Of course, they grilled me on the specifics, but I managed to smooth things over for now," Devonshire revealed. Curtis grew concerned. "Could the leak have come from someone at the meeting?"

"You never know, but I guess that it might have come from one of the women that night. You know how they like to gossip. Perhaps she mentioned it to a friend, and the information reached higher-ups," Devonshire pondered.

"Do you think it would reach them that quickly?" Curtis questioned skeptically.

"You'd be surprised," Devonshire replied. "Anyway, that's why I called you that night—to give you a heads up. They might reach out to you and Haddonfield for further clarification."

Curtis sighed. "Couldn't it have waited?"

"I prefer to address things promptly. No point in waiting and risking things falling through the cracks," Devonshire explained. "Your wife must be concerned about your continued involvement."

"She is, and it's got me thinking. It might not be safe for Katherine and me to stay here. If something were to happen while I was away, she would be alone. I don't know what I would do if she got hurt because of me," Curtis confessed.

Devonshire offered a suggestion. "What's your plan then? I can arrange for patrols to check on your house a few times a day."

"Thank you, but I think we should take a short holiday in Stratford," Curtis proposed. Confused, Devonshire asked, "Why Stratford?"

Curtis suggested staying at Edna Braithwaite's bed and breakfast in Stratford as a safety measure and for information-gathering purposes. Katherine expressed hesitation but eventually consented, albeit with a single condition. "And what might that be?" Curtis inquired, a tinge of regret creeping into his voice.

"Two weeks, and if this is not resolved, you promise to walk away from the investigation," she said firmly.

"Don't you think that is a bit unreasonable?" Curtis queried.

"Two weeks or else I stay here," Kathrine said unflinchingly.

"Okay," Curtis responded, "Two weeks, and then I am done."

After some time, Curtis returned and announced, "I have just spoken to Edna Braithwaite. We can move in towards the end of the week."

"I am really not looking forward to living in a small room, even if it is only for a week or so," Katherine reluctantly admitted. She noticed a wry smile on Curtis's face and asked, "What is it now?"

"It seems that Edna has a cottage at the bottom of her garden that is unoccupied at present. I have booked that out, and here's the even better part. She has agreed to let us stay free of charge as long as we take care of our laundry and meals," he said triumphantly.

Her eyes narrowed, suspecting something. "How did you manage to do that?"

"I may have told her that I was writing a book on the farmhouse murder and wanted to stay in the area for research. I think she saw an opportunity to get her name in print," he replied gleefully.

"Oh, Curtis! You and your ruses. One of these days, you're going to get caught," she admonished him.

"You have a point. I need to start writing. Let me go and call Richard to get the ball rolling," Curtis said thoughtfully.

"I'll contact the house sitters and see if they can accommodate us on short notice. How long do you think we'll be away?" Katherine asked.

"Well, considering you've given me a two-week deadline to wrap this up, I'd say from Friday until the following Sunday," he estimated.

Gazing out of his study window at the serene back garden, Curtis embraced a profound sense of tranquility. It was in moments like these that he realized the true meaning of "home is where the heart resides."

Feeling compelled, he reached for his mobile phone and dialed Richard Smith's number.

"Richard speaking, how can I help you?" Came the familiar voice. "Curtis here, how are you doing?"

"Better than you, from what I hear. I feel awful for convincing you to stay in that place," Richard expressed with regret.

"It's not the place that decided to give me a thump over the head," Curtis replied jokingly.

"Good to hear you're in good spirits, my friend. I guess we have no article to write, although we hardly had one in the first place, to be fair," Richard responded.

"That's not necessarily entirely true," said Curtis.

After a few minutes discussing his move to the bed and breakfast in Stratford, Curtis suggested, "Why don't I write an article about the farmhouse murder? I can include the ghost angle. I think it could generate a lot of public interest."

There was a pause, and then Richard replied, "Okay, it's worth a shot. Can you have something for me by the middle of next week?"

"I should have," said Curtis, "Sorry, Richard, I have to cut you short. I have another call coming in. I'll talk to you soon."

He switched to the other incoming line, "Hello, Curtis Styles speaking." "Curtis, this is Lyndon Whiteford. I need to see you. I'll phone you in a day or two and give you a meeting place. Tell no one that I called. Your life could depend on it." With that, the call ended abruptly.

Curtis observed that the call had come from a private number and, unable to contain his excitement, rushed to find Katherine in the laundry room at the bottom of the garden, exclaiming, "You'll never guess who just called me."

"Who?" she inquired with curiosity.

Curtis gazed at her intently, awaiting her reaction, before finally revealing, "Lyndon Whiteford!"

Her jaw dropped in sheer amazement, a mix of surprise and intrigue dancing in her eyes.

"He wants to meet me, but I've been instructed not to tell anyone," Curtis deliberately omitted the part about his life depending on it.

"I don't like the sound of this, Curtis. Forget what I said before. This stops now!" She demanded forcefully.

"Let's calm down and think about this for a minute," he replied soothingly.

"Are you seriously suggesting we meet this guy in secret, even considering the possibility that he could be a murderer?" Katherine exclaimed; her voice filled with disbelief.

"Firstly, we can't jump to conclusions and assume he's the murderer," Curtis countered. "And secondly, how can he be so certain that I wouldn't divulge anything?"

"I'm sure he has ways of finding out," she responded cynically.

"Look, he's going to call back, so let's wait and see where he wants to meet. We can decide from there," he reassured her calmly.

"You won't tell anyone else about this?" She asked, agitated.

"Not for now," he replied. "Only you need to know. You wanted to be more involved, so here you go."

"First, we received a warning note, and now this mysterious call. Something doesn't feel right," she said, folding the laundry with more force. Spotting his sheepish expression, she added, "What is it? I can tell you're hiding something."

"Don't overreact, but he did mention that my life could be at stake if I told someone," Curtis revealed softly.

Katherine let out a shriek of terror. "What have you gotten us into, Curtis?"

"Who was that on the phone?" Katherine inquired with curiosity. "Just Haddonfield. He's going to meet Gabriella Atkins' parents later today, and he asked if I wanted to join him," Curtis responded. "Then why the frown?" Katherine asked.

"I was just thinking about all the people we've interviewed so far," Curtis said. "Every time, you go in hoping to find definitive answers, but somehow we always end up with more questions."

"Thanks for picking me up. You didn't have to," Curtis said appreciatively to Haddonfield as he fastened his seatbelt.

Haddonfield brushed it off, saying, "Don't mention it. Sometimes I'm just glad for the drive. Helps clear the mind."

Curtis approached Haddonfield earnestly, asking, "Do you mind if I ask you something?"

Haddonfield responded casually, "Shoot, pal."

"How do you handle this? You often deliver bad news or information that people don't want to hear," Curtis queried.

Haddonfield contemplated Curtis's question and replied, "Life frequently brings heartache, and I believe providing a degree of closure, even if it can't erase all the pain, carries importance."

As they reached their destination, Curtis was reminded of the challenging mission ahead: meeting with parents who remained in the dark, seeking answers.

"Agreed," Curtis replied, dismissing his contemplation. "Enough philosophizing. Time to get down to business."

A middle-aged man with glasses and a stocky build opened the front door.

"Hello, Dave," Haddonfield greeted. "This is my partner, Curtis Styles."

Curtis shook Dave's hand. "Pleased to meet you."

"Likewise," Dave Atkins replied. "Let me call Shirley. She's out back watering the garden." He disappeared briefly and returned with a woman, short and with long grey hair.

The pain in Shirley's eyes struck Curtis immediately. After exchanging brief introductions, they all retired to the living room.

"Would anyone like something to drink?" Shirley offered. Both Haddonfield and Curtis politely declined.

Without waiting for her husband's response, Shirley said pleadingly, "Please tell me you have some news about Gabriella."

Curtis observed the uneasy expression on Haddonfield's face.

"I'm afraid not," Haddonfield replied. "But there have been developments since we last spoke."

"Such as?" Dave inquired.

After summarizing the recent events, Haddonfield took a deep breath and said, "I don't know how to say this, so I'll be direct. We have reason to believe that Gabriella may have been pregnant when she disappeared."

Curtis watched the pair keenly.

Shirley sat silently; her gaze fixed ahead. But Curtis noticed anger flushing Dave's face as he blurted out, "What nonsense is this, Haddonfield? We're not paying you for baseless information!"

The room fell silent.

Shirley placed her hand on her husband's leg and, with remarkable composure, said, "I think you need to talk to Tiana Taylor. She was Gabriella's best friend."

Driving away from the Atkins' residence, Haddonfield asked Curtis, "What do you make of that?"

"The husband clearly doesn't want to consider that possibility, which is understandable. No father wants to think his teenage daughter had an unwanted pregnancy," Curtis replied. "But the mother's reaction is different. I expected a similar response, but she seemed to believe it could be true."

"I agree with you on that," Haddonfield said.

"Have you heard of this Tiana Taylor before?" Curtis asked, puzzled. "I would've thought Gabriella's closest friends would be the first leads we'd get."

"I would've thought so too," Haddonfield admitted. "I'm not sure. Let's give her a call and arrange a meeting."

Curtis dialed the number Shirley Atkins had given them, bracing himself for the conversation.

"Hi, how can I help you?" A female voice answered. "Hi, is this Tiana? My name is Curtis Styles, and I'm investigating the disappearance of Gabriella Atkins. Her mom gave me your number, and she said you might be able to help with my inquiries," Curtis explained.

There was a brief pause before the voice on the other end responded, "Are you a cop? I can't talk to the police."

"No, I'm not," Curtis reassured her. "Her parents hired us for a private investigation."

There was another pause, and Tiana continued, "Look, he'll kill me if he finds out I'm talking to anyone associated with law enforcement."

"As I mentioned, we're not involved with the police," Curtis assured her gently.

Tiana hesitated; her fear evident in her voice. "Even so, he won't take it lightly. He'll be furious."

Curiosity piqued; Curtis pressed further. "Who exactly are we talking about here?"

"It doesn't matter. Can you meet me later at Crowhurst Park? Around 9 PM. I don't want to meet during daylight when anyone could see us," she said abruptly.

"Crowhurst Park?" Curtis repeated, looking at Haddonfield, who gave him a thumbs-up sign.

"Do you not know the place?" Tiana asked.

"It's alright, my partner knows it well. We'll meet you there at nine PM tonight," Curtis replied confidently.

The line went abruptly dead.

"Well?" Haddonfield asked, seeking clarification. Curtis shook his head. "It's strange, just bloody strange."

Entering through the front door, Curtis briefed Katherine on his meeting with the parents, describing it as yet another perplexing puzzle. He then shared their upcoming plans to meet with Haddonfield and expressed his concerns about leaving her alone at night in light of recent events.

During the drive to Haddonfield's place, Katherine emphasized the importance of their family's safety and granted Curtis a two-week concession to continue his investigation. Curtis appreciated her support and discussed his aspiration to make a meaningful impact on this case.

Upon arriving at Haddonfield's destination, Curtis commented on its proximity to their home. Haddonfield explained that it was known as a local teenage hangout due to its dimly lit and secluded setting.

Curtis surveyed the deserted park, a chill creeping over him. "Brr," he shivered. "If I were a teenager, I certainly wouldn't bring my girlfriend here. It's too risky with potential unsavory characters lurking around."

Suddenly, a figure emerged from the shadows, a woman with long hair wearing what seemed to be a raincoat. She approached and tapped on the driver-side window.

As the window rolled down, she inquired, "Curtis Styles?" From the passenger side, Curtis responded, "Tiana, is that you?"

"It is," she confirmed. "And who's this with you?"

"This is my partner, Tom Haddonfield," Curtis introduced. Before

Haddonfield could reply, Tiana Taylor interrupted, "Before I get in and talk to you, it'll cost you two hundred dollars. Are we okay with that?"

Curtis started to respond, but Haddonfield promptly replied, "Sure, please get in."

Tiana got into the backseat and instructed them to drive to a secluded cul-de-sac nearby. Once they parked, Haddonfield began, "So, Tiana, Shirley Atkins...I believe you can help us."

"Money first!" Tiana asserted abruptly.

Curtis still felt uncertain about the transaction before him. Tom Haddonfield took out his wallet and handed over the two hundred dollars.

"Thank you," Tiana acknowledged. "So, how does Mrs. Atkins think I can assist you?"

"We have reason to believe Gabriella may have been pregnant when she disappeared," Haddonfield explained. "Shirley immediately mentioned that we should speak to you, considering you were her best friend."

Tiana spoke candidly, "She never liked me much. Thought I was a bad influence on her daughter. I'm surprised she brought me up."

"To be honest, they didn't mention you as Gabriella's friend when they hired us," Haddonfield disclosed.

"They wouldn't," Tiana responded matter-of-factly. "They didn't want people to know their daughter was friends with a call girl. Now that she's been missing, suddenly they mention me."

Curtis and Haddonfield met with Tiana, who revealed that her friend Gabriella had been seeing someone she met online named Eddie. Gabriella hadn't shared many details about Eddie, and surprisingly, Tiana was unaware of Gabriella's pregnancy. After the conversation, Haddonfield remained suspicious about Tiana's level of knowledge.

Upon returning home, Curtis and Katherine noticed that the living room light was on, a detail they couldn't recall from their departure. Curtis instructed Katherine to turn off the car and the lights while he took it upon himself to investigate. He approached the house stealthily, discovering that the front door was slightly ajar and unlocked. Curtis entered the house cautiously, using the flashlight on his phone. He found no immediate threats, but an unsettling silence hung in the air. Curtis proceeded to inspect each room for any signs of unusual activity.

Glancing at the front door once again, he felt a foreboding sensation. In that instant, he decided to retreat to the car. With a sense of urgency, he entered the passenger seat and exclaimed, "Someone has definitely been inside. The front door is open. We didn't notice because the porch light isn't very bright."

"What!" Katherine exclaimed anxiously. "Oh, my God! What should we do, Curtis?"

"First things first, let's try to keep calm," he reassured her, his voice steady and reassuring. "I'll contact the police immediately and request that they send someone over. It's not safe for us to go inside in case the intruder is still present."

While standing on the front lawn, speaking to a police officer who had responded to the burglary report, Curtis noticed Paul Harlow's bulky frame approaching. Harlow greeted Curtis before addressing the officer. "McCormack, what's the situation?"

"Evening, sir," Sergeant McCormack replied. "We thoroughly searched the house and the grounds. Everything seems clear, and there's no sign of any theft."

"Where's Katherine?" Harlow inquired.

"She's in the kitchen making coffee for us," Curtis answered.

"Don't worry, sir. Sergeant Harper is with her," McCormack reassured Harlow, noticing his puzzled expression.

"Let's go inside and have another look around. Perhaps you missed something. Is that alright with you, Styles?" Harlow proposed.

"Fine by me," Curtis agreed.

As they ascended the porch steps toward the front door, Harlow asked, "Are you okay, Styles?"

"I'm a bit shaken up, to be honest." After meticulously combing through each room, Curtis remarked, "It seems like nothing is missing. Why break into someone's home and take nothing?"

"They might have been startled by your arrival, prompting a quick escape through the back," Harlow speculated. "Harper, McCormack, did you check the garden for footprints?"

"We did, sir," Harper replied. "We found no footprints or any signs of disturbance in the flowerbeds."

"The phantom strikes again!" Curtis quipped.

Harlow, McCormack, and Harper stared at him with puzzled expressions.

"Pay no attention to me," Curtis said. "It's an inside joke."

An hour later, Curtis and Katherine sat on the front porch, sipping brandies. "I really need this," Katherine admitted. "My nerves are completely shot. I doubt I'll sleep a wink tonight."

"Is it possible we forgot to turn off the lights and properly close the front door?" Curtis wondered.

Katherine looked at him with disbelief. "In all the time we've lived here, has that ever happened?"

"No," Curtis replied despondently. "You don't have to say it. I understand."

"You should try to get some sleep," Curtis suggested as they climbed into bed. "It's nearly two in the morning. I'll read for a bit. Just try to rest."

"I doubt I'll be able to. Bloody hell, Curtis, I'm afraid to fall asleep in my own bed," Katherine vehemently expressed.

"I know tonight has been incredibly shocking, but let's at least try to get some rest, and we can discuss this in the morning," he reassured her as best he could.

Turning away from him, Katherine sighed. "This is unacceptable. You realize that, don't you?"

"We'll talk about it in the morning, love," Curtis responded. He picked up his book from the nightstand and, as he flipped through the pages to find his place, a piercing cry escaped his lips.

Startled, Katherine turned towards him. "What's wrong?" Slowly unfolding a piece of paper, Curtis began to read aloud:

*"YOU SHOULD CHOOSE A BETTER PASSWORD!
THERE ARE A LOT OF HACKERS AROUND, AND YOU DON'T
WANT YOUR PERSONAL INFORMATION TO FALL INTO THE
WRONG HANDS!"*

"It's my laptop!" He exclaimed. "They were after something specific on my laptop!"

CHAPTER 7: THE ATTIC

Curtis had been fixated on the screen for hours. Katherine, growing increasingly concerned about his extended work hours deciphering the intruder's intentions suggested a coffee break in the kitchen.

After a brief pause, Curtis nodded, closed his laptop, and conceded, "I guess you're correct."

Sitting in the kitchen, Curtis sipped his coffee. "There has to be something I'm missing. Whatever they were searching for should be obvious, shouldn't it?"

Katherine thoughtfully considered his words. "Maybe that's the point. We assume it should be apparent, but perhaps the laptop is just a decoy. Maybe the intruder was looking for something else, or maybe they were just trying to scare you. After all, a home invasion is a deeply personal violation."

Curtis stared at her. "So, you mean the laptop is a red herring?" "Exactly," she responded excitedly. "Either they had another motive, or it was all a deliberate attempt to mislead you. This whole situation is becoming overwhelming."

"Well," Katherine suggested, "we're about to move into the guesthouse in Stratford. Why don't you take a day or two to relax and clear your mind before we go? Recharge your batteries."

Curtis sighed, slightly exasperated. "Why do you always make so much sense?"

She chuckled. "The wife always knows best." With the suitcases packed in the car's trunk, Curtis called out, "Katherine, are you ready to go? Everything's packed."

"Coming!" She shouted back. "Just give me a minute. I want to double-check everything."

Curtis and Katherine are getting ready for a trip, but Curtis has a feeling of unease. Katherine reassures Curtis by telling him that Kent Devonshire will be taking him out for a few hours to give her some peace and quiet during the trip. Curtis is taken aback but ultimately agrees. As Kent arrives, Curtis can't help but wonder about the surprises that may await him during this unexpected outing with Kent.

"What is this place?" Curtis asked, trying to make sense of his new environment.

"Welcome to Stratford Forest," Devonshire replied.

"I still don't understand why you had to come and keep an eye on me," Curtis said. "If Katherine wanted to unpack alone, she could have told me. I could have gone to the pub for a while."

"I think she's just worried about you. It has been quite eventful these past few days," Devonshire replied.

Curtis and Kent Devonshire engage in a conversation while taking a stroll, during which Curtis voices his concerns regarding security matters. Devonshire suggests convening another committee meeting to address these issues and mentions that Richard is eager for Curtis to get in touch. Subsequently, Curtis receives a discreet meeting request from Lyndon Whiteford at the train tracks, to which he agrees, placing a strong emphasis on maintaining secrecy.

Later, Curtis discloses to Devonshire that the call was from the house sitter.

Curtis and Katherine arrive at a charming cottage, and Curtis expresses his admiration for it. However, Katherine appears somewhat pessimistic. Curtis takes some time to explore the cottage and finds it appealing, but Katherine responds with caution. They proceed to discuss Curtis's meeting with Devonshire.

"You were right," he replied. "It was exactly what I needed. He took me to the forest on the outskirts of the village. We went for a walk, and it was refreshing, albeit a bit eerie. I wouldn't want to be there alone, though."

Katherine stared at him; her mouth slightly open. "What's wrong?" He asked.

She shuddered. "When you mentioned the forest, for a moment, I imagined the missing girls being buried there. I must be watching too many bad movies."

Curtis looked at her, realizing she might be onto something. "You know, I didn't think much of it at the time, assuming the police would search places like that first. But it might be worth discussing with Devonshire and Harlow."

"I don't want to think about that now. It gives me the creeps," she said, her voice tinged with unease. "So, what did you and Devonshire talk about?"

"Not much, really," he replied. "Oh, he wants to have another committee meeting on Sunday. I need to call Haddonfield and check if he's available."

"Anything else interesting?" She inquired.

Curtis felt a dryness in his throat for a moment. "Well," he started, "there is something, but don't freak out, okay?"

"Now that you're telling me not to freak out, I'm definitely getting worried," she responded, her voice rising.

He took her hands in his, trying to reassure her. "I promise it's nothing to get overly worked up about. But when I tell you, please try not to jump to conclusions."

"Just tell me," she said firmly.

"Just as we were about to leave the forest, Lyndon called me. He wants to meet later tonight," he said softly.

"Where?" She asked bluntly.

He averted his gaze. "Next to the Salem River Bridge, by the railroad tracks."

"Bloody hell, Curtis!" She exclaimed. "Isn't that where Nikita Marsh died?"

"Yes, but I think you're reading too much into it. He just wanted to meet somewhere quiet, where he wouldn't be seen," Curtis replied.

Before she could reply, a knock sounded at the door. Katherine moved to answer it. "We're not done talking about this, Curtis."

He breathed a brief sigh of relief.

A moment later, Edna Braithwaite entered the living room. "I thought I'd come and see how you're settling in. I also brought these freshly baked chocolate chip cookies for you."

"That's very kind of you," Katherine said, turning to Curtis. "Isn't it lovely, Curtis?"

"Too kind," he replied. "Sorry, ladies, if you don't mind, I need to make an urgent phone call."

Taking the opportunity, Curtis stepped out of the cottage and walked across the lawn, ensuring he was out of earshot. A few minutes later, he returned to find Katherine and Edna enjoying coffee in the living room.

"I didn't know how long you'd be, so I didn't pour you a cup," Katherine apologized.

"It's fine for now," Curtis said. "So, what have you two been talking about?"

"Your fascination with these missing women cases," Katherine replied bluntly.

Taken aback, Curtis responded, "I wouldn't call it a fascination exactly." He could feel his face reddening as he spoke.

"Oh, I find it quite thrilling," Edna Braithwaite chimed in.

Curtis glanced at her and realized that she would indeed find it exciting. It was clear that anything that stirred up gossip would be right up her alley.

"I would be extremely happy if I could play a part in providing closure to the families," he said.

After Edna Braithwaite left, Curtis told Katherine, "Get used to these impromptu visits. The term 'village gossip' was coined for people like her."

"Don't be unkind," Katherine said. "She's very sweet, albeit a little nosy. She's probably just lonely."

"Lonely?" Curtis questioned. "How can she be lonely when she runs a guesthouse? She must have people around her most of the time."

"It's not the same, and you know it," Katherine replied. "By the way, did you reach Tom Haddonfield?

"I did, and he's available on Sunday. I just need to take a quick bath. That walk with Devonshire left me all sweaty," Curtis replied.

"Not so fast. We have something to discuss first," Katherine said firmly. "Do we have to?" Curtis asked. "Everything will be fine."

"I don't think you've thought this through properly," she replied. "Clandestine meetings in the middle of nowhere at eleven o'clock at night. How does that sound to you?"

During a tense discussion, Curtis grappled with the idea of dismissing a potential lead. Katherine suggested bringing along additional support, but Curtis hesitated. They even made light of the notion of hiding someone in the car's trunk before Katherine proposed a more practical solution. She warned that she would involve someone named Devonshire if Curtis refused. With reluctance, Curtis agreed, stressing the importance of the person being unrelated to the case. Katherine hinted that she had the perfect candidate in mind, leaving Curtis both intrigued and cautious. Ultimately, he chose to place his trust in Katherine's judgment and left the decision in her hands as he prepared for the unknown.

"I can't help but feel a bit worried," Curtis said thoughtfully. "The person you've brought with me tonight... I shudder to think who it might be."

"You won't have to wait long to find out," Katherine replied firmly. "They should be here any minute now."

A few moments later, the doorbell rang.

"There we go," Katherine said. "Our guest is right on time."

As Curtis opened the door, he was met with the familiar figure of Matt Jeffery. "You!"

"Good evening, Curtis," greeted Matt Jeffery.

Turning to Katherine, Curtis asked, "Should I even ask?"

Katherine explained, "I got the idea from Edna. She was chatting with me while you were out with Kent Devonshire. Matt's name came up, and she mentioned that she knew him quite well. That planted a seed in my mind. To be honest, the idea of someone accompanying you only occurred to me later when we were talking after your walk. So, when you went for a bath, I went to Edna to ask for Matt's number, and the rest is history."

Curtis faced Jeffery, questioning his involvement. "And you agreed to go along with this crazy scheme?"

Jeffery smiled and replied, "What can I say? I used to be a reporter, just like you. We have that innate curiosity to venture into situations others wouldn't."

After finishing dinner, Jeffery thanked Katherine. "That was a lovely meal. Thank you so much."

"It was my pleasure," replied Katherine. "Just promise to keep an eye on my husband."

"I will do my best," responded Jeffery.

"Now," said Katherine, "I'll go and do the dishes. I'll leave you two alone to talk."

During an uncomfortable silence, Jeffrey offered to go along with Curtis to meet Lyndon Whiteford at a secluded spot. They discussed when to leave and the importance of keeping things confidential. While they waited for Lyndon to show up, they briefly reflected on a past incident involving a young woman and dismissed any thoughts of self-harm at this location. When Lyndon arrived, Curtis greeted him, and Lyndon explained the necessity of discretion, even though he wasn't a primary suspect in the disappearances.

"What individuals? Haddonfield?" Curtis inquired, perplexed.

"That doesn't matter right now," Lyndon firmly stated. "There are more urgent matters to discuss."

"Alright then, let's hear it," Curtis said, trying not to show his uneasiness about the situation.

"I was working on a case in Montpelier when it led me to Stratford and the string of disappearances in this area. Long story short, I strongly believe that my case and the happenings here are connected," Lyndon explained.

"Okay, I can buy into that," Curtis replied.

"For reasons I can't disclose at the moment, it has become crucial for me to stay out of sight," Lyndon continued.

"That must be really tough," Curtis empathized.

Without acknowledging the comment, Lyndon went on, "I heard about your involvement in these cases, so I reached out to a friend to gather some background information on you. He didn't know you personally, but being in the same profession made it easier for him to find out a few details. According to all available information, you are regarded as a trustworthy individual."

"I assume you didn't bring me here just to tell me that," Curtis curtly remarked.

Lyndon chuckled at the suggestion. "The truth is, I need someone I can trust entirely to assist me."

"It seems I'm not alone in that regard," Curtis replied. "Being cast as the sidekick appears to be the trend for me lately."

Lyndon laughed again. "I'd take that as a compliment if I were you. Reliable people aren't easy to come by."

"Thanks, I think," Curtis said.

"Anyway, getting back to the point," Lyndon resumed, "Things have reached a stage where I really need someone to help me. I have to leave town for a week, and unfortunately, it can't be postponed. But I don't want to leave things hanging while I'm away. I'm more convinced than ever that the responsible party is becoming unsettled. And when people are rattled, tragedy often follows," Lyndon explained.

"Why do you think they're rattled?" Curtis questioned. "Walk with me," Lyndon replied. "I'll show you."

Lyndon turned and began walking toward the bridge that crossed over the Salem River. Curtis felt a chill creep up his spine, wondering if this was the moment of truth and if Lyndon intended to throw him off the bridge.

"Are you coming?" Lyndon asked.

Curtis felt as if his feet were glued to the ground. "Come on," he muttered under his breath. "You're letting your imagination get the best of you."

"I'm coming," Curtis replied. "This had better be worth it."

As they reached the middle of the bridge, Lyndon abruptly stopped and said, "Look over the side and tell me what you see."

Curtis meets Lyndon Whiteford on a remote bridge, engaging in a conversation about the likelihood of suicide in that place and the potential involvement of foul play. Lyndon alludes to a task he has in mind for Curtis and mentions a friend who can provide clarification.

To Curtis's shock, Lyndon beckoned his friend to join them, revealing an unexpected connection between Lyndon and Matt Jeffery. Overwhelmed and incensed by this disclosure, Curtis opted to distance himself from them and drove away, seeking solace in the comforting embrace of music.

"We're slowly approaching the bewitching hour. Let's take you there with our midnight fourplay. Four songs in a row, starting with this one from 'Talk Talk.'"

As the melodic intro of the song filled the night air, Curtis felt a wave of calm washing over him. He listened intently as the lyrics reached the chorus:

"It's a shame

Number me with rage

Curtis finds himself haunted by the song lyrics and is reminded of a book titled "The Dice Man," in which choices are determined by the roll of dice. This leads him to contemplate the sharp contrast between his systematic investigation and the unpredictable nature of chance. As he heads back to the cottage, he readies himself for the questions Katherine may have.

She glanced up, "How did it go, love?"

"Don't ask," he replied, tossing his car keys onto the entrance table. "Did you know that Lyndon and Jeffery knew each other?"

She looked shocked. "No, I had no idea. If I had known, do you think I would have asked Jeffery to go with you? What happened exactly?"

"I'm too furious right now to discuss it," he said, his frustration palpable. "But I discovered that they're friends. Jeffery knew about the meeting all along, and he dared to sit with us, pretending the whole time."

"I'm sorry," she said, filled with regret. "By the way, where is Jeffery?"
"I left him and Lyndon at the meeting spot. I never want to see or hear from that man again," Curtis declared vehemently.

Katherine's tone turned rueful. "That might be difficult." Confused, Curtis asked, "What do you mean?"

"He left his car here, for one. And he also forgot his car keys, so avoiding him won't be easy," she explained, her voice tinged with resignation.

"You answer his calls, and you can tell him that his keys will be with Edna in the main house. He mustn't come near me. I can't guarantee my actions if I see that man," Curtis firmly stated.

As they spoke, an abrupt knock at the door disrupted them. In response, Katherine swiftly seized the car keys and made her way to the door, where she heard Jeffrey's voice calling out.

"Hi Katherine, could I have a word with Curtis, please?"

"Now isn't a good time," Katherine replied, her voice reaching Curtis. "I'll ask him to call you."

"Thanks," Jeffery responded. "Please let Curtis know that tonight wasn't what he thought it was. If he calls me, I can explain and clear things up."

Katherine returned to the living room, joining Curtis. "You heard that," she said. "Maybe you should give him a call tomorrow once things have settled down. I don't think this was some elaborate plot."

Curtis nodded, realizing his hasty reaction. "You're probably right. In the heat of the moment, I didn't wait for an explanation. I should have."

Katherine seemed somewhat puzzled. "That's quite a change of heart. What made you reconsider?"

Curtis thoughtfully replied, "When I heard him talking to you just now, he didn't sound like someone trying to deceive me. It occurred to me that he might not be as guilty as I initially thought."

Katherine chuckled softly. "He definitely doesn't seem like a dangerous person."

Trying to stifle his laughter, Curtis agreed, "Not at all." He burst into laughter.

Curtis, still preoccupied with the recent events involving Matt Jeffery and Lyndon Whiteford, found himself seated on the cottage patio, replaying the sequence of events in his mind. Katherine interrupted his thoughts by bringing him a cup of coffee and asking about his restless night. She suggested reaching out to Jeffery to clear things up, but Curtis had another call to make first.

Later, he dialed Richard Smith's number. Richard had requested an article about the missing women and hinted at a significant revelation during his visit on Wednesday. Curtis agreed to write the article and discussed the need to keep it from Devonshire and Harlow for the time being. After their call, Curtis discussed the situation with Katherine, and they also contemplated Edna's gardening plans.

Katherine proposed calling Jeffery again, but Curtis hesitated, believing that Jeffery would initiate contact if he wanted to talk. However, their conversation was abruptly interrupted by a sudden knock on the door. It was Edna, standing there, visibly distraught. She sought their assistance in driving her to the hospital as she had found Matt Jeffery unconscious in his driveway that morning. Curtis and Katherine exchanged surprised glances as they absorbed the shocking news.

Curtis couldn't help but regret his past decisions concerning Jeffery and Nikita Marsh. As Katherine updated him on Jeffery's condition and the police observation, his concern grew. Edna's request for help added another layer of complexity to their day. Curtis contemplated delaying his committee meeting, but Katherine encouraged him to attend, assuring him they would gather more information soon.

Although reluctant to contact Lyndon, Curtis ultimately agreed to the meeting. The following day, Edna asked him to check on Jeffery's house. He conducted a thorough search but found no signs of disturbance. However, his search did reveal a mysterious trapdoor.

With curiosity piqued, Curtis muttered to himself, "An attic... Hmm." Despite his reservations, he allowed curiosity to drive him as he explored the attic. To his shock, he found it filled with photographs of missing women. The attic was well-furnished, suggesting it served a purpose beyond mere storage. It featured a desk with a laptop and a bookcase filled with books about serial killers.

Curtis suspected that Lyndon may have been operating from this attic and regretted not pursuing more information from Matt Jeffery. He decided to take the laptop but refrained from turning it on. Returning to the cottage, he was aware that he had entered a more complicated and dangerous path. Haunting song lyrics lingered in his mind: "Number me in haste (such a shame) This eagerness to change. It's a shame."

Driven by a desire for change, Curtis planned to use the skills of a hacker friend to access the laptop later. Respecting Katherine's disapproval, he stashed the laptop bag in an unassuming, lockless chest in the bedroom before receiving a call from Haddonfield.

"Just give me a minute, and I'll be there," Curtis replied. "Could we make a quick stop at the hardware store? Katherine isn't home, and I need a secure place to store some valuables. There's no safe here, but I found a chest I can use. The only issue is it's missing a lock, and I don't feel comfortable leaving things unsecured."

"Sure," Haddonfield concurred. "We can stop by the hardware store. I suppose you'll want to head back to the cottage afterward?"

"Yes," Curtis confirmed, "I'll inform Devonshire that we'll be about forty-five minutes late."

"Let's not waste any more time, then, pal," Haddonfield urged. "Otherwise, we'll never make it to this damn meeting."

"On my way," Curtis replied, "You're a true lifesaver, Tom!"

"Alright, gentlemen, that's a wrap," declared Kent Devonshire. "Curtis, could I have a moment with you before we join the others outside?"

"Sure," Curtis replied, sensing the gravity of the situation. "Sounds serious."

Devonshire chuckled. "Nothing overly dramatic, but I thought it would be best to share the news in person."

"Okay," Curtis said, giving his full attention. "I'm listening."

"I'll be leaving at the end of the month," Devonshire revealed. "There's an opening in Miami, and I've decided to take it."

"Whoa!" Curtis exclaimed, caught off guard. "I didn't see that coming. What made you decide to leave?"

"It's been in the works for a few months now," Devonshire explained. "My father-in-law's health has been deteriorating for about six months. I promised my wife that if an opportunity came up and I got accepted, we would move. As much as I'd love to stay here and find the person responsible for these disappearances, family comes first. You understand, right?"

Curtis nodded understandingly. "I do. I'm just surprised, that's all. I always felt this case was deeply personal to you, especially after what happened with the Jessica Stones case."

"It is," Devonshire acknowledged. "But history has taught me to take a step back and look at the bigger picture. This case could take years to solve, or it may never be resolved. Our time on this earth is limited. I don't want to deprive my wife of the chance to spend what time is left with her father."

"I completely understand," Curtis said. "Honestly, I commend your decision. Family should always come first. By the way, have you considered commuting?"

"No," Devonshire replied firmly. "My work here is done. I need to be there for my wife and family. It may seem like a failure to some, but I believe I've laid a solid foundation for my replacement. There's a strong team working on this case, and with people like you and Haddonfield actively involved, I have a feeling you'll eventually get to the bottom of it."

"You didn't mention it earlier, but what will happen to these committee meetings?" Curtis inquired.

"To be honest," Devonshire confessed, "As you can see from today's discussion, very little progress seems to have been made. We spent most of the time rehashing what we already discussed in the first meeting."

Curtis agreed, "That's true. Do you think we've hit a dead end?"

Devonshire looked thoughtful. "I don't think so. This case is challenging, no doubt about it, but I believe there have been developments. People either don't want to share them or don't realize their significance. When I formed this committee, I wanted to bring together like-minded individuals to share information and brainstorm ideas. But perhaps I didn't think it through properly."

Curtis raised an eyebrow. "Are you trying to tell me something?"

Devonshire smiled wryly. "I want you to take charge of the committee and shape it as you see fit. I admire your focus and determination."

Curtis felt honored. "Thank you, Devonshire. That means a lot. But what about Harlow and Haddonfield? They have more experience, and I'm not sure they would want me in charge. And what does Harlow think about your departure?"

"Nobody else knows about me leaving yet," Devonshire disclosed. "The authorities thought it best if I waited to inform them. They wanted to select the right candidate and have them present during the announcement. It turns out the chosen candidate is a woman, and she'll be here later this week."

Curtis and Devonshire delved into discussions about community efforts and Devonshire's role in them. Curtis expressed some doubts about his suitability for the role. Katherine reassured him to take his time and consider it carefully. Then, Curtis had a sudden realization and expressed his desire to visit The Stables, which took Katherine by surprise.

Curtis hesitated for a moment, contemplating his decision. "You know what? Never mind. It can wait until tomorrow morning. There's something else I need to look into first."

Katherine let out an exasperated sigh. "Make up your mind, Curtis. Your impulsive behavior is going to get us into trouble one of these days."

Apologetically, Curtis replied, "I'm sorry. You know I tend to act on impulse sometimes."

"That's an understatement," Katherine retorted, her annoyance evident in her voice. "Impulsive behavior seems to be your default setting."

As they settled back into the cottage, Katherine couldn't contain her curiosity any longer. "So, care to explain what that was all about in the car earlier?"

Curtis took a deep breath before explaining his thoughts. "I know what I'm about to say might sound far-fetched, but just hear me out."

Katherine nodded her full attention to him. "Go ahead. I'm listening." "When you mentioned that I didn't seem pleased about Devonshire asking me to lead the committee, I admitted that I wasn't. The truth is, both Harlow and Haddonfield are more qualified in law enforcement than I am. I've only written about investigations; I've never actually conducted one."

"Alright, I see your point," Katherine acknowledged. "But I don't understand why that matters. Experience isn't everything."

Curtis continued, "I understand what you're saying, but let me explain further. Despite my lack of experience, I've always relied on my instincts throughout my career, and they've served me well. That brings me back to Devonshire." He paused, noticing Katherine's attentive expression, and debated whether to proceed. Ultimately, he decided to share his thoughts. "I don't believe Devonshire asked me to lead the committee because he genuinely thought I was the best person for the job. I think he has reservations about the other two."

"You mean Haddonfield and Harlow, not Richard," Katherine interjected.

"Exactly," Curtis affirmed. "Devonshire might have asked Richard if he were closer, but since he isn't, I became the available candidate."

Curiosity piqued, Katherine asked, "What reservations are you referring to?"

"That's what I don't know yet," Curtis replied, frustration creeping into his voice. "All I know is that Devonshire asked me to stay behind, not Haddonfield or Harlow. He wants me to continue with the committee, but not necessarily in its current structure. He knows they're unlikely to agree to that. I just happened to be the convenient choice."

Surprisingly, Katherine responded, "It makes sense, but there's a sticking point."

"What's that?" Curtis inquired.

"Wouldn't he have told you if he had suspicions about them?" Katherine asked.

"Not necessarily," Curtis replied. "It would have been nice if he had, but I think his suspicions might be just that—suspicions. He might not have concrete evidence. I don't think he wanted to tip his hand, so he didn't say anything. It's more like keeping your enemies close, you know?"

Katherine's expression changed, a realization dawning on her. "Wait, are you suggesting what I think you're suggesting?"

Curtis raised an eyebrow. "What do you think I'm suggesting?"

"That either Haddonfield or Harlow might be involved in these disappearances?" Katherine questioned. "At first, I thought you meant he didn't trust them, but now it sounds like you suspect something more."

"Bingo!" Curtis confirmed.

Taking a moment to gather her thoughts, Katherine responded cautiously, "I'm not going to disagree with you, but we need to be careful, Curtis. Harlow is your friend, and I know you've grown fond of Haddonfield. Whether or not it started that way, you have a connection with them. If they were to catch wind of your suspicions, it could lead to trouble."

Curtis nodded in agreement, realizing the potential complications.

Katherine shifted gears, bringing up another topic. "What did you mean by that comment about there being four?"

Curtis felt his face redden. "Oh, that. It was nothing, really."

"Don't hold back, Curtis Styles! That wasn't 'nothing'," Katherine replied firmly.

"Okay," Curtis relented. "You know how sometimes when we're in a group, someone slips away unnoticed, and nobody seems to notice their absence?"

"What does that have to do with Devonshire?" Queried Katherine.

Curtis continued, "Not directly related to him, but it just popped into my head when Devonshire left. It made me think about the night I was attacked at The Stables. We assumed someone was waiting for me outside, but that doesn't make sense. How would they know I would go outside that night? It seems more likely that someone from inside the pub followed me out. If they didn't pass by the receptionist, how could they slip away without being seen? We've been interviewing a whole list of people from that pub, including Haddonfield, Harlow, and even Jeffrey was there at some point. I wanted to ask Frankie about it. There must be another way out."

Katherine put her head in her hands, sighing deeply. "I'm sure there must be another exit, but sometimes I don't know how your mind works, Curtis. You follow one train of thought, and then suddenly, you impulsively switch tracks. It's going to get you into trouble one day. Well, let me correct that—it already has."

Curtis raised his hands in surrender. "I'm sorry, sometimes my mind works in overdrive. One thought leads to another, and I feel the need to address them immediately."

"You really need to calm down and think things through, one step at a time," Katherine advised. "But for now, I'm going to take a quick bath before bed. It's been another exhausting day."

As Katherine left the room, Curtis reached for the brandy. Just as he was about to pour himself a drink, he heard Katherine's voice calling him from the bedroom. "Curtis, come into the bedroom for a minute, please. There's something I want to ask you."

His heart skipped a beat. "Oh God," Curtis thought to himself. "She must have noticed the lock on the chest."

CHAPTER 8: COFFEE WITH JANE

Curtis entered the bedroom with a sense of apprehension. He hoped that she would inquire about something other than the mysterious lock on the chest, but deep down, he knew it was unavoidable. "Yes, dear," Curtis said, anticipating her question. "You wanted to ask me something."

She pointed directly at the chest in the corner. "There wasn't a lock on that chest before. Do you happen to know how it mysteriously appeared there?"

"I honestly have no idea," Curtis admitted sheepishly. "To be honest, I didn't pay much attention to that chest before, so I wouldn't know if it had a lock or not."

She scowled at him. "There was definitely no lock on it before. I'll give you one last chance to tell me what it's doing there."

Curtis furrowed his brow. "It's not what you think."

"I'm waiting," she said impatiently, "But I must warn you, I don't expect to be happy with your answer."

Slowly, Curtis began explaining the events of that morning. He recounted everything in detail, hoping to provide some clarity.

Once he finished, Katherine responded sternly, "Firstly, tomorrow morning, we're going to return the laptop to where you found it. You can't just take someone else's belongings without permission, even if you believe it's for a good cause. Secondly, I'll talk with Edna. It's one thing for you to ask her not to tell me about your little escapade, but it's clear that your trustworthiness is in question."

"I'm sorry," Curtis admitted, feeling chastised as if he were back in school, caught misbehaving. "I didn't think it through properly."

"I hate to sound like a broken record," Katherine sighed in exasperation, "But weren't we just discussing your impulsive behavior not ten minutes ago?"

"Message received," Curtis replied, retreating from the room. "I'll go and return the laptop in the morning."

The next morning, as Curtis stepped into the living room, the delightful aroma of breakfast being prepared by Katherine welcomed him. "That smells fantastic!" He exclaimed.

"Thank you," Katherine responded. "After breakfast, we're going to Matt Jeffrey's place to return the laptop. Then we've been invited for coffee at Jane Thomas's. Is that okay with you?"

Knowing it wasn't the time to argue, Curtis replied, "That's fine, love. Although I don't have Jeffrey's house keys. I returned them to the receptionist yesterday."

"Lucky for you, I have them right here," Katherine replied bluntly. "How did you..." Curtis began.

"I went to see Edna first thing this morning to ask if she wanted to go to the hospital this afternoon. I also mentioned that you seemed to have misplaced your phone and thought you might have left it at Jeffrey's house."

"Very clever," Curtis acknowledged. You didn't tell her about me taking the laptop, did you?"

"No need to make the situation any more embarrassing than it already is," Katherine assured him. "Are you ready to eat?"

As they arrived at Jeffrey's house, Katherine burst into laughter. "What's so funny?" Curtis asked, puzzled.

"You do the silliest things sometimes, but I can't help but admire your audacity!" Katherine replied.

"Thanks, I think," Curtis chuckled. "Wait in the car while I return the laptop. It might take a few minutes, as I'll need a ladder for this job."

Katherine smiled affectionately, and Curtis couldn't help but return the gesture. "She may give me a hard time, but I know she does it because she loves me," he thought to himself.

A few minutes later, Curtis hurried back to the car with the laptop bag still slung over his shoulder.

"What happened?" Katherine asked, concerned.

"I'm pretty sure someone broke in!" Curtis exclaimed. "Why do you say that?"

"For one thing, there's a broken window on the side of the house, and secondly, the ladder wasn't where I left it yesterday," Curtis explained frantically.

"Could the window have been broken before, and Jeffrey simply hadn't gotten it fixed yet?" Katherine suggested.

"It's possible, as I didn't pay much attention yesterday. But I'm certain the ladder was moved. Unless it's an extraordinary coincidence, someone has broken into the house," Curtis concluded.

"We need to call the police," Katherine stated firmly.

"Agreed," Curtis replied. "But we might have a problem with the laptop."

"Why?" Katherine inquired.

"I don't know what the police will do when they arrive, but what about fingerprints on the laptop?" Curtis pondered. "Now I'm starting to feel like someone guilty. Edna asked you to come and make sure everything was alright yesterday. You had a legitimate reason to be here. You can simply say you decided to do a thorough check and went up to the attic as well."

Curtis looked unconvinced, but Katherine reassured him, "I suppose you're right. Should I put it back before we call the police?"

"That would be a sensible thing to do. While you do that, I'll call Jane and explain that we'll be running late," Curtis suggested.

A little while later, Curtis returned to find Katherine waiting by the car. "I've put the laptop back, so I suppose we should call the police now," he said, his uncertainty evident in his voice.

"You seem hesitant to call them. What's the problem?" Katherine asked.

"I know it's the right thing to do, but I have a strange feeling about it," Curtis admitted.

"What kind of feeling? This is what the police are here for, Curtis," Katherine reasoned.

"I know," he responded. "I just wish I had spoken to Jeffrey the other night. I can't shake the feeling that all of this could have been avoided somehow."

"You're overthinking things," Katherine assured him firmly.

"Mark my words," Curtis said with conviction, "There's more to all of this than meets the eye."

"What wasn't so bad, was it? The police conducted a thorough search of the place, and now they are going to talk to Jeffery at the hospital. It is out of our hands," Katherine said as the car made its way out of Matt

Jeffery's driveway.

"Yeah, yeah, good Samaritans and all that. I still wish I had spoken to him before, though," replied Curtis. "When do you think I could come and see him?"

Katherine shifted her gaze towards him. "Let's find out how he's doing this afternoon when I accompany Edna. Oh, and I completely forgot to mention it last night, given all that transpired, but do you recall me saying I had something important to discuss with you?"

"Now that you mention it, I do remember. What is it?" Asked Curtis. "I managed to get Lyndon Whiteford's number for you."

Curtis exclaimed delightfully, "I thought you weren't interested in doing that. How did you manage to get it?"

"Let's not worry about that. Just say that I changed my mind. Now let's get over to Jane's house. We are really late," stated Katherine.

Sitting in the living room, Curtis sipped his coffee and listened to Katherine and Jane talking. He could sense the pain and anguish that Jane was going through. He thought it best to add as little to the conversation as possible at this point.

He wanted to wait until the time was right. He knew he had a few things to ask Jane, but he felt it would be better to wait until they were about to leave.

An hour and a half later, which had seemed like an eternity, he could sense that the moment had arrived. "Jane, I just want to say how sorry I am that you have to go through this."

Both women looked at him as if they had seen an apparition. He hadn't realized just how silent he had been.

Tears welled up in Jane's eyes. "Thank you, Curtis! I pray every day that my baby girl will come back to me safe and sound."

It was this very reaction that had prevented him from speaking out sooner. Still, he could relate to and understand it. He thought momentarily about what the loss of one of his children would feel like, and almost instantaneously, he gave an involuntary shudder.

"We may not have gotten to the bottom of this yet, but I can assure you that we are doing everything in our power to bring these disappearances to a resolution," he said kindly.

She nodded. "I know you are, and I can't thank you enough for all your effort. Katherine has told me how invested you are in getting to the bottom of this."

Jane's emotional response to Nikita Marsh's final moments moves her to tears. Curtis, sensing her discomfort and not wanting to exacerbate her distress, decides to refrain from further questioning for now. However, he makes a mental note to approach Jane with a well-thought-out question at a more appropriate time.

As Jane gradually regains composure, she excuses herself briefly to freshen up. Katherine advises Curtis to be sensitive and cautious when discussing delicate matters with Jane, given her current fragile state. Curtis agrees, acknowledging the need to handle the situation with care.

Just as Jane walked back into the room, Curtis said regretfully, "I'm so sorry for upsetting you, Jane."

"Don't be silly. You're only trying to help me. I just find it so hard to keep it together sometimes," Jane said emotionally.

"I don't want to add to your stress, but would you mind if I asked you a question?"

"Of course, you can, Curtis. All I want to do is find my little girl. Anything I can do to help, I will."

Curtis paused and said, "How often did Chloe come home to visit?"

He saw Jane looking at him with a puzzled expression, often indicative of someone who doesn't understand the question correctly.

"Sorry, let me rephrase that," Curtis continued. "The other women who have gone missing were all deeply connected to the local community when they disappeared. I know Chloe is away at college, so I was wondering if she still has close ties to people in the area."

"She has some friends here if that's what you mean. But she doesn't come home very often, so it's more of an occasional get-together when she's here," Jane replied.

"Is she still close to any of them?" Asked Curtis.

"I wouldn't say so," responded Jane. "She had a group she hung out with at school, and, as I mentioned, she does make time to see them when she's here. But from our discussions, I think the majority of her friends are people she met at college."

"That's what I thought," said Curtis thoughtfully.

"Do you mind me asking why that's important?" Queried Jane. As Curtis was about to answer, the doorbell rang.

"Sorry, hold that thought for a moment. Let me see who's at the door," said Jane.

Curtis and Katherine sat quietly, listening as Jane opened the door. "Hello, Frankie!" They heard Jane say. "How nice to see you. What brings you over?"

Curtis and Katherine exchanged surprised glances.

"I didn't see that coming," said Curtis. "Frankie never mentioned knowing the Thomases."

Frankie approached Jane, holding a bag of clothes. "My mother asked me to drop these off," she said.

Jane gratefully responded, "Thank you, dear. The people at the shelter will be extremely grateful. Would you like to come in for some coffee?"

"Thanks, Mrs. Thomas, but I really need to get back home. My shift starts in an hour," replied Frankie.

Curtis swiftly rose from his chair and made his way towards the front door. He arrived just as Jane was about to close it.

"Sorry," Curtis apologized, "I couldn't help but overhear Frankie's voice. I just need to have a quick word with her before she leaves."

Hastily traversing the garden path, Curtis called out, "Frankie!" She spun around, astounded. "Mr. Styles... Fancy seeing you here."

"Do you have a moment? I really need to ask you something," Curtis said.

"Sure," Frankie responded, "How can I help?"

"I was wondering how many exits there are out of the bar at The Stables?" He asked directly.

"Two," she answered, "One leading into the reception hall, and a fire exit on the other side of the bar."

"Thank you," Curtis replied. "By the way, how are you doing?"

If Frankie felt any curiosity about his question, she didn't show it. Instead, she replied, "Carrying on... I suppose that is all one can do, given what has happened around here lately. I think I should be asking you that question, especially after what happened to you at The Stables."

"I'm alright," Curtis reassured her. "Fortunately, it was only a bump on the head. No lasting damage."

"I'm really sorry about that," said Frankie. "I know Jim is still feeling terrible about the whole incident."

"It's forgotten," replied Curtis. "Sorry, I know you're in a rush, so I won't keep you any longer." After exchanging farewells, Curtis returned to the house.

Inside, he found Katherine preparing to leave.

"She's a lovely girl," Curtis remarked. "I wasn't aware that you knew her, Jane."

"Family friends," Jane Thomas replied. "Known them for years."

As they drove back to the cottage, Curtis spoke to Katherine, "I'm sorry if I upset Jane. It really wasn't my intention."

"As it turns out, you may have done some real good back there. When you were talking to Frankie, Jane was singing your praises. She truly believes that you are going to find out what happened to her daughter."

In that moment of pride, Curtis fully grasped the bigger picture. Yes, there seemed to be endless frustrations on this journey, but this isn't about me.

Upon returning to the cottage, Katherine said, "I won't have enough time to cook lunch before I take Edna to the hospital. Will you be able to manage on your own?"

"I'll be fine," Curtis assured her. "I need to work on the article before Richard gets here. I'll make myself a sandwich. Can I have Lyndon Whiteford's phone number before you leave?"

Reaching into her bag, Katherine handed him a piece of paper. "I'll freshen up quickly before I leave," she said. "Curtis, I'm proud of you for what you're trying to do here. I may not always say it, but I am."

"I know you are." He watched as she left the living room.

Observing Katherine's departure from the cottage, Curtis realized he needed to write the article for Richard Smith. But first, he needed to call Lyndon Whiteford. Taking out the piece of paper Katherine had given him; he dialed the number on his mobile.

After just two rings, the call was answered. "Hello?"

"Lyndon?" Curtis questioned, "Is that you?" "Curtis, hello. I'm glad you called," Lyndon responded. "Look, about the other night," Curtis began.

"Forget it," Lyndon interrupted. "Your reaction was reasonable given the circumstances."

"Thanks," said Curtis. "Did you know that Matt Jeffery is in the hospital?"

"I do," Lyndon confirmed. "I spoke to him this morning. He told me that he had given your wife my number."

"Oh!" Curtis realized. "I wanted to talk to you about what you asked me the other night."

"Good stuff," Lyndon acknowledged. "But before we do that, I have a massive favor to ask you."

"Okay, ask away," Curtis consented.

"I heard there was a break-in at Jeffery's house. I think I know what they were looking for. In the attic, I've set up an office. In the top drawer on the right-hand side of the desk, there should be a folder marked confidential. I need you to go and see if it's still there. If it is, please take it with you."

"Okay, but how will I..." Curtis started to ask.

"Edna Braithwaite has a set of keys for the place. When you get to Jeffery's house, I want you to phone me. I'll tell you where I keep the keys to the drawers hidden," Lyndon instructed.

"Alright," said Curtis. "I have to wait for my wife and Edna to get back from the hospital first, though, so I can get the keys and the car."

"I understand, but please do it as soon as they get back. The information in that folder cannot fall into the wrong hands," Lyndon emphasized.

"As soon as they get back, I'll go," Curtis promised.

"Thanks," Lyndon said, his tone tinged with an ominous note. "Take care, Curtis. Be cautious!"

Curtis discovered tranquility on the peaceful patio after his conversation with Lyndon Whiteford, truly appreciating the serene environment. It was during this moment of reflection that he came to the realization that his partnerships were lacking in genuine foundations. The committee, he thought, felt more like a business networking group.

Nevertheless, his interaction with Lyndon filled him with hope and inspired him to embark on an article written from the depths of his heart. Curtis made a firm decision to cast aside conventional editorial norms and write with impassioned sincerity, adopting a pseudonym for this endeavor. With newfound clarity and determination, he set his finger on the keyboard and began crafting his piece.

SHROUDED IN MYSTERY – LOCAL WOMEN VANISH INTO THIN AIR
BY LLOYD PARKER (GUEST COLUMNIST)

The community spanning from Erinsdale to Stratford lives in fear as four young women mysteriously vanish without a trace. Another tragedy unfolds as one drowns in the Salem River. The absence of answers has residents constantly looking over their shoulders, especially young women who wake up each day wondering, "Could I be next?"

Jemma Anderson, a beer representative, disappeared after a night out at The Stables Lodge. Last seen on her way back to her nearby bed and breakfast after a launch party, she vanished without a trace. Sophie Hunt, who worked in Erinsdale, never made it home after a few drinks with a friend at a local watering hole. Gabriella Atkins went out for coffee with a friend,' and her whereabouts remain unknown. Lastly, Chloe Thomas went for an afternoon jog and seemingly disappeared into thin air. These young women, leading ordinary lives, were abruptly torn from the heart of our community.

Nikita Marsh, a former receptionist at The Stables Lodge, was found drowned in the Salem River. An inconclusive autopsy raises questions about whether it was a tragic suicide or the result of sinister acts. The answer to this remains elusive.

What we do know is that, for now, we are left clueless about the how and why. But if we pause and consider, this is spine-tingling. Amongst us hides a predator, possibly disguised as the friendly neighbor next door. And what's even more chilling is the thought that there might be more than one perpetrator involved.

Having had privileged insight into this investigation, I can honestly say that the efforts of law enforcement and all involved parties

Curtis shut his laptop, a surge of pride washing over him for his tenacious writing. His mind drifted to the upcoming meeting with Lyndon Whiteford, haunted by memories of his third visit to Matt Jeffery's house and the foreboding words Lyndon had shared. As Katherine walked in, Curtis steeled himself for the challenges that awaited.

Curtis asked with genuine concern, "How is Jeffrey?"

"He's improving every day. He actually asked if he could see you tomorrow," Katherine replied, conveying the hopeful news.

"That's great," Curtis responded. "That leads me to something I need to discuss with you." He felt uneasy as Katherine stared straight at him. "I, umm..."

"If you're going to bring up another visit to Jeffery's place, I'm already aware," Katherine interjected straightforwardly.

"You're either a mind reader or Jeffery has spoken to you. I assume it's the latter," Curtis said.

"He mentioned it, and I must say that it sounds dangerous," replied Katherine.

"I've already made two trips there, so how bad can it be?" Curtis argued. "That was before you knew about the break-in," Katherine pointed out.

"That's true, but just one more trip, and then I'm done with it. I promise," Curtis reassured.

"I'm going with you," Katherine stated firmly. "Before you say anything, this is non-negotiable."

Curtis nodded. "Okay, then. We should get going." At that moment, there was a knock at the front door.

Curtis answered the door to find Paul Harlow standing there. "Paul," Curtis greeted him. "This is an unexpected surprise! Come on in."

As Harlow entered, he said, "I'm sorry to bother you, but I just came from Devonshire's place. He told me about his move to Florida. He said he already informed you."

"He did," Curtis replied. "Coffee?"

"That would be great," Harlow said. "Hello, Katherine. I didn't see you there for a minute."

"Hello, Paul," Katherine responded. "You guys sit. I'll make the coffee."

Curtis turned his attention back to Harlow. "What did you want to talk to me about?"

"There's been a delay in finding Devonshire's replacement. That's the main reason he wanted to speak to me. I'll be temporarily taking over for a month until she arrives," Harlow explained.

"That's great, Paul, but I'm not sure how that concerns me," Curtis said. "I thought we should discuss this investigation," Harlow stated. "I think you should leave it alone."

"Where is this coming from, Paul?" Curtis questioned.

"Let me get straight to the point. I went along with everything until now because it wasn't my decision to make. But now I'm asking you to back off and let the police handle it. At least for the month while I'm in charge."

Gazing at him, Curtis responded, "Consider it accomplished. I've got another project keeping me occupied, anyway." Curtis shared his tactical choice with Katherine, aiming to divert attention away. Despite Katherine's unease about the darkness, Curtis insisted on an immediate visit to Jeffrey's place, armed with flashlights.

Approaching the house, Katherine suggested returning in the morning due to her discomfort with the darkness, but Curtis pushed forward. As they entered the house, an eerie sound reached Curtis's ears, and he caught sight of a shadowy figure through the living room window, sending a shiver down his spine.

Worried about Katherine's safety, Curtis retreated cautiously, slipping out of the house as quietly as he could, his heart racing, and quickly made his way back to her side.

"Wow, that was fast! What's wrong?" Katherine asked, her worry evident in her voice.

"Stay calm, but there's someone inside the house,"
Curtis replied, his breath still labored from his recent endeavor.
Katherine gasped audibly. "What do you mean, someone inside the house?"

"Just as I entered, I heard a noise and caught sight of a figure in the living room window," Curtis explained, trying to maintain his composure.

"Oh my God, Curtis! I knew it was a mistake to come here tonight. Let's leave! I won't stay a minute longer," Katherine fervently insisted.

At that moment, the roar of a motorcycle engine filled the air. They sat in the car, witnessing the headlight beam followed by the sight of a motorcycle zooming past them down Matt Jeffery's driveway.

After a few moments to collect his nerves, Curtis spoke up, "So, I wasn't imagining things after all."

"This is no time for jokes!" Katherine reprimanded him. "Let's go!" "He's gone now, so maybe I should go back inside," Curtis suggested.

"He must have heard me entering or leaving. Let me return and see if I can find the document Lyndon asked me to search for."

Katherine stared at him in disbelief. "Have you lost your mind?" "Please, my love, try to calm down and think about it. Whoever that was, they're gone for now and unlikely to return anytime soon. This is our best opportunity to go back inside and search. Give me just ten minutes, and if I find nothing, we can leave," Curtis proposed.

"Ten minutes, and that's all," Katherine replied firmly. "Did you manage to get a good look at the person inside?"

"I could only see a figure in the window, and their motorcycle helmet had a black visor when they passed us. Unfortunately, that's all," Curtis replied dejectedly.

"Fine," Katherine said, relenting. "Ten minutes, Curtis. Please hurry... I don't feel safe in the car anymore."

As Curtis reentered the house, he dialed Lyndon Whiteford's number. After a brief explanation of the recent events, Curtis said, "Let's pray that the document is still there. Where can I find the key to the desk drawer?"

After listening to Lyndon's instructions, Curtis responded, "Okay, let me handle it. If I encounter any problems, I'll call you back. If all goes well, I'll contact you when I get home."

Ending the call, Curtis proceeded inside the house. Lyndon's directions proved accurate, and Curtis quickly located the specified bedroom. However, he chose not to turn on any lights, fearing it would attract unwanted attention from passersby on the road.

With the illumination of his flashlight providing enough light to navigate, Curtis eventually found the wall safely concealed behind a tall statue. "Not very well hidden," he muttered to himself.

Using the code provided by Lyndon, Curtis opened the safe door and discovered a pile of papers along with a set of keys. Retrieving the keys, he closed the safe and returned to the living room.

Picking up the ladder he had left behind, Curtis ascended to the attic. Directing his flashlight toward the ceiling, he confirmed that the trapdoor remained undisturbed. He felt a glimmer of hope that no one had been there that evening.

"Alright," Curtis declared aloud. "Time to search for this damn document."

In the attic, Curtis used Lyndon's keys to unlock a drawer marked "confidential." Inside, he discovered an envelope. His heart raced with excitement, but he reminded himself to remain composed.

As he hurried to depart, he momentarily forgot to secure the drawer and had to return to do so. Afterward, he descended the ladder carefully, a sense of tranquility washing over him.

However, his serenity was shattered by a blood-curdling scream that caused him to lose his grip on the ladder and tumble to the floor below.

"Katherine!" Curtis exclaimed, rushing to the front door and flinging it open. He found Katherine nervously pacing by the side of the car.

"What the hell was that?" Curtis exclaimed loudly. "I thought you were in danger or something."

"Damn right you'd deserve it if something had happened to me," retorted Katherine, her anger evident. "You were in there for over twenty minutes. Let's just go home now, please."

"Okay," Curtis responded, sensing her frustration. "Do you have any idea what that scream was?"

"Probably just some wild animal. Can we please leave now?" Katherine replied impatiently.

"Let me go back and lock up, and then we can go," Curtis said, relieved that his wife was unharmed. They drove home in silence. Curtis was aware that Katherine was simmering with anger. Nevertheless, he decided that confronting the issue would only likely exacerbate it, so waiting for the inevitable blow-up was the wisest choice.

They drove home in silence, both aware of the simmering anger between them. Curtis decided it was best to avoid confrontation for now, knowing that addressing the issue would only make it worse. He recalled advice from a friend during the early days of their marriage: "Sometimes it's best to let them vent and say as little as possible until they tire themselves out." While not entirely true, it has proven helpful over the years. Finally, they arrived at their familiar bed and breakfast, and Curtis breathed a sigh of relief.

Once inside, Katherine announced, "I'm going to bed. If you're hungry, fix yourself something to eat."

"No problem, dear," Curtis replied. "I won't be long." Although Curtis was well aware of his limited culinary abilities, he believed that preparing a simple toast was a much preferable choice compared to the cacophony of Katherine's clattering pans in the kitchen.

She left the room without another word, leaving Curtis standing in the middle of the living room, holding an envelope.

"Well," he muttered to himself, "She must be angrier than I thought. She hasn't even asked about this envelope." He grabbed a beer from the fridge.

Retreating to the porch, he dialed Lyndon Whiteford's number on his mobile. When Lyndon answered, Curtis said, "I retrieved the document safe and sound."

Relief washed over Lyndon's voice. "Thank goodness for that. Can you bring it to Jeffrey at the hospital tomorrow? He'll explain more to you. I'll be back at the end of the week, and we'll arrange another meeting then."

"Sure thing," Curtis replied. "I'll talk to you soon."

After ending the call, Curtis contemplated opening the envelope but decided against it. Instead, he slumped into a chair and placed the envelope on the nearby table. Taking a long swig of beer, he enjoyed the refreshing coolness of the warm evening. As he stared into the garden, a figure caught his eye in the porch light. He squinted to see Tom Haddonfield purposefully approaching.

"Tom?" Curtis asked, surprised. "What brings you here at this hour?"

"Hey, Curtis," Haddonfield replied. "Sorry to bother you. I would have called, but I thought it would be better to talk in person."

"Okay," Curtis said, gesturing for Haddonfield to take a seat. "Want a beer?"

"That would be great," Haddonfield accepted. "This heat tonight is something else."

Curtis noticed Haddonfield's gaze on the envelope but chose not to acknowledge it. He said, "Let me get that beer for you. I'll be right back." He hurried inside and stashed the envelope in a kitchen drawer before returning with the beer. "So, what's so urgent, Tom, that you needed to see me in person tonight?"

"I stopped by The Stables earlier for a drink on my way home and ran into Paul Harlow. He told me you decided to step away from the case. Is that true?" Haddonfield asked.

"I'm afraid so," Curtis confirmed. "That warning letter really upset Catherine, so I figured it's best to keep my distance for now, at least."

He could see Haddonfield staring at him intently.

Haddonfield stared at Curtis intently. "I suppose that makes sense. We haven't worked as closely as we could have, but I'll miss having you as my partner."

Curtis caught a hint of insincerity in Haddonfield's voice but shrugged it off.

Curtis detected a hint of insincerity but dismissed it. "I'll miss working with you too, but I can't risk anything happening to Katherine because I didn't back off. How have things been going for you?"

"With the case, you mean?" Haddonfield clarified.

Curtis nodded. "Besides the committee meeting, it seems like everyone's keeping their cards close to their chests."

"Yeah, I got the same impression. So, have you discovered anything recently?" Curtis inquired.

Haddonfield chuckled. "Easy there! You're not on the case anymore, remember? It's probably better if you don't know."

Curtis bit his lip, resisting the urge to say what he truly wanted to. He felt like Haddonfield was intentionally trying to provoke him, and he refused to take the bait. Instead, he laughed along, saying, "You got me there, mate! Old habits die hard."

Haddonfield finished his beer. "I should be heading home. Penny's probably worried. By the way, I support your decision. Are you sure you won't have second thoughts?"

Curtis tilted his head. "What do you mean, 'second thoughts'?"

"Maybe I'm reaching, but I couldn't help but notice the envelope you had earlier, the one labeled 'confidential,'" Haddonfield remarked.

"Oh, that," Curtis responded casually. "Just some financial paperwork I need to sort out."

As Haddonfield departed, Curtis couldn't shake the suspicion that Haddonfield's visit had ulterior motives, possibly seeking information. A sense of unease crept over him as he watched Haddonfield's departure, leaving him with a foreboding sensation.

Curtis then stepped onto the porch, inhaling the brisk morning air deeply as he savored his coffee. The rejuvenating sensation washed over him, and he felt invigorated, fully prepared to embrace the day ahead.

Unexpectedly, Katherine's voice broke the peaceful moment. "Good morning. You're heading to see Matt Jeffery this morning, right?"

Curtis nodded a hint of surprise in his eyes. "Absolutely. What time do visiting hours start?"

"They begin at ten o'clock, but if you arrive a bit early, it shouldn't be a problem," Katherine replied.

He studied her intently, realizing he hadn't anticipated such a warm reception. "Are we okay? I know you were upset with me last night, and I can't blame you."

Katherine sighed; her anger still evident. "Oh, I'm still angry, but we can discuss that later. I thought I'd spare you a scolding for now since you're going to see Jeffery this morning. Is Richard not coming by this afternoon?"

Curtis nodded. "He should be here around two. Impressive memory, my love."

"Don't try to butter me up, Curtis. Now, what would you like for breakfast?"

As Curtis made his way through the sterile hospital corridor to Matt Jeffery's room, he couldn't help but ponder his aversion to hospitals. The clinical atmosphere always served as a stark reminder of illness and suffering.

Pushing aside his negative thoughts, Curtis prepared himself to see Matt Jeffery for the first time since their encounter on the Salem River Bridge. Stepping into the room, he found Jeffery sitting up in bed, engrossed in a newspaper.

"Morning, Matt," Curtis greeted him. "Good to see you looking healthy. You had us worried for a moment there."

Jeffery chuckled. "Morning, Curtis. I'm glad you came. Getting bashed over the head isn't something I'd recommend. Though I can't complain too much. You had a similar experience not too long ago."

Curtis acknowledged the truth. "That's true, but I got off easier than you did. So, when do they plan on releasing you?"

"Tomorrow, or so they've told me," Jeffery replied.

"That's great news. But considering recent events, do you think it's wise to go back home right away?" Curtis inquired.

Jeffery shook his head. "With everything that has happened, the break-in and all, I've decided it's not the best idea for now. Edna kindly offered me a room at the bed and breakfast until I felt safe enough to return home. So, old man, you'll unfortunately be seeing a lot of me over the next week or two."

Curtis laughed. "Matt, about the other night..."

"Forget about it," Jeffery interjected. "Water under the bridge, as far as I'm concerned." He gestured toward the envelope in Curtis's hand. "Is that for Lyndon?"

Curtis handed it over to him. "Yes, it is."

Jeffery tucked it into the drawer of his bedside table. "It just occurred to me. Since I'll be at the bed and breakfast tomorrow, you could have given it to me then."

Curtis shrugged. "True, but someone will be coming to collect it later this afternoon."

"Okay," Curtis said, a note of curiosity in his voice. "Sounds rather mysterious. Do you know what's inside?"

Jeffery replied honestly, "Truthfully, I have no idea. Hopefully, Lyndon will fill us in when he returns to town. After all the recent shenanigans, he owes us that much."

Curtis pressed on. "I take it the envelope wasn't the only reason you wanted to see me?"

"You're right," Jeffery said solemnly. "I need to fill you in on what's been happening."

Curtis nodded. "That would be nice. Lately, it feels like I've been stumbling around in the dark."

"To begin, I met Lyndon a few years ago while working on a case in New York. He was involved in the investigation and became a valuable source of 'off the record' information. We quickly became friends," Jeffery began.

Listening to Jeffery speak, Curtis couldn't help but reflect on their encounter on the bridge and his own overreaction. He realized now the sincerity behind Jeffery's words.

Continuing, Jeffery said, "Long story short, Lyndon reached out to me a few weeks ago, saying he needed a place to stay while he worked on a case in this area. I was more than happy to help."

Curtis nodded, wanting to understand his role in all of this. "So, are you involved in the investigation too?"

"Not directly. However, he has shared some information with me," Jeffery replied.

Curiosity brimming, Curtis asked, "Like what?"

"What I do know is that Lyndon is working on a case in Montpelier. The details are still hazy, but it seems to be connected to the recent disappearances of women in this area."

Curtis nodded, seeing the connection. "That makes sense. So, where do I fit into all of this?"

"Lately, Lyndon has lost trust in the local law enforcement. He suspects they might be setting him up. That's why he's been laying low at my place," Jeffery explained.

Curtis understood. "I gathered that much from the meeting the other night. He wanted to meet me. What now?"

"Lyndon feels he needs someone he can trust, someone who can assist him in his local investigations. He heard about your involvement through the grapevine and was determined to meet you. You know the rest," Jeffery explained.

"Alright," Curtis said, considering the request. "So, do I wait for him to return and go from there?"

"No," Jeffery replied. "Let me tell you, when he says to expect him, it's not always the case. He has a bit of a maverick nature."

"I sensed that the other night," Curtis recalled.

"If you're willing, Lyndon wants you to go to Montpelier tomorrow. He has an associate there who will fill you in on the case. From there, you'll likely receive further instructions on how to proceed," Jeffery revealed.

Curtis pondered the request for a moment. "Alright, count me in. Do you have the details for the person I'll be meeting?"

Jeffery retrieved his wallet from the bedside table and handed Curtis a tightly folded piece of paper. "Here you go."

Checking his wristwatch, Curtis realized time was slipping away. "I should be on my way. It's good to see you on the mend. We'll catch up soon."

With that, he shook Matt Jeffery's hand and turned to leave the room, brimming with a mixture of anticipation and determination.

"What's your take on this?" Curtis asked Richard, looking for his opinion.

Richard Smith, with a sincere expression, responded, "It's not what I expected, but I'll run it. It's a good article, despite my initial surprise."

Curtis smiled and remarked, "I'm not certain if that's a positive or negative response, but since you'll be publishing it, I won't ask any more questions."

Richard chuckled and agreed, "Let's leave it at that. By the way, I was surprised to hear that Devonshire is leaving."

Curiosity piqued; Curtis questioned Richard. "Why do you say that?"

Richard responded, recalling past conversations. "Just some things he mentioned during our discussions."

Curtis pressed for more details. "What things?"

Richard paused, choosing his words carefully. "I had the impression that Devonshire would stick around no matter what and see this investigation through to the end."

Curtis nodded, realizing he had a similar feeling. "Now that you mention it, I felt the same way. But I suppose things are as they are."

A silence settled in the living room until Katherine entered, breaking the stillness. "Hello, Richard. How have you been?"

Katherine's entrance punctuated it. "Hello, Richard. How have you been?"

Richard greeted her politely. "Hello, Katherine. Can't complain. Speaking of which, when I was at the conference in Montpelier, I saw Tom Haddonfield at the hotel I was staying at. He was having quite an argument with the receptionist."

Curtis inquired, "Did you speak to him?" Richard replied, "Funny thing is, I was in a rush and couldn't talk then. But later in the afternoon, I crossed paths with him in the lobby. I greeted him, but he completely ignored me like a stranger. Strange fellow, I must say."

Curtis shared his own encounter, "You know, Haddonfield showed up at the cottage last night out of nowhere, asking if I was leaving the investigation. It struck me as odd that he didn't just call me. Something seems off about him."

Surprised, Richard asked, "Are you actually leaving the investigation?"

Curtis confirmed, "Yes, I'm afraid so. It's not really my thing. I think it's time for me to pursue something less intense."

Richard laughed and added, "First, Devonshire leaves, then you quit the investigation. The surprises keep coming. Speaking of which, I better get going. Devonshire is determined to play nine holes of golf this afternoon."

Curtis joined the laughter and chimed in, "Golf, now that's something I should think about."

After Richard left, Katherine confronted Curtis, "I see you're determined to tell everyone that you're giving up the case. Too bad you're not actually going to do it."

Curtis decided not to engage in an argument at the moment. He knew Katherine was still upset about the previous evening's events, but he had an urgent matter to attend to. "I just need to make a quick phone call, love, and then you can give me a piece of your mind."

He picked up his mobile phone and dialed the number Jeffrey had given him earlier that morning, patiently waiting for someone to answer. Finally, a voice on the other end said, "Afternoon, Parker Hayes speaking."

"This is Curtis Styles speaking," Curtis said. "Lyndon Whiteford asked me to get in touch with you."

"Hello, Curtis. I've been expecting your call," Hayes replied. "Would tomorrow at twelve be convenient for you?"

"That works for me," Curtis confirmed. "Could you email me the directions?"

Hayes offered an alternative, "Actually, I've been meaning to visit Stratford. Let me come to you."

Feeling relieved, Curtis replied, "That would simplify things. Are you familiar with The Stables Lodge?"

"I do," Hayes confirmed. "I'll see you at twelve then. I'll give you a call when I arrive."

As Curtis walked back into the cottage, he told Katherine, "I'm all yours now. You can...," But he stopped mid-sentence, noticing her expression.

"Katherine, what's wrong? What happened?"

She responded with concern, "Penny, Tom Haddonfield's girlfriend, just called me. She couldn't reach you. Tom is missing!"

Surprised, Curtis raised his voice, asking, "What do you mean he's missing?"

Katherine explained, "She hasn't seen him since yesterday afternoon, and his phone is off. She's extremely worried. You should call her."

Curtis let out a deep sigh, his head sinking into his hands. "It seems like there's always something," he murmured. "Maybe I should consider taking up golf and steering clear of all this secretive business."

After the phone call, Curtis reassured Katherine that Haddonfield was probably fine despite Penny's concerns. When he noticed Katherine was lost in thought, he gently brought her back to the conversation. Curtis explained that he had comforted Penny and advised her to remain calm, but he remained uncertain about Haddonfield's situation.

Katherine acknowledged that Haddonfield could be thoughtless but should have considered his girlfriend's feelings. Curtis mentioned that if there were no updates from Haddonfield by the end of the next day, he would contact Devonshire.

Katherine then stressed that they were both in their sixties and shouldn't be entangled in a detective story. Curtis realized it was time to address their differences and stood his ground, stating that he needed to see this through despite her ultimatum.

He expected her to explode, but to his surprise, she responded, "Alright, I admit I might have been too forceful. But it's for your own good. The way you're going, one or both of us could get hurt. I can't allow that, Curtis!"

Rubbing his temple, Curtis realized things weren't going well. "Katherine, please be reasonable."

"Let me explain," Katherine interjected. "I should never have let you get involved in the first place, but I did. I knew you were struggling with retirement, and I thought this would keep your mind occupied. I should have known better. But what's done is done. I'll support you in seeing this through."

Curtis felt a surge of elation and immediately embraced her warmly. "Not so fast," Katherine interrupted. "There are conditions, though."

Composing himself, Curtis replied, "Okay, I'm listening."

"After this is over, we'll live a calm life. No more running around playing detective. This will be the end of it," Katherine declared.

Taking a deep breath, Curtis responded, "That's fair. I promise you, once this is over, I'm all yours."

"What was that important call you just made?" Katherine asked curiously.

Curtis explained his visit with Jeffery at the hospital and his upcoming meeting with Parker Hayes. "Would you like to come with me tomorrow when I go to meet him?"

"You go," Katherine replied. "I'm taking Edna to the hospital to pick up Matt Jeffery. Seems like you'll have a friend to chat with."

Curtis chuckled. "You know, I have a feeling tomorrow might be the day things finally start changing for the better in this case."

"Now, don't get ahead of yourself. One step at a time, dear," Katherine cautioned.

The next morning, Curtis rose from bed and headed to the kitchen to make himself a cup of coffee. Stepping onto the porch, he surveyed the gray skies filled with dark clouds, replacing the previous days' bright sunshine.

"If I believed in omens, then so much for today being the start of something better," he muttered.

Arriving at The Stables Lodge, Curtis glanced at his wristwatch. It was still a quarter to twelve, but he preferred being early. Uncertain about Parker Hayes' personality, he decided to abandon any preconceived notions. Walking into the reception, he was greeted by the smiling face of Frankie behind the front desk.

"Morning, Mr. Styles, and how are you today?" Frankie asked. "All the better for seeing you," Curtis replied.

Frankie inquired, "What brings you here today?"

"Just meeting a friend for a drink and some lunch," Curtis replied. "Enjoy," said Frankie. "We are very quiet today, so you should be able to dine in peace."

After requesting a beer for himself, Curtis settled at a secluded corner table. "Cor blimey!" He exclaimed aloud, his voice echoing through the emptiness of the establishment. "Not a single soul in sight."

Deciding it was wise to distance himself from the bustling bar area, he sought a seat as far away as he could. Anticipating the influx of lunchtime patrons, he aimed for a secluded spot. As he sat down, his mobile phone rang.

Answering the call, he heard Parker Hayes' familiar voice. "Hi, I have just arrived. Where can I find you?"

"I am in the bar. It's on your right as you enter the reception area. I won't be hard to spot. Besides the barman, I am the only other person here," Curtis replied.

A few minutes later, a lean and neatly dressed man in his thirties, wearing glasses, walked into the bar. Curtis sensed an intellectual air about him. Catching Hayes' eye, Curtis raised his hand in acknowledgment, prompting the man to approach his table.

Standing up, Curtis extended his hand. "Parker Hayes, I take it?" After exchanging greetings, Curtis offered, "Would you like a drink?"

"A bit early for me, but what the heck, I will have a beer, thanks," Hayes replied.

Returning with the beer, Curtis took his seat and asked, "So, how can I be of service?"

Hayes laughed. "You don't beat around the bush. Cut straight to the chase."

Curtis smiled. "Sorry, years of investigative journalism have somewhat stunted my small-talk abilities."

"No need to apologize," responded Hayes. "I think it can be a very good quality."

"To get straight to it then," began Parker Hayes, "I know you have already had a meeting with Lyndon. I also know that he is keen to work with you."

Curtis raised his hand to pause Hayes' explanation. "If you don't mind me asking, why is he so keen to work with me?"

"He has never given me a specific reason. From what I know about Lyndon, if he gets a good vibe about a person, then he is all in. I don't know if that adequately explains it?" Explained Hayes.

"It will do," said Curtis. "Sorry, and before you go on, what is your relationship with Lyndon?"

"I have known him for years, even before he became a private investigator. He is a friend, although I assume you are asking more about our working relationship," Hayes clarified.

Curtis nodded and waited for Hayes to continue.

"Let's just say I know my way around the digital world," Hayes concluded.

Curtis pondered for a moment. He admired the energy and intellect of the stranger before him, but another thought crossed his mind. Observing Parker Hayes' brooding brown eyes, he sensed a potential for rapid mood swings.

"Mercurial!" Curtis blurted out.

"Sorry, I don't understand?" Hayes responded.

"Forgive me," said Curtis. "Things just pop into my head, and I have a bad habit of saying them out loud. It was nothing, really. Please do carry on."

"Basically, Lyndon asked me to talk to you about the case in Montpelier. I suppose you could have researched it yourself, but he wanted to provide you with a more personal insight from his perspective," said Hayes.

"I am definitely intrigued," said Curtis.

"I am not a hundred percent familiar with the exact timelines, but I know that the case led him here. The girl in question was a twenty-year-old named Annie Soles. I don't know if you are familiar with the case?" Explained Hayes.

Curtis shook his head. "It doesn't ring a bell."

"Annie was a hairdresser in Montpelier. She had recently moved apartments. One Saturday, she went back to her old apartment in the afternoon to finalize some matters with her former roommate. They had a dispute over the security deposit and other bills. The discussion grew heated, and Annie left. That was the last time anyone saw her. She vanished without a trace," Hayes detailed.

"Wouldn't the roommate be a person of interest?" Curtis asked.

"One would think so. The apartment complex had CCTV cameras at all entrances and exits. Annie was seen leaving the complex alone. Her previous roommate didn't leave the building until the next morning. All cameras were functioning, so unless there was another way for someone to leave undetected, the roommate was ruled out," stated Hayes.

"Whoa, that's strange," said Curtis. "How did Lyndon conclude that this case was connected to the local disappearances?"

"At first, it didn't, but then Lyndon received an anonymous phone call suggesting he look into the cases in this area, linking them to Annie Soles' disappearance," Hayes revealed.

"Naturally, he would pursue that lead. But couldn't it have been a prank call?" Curtis questioned.

"It's a possibility, but then Lyndon discovered Annie Soles' connections to this area. She grew up here and attended school nearby. I believe that immediately raised red flags," Hayes explained fervently.

"I can see the connection, but it could still be coincidental," Curtis mused.

"Wait, there's more," Hayes continued.

Curtis took a deep breath as he waited to hear Hayes' additional information.

"Her new apartment building is only a five-minute walk from her old one. During inquiries, it was discovered that their CCTV cameras weren't operational at the time. Moreover, she was supposed to visit her parents that night in Big Bear. Lyndon developed a theory that she returned to the apartment, gathered her belongings, and drove straight here," Hayes elaborated.

"Are you saying what I think you are saying?" Curtis asked.

"That her disappearance took place around these parts and not in Montpelier," confirmed Hayes.

"Holy smokes! There could be another missing woman that no one knows about," exclaimed Curtis.

"Correct," said Hayes. "However, the case becomes more complicated. Her car was found abandoned on the outskirts of Montpelier, with no signs of foul play."

"That's why the local law enforcement never actively pursued her case?" Curtis questioned.

"It seems that way because, from what I understand, they are well aware of it," said Hayes.

Curtis let out a whistle. "Where can I help, then?"

"For now, Lyndon would like you to gather local information about her," Hayes requested.

"Where should I start? I assume Lyndon already spoke with the family," Curtis inquired.

"The family sought his involvement in the case. This involves a group of young individuals who frequent this very establishment. Do the names McIntyre and Lassiter ring a bell?" Hayes asked.

Curtis widened his eyes at the mention of those names. "Yeah, I know who they are," he said. "I've already interviewed them, and I doubt they'll be forthcoming if I visit them again."

"I think I didn't explain myself clearly," said Hayes. "It's not just about inquiries. Lyndon would like you to conduct surveillance on them over the next few days until he returns. There are a few more details, but all will be explained in greater detail once you take a look at this." Hayes retrieved a memory stick from his coat pocket. "There's a substantial amount of information on here."

Accepting the memory stick from Hayes, Curtis said, "Katherine is going to lose her mind over this. Good Lord! What have I gotten myself into?"

After concluding his meeting with Parker Hayes, Curtis returned home, only to find Katherine pacing anxiously in the living room.

"Honey, has something happened?" Curtis asked, concern evident in his voice.

Katherine, visibly shaken, replied, "Penny called half an hour ago. They found Tom's car in Stratford Forest, but he's nowhere to be found."

"Good grief! This is not good," Curtis exclaimed. "Who found the car?"

"Some walkers discovered it early this morning," Katherine explained. "The driver's and passenger doors were open, and when they couldn't find the occupants, they contacted the police."

Curtis took a moment to absorb the information.

"Let me call Devonshire and see if he has any updates."

"Is he not answering?" Katherine asked nervously.

"No, it went straight to voicemail. I won't bother trying Harlow after our conversation the other night," Curtis replied. "Listen, is Matt Jeffery at the main house?"

"He is," Katherine confirmed. "He's probably busy unpacking and settling into his room. Why do you ask?"

"I promise I'll explain everything when I get back," Curtis assured her. "I just need to make a quick stop."

"Oh, Curtis! Not again," Katherine sighed in exasperation. "Fine, if you must. By the way, what happened in your meeting with Parker Hayes?"

"I'll provide a full explanation when I get back," Curtis stated as he headed out the door.

Arriving at Matt Jeffery's room, Curtis greeted him warmly. "Matt, good to see you. Listen, I don't have time to explain, but are you well enough to accompany me on a trip?"

"Hello, and good to see you too," Jeffery replied. "And to answer your question, I am. May I ask where we're going?"

"We're going to search for a missing detective," Curtis replied.

As the car sped along, Curtis briefed Matt Jeffery on the details of Tom Haddonfield's disappearance. When he finished, Jeffery let out a whistle. "I'm getting too old for this!"

Curtis turned to him, realizing his oversight. "Geez, I didn't think. Let me take you back to the bed and breakfast. You took a nasty knock a few days ago, and here I am dragging you back into the battlefield."

Jeffery burst into laughter. "Don't you dare! I meant that I know I shouldn't be involved in this stuff, but honestly, I wouldn't have it any other way."

Joining in the laughter, Curtis agreed, "I know what you mean. We're a pair of stubborn old fools."

"Are we heading to the forest?" Jeffery asked.

"Yes, we are," Curtis confirmed. "But before that, I need to make a quick stop." He pulled into the parking lot of The Stables Lodge and said, "I won't be long. I just need to speak to someone inside."

"Take your time," Jeffery replied. "I'll be here when you get back."

Entering the lodge, Curtis encountered an unfamiliar face at the reception desk. "Sorry to bother you," he said. "I'm looking for Frankie."

"It's her day off. Can I take a message?" The receptionist offered.

"No need to worry," Curtis replied. "It can wait." He turned around and headed to the courtyard, lost in thought. After a moment's contemplation, he made his way down towards Frankie's living quarters.

Knocking on the door, he waited patiently but received no answer. Trying again, he grew convinced that she wasn't home and decided to return later. As he started to walk back up the hill, a voice called out from behind him. "Mr. Styles, is that you?"

Turning around, Curtis saw Frankie standing in her doorway, dressed in a robe. "Hi, Frankie. Sorry to disturb you," he apologized. "I just need to ask you something, if it's alright."

"Sure," she replied. "Is everything alright?"

"Tom Haddonfield is missing. You know Tom, right?" Curtis inquired.

"Yeah, the detective guy. Oh God, that's terrible news. What do you want to ask me?" Frankie responded.

"Were you working two nights ago?" Curtis asked directly.

"I was. I've been on night shift for the last four nights," she confirmed. "Did you see Tom Haddonfield here?" Curtis pressed.

"I did. He was with that big police guy," Frankie recalled. "Paul Harlow?" Curtis questioned.

"That's the one. Paul Harlow left early, though, and then another police guy joined him," Frankie shared.

"Another police guy? You mean Kent Devonshire?" Curtis asked, excitement creeping into his voice.

"I think so. I just know he's the main guy around here, or so I've been told," Frankie replied earnestly.

"Thank you. You've been a tremendous help," Curtis expressed his gratitude.

"Glad I could assist. By the way, why didn't you just call and ask instead of coming all the way here?" Frankie wondered.

Pausing for a moment, Curtis finally responded, "Frankie, I wish I could answer that question. All I know is that my mind isn't functioning clearly these days."

With that, he turned and left, determined to uncover the truth behind Tom

Haddonfield's disappearance.

"Where are we heading?" Matt Jeffery inquired. "Change of plans," Curtis replied.

As they pulled into the White Horse Inn, Jeffery expressed his appreciation, "I like your thinking. I could really use a beer right now."

Sitting at the bar, enjoying their drinks, Curtis turned to Jeffery and asked, "Mind if I share a story with you, Matt? A story that actually began right here in this very pub."

"Sure thing," Jeffery replied. "I've been told I'm a good listener."

Curtis began recounting the events of the past few weeks, from the initial phone call from Jane Thomas to Tom Haddonfield's sudden disappearance.

"You see," Curtis explained earnestly, "after my conversation with Frankie, I realized that I've been manipulated throughout this whole affair."

"What do you mean?" Jeffery questioned.

"On the surface, it seemed like my involvement in this investigation was valuable, but it wasn't. Just the other night, Paul Harlow tells me to stay out of it, and then Haddonfield arrives later, praising my decision to step away," Curtis stated passionately.

"I'm sorry, but I'm not sure I follow," Jeffery responded politely.

"Don't you see?" Curtis urgently asked. "People have been keeping me close not because they valued my involvement, but because they wanted to know what I knew. You know how they say, 'Keep your friends close and your enemies closer.'"

"I think I'm starting to understand," Jeffery replied. "But what does this mean for our investigation?"

"In simple terms, one of these so-called allies is, in fact, my secret adversary. I believe one of them is responsible for these disappearances, and I have a strong suspicion that I'm getting close to the truth," Curtis explained with conviction.

"Okay, now you're losing me again," Jeffery said, wearing a bewildered expression.

"I'm talking about Harlow, Haddonfield, Devonshire, or Lyndon. It has to be one of them," Curtis declared.

"Whoa! Maybe you need to take a step back and reconsider what you're saying," Jeffery reacted, visibly shocked.

"No!" Curtis responded vehemently. "Listen, Matt, call me crazy, but I think you're the only one I can trust here."

Jeffery raised his hands in surrender. "I'm flattered, Curtis, but I think you are way off base with this. I mean, Lyndon, for starters... That just sounds insane!"

Without warning, Curtis interrupted, "Finish your drink. We need to go."

As they drove back to the bed and breakfast, Jeffery spoke up, "Let's assume for a moment that you're right, and one of them is the culprit. You're treading on dangerous ground. You left your house to keep Katherine safe, but these people know where you live. Wouldn't it be better to call it quits now?"

"Don't you see," Curtis said excitedly, "all of them, except Lyndon, think I've stepped away from the investigation. I haven't told Devonshire in person, but I imagine Paul Harlow has. I need you to speak with Lyndon and inform him that I can no longer be involved."

Jeffery raised an eyebrow. "What should I say to him?"

"You'll think of something, old boy," Curtis replied confidently. "Do I have a choice?" Jeffery asked.

Curtis chuckled, "No, you don't."

Jeffery sighed. "Alright, you win. But what comes next?"

"Then, my friend, you and I get to work and seek justice for these families. Two retired reporters like us, no one will see us coming."

With that, Curtis pressed his foot on the accelerator, and the car sped through the countryside.

"I'm confused," Katherine said with a perplexed expression. "You've changed your mind about working with Lyndon Whiteford. Now you believe Jeffery is the one who can help you solve these cases."

"Exactly!" Curtis replied. "I know it seems like I keep changing my mind, but I truly feel like I have clarity for the first time since I started this investigation."

Katherine pursed her lips. "How did you come to this conclusion?"

"Let me explain," Curtis began. He recounted his meeting with Parker Hayes, his discussion with Frankie, and their visit to The White Horse Inn. Afterward, he asked triumphantly, "Can you see it now?"

Katherine shook her head. "I have no idea, but please continue. The sooner we wrap this up, the sooner we can move on with our lives."

While Katherine busied herself with dinner preparations, Curtis retreated to the bedroom to check his emails, comfortably lounging on the bed. As he stared at the laptop screen, a sudden recollection struck him— Parker Hayes had given him a memory stick earlier that day.

Reaching into his pocket, Curtis pulled out a small metallic object. "Alright," he said aloud, "I might not be working with you anymore, Whiteford, but there's no harm in seeing what's on here."

Inserting the memory stick into the drive, Curtis patiently waited for it to load and began retrieving the information. To his surprise, there was only one folder, labeled *'Novel.'* Opening it, he came across a title page that read, *'The Forest Murders – A Novel by Lyndon H. Whiteford.'*

"What in the world?" Curtis exclaimed.

"Is something wrong, Curtis?" Katherine shouted from the kitchen.

Curtis responded loudly, "Everything's fine. I'm just going to wash up before dinner."

He stared at the page for a few moments, then impulsively decided to save the document. After closing the laptop, he headed to the bathroom to wash his hands, then joined Katherine in the dining room to eat.

As they finished their meal, Katherine noticed Curtis's unusual silence. "Is something bothering you?"

Curtis looked at her. "I forgot to mention earlier that Parker Hayes gave me a memory stick. While you were cooking, I decided to take a look and see what was on it."

Interrupting, Katherine nervously said, "I have a feeling I shouldn't ask."

"That's the thing," Curtis replied. "I had the same thought when I opened it. I can't say I knew what I expected to find, but I definitely wasn't prepared for what I did."

There was a pause, and Katherine encouraged him, saying, "Alright, don't keep me in suspense."

"It turns out Lyndon Whiteford is an aspiring author," Curtis revealed.

"What do you mean?" Katherine asked.

"The only thing on the memory stick was a novel he wrote," Curtis clarified.

"What kind of novel?" Katherine inquired.

"It seems to be a murder mystery of some sort. I didn't read any of it; I only saw the title, *'The Forest Murders,'*" Curtis recounted.

"That's strange," Katherine said thoughtfully. "Perhaps you received the incorrect memory stick by accident."

Curtis pondered for a moment. "You might be right. I didn't consider that. Anyway, I'll give the memory stick back to Jeffrey tomorrow, and he can return it to Lyndon."

"I've prepared brownies for dessert," Katherine announced as she rose from the table to gather their empty plates. "Is that okay with you?"

"Sounds delicious, love," Curtis replied. "I'm just going to stretch my legs in the garden before bed."

"Don't take too long," Katherine cautioned. "It's cold outside tonight."

Walking into the garden, Curtis gazed up at the clear night sky. Despite its beauty, a definite chill lingered in the air. He contemplated the events of the day for a few moments but concluded that it was too cold to stay outside.

Curtis was about to head indoors when he received a private call from Lyndon Whiteford, who asked about Curtis no longer assisting him due to recent developments. Curtis apologized and expressed his intention to step away.

Lyndon surprised Curtis by mentioning the memory stick from Parker Hayes. He revealed it contained a novel he had written and asked Curtis to read it and share his opinion, promising it would be worthwhile. Curtis hesitated, explaining his background as an investigative journalist, but Lyndon insisted it was worth reading.

Curtis made his way up to the main house after breakfast to meet Matt Jeffery. He found him sitting in the dining room, finishing his breakfast. Jeffery looked up from his cereal and greeted Curtis, "Morning, Curtis. What brings you here so early?"

"I just wanted to thank you personally for talking to Lyndon," Curtis replied.

"Don't mention it," Jeffery responded. "You would have done the same for me."

Curtis began, "About our discussion yesterday-"

Jeffery interrupted, "Just forget about it. This whole situation has been emotionally draining for you."

Curtis studied him closely. "I meant what I said, Matt. I also wanted to make sure you're still on board with our discussion."

"Okay," Jeffery started, "I honestly thought you were just speaking in the heat of the moment. I didn't expect you to want to follow through with it."

"I was serious, Matt," Curtis affirmed. "You and I can get to the bottom of this without the others. In fact, one of them is not a very nice person, to say the least."

Jeffery rubbed his chin. "I'm still not convinced because you haven't shown me any concrete proof to support this theory. However, I think my job here is to prevent you from self-imploding. So, count me in. What's your plan?"

"After you finish breakfast, meet me down at the cottage, and we can discuss it," Curtis suggested.

An hour later, the two men sat on the porch, sipping their morning coffee. Jeffery said, "Alright, you have my full attention."

Curtis began, "I want to make it clear that I'm not a detective and I'm not trying to be one. I thought I should mention that in case you think I'm running around playing Magnum PI."

"Valid observation," Jeffery responded. "Honestly, it's never crossed my mind before." "You may be impulsive, but your heart is in the right place."

"All I want to do is bring closure to these families," Curtis declared vehemently.

"I understand that, but pointing fingers at four people who are supposedly on the same side as you seem like a stretch," Jeffery pointed out.

"On the surface, you're right. I can't provide you with evidence to support my theory. But it comes down to a hunch. Throughout this investigation, I've had a feeling that the truth is closer than I'm willing to acknowledge. Eventually, you can't ignore that feeling. There must be something to it," Curtis explained purposefully.

"Supposing you're right, how do you suggest we proceed?" Jeffery asked. "We can't just interview them as suspects. They have the authority in this investigation."

"You hit the nail on the head. We need a strategy that plays to our strengths," Curtis said.

"What are those strengths?" Jeffery looked puzzled.

"We're both retired investigative reporters. Our strengths lie in finding interesting angles, researching them, and engagingly presenting them. That's what we need to do," Curtis explained with excitement.

"That sounds a bit convoluted, but I'll play along," Jeffery responded.

"We need to look at each of the four individuals and find those angles." "We have to dig as deep as we can because digging for information is our expertise," Curtis said proudly.

"I'm leaning in your direction," Jeffery replied. "Do you have a particular idea in mind?"

Curtis laughed. "When you put it that way, no, I don't. I have a lot of thoughts floating around in my head. I need to put them down on paper, and then we can progress from there."

Jeffery shook his head. "Look, I know I won't talk you out of this, so when do we start?"

"I'll get started today. Should we meet back here tomorrow morning at the same time, if that's convenient for you?" Curtis suggested.

"Well, it's not like I have anything better to do, although I wish I did," Jeffery replied ruefully.

Curtis laughed again. "Come on, Matt. I know you're drawn in by the excitement."

"I'm not sure if that's how I would explain it, but see you tomorrow morning. Let me enjoy the rest of the day in peace. I don't know how many peaceful days I have left," Jeffery replied sarcastically.

After Jeffery left, Curtis returned to the cottage. He spotted Katherine in the kitchen and asked, "What's for lunch, honey? I'm feeling quite hungry."

"You seem very cheerful this morning," Katherine observed. "What has put you in such a good mood?"

He grabbed a beer from the fridge. "Let's just say I think the end is in sight, dear."

The next day, the two men found themselves once again sitting on the porch of the cottage, enjoying their morning coffee.

"Feels like déjà vu," Jeffery chuckled, breaking the silence. "So, what have you got for us?"

Curtis powered up his laptop and opened a file labeled 'NW.' "Bear with me, the notes are a bit rough," he warned before proceeding to read aloud to Matt Jeffery.

Paul Harlow

Occupation: Former police commander for the Erinsdale to Stratford area, currently retired but temporarily back on the missing women's task force. Recently promoted to his former position until a permanent replacement for Kent Devonshire arrives.

Motives: In-depth knowledge of police procedures and the areas where the women disappeared, allowing him to gain their trust based on his previous and current roles.

Areas to investigate: Any connections he may have with the missing women and his whereabouts during their disappearances. Notably, he contacted Nikita Marsh before she went missing and was later found dead.

Kent Devonshire

Occupation: Current commander of the Erinsdale to Stratford area, soon to relocate to Florida and step down from his role. Leads the current task force.

Motives: Similar to Harlow, though his familiarity with the area may not be as extensive.

Areas to investigate: Same as Harlow. Pay special attention to the murder of Victoria Stones, as Devonshire is confirmed to be her father. Could there be a long-standing grudge or resentment behind these recent events?

Lyndon Whiteford

Occupation: Self-employed private investigator.

Motives: He was employed by the family of the first missing woman, suggesting a potential fallout leading to subsequent events. Working as a private investigator could also facilitate gaining victims' trust.

Areas to investigate: Throughout the investigation, Whiteford's name has emerged, but he has managed to stay mostly hidden. He is involved in the current investigation in an undisclosed capacity. His past connections with Tom Haddonfield, currently missing, should be explored. Additionally, his timeline from the beginning needs verification, as well as his genuine interest in these cases. He has mentioned having enemies in law enforcement—further exploration is necessary.

Tom Haddonfield

Occupation: Self-employed private investigator.

Motives: Haddonfield has ties to the area dating back two years when his partner moved to Big Bear Falls. He possesses the ability to gain victims' trust, much like the other three individuals.

Areas to investigate: Haddonfield is currently missing, and determining his whereabouts is urgent. It is crucial to examine why he left his advertising career, his relationship with Lyndon Whiteford, and any connections he may have to the missing women.

After finishing his recitation, Curtis looked at Jeffery and asked, "What do you think?"

Jeffery pondered the information for a moment before responding, "Honestly, it's thin. We don't have much to go on except for a strong hunch."

Curtis sighed and rubbed his temples. "I have to agree with you. It feels like I'm grasping at straws in desperation to solve this case."

Jeffrey's gaze was fixed on Curtis. "Here's the thing: You're not a private investigator, and you're not pretending to be one. If you were working as an investigative journalist again, what would your gut instinct be telling you?"

Curtis pondered the question. "I would dig deeper into the four individuals I just mentioned. What's your point?"

Jeffrey asserted, "We were investigative journalists once, and following our instincts is in our blood. Let's stop pretending to be police officers and go all in. If we're wrong, so be it."

A renewed sense of enthusiasm surged within Curtis. "You know what? Let's do it. What's the worst that can happen?"

Jeffrey's expression darkened. "I don't think we want to dwell on that. Whoever is behind this is dangerous, but if it's someone who should be upholding the law, it's even worse. Who can we trust if we find ourselves in trouble?"

Curtis and Jeffery contemplated their daunting task ahead, recognizing the challenges that lay in uncovering the truth. Curtis asserted they should start by focusing on Tom Haddonfield, given his disappearance could hold the key to the mystery. They discussed their plan to gather information about Haddonfield, with Curtis arranging a meeting with his partner, Penny, while Jeffery collected data online.

The next morning, Curtis reassured Katherine before heading to Ashbury to meet with Penny, determined to solve Haddonfield's disappearance. Her words about the fragility of life weighed on him.

As he parked his vehicle outside Penny's store, Curtis mentally steeled himself for the forthcoming conversation, his thoughts drifting to Jane Thomas's evident distress. He harbored hopes that this meeting would mark the beginning of the end for the dark events that had been haunting their community. Upon entering the store, he approached Penny and greeted her warmly.

She spun around, and upon seeing him, tears immediately welled up in her eyes.

He approached her gently and wrapped his arms around her. "I promise you; we'll find him."

After a few moments, Penny regained her composure. "Let me just put a 'closed' sign on the door. Then we can talk without any interruptions."

A few minutes later, they sat in her back office, sipping coffee. "I know this is an incredibly difficult time for you. I just need to ask you a few questions," Curtis said with empathy.

Penny nodded. "Anything to bring Tom back. Please, Curtis, you have to find him."

"Can you recall anything unusual or out of the ordinary before his disappearance?" Curtis asked.

She shook her head immediately. "Nothing specific that I can pinpoint. Tom and I didn't discuss his cases much. He always believed it was better for me not to know, for my safety. Now I realize the full weight of those words."

Curtis pondered her response for a moment before asking candidly, "Let me rephrase it. Can you think of anyone who might have wanted to harm Tom?"

This time, Penny took her time before responding. "It may sound strange given his line of work, but no. Tom may have come across as arrogant at times, but people generally liked him."

Curtis studied her carefully. "That's surprising because, in his line of work, he could have upset people. Breaking up marriages, sending people to prison, and so on. Surely, there must have been a few individuals with a serious grudge against him."

Penny seemed taken aback. "I understand where you're coming from, but I honestly can't recall any instance where Tom feared for his safety. Believe it or not, he was a sensitive soul. He had a job to do, but he wasn't the reckless type who trampled over anyone."

Curtis found this revelation somewhat startling. There are always two sides to every coin, he thought to himself.

"I'm sorry," Penny said, her frustration evident. "I'm not being of much help, am I?"

"On the contrary," Curtis replied gently. "We often only see someone's public persona. Getting a more detailed understanding of who they are behind closed doors can be immensely helpful."

"There are just two more questions I'd like to ask," Curtis continued. "As I said before, ask me anything if it will help bring Tom back," Penny fervently replied.

Curtis inquired, "Tom mentioned having a career in advertising before becoming a private investigator. Do you happen to know the agency he worked for?"

"He worked at Synergy in Los Angeles," she answered promptly. "Why do you ask?"

Curtis looked at her and said, "Not directly related, but I thought I might give them a call to gather information about Tom's past."

"You think it might be connected to something that happened years ago?" Penny asked, her voice trailing off.

Curtis sensed her hesitation. "Did something happen during his time there?" He pressed.

"No, no, nothing like that," Penny stammered. "It was a slip of the tongue. I didn't mean it the way it sounded."

"Of course, I understand," Curtis assured her, making a mental note to follow up on this lead. "Lastly, earlier, you mentioned that you and Tom rarely discussed his work. Can you think of anyone he might have confided in?"

She took a moment before responding. "I thought he confided in you. But if you're thinking of someone else, then yes, there's Barrington."

"Your brother?" Curtis asked, clearly surprised.

A faint smile graced Penny's face. "I know they weren't close before, but something changed the last time Barrington visited. They started getting closer, even calling each other, which took me by surprise."

"In that case, I'll give your brother a call. Perhaps Haddonfield confided in him," Curtis suggested earnestly.

"He'll be visiting this weekend. Why don't you come around and speak to him in person?" Penny offered.

"If that's okay with you, I'll do that," Curtis accepted. With that, he stood up and embraced Penny. "I know it's difficult, but I promised you I'll find him. And I intend to keep that promise."

As Curtis walked out of the trading store, he gazed across the road at the park. His attention was drawn to a lone woman walking her dog. He observed for a moment as the dog began digging energetically at the ground.

Speaking aloud to himself, Curtis mused, "The answers are often right in front of us. We just need to know where to dig."

The morning sun streamed through the window, casting a warm glow in the room. Curtis could hear the familiar sounds of his wife bustling in the kitchen, preparing breakfast. Amidst the peaceful silence, a voice broke through, instantly recognizable.

"Hello, Matt. How can I help you?" Katherine's voice carried to Curtis's ears.

"Hi, Katherine! I'm here to see Curtis," Jeffrey exclaimed with a joyful tone.

Curtis stood up, anticipating Jeffrey's arrival, and made his way to greet him. "Hello, Jeffrey. What brings you here today?"

"Just wondering if you have any updates from your meeting with Haddonfield's missus," Jeffrey inquired.

Curtis contemplated for a moment before deciding on transparency. He trusted Jeffrey and believed he should share the information he had discovered. Curtis explained the meeting with Penny and the growing connection between Haddonfield and his brother-in-law. He mentioned that Penny couldn't think of any possible enemies and saw Haddonfield as a completely different person from the one they knew.

Jeffrey listened intently, processing the information before speaking abruptly. "So, we have no leads, basically?"

"Well, pretty much. But I think it's worth speaking to this Barrington. He's coming for a visit this weekend, as Penny mentioned. Initially, I agreed to speak to him then, but I think it might be better to approach him sooner," Curtis replied.

"Agreed," Jeffrey nodded, interrupted by Katherine entering the room. I've prepared pancakes," Katherine announced.

"Please stay and join us, Matt."

Jeffery enthusiastically devoured a stack of syrup and berry-covered golden pancakes, appreciating Katherine's culinary skills. Once they finished their breakfast, Curtis and Jeffery headed toward the front door, but

Curtis noticed Katherine's puzzled expression as she watched them.

"And where do you think you're going?" She asked.

"We just need to follow up on a lead, love. Matt is with me, so I won't be alone. I'll fill you in when I get back," Curtis reassured her with a comforting look.

"You really think he's up for playing detective?" Katherine questioned.

Jeffrey smiled. "I'll be fine, Katherine. There's still some life left in this old dog."

With a hesitant nod, Katherine bid them farewell. Opening the door, Curtis and Jeffrey ventured out, making their way toward Curtis's car.

"So, are we going to see Barrington?" Jeffrey asked, curiosity etched on his face.

Curtis nodded, starting the engine as the car roared to life. The two men drove in silence, modern songs blaring from the radio, unfamiliar to both of them.

After forty-five minutes of driving, they reached a long gravel driveway leading to a small, crooked cottage.

"This must be it," Curtis declared, bringing the car to a halt. He turned the key, silencing the engine completely.

Curtis and Jeffrey exited the car and headed to the front door. Curtis pressed the doorbell, their anticipation growing with every passing second. After what felt like an eternity, they spotted a figure slowly approaching the door, its silhouette distorted by the weathered glass.

As the figure drew nearer and the door creaked open, Curtis couldn't help but notice a distinct change in Barrington's demeanor. Fear, nervousness, and an undeniable sense of sheepishness filled his eyes as he sized up the two men.

"Hello, young chap. We heard about what happened to Tom, and we really need to speak to you regarding his disappearance. I'm Curtis, and this is my friend Matt, who knows about your brother-in-law's predicament," Curtis eagerly introduced themselves, hoping Barrington would allow them in.

After a brief pause of reflection, Barrington swung the door open wider, extending an invitation for them to enter.

Curtis mused to himself, "I expected this to be more challenging," as he entered the run-down cottage, closely followed by Jeffrey.

Barrington gestured for them to enter a small, dated sitting room.

Once seated, Curtis was about to speak, but Barrington beat him to it. "So... How do you think I can help you?"

"We spoke to your sister, Penny, and she believes that if Haddonfield confided in anyone, it might be you," Curtis replied, noticing the sweat forming on Barrington's forehead.

"I have no idea why she would say that. I'm not particularly close to him, so it's unlikely he would share much with me. It's sad what happened to him, but he does have a lot of skeletons in his closet. Shouldn't you be talking to the people he's upset?" Barrington responded; his words tinged with nervousness.

Curtis paused, preparing to speak, but Jeffrey had the same thought and quickly interjected with a puzzled expression. "Sorry, but what do you mean by 'it's sad'?"

"Well, you know... He's probably dead or something... Maybe even worse," Barrington mumbled.

Curtis asked, intrigued, "And why do you think he's dead, sir? What could be worse than death?"

Realizing he had said too much, Barrington stood up, stuttering. "I... I... I just have a feeling. With all these missing women and the death of Nikita, things aren't as they seem here. But what do I know? I probably know far less than two professionals like yourselves."

Sensing Barrington's nerves and reservations, Curtis decided it was best to let the matter rest for now. "Well, thank you for your help," Curtis said confidently, offering a smile.

"Wait—" Jeffrey began.

Curtis interrupted, "Come on then, Jeffrey, let's go."

With a confused look, Jeffrey followed Curtis, and they made their way to the door. Once outside, Jeffrey touched Curtis on the shoulder.

"Mate, what was that about? He was so close to breaking. He definitely knows more than he's letting on."

Curtis turned and smiled at his friend. "I know, buddy. I know." And with that, he got into the car, ready to continue their investigation.

By mid-afternoon, Curtis sensed Jeffrey's confusion and could barely contain his excitement at his discovery.

Arriving at the bed and breakfast, Curtis noticed Edna Braithwaite tending to her roses and decided it was time to update Jeffrey on his findings. Curtis emphasized the importance of their mutual information-sharing.

"When Jeffrey questioned Barrington about Haddonfield's death, Barrington's eyes flicked towards a coffee table with an identical envelope to the one Curtis gave Jeffrey for Lyndon," Curtis revealed.

Jeffrey's curiosity grew, wondering if Lyndon was connected to Barrington. Curtis remained uncertain but suspicious, citing their history of unexpected twists.

Recognizing the gravity of the situation, Jeffrey agreed to further investigation. Curtis suggested capitalizing on the upcoming weekend when Lyndon's place would be empty. Jeffrey enthusiastically joined the effort.

Surprised and pleased by Jeffrey's commitment, Curtis returned to Katherine, knowing he was risking her safety but keeping his promise of transparency. He recounted the morning's events, including the envelop Barrington's assumptions about Haddonfield, and his growing suspicions.

Katherine listened calmly and responded, "I understand your need to find out what happened, Curtis, but please be careful. These people are clearly dangerous. I've come to expect such risks with your work as an investigative journalist."

Curtis was surprised by Katherine's understanding, recalling her years of experience with his involvement in complex and perilous cases. He continued setting the table for dinner when he heard a knock on the door.

"I've got it!" Curtis called out, rushing to open the door. To his delight, it was his dear old friend Harlow standing there.

"Harlow, pal, what brings you here?" Curtis greeted him warmly.

Harlow glanced inside. "It's a sensitive matter, mind if I come in?"

Curtis gestured for him to enter. They settled into armchairs, basking in the sunlight that streamed through the windows. Curtis noticed Harlow's scuffed and bloody knuckles gripping the armchair.

Harlow noticed Curtis's gaze and hastily covered his hand. "Work related incident, unpleasant business. But that's not why I'm here," he said, cutting through the silence. "You agreed to step back from all this, yet I've heard that you've been questioning Barrington about Haddonfield's disappearance. He feels suspicious of you."

Curtis was taken aback by the accusation. "Questioning him? I'm afraid there's been a misunderstanding."

Harlow's tone grew forceful. "He felt suspicious after your questioning about Haddonfield's disappearance. You need to leave this alone, old friend. It's not your concern anymore, and you should let sleeping dogs lie. For Katherine's sake."

Alarmed, Curtis wondered what Harlow meant by "Katherine's sake," but decided not to question it. "Understood, boss," he replied, with a hint of sarcasm slipping through unintentionally.

Harlow's departure left Curtis deep in contemplation. He meticulously briefed Katherine on the unfolding events, sharing every detail and his mounting suspicions regarding Harlow and the committee members. To his surprise, Katherine concurred with his concerns.

That night, Curtis wrestled with sleep, troubled by Harlow's evident worry for Katherine's well-being. At 4 AM, he surrendered to restlessness and delved into Lyndon's captivating novel, stoking his determination to unveil the truth.

With weary eyes, Curtis eventually closed his laptop, his mind reeling from the unsettling information he had absorbed. Aware that it was too early to rouse Jeffrey, he returned to bed alongside Katherine, eventually succumbing to sleep.

Suddenly, Curtis was jolted awake by a loud thumping noise emanating from the front door. Katherine was nowhere to be found.

"I'm coming! Hold on!" Curtis shouted as he hurriedly got up and made his way to the door.

He swung it open to find a pale and panicked Jeffrey standing there. "What's wrong, buddy? Is everything okay?" Curtis asked with concern. As Jeffrey stepped inside, Curtis noticed the color draining from his face.

"We don't have time. Barrington called me. He said we need to get over there immediately for Katherine's sake. He even mentioned her by name. How does he know?" Jeffrey exclaimed. "I was going to ask him the same question, but he hung up. I rushed straight here."

Curtis grabbed his keys and dashed to his car, not even realizing he was still in his pajamas. He sensed the gravity of the situation, something ominous unfolding that deeply troubled him.

The drive to Barrington's house was somber, with little conversation between the two friends. It was an unspoken agreement that they were facing an urgent crisis.

When they arrived at Barrington's address, they were greeted by a wide-open front door. Curtis and Jeffrey exchanged horrified glances. Without a second thought, Curtis rushed into the house, finding it eerily silent.

"Barrington? Where are you?" Curtis called out. He heard sobbing coming from the sitting room where they had gathered the previous day and hurried inside to investigate.

"Oh, my God!" Curtis screamed; his voice filled with terror. "Jeffrey, hurry, come in here!"

A few moments later, Jeffrey burst in, shocked. Barrington sat hunched in a corner, drenched in blood, cradling a lifeless body on the floor. The anguished cries of a broken man echoed through the desolate cottage.

"Is he... Is he dead?" Jeffrey asked, his voice trembling. "Barrington?"

Barrington lifted his head, tears streaming down his face and staining his blood-soaked shirt. "I think so," he choked out. "This isn't what you think." He continued to hold the body tightly, refusing to let go.

Curtis finally noticed the face of the lifeless man—it was his ex-colleague Haddonfield. The gruesome scene overwhelmed him, but he managed to gather his thoughts enough to speak. "Barrington, what does this have to do with Katherine? Why did you bring us here for her sake?"

Barrington continued to sob, offering no answers to Curtis's questions. Jeffrey took out his phone and began dialing 911, but Barrington shot him a desperate glance. "No!" He exclaimed. "You can't call them. We can't trust them anymore. Look, I can't explain, but we're running out of time. If you want to save your wife, Curtis, you'll have to trust me."

Curtis felt a wave of apprehension. He had a sinking feeling about the situation, but the thought of anything happening to Katherine was unbearable. With a heavy heart, he sank to his knees, realizing that he couldn't afford to have more blood on his hands.

"What was that envelope on your coffee table yesterday?" Curtis asked, his voice trembling as he tried to compose himself.

Barrington wiped the tears from his cheeks, visibly attempting to gather himself. "You have to understand, that Haddonfield's death wasn't my doing. I loved him like a brother," Barrington said, his voice filled with anguish.

Curtis focused on Haddonfield's brutal throat wound, a chilling sight that sent shivers down his spine, filling him with fear and anxiety. It was at this moment that he truly grasped the gravity of the situation he had unwittingly stumbled into.

He noticed Jeffrey's conspicuous absence and hurried outside, discovering his friend pacing the driveway, clearly in distress. Curtis observed him from the doorway until their gazes locked.

"Who did you call?" Curtis inquired; his concern evident.

"I know you won't be pleased, but I reached out to Lyndon, and..." Jeffrey began, but Curtis interrupted with a shocked outburst.

"You did what?!" Curtis exclaimed, incredulous. "Why would you contact him? We agreed it's just us now. We can't trust Lyndon."

"I know you don't trust him, but this situation is far more complicated and dangerous than we initially thought. Lyndon might have answers that could help us," Jeffrey explained.

Curtis's patience wore thin. "How can Lyndon be of any help? He seems entangled in all of this," he said, feeling the weight of the situation.

"We don't have all the facts yet. There are pieces to this puzzle that have eluded you, but I genuinely believe that Lyndon holds the key to unraveling it," Jeffrey insisted. "Come on, let's return inside to Barrington."

Curtis locked eyes with Jeffrey, a mixture of shock and concern mirrored on both their faces. Haddonfield remained sprawled on the floor, while Barrington had vanished without a trace. "What do we do now?" Curtis asked, searching Jeffrey's face for answers.

Jeffrey shrugged, uncertain about how to proceed in the face of the grisly scene before them. "You know what we should do. Lyndon."

Curtis shifted his gaze to Haddonfield's lifeless body. "But what about Haddonfield? I promised Harlow I'd leave him alone. How do I explain our presence here, with a dead body, and the person we found covered in blood is now missing?"

"I honestly don't know, mate. But first, you need to call Katherine and make sure she's okay," Jeffrey advised.

Curtis felt a wave of sickness wash over him. Amidst the chaos, he had forgotten that Katherine hadn't been around when he woke up that morning. He had assumed she was assisting Edna Braithwaite with her gardening, but now he couldn't help but entertain the thought that something might have happened to her.

After three unsuccessful attempts to reach Katherine, Curtis turned to Jeffrey, distress evident in his eyes. "No answer. She's not picking up. If anything has happened to her, I swear I'll personally bring Harlow down, along with anyone else responsible for these horrors. I'll make them pay."

Minutes passed in a deafening silence that felt like an eternity. Jeffrey stood up and reached for his phone, leaving Curtis unsure of his next move. "Alright, we need to get out of here and act like we were never here," Jeffrey said calmly, his face composed.

"What? Are you serious? There's a crime scene here," Curtis spat, incredulous.

"I know, I know," Jeffrey replied. "But if the police are covering something up, they'll know we're onto them. And the last thing we want is to be implicated in this mess."

Curtis hesitated for a moment but eventually nodded in agreement. "Fine. What's the plan, then?"

"Lyndon said to meet him at an address in fifty-five minutes. It should take us about forty minutes to get there, so we should leave now. And remember, don't touch anything," Jeffrey instructed.

Slowly the two men left the cottage and headed towards the car being very careful not to leave any residual presence of them in the cottage.

Carefully, the two men exited the cottage, making sure not to leave any traces of their presence behind. Curtis took a deep breath as he got into the car, tears streaming down his cheeks. He turned away from Jeffrey, attempting to hide his despair, but suspected his friend could sense the tears anyway.

With the engine running, Curtis began to drive. The supposed forty-minute journey took them only thirty-five, their haste apparent in the occasional "Slow down, mate" from Jeffrey.

As Curtis brought the car to a halt, he looked out the window and recognized the address they had arrived at, though he couldn't recall where he knew it from.

Moments later, a sleek black car pulled up beside them, its windows heavily tinted. Curtis caught a glimpse of a figure in the driver's seat. "Come on," Jeffrey said, stepping out of their car and walking toward the black vehicle.

Jeffrey opened the back right door and got inside, prompting Curtis to follow suit and enter the back left side. As he settled in, he saw Lyndon in the driver's seat, looking composed and professional despite the morning's events.

"Look, Lyndon, I have no idea what's going on here, but Jeffrey seems to think—" Curtis began, only to be abruptly interrupted by Lyndon.

"I know you must have countless questions, Curtis. I also know you pretended to step back from all of this, but right now, you have to trust me, okay?" Lyndon spoke calmly, his eyes fixed on the road ahead.

With countless questions swirling in his mind, Curtis nodded and fought to suppress the sickening feeling in his stomach whenever he thought of Katherine.

"So, what happened when you arrived?" Lyndon inquired. Curtis glanced at Jeffrey. "Go on, tell him," Jeffrey urged.

Realizing he had little to lose, Curtis proceeded to recount every detail from the open front door to Haddonfield's lifeless body, the slit throat, Barrington's disappearance, and Barrington's cryptic words.

Lyndon raised an eyebrow and turned to face Curtis over his shoulder. "Interesting."

"Interesting? Is that all you have to say?" Curtis exclaimed.

"Well, before we do anything else, we need to track down Barrington. Any idea where he might be?" Lyndon asked.

"Why would I..." Curtis stuttered.

"What is it?" Jeffrey asked, sensing Curtis's hesitation.

"He mentioned visiting his sister tomorrow. Penny, you know her," Curtis replied, momentarily forgetting Lyndon and Penny's past romantic involvement.

"That's where we start then. You need to go visit Penny and hope Barrington is there," Lyndon suggested.

Just as Curtis pondered their next move, his phone buzzed in his pocket.

He glanced at the screen, which displayed Katherine's name. "Sorry, I need to take this," Curtis said, answering the call. "Love, where are you?"

Curtis listened intently, hearing heavy breathing on the other end of the line. After a few seconds, the call abruptly ended, leaving Curtis with a sinking feeling in his chest.

"Well?" Jeffrey inquired; his voice filled with concern.

Curtis leaned his face against the backseat window, tears streaming down his cheeks. Through sobs, he recounted the phone call and noticed a worried expression on Lyndon's face.

"What's wrong?" Curtis implored, desperate for answers.

"Mate, I'm concerned about Katherine. We had a feeling something like this might happen," Lyndon said.

"We? Who's we?" Curtis questioned.

Lyndon looked at Jeffrey and let out a sigh. "Jeff, tell him."

"Pal, I've been working with Lyndon all along. He can be trusted, Curtis. He's on our side in this. He wants to uncover the truth just as much as we do," Jeffrey explained.

Curtis couldn't help but feel a pang of betrayal, but he knew his options were limited. "Alright. What do we do now?"

In the midst of a restless night, Curtis braced himself to fetch Jeffrey, eager to see Penny and, hopefully, find Barrington. Being apart from Katherine, his long-time wife, worried him deeply. He couldn't shake the fear of her falling into harm's way.

Curtis felt responsible for the sadness that engulfed him after hearing about Jane Thomas. His journalistic curiosity had intertwined the fates of these missing women with his own life. His initial instinct was to involve the police in finding Katherine, but an inner voice pushed him to take a different path, to go rogue, believing it was the only way to uncover the truth and save Katherine.

Jeffrey noticed Curtis's worry beneath his brave facade. They quickly got to work upon meeting, arriving at Penny's storefront. Curtis took a deep breath before opening the door, and to his surprise, Barrington stood by the counter.

"Barrington?" Curtis exclaimed; his voice filled with surprise. Barrington turned towards him and greeted him casually. "Oh, hello, old chap. How are you?"

Curtis and Jeffrey exchanged bewildered glances. Barrington then motioned for them to follow him to the back room, leaving them confused yet intrigued.

"What is going on, Barrington? You disappeared without a trace," Curtis questioned.

Barrington sighed, explaining his actions. "I know, I know. I just couldn't stay. When I saw Jeffrey on the phone outside, I thought he might be calling the police, so I had to make myself scarce."

Unable to contain his curiosity, Curtis blurted out, "What was in that envelope, Barrington? And why were you so concerned about Katherine? What do you know?"

Barrington's confidence wavered, and he hesitated before responding. "I've had my suspicions for a while, but I'm not sure if I can trust you, Curtis, or you, Jeffrey. You need to talk to Frankie Walsh. That's all I can say."

Puzzled, Curtis pressed for more information. "But why Frankie? How is she connected to all of this?"

"It's not for me to say. Just follow the trail, and you'll find yourself in a forest," Barrington cryptically replied.

Accepting the enigmatic advice, Curtis nodded and prepared to leave the shop. However, he couldn't resist asking one more question. "Barrington, what will you do about Tom's body?"

Barrington looked at him with a puzzled expression. "Don't worry, it's taken care of."

Confused by Barrington's response, Curtis turned to Jeffrey. "What do you think he meant by 'it's taken care of'?"

Jeffrey shrugged. "I honestly have no idea, buddy. But maybe it's best not to dig too deep right now."

Though in agreement, Curtis couldn't shake the unease settling in his gut. As they arrived at the bed and breakfast, a cluster of police cars and officers caught their attention. Curtis rushed over to Edna Braithwaite, seeking answers.

He hurriedly jumped out of the car and ran to Edna Braithwaite, demanding answers. "Edna, what happened?"

"I heard glass shattering, and when I looked, I saw the door to your cottage had been smashed. Someone had forced their way in, so I called the police," Edna explained with a tremor in her voice.

A familiar voice called out to Curtis. It was Paul Harlow. "Hello, Curtis. As soon as Ms. Braithwaite alerted us, we sent some units over. It seems nothing has been taken... Where's Katherine?" Harlow inquired.

Curtis hesitated for a moment before replying, trying to appear composed, "She's out with a friend." Harlow smirked, "Hmm, okay. Well, we're done here, but I suggest you secure that door. There have been all sorts of incidents in this area recently." Curtis couldn't shake the feeling that Harlow doubted his explanation and that something wasn't right about him. As he entered the cottage, he immediately noticed the absence of something important. "The laptop!"

The laptop was gone, stolen by the intruder who seemed to know exactly what they were looking for. While there might not have been much confidential information on it, Curtis worried about Lyndon's novel stored within. Whoever had the laptop could potentially crack the password and access its contents.

Realizing he hadn't discussed Barrington with Jeffrey, Curtis decided to visit his neighbor. However, his attempts to reach Barrington were met with silence. Just as he was about to give up and return to his cottage, his phone began to ring.

"Hello, Curtis. It's Jane Thomas. I really need you to come over."

"Of course, I'll be there within the hour," Curtis replied, ending the call. Forty-five minutes later, Curtis found himself standing at Jane Thomas's doorstep, the mother of the missing woman Chloe. The disheveled and distraught woman opened the door, appearing a mere shadow of her former self.

"Hello, Jane," Curtis greeted her warmly.

"Um... Hi, Curtis. Please, come in," Jane stammered.

Curtis entered the house and settled at the solid oak table positioned in the center of the kitchen. He couldn't help but notice Jane's slurred speech and her slightly intoxicated state. He inquired, "Have you been drinking?"

Jane produced a half-empty bottle of vodka and poured herself another stiff drink. She downed it swiftly, emitting an audible sigh. Jane poured herself another glass and hesitated before speaking. "Well, it might be nothing, but... Oh, never mind."

"No, please continue. Any information could be helpful. We want to find Chloe," Curtis urged, his curiosity piqued.

"I'll show you. Just a moment," Jane mumbled and stumbled out of the kitchen. Uncertain whether to follow, Curtis waited. After a few minutes, Jane returned with Chloe's phone in a glittery case, displaying photos. Curtis initially thought it was an ordinary phone until he saw Chloe's picture, confirming it was hers. Jane then showed him a contact labeled "Mom" with her number, explaining it was Chloe's phone retrieved from the police.

As Curtis replayed the unsettling voicemail message, a shiver ran down his spine. It was the identical message he had listened to on the night he was scheduled to meet Nikita, who had ultimately failed to appear. Curtis had dialed her number repeatedly, each time confronted by that eerie and haunting message.

Confusion overwhelmed Curtis about Chloe's connection to Nikita and the "Mom" contact. Jane was too intoxicated to provide answers. Curtis asked to see Chloe's call history, but it was empty. "Someone must have deleted them," he thought, leaving puzzled.

The connection between the two troubled him, but he couldn't approach Harlow, as he had promised to step back, not wanting to raise suspicions. As Curtis drove back, the sunset cast a darkening hue. Near a junction, a screech and everything went white and hazy.

"Are you okay, mate?" An unfamiliar voice asked.

Confused and disoriented, Curtis found himself slumped over the steering wheel, feeling a cold breeze and what seemed like shards of broken glass on his body.

Lifting his head, Curtis saw a blurred figure wearing a black balaclava next to his car. As his vision cleared, he realized the person had covered everything except their eyes.

Panicking, Curtis tried to start the engine to escape the terrifying individual, but he was too slow. The masked stranger reached through the broken window, snatched the keys from his hand, and spoke in a gruff voice, filled with menace.

"Listen to me carefully. If you want to see your wife again, you'll stop. Leave this alone. Don't dig any further. Forget everything you've looked into."

"I promise. But where is Katherine?" Curtis asked nervously. "Where is my wife?"

The stranger's gruff voice issued a warning. The stranger handed Curtis a large brown envelope with a bold question mark drawn in red pen. You're familiar with Lyndon Whiteford. "Listen carefully. Take this package to him and make it seem relevant to the investigation. Then leave swiftly. Understand?"

"I think so," Curtis replied, his mind filled with uncertainty about the mysterious package.

"Now is not the time for thinking." The stranger threw the keys back into the car, walked away, hopped onto a motorbike, and sped off.

Curtis was in shock. He didn't know what to do, but he knew that this confirmed someone had Katherine, and he would do whatever it took to get her back. He remembered her warning about the messiness and danger but regretted not heeding her advice.

Picking up the keys from the floor, Curtis started the car and drove back to the bed and breakfast. To his surprise, Jeffrey was standing at the cottage doorway.

Jeffrey rushed over when he saw the state of Curtis' car. "Curtis, what happened? Are you okay?"

Curtis stepped out of the car. "Yes, I think I am. I took a turn too fast and went off the road, but I'm fine."

"Well, now might not be the best time, mate, but I've been thinking about what Barrington said regarding Haddonfield's body. Maybe we should tell the police," Jeffrey suggested.

"No!" Curtis shouted. "We can't do that. There's too much at stake." "But we don't know what happened to Haddonfield, do we? What if Barrington was involved?" Jeffrey questioned.

"Trust me. I have something that could help the investigation, but I need to talk to Lyndon first. You have to trust me," Curtis insisted.

"If you say so, pal. I'll trust you, but I hope you're right," Jeffrey reluctantly agreed.

With that, Curtis pulled out his phone and called Lyndon, who picked up immediately. Curtis explained the evidence he had and stressed that he couldn't discuss it over the phone; they needed to meet in person.

Lyndon agreed, sounding hopeful, which made Curtis feel guilty for deceiving him. However, he knew he had to do it for Katherine's sake.

The next day, Curtis drove with Jeffrey to Crowhurst Park, the place where he had previously met Tiana Taylor, Gabriella's best friend, along with Haddonfield. It still felt eerie, a rough place to be. Curtis wondered if Lyndon had intentionally chosen it as a meeting point or if it was a mere coincidence.

Before he could dwell on the thought, Lyndon's car pulled up beside them. This time, Curtis didn't freeze. He confidently got out of the car and joined Lyndon in the backseat, with Jeffrey following suit.

"Well?" Lyndon turned to look at Curtis in the backseat.

Silently, Curtis handed him the package, watching as Lyndon carefully opened it and examined its contents. After resealing it, Lyndon simply said, "I see. Thank you, Curtis."

Curtis desperately wished he had looked inside the envelope himself, as Lyndon did not indicate what was inside.

"It's probably best for Jeffrey to stay here with me now, Curtis. Thank you for this, but we have some business to discuss," Lyndon said, unlocking the car doors with a switch.

Confused by the sudden turn of events, Curtis nodded and stepped out of the car. He returned to his own vehicle and started driving off. As he was about to leave Crowhurst Park, he noticed a vehicle parked with its lights off and two figures standing nearby.

Drawing closer, Curtis could make out the silhouettes of a stocky man and a petite woman engaged in a heated argument. Trying not to appear too nosy, he glanced out of his window as he approached, only to realize that he knew both of them.

The woman, he was certain, was Tiana Taylor, Gabriella Atkins' best friend. To his surprise, the male figure turned out to be his "old friend" Paul Harlow.

"This makes no sense. The police don't know that Tiana is Gabriella's best friend. Haddonfield and I just found out, and that was only by accident," Curtis muttered aloud.

Convinced that Katherine was out of harm's way, Curtis parked his car discreetly around the corner to keep an eye on the unfolding scene.

He watched as Tiana and Harlow continued to argue for a few more minutes before Tiana eventually started walking away.

Harlow forcefully grabbed her arm and pulled her back, reaching into his pocket to hand her something. Then, he swiftly got into his car and sped off, leaving Curtis puzzled by the peculiar encounter.

Once the coast was clear and Harlow was gone, Curtis turned on his car headlights and flashed them, hoping to catch Tiana's attention. After a few flickers, he saw her approaching his vehicle.

"It's you again. What do you want?" Tiana asked suspiciously as she neared the car.

Curtis was surprised she remembered him but tried to play it cool. "Get in, love. It's cold out."

"What happened with that man you were meeting? I saw you," asked Curtis.

Tiana eyed him skeptically for a moment before circling around the car and getting into the passenger seat.

Tiana fumbled in her pocket and pulled out a small bag. "Look, if you want information, it's going to cost you three hundred dollars."

Curtis reached for his wallet and began to pull out some cash. "Last time, it was two hundred dollars."

Tiana poured out a powder from the bag onto the car's dashboard. "The stakes are higher now."

Curtis realized it was drugged and observed as Tiana took the money from his hand, rolled up a note, and snorted a line of the mysterious powder. She sniffed loudly, then stuffed the bag and money into her pocket.

"He's a friend of Gabriella's. He likes the working girls. He likes to make sure they're okay," Tiana said, glancing around outside to ensure their privacy.

"But Gabriella wasn't a working girl. You said that yourself. You said her parents didn't like her being friends with you because..." Curtis trailed off, questioning Tiana's previous statement.

"Because I'm a prostitute, you mean? Because I sell my body for money? Just say it, man. We all know what you're thinking," Tiana replied defensively.

Curtis felt remorseful for his prejudices. "Well, yes, I suppose so."

"We all have our skeletons in the closet. Gabriella was no different. Eddie knew what she was, and he looked after her," Tiana disclosed.

"Eddie? That name rings a bell. Eddie. That's who you said Gabriella had been meeting with, someone she met online," Curtis realized, connecting the dots.

"I thought you didn't know who this Eddie was?" Curtis felt rather pleased that despite everything going on, he had retained such crucial information.

Tiana explained, "I didn't lie. I didn't know who he was until a few days ago. He approached me, asking if I was a working girl. When I confirmed, he introduced himself as Eddie. I thought it might be a coincidence, but when I mentioned being Gabriella's best friend and knowing all about him, he said he would look out for me like he did for her."

"But I thought Gabriella met Eddie online," Curtis said, seeking clarification.

"Yes, that's what I thought too. But considering she usually met clients online, I figured she said that because she didn't want me to know she was working the streets. It's seen as less respectable in our line of work, as I'm sure you understand," Tiana explained.

As Curtis was about to respond, he noticed Tiana sweating profusely, her body trembling. Alarmed, he asked, "Tiana, are you okay?"

There was no response.

At that moment, Curtis realized that the drugs had harmed her, and he needed to get her to a hospital. He leaned over, fastened her seatbelt, and sped off toward the nearest medical facility.

Upon arrival, Curtis rushed inside, calling for help and attention. Within moments, a group of nurses and doctors hurried to assist. Curtis led them to Tiana in the car, and they swiftly unstrapped her and placed her on a stretcher.

Curtis stood in shock as he watched Tiana convulsing violently. He remained rooted in the waiting room until a nurse approached him. "What's her name, and what happened to her?"

Curtis provided Tiana's name and explained that she had snorted an unknown powder, unsure of its contents. Still in a state of shock, Curtis sat in the waiting room, anxiously awaiting news, praying for Tiana's recovery.

After a night of fitful dozing in an uncomfortable metal chair, it felt like an eternity when Curtis was awakened by a nurse calling out his name. "Curtis Styles, I'm looking for Curtis Styles!"

He stood up and walked toward her, confirming his identity. She then led him to Tiana's private room. "Am I okay to share what has happened with, I assume, her father?"

Before Curtis could correct her assumption, Tiana weakly sat up and croaked, "Yes," in agreement.

Curtis was taken aback by Tiana claiming him as her father but listened attentively to the conversation.

"It appears that whatever drugs you took were clearly laced with something. I don't know if the person who gave them to you intended to harm you or if it was simply cut with harmful substances," the nurse explained. "But one thing is certain, Miss Taylor, you were very lucky. If you hadn't arrived at the hospital when you did, you could have been dead by now. Surviving such a lethal dose of the substances in those drugs is remarkable."

Tiana's eyes welled up with tears as she expressed her gratitude to the nurse. Then she turned to Curtis and said, "Pass me my coat," pointing to a chair in the corner of the room.

Curtis leaned over, retrieved the coat, and handed it to her.

Tiana reached into the pocket and pulled out the wad of cash Curtis had given her twelve hours earlier. "Here, take that back. You saved my life, Curtis," she said, holding out her hand.

"No, Tiana, keep it. You need it more than I do, and you've taken a significant risk by talking to me," Curtis replied, feeling sorry for her situation.

Exhausted, Curtis slouched at the kitchen table, battling to remain alert. A glimmer of light from outside seized his attention. He blinked, half-convincing himself that it was a sleep-deprived mirage, yet a presence lingered.

Curtis was overcome by a mixture of curiosity and a touch of unease. Just as he was about to investigate, a soft knock reverberated on the door. Assuming it was Jeffrey, he called out, "Please, come in. It's not locked," and resumed his reading.

"Love?" A familiar voice called out, sending a jolt of surprise through

Curtis.

He looked up and saw his wife, Katherine, standing in the doorway. Overwhelmed with emotion, Curtis jumped up from his chair, knocking it to the floor, and rushed to embrace her. He held her tightly, burying his face in her hair, unable to believe she was finally home. Questions poured out of him, desperate for answers about her disappearance. "What happened? Where have you been? Who took you?"

After a prolonged embrace, Katherine sat down and proceeded to explain everything to Curtis. She assured him that she was unharmed, having been fed and taken care of, but the captors always wore masks, and balaclavas, as she remembered.

Curtis, his eyes welling up with tears, expressed his overwhelming relief, "I'm just so glad to have you home. I've missed you more than words can say."

"And I to you, my love," Katherine replied, wiping away her tears.

Curtis proceeded to narrate the occurrences of the preceding 48 hours, beginning with the discovery of Haddonfield's lifeless body at Barrington's residence, followed by the collision with his car by the masked attacker, the mysterious envelope he had been compelled to deliver to Lyndon, and the disconcerting encounter with Tiana.

"Well, I'm stunned," Katherine remarked. "You've truly been investigating, haven't you? Listen, now I need you to approach this with an open mind. Think outside the box."

"Okay," Curtis replied, patiently waiting for his wife's insight. Katherine continued, her voice filled with determination, "The thing is, I don't think we can trust the police right now. Not any of them. When I was held captive, I cried out for help, and one of the men told me that nobody could save me, not even the police. At the time, I thought it might be meaningless, but after what you've told me about Paul Harlow, I believe there might be some truth to it."

Curtis intrigued, asked, "Agreed. But what about me stepping back?" "For the sake of the mothers," Katherine said, locking eyes with Curtis. "You need to do this for them if nothing else."

Curtis nodded, taking his wife's hand. He kissed it gently and stood up. "Cup of coffee, love?"

"I would love one," Katherine replied, settling back into the chair.

As Curtis prepared the coffee and sat back down, they heard a knock at the door.

"What now?" Curtis muttered aloud, rising to his feet and heading towards the door.

Opening it, he heard Jeffrey's urgent voice, "It's Barrington. You need to come now."

"Look, Jeffrey, I'm done with this. Enough is enough," Curtis protested.

Jeffrey's tone escalated, "Unfortunately, you don't get to tap out of this game, pal. Listen, Barrington called me five minutes ago. The police are after him. They think he killed Tom. They think he killed Haddonfield!"

"We don't know that he didn't," Curtis retorted.

"We also didn't know that he did," Jeffrey replied.

Curtis was about to say something when Katherine leaned in and whispered, "I'm going for a shower. Boys will be boys, but tell me everything later."

"Okay, love," Curtis acknowledged as he grabbed his keys and headed toward his car.

"Where are you going?" Jeffrey inquired.

"To see Barrington, I suppose. Get in," Curtis replied, unlocking his car.

Jeffrey directed Curtis to an abandoned car park, where they spotted an old, rundown blue estate car tucked away in the darkest corner.

"Guess that's him," Curtis remarked. "Looks like it," Jeffrey agreed. "Let's go."

Exiting the car, they made their way towards the vehicle. A sense of unease hung in the air, noticeable to Curtis, but he refrained from mentioning it. As they approached, moans emanated from inside.

"Jesus, what happened?" Jeffrey exclaimed dramatically.

Curtis widened his eyes as he peered into the car. Barrington sat slumped over, groaning in pain, a gunshot wound visible on his abdomen.

"I... I don't have much time, but I know I can trust you. I didn't kill Tom. I loved him like a brother," Barrington moaned.

"We know, man. We know," Jeffrey assured him.

In Curtis's mind, he silently acknowledged that they didn't actually know, but he allowed the conversation to proceed.

"I'm being framed, I tell you," Barrington cried.

Curtis, trying not to step on anyone's toes, asked, "How did you get shot, mate?"

"I was at Penny's store when the police came looking for me. I hid in the back, but I accidentally knocked over some stock, and they heard me. The next thing I knew, I was running and being chased. Shots were fired, and one happened to hit me. I managed to fire back a couple of shots, but it only gave me a minute to escape," Barrington explained with a hint of bitterness.

As Barrington explained how he had been shot during the intense police chase, Curtis noticed the severity of his condition. Concern etched on his face; Curtis realized that too many lives had been lost already. The time for justice had come.

Curtis grew increasingly concerned and turned to Jeffrey; his voice filled with urgency. "We have to get him to a hospital immediately. If we don't, he won't survive out here."

"No!" Barrington shouted, panic in his voice. "I can't go to a hospital. I'm not safe there. I'm not safe anywhere."

Curiosity getting the better of him, Curtis couldn't help but ask about the contents of the envelope from the day Tom died. "By the way, what was in that envelope?"

Barrington was about to respond when a fleet of police cars pulled into the parking lot. "Damn it! They must have been tracking my phone. I can't hold on much longer," Barrington said, struggling to stay conscious.

"The envelope, Barrington!" Curtis called out; his voice urgent.

"In due time, my friend. This is bigger than the three of us, and you hold the power to solve it," Barrington gasped.

As the police officers surrounded the car with their guns drawn, Jeffrey and Curtis quickly raised their hands above their heads and complied with their instructions to lie on the ground, hands behind their backs.

"Nice work, Curtis. I knew he would contact you. That's why I tapped your phone," a familiar voice said.

Curtis immediately recognized the voice. "Harlow?"

"The one and only, pal. Thanks to you and us, we caught him. He'll be taken to the hospital for his gunshot wound and then charged with the murder of Tom Haddonfield and the kidnapping and murder of the missing women," Harlow said, jubilant. "You can stand up now. Both of you."

As they rose to their feet, Curtis and Jeffrey watched as Barrington was lifted into an ambulance, accompanied by two police officers. The door closed, and the ambulance sped away with its sirens blaring.

"I don't understand. Barrington did all of this?" Curtis questioned, bewildered.

"That's right, my friend. We had our suspicions, and it seems his brother-in-law, Haddonfield, caught onto him, which led to Barrington killing him. Sad, really," Harlow explained.

"But where are the bodies?" Curtis inquired.

Harlow chuckled. "Not yet, but with enough pressure, Barrington will spill information like a leaking pipe."

Exhausted and somber from the day's events, Curtis and Jeffrey rode back to the bed and breakfast in silence. Curtis invited Jeffrey into the cottage, where they poured themselves whiskeys. Sensing the serious atmosphere, Katherine quietly left them alone.

"Do you really think it could have been Barrington?" Curtis asked, seeking Jeffrey's thoughts.

"Do you?" Jeffrey replied.

Curtis spoke cautiously. "There's something I need to tell you." "I'm listening," Jeffrey said.

Over the next two hours, Curtis recounted every detail of the past seventy-two hours to Jeffrey. From Katherine's abduction to the masked man and Harlow's connection to missing woman Gabrielle Atkins and her friend Tiana.

"So, you're telling me this Tiana woman met up with this mysterious Eddie character, who turned out to be Harlow?" Jeffrey asked, trying to piece it all together.

Curtis took a long sip of his whisky. "Exactly. And I can't shake the feeling that Harlow might have drugged her, almost causing her death."

"Drugged her to keep her quiet?" Jeffrey questioned.

"I don't have concrete proof, but we can't rule it out," Curtis admitted.

Jeffrey took a sip of his drink. "Interesting, very interesting."

"I don't suppose you know what was in the envelope I gave to Lyndon?"

Curtis asked.

"Do you?" Jeffrey countered. "Lyndon thought it was a show of force, directly from you."

"What?" Curtis exclaimed. "I didn't even know what was inside. I swear."

"Well, I suggest you make that clear to Lyndon because he strongly advised me to stay far away from you at all costs," Jeffrey calmly stated.

Curtis wondered if someone had threatened Lyndon, just as they had threatened him and Katherine. But he realized he didn't even know if Lyndon had family. All he knew was that Lyndon had a girlfriend, but they had broken up, and he was deeply committed to his job.

That evening, Curtis shared the events with Katherine, leaving her shocked. He explained Barrington's suspicions about the police force and how their inside knowledge had played a role in the missing women cases. Katherine expressed her thoughts, and what struck Curtis was her belief that Barrington might be right, that he could be a mere scapegoat.

Curtis described how Lyndon took the envelope as a personal attack, assuring Katherine he had no idea what it contained. Still, he couldn't help but wish he had peeked inside.

"Life is full of 'what ifs,' love. You couldn't have known if whatever was in that envelope was harmful. It could have been anthrax or some other poison. You never know with these people," Katherine said.

Curtis chuckled. "You're right. I suppose I just need to find out what was inside. Lyndon is so invested in his career; it must have been something grave to make him step back like this. He's even writing a novel about it."

"A novel?" Katherine questioned.

Curtis laughed. "Yes, I forgot to mention. I started reading the 'novel' on the pen drive from Lyndon, and it's focused on this investigation. I'm not sure why he specifically wanted my opinion; after all, I'm a journalist, not a novelist."

"Don't underestimate yourself, love. There must be a logical explanation. Just talk to him tomorrow," Katherine sighed. "Anyway, I'm exhausted. These past few days have taken a toll on me."

With that, she bid Curtis's goodnight and headed to bed. Curtis glanced at the paper he had started earlier but decided to leave it for tomorrow. He changed, brushed his teeth, and climbed into bed.

Curtis embraced Katherine tightly, relishing her presence. That night, he didn't need to read himself to sleep; he peacefully drifted off with her by his side, determined never to let her go again. When he woke up, he panicked, thinking she was gone, but found her casually making pancakes in the kitchen as if it were any ordinary day.

Setting a plate of pancakes on the table, Katherine greeted him, "Good morning, honey."

Curtis smiled and sat down, eagerly preparing to tackle the generous stack in front of him. Katherine joined him at the table, reminding him, "Don't forget to call Lyndon."

Nodding with a mouthful of pancakes, Curtis managed to paint a smile across his face. For a brief moment, it felt like everything was back to normal as if the past few weeks and the ongoing missing person's case didn't exist. It was a temporary reprieve from the chaos that surrounded him.

Later that morning, Curtis dialed Lyndon's number, but all he heard was a series of beeping sounds. He tried again, hoping for a different outcome, only to realize that the number was no longer in use. Frustrated, he dialed Jeffrey's number and waited for him to pick up.

"Hi Jeffrey, I tried reaching Lyndon, but it seems his number is no longer active," Curtis informed him.

"I know, mate. I had the same experience," Jeffrey replied.

Curtis inquired, "I assume you don't have any other contact information for him, do you?"

"Sorry, pal, that was the only number I had for him," Jeffrey regretfully admitted.

"Alright, no worries. I'll try another approach then. Thanks, mate," Curtis concluded the call. Turning to Katherine, who had been listening from the bedroom door, he informed her, "No luck, love."

Curtis let out a sigh and continued, "I'm going to try Penny. Maybe she has a way to reach him. Plus, I think she could use some support, especially now that Tom's death is likely public knowledge."

Katherine expressed her concerns, "Okay, but don't take too long, and be cautious. She's probably in a fragile state. I plan to visit Jane later today, so make sure you're back by three because I'll need the car."

"Yes, boss," Curtis playfully replied, waving as he left the cottage.

As Curtis arrived at the store, an overwhelming sense of dread washed over him, reminiscent of his visit to Jane, Chloe's mother. Taking a deep breath, he pushed open the door, hoping to find Penny. To his surprise, she was indeed working in the store, looking exhausted and tear-stained.

"Hello Penny, how are you?" Curtis greeted her.

Penny appeared taken aback as if she had seen a ghost. "Oh, hi, Curtis. I'm holding on. I can't believe he's gone."

"It's truly awful. A tremendous loss. He was a good man, Penny, and he'll be deeply missed," Curtis expressed genuinely.

Penny, overcome with emotions, sobbed, "I can't believe I'll never see him again."

"I'm so sorry, Penny. How's your brother holding up?" Curtis inquired cautiously, unsure if he should bring up the topic.

Penny wiped away her tears and looked directly at Curtis. "I know... I know you were there."

Curtis didn't know how to respond, realizing that denying Penny's words would be pointless. It seemed she had learned about his involvement from a reliable source.

Penny fixed him with a stern look. "I know my brother didn't do it, but I want to know why you were there."

Curtis explained, "Your brother... He called me, us, and asked for our help. He said he needed to talk to us."

"He got himself tangled up in all of this, especially when he became obsessed with that working girl, Sophie Hunt, I think her name was. He put himself right in harm's way. And of course, he was there when the woman from the brewery went missing. Connecting the dots isn't hard, Curtis. Two out of four... It's not a coincidence," Penny revealed.

Curtis was astonished by Penny's knowledge. Haddonfield had always kept his work private, rarely discussing the cases in detail. Both Penny and Haddonfield had stressed the importance of confidentiality, which made Penny's insights even more puzzling. Barrington must have shared this information with her.

Penny continued, undeterred by Curtis's silence. "I really think it's time for you to step back from all this, assuming you are who you claim to be."

"What do you mean?" Curtis asked, his confusion mounting.

"You approached Tom, got cozy with that Harlow guy, and seemed to have connections with the police. I can't help but wonder if my brother and Tom might have avoided such a tragic fate if not for your interference. You uncovered too much, dug too deep," Penny accused.

Curtis chose to ignore the insults and accusations thrown at him. "One last question, Penny. Do you happen to have Lyndon's contact details? I really need to speak with him." Penny's response was filled with anger. "Are you joking? I know what you did to Lyndon, to us. You think you're clever, don't you? Well, you got your way."

Realizing the conversation was going nowhere, Curtis abruptly left the store without pressing Penny any further. He couldn't decipher what Penny meant by questioning his identity and what he had supposedly done to Lyndon.

He had always thought of himself as *"the good guy"* but after recent events how found himself really questioning whether he was the good guy anymore, whether there even were any good guys left, it really didn't feel like there were.

Glancing at his watch, Curtis realized it was approaching three o'clock, and Katherine needed the car to visit her friend Jane. He hurried back to the cottage, where Katherine was waiting. As he handed her the keys, he realized he hadn't informed either her or Jeffrey about his meeting with Jane.

He quickly recounted how Chloe's phone had Nikita saved as "Mom" and the suspicion it had raised. Katherine found it odd and suggested they visit Nikita's roommate. Curtis agreed, planning to discuss it with Jeffrey and hopefully accompany him to the meeting.

Jeffrey expressed his concern. "While I agree with you, and it is indeed strange, should we really get involved with Frankie?" "Have you seen today's newspaper?" He asked Curtis.

Curtis glanced at the paper on the table and read the front cover.

"Barrington arrested for the abduction and suspected murder of four missing women. Also arrested for seriously injuring a police officer and murdering his girlfriend's brother, Tom Haddonfield."

"Oh, I just saw it. I know it's a sensitive subject right now, but we need to find out how Nikita knew Chloe. It could be the key to uncovering crucial information," Curtis said, unsure of Jeffrey's response. Would you be willing to visit Frankie, or would I have to embark on this journey alone again?

"Well, you're persistent, I'll give you that, old chap. Okay, I'll come," Jeffrey finally agreed.

"Great, we'll have to use your car since Katherine has ours. She went to see Jane, Chloe's mother," Curtis explained.

"That's fine, pal. I'll pick you up in ten," Jeffrey confirmed.

Later, Curtis heard the sound of Jeffrey's car pulling up outside. He locked the door and made his way to the vehicle. The journey to The Stables Lodge, where Frankie both worked and lived, seemed to stretch on endlessly.

Curtis couldn't shake Penny's accusatory words from his mind. She held him responsible for everything, despite his sincere efforts to assist a distressed mother in finding her daughter. His good intentions had been misconstrued, casting him as the villain while the true wrongdoers remained at large.

Upon entering the lodge's reception area, Curtis spotted Frankie. Initially, he didn't recognize her, but as she spoke softly to a lodge guest, he realized it was indeed her.

"Hi, Frankie. Can we have a word, please?" Curtis asked politely. "Hello, I have a break in ten minutes. I can meet you at my place then if you're willing to wait," Frankie responded.

"That's fine, we'll meet you then," Curtis said as he and Jeffrey walked back out the door. Curtis couldn't believe how different Frankie looked. She had lost a significant amount of weight and appeared exhausted as if she hadn't slept in days.

To pass the time, Curtis and Jeffrey walked around the lodge grounds, engaging in small talk. Eventually, they made their way to Frankie's residence and patiently waited for her.

Within a couple of minutes, Frankie arrived. "Well, you'd better come in, I suppose, although I'm not sure how much more I can help you," she said, unlocking the front door and switching on a small wall heater.

"This may sound odd, but did Nikita ever mention knowing a Chloe

Thomas to you?" Curtis asked, feeling a bit awkward and direct.

"I had a feeling this would come up sooner or later. Yes, Nikita knew her, but I'm not sure if it's my place to share," Frankie replied sheepishly.

"I understand that it can be difficult to disclose a friend's secrets or private matters to others, but we genuinely want to find out what happened to her," Curtis assured her.

"I saw that they found the killer of the missing women today, but no news about Nikita. It seems like they didn't care as much about her as they did about the other girls," Frankie sighed. "By the way, who's your friend? I haven't met him before. He's not... Police, is he?"

"No, he isn't. He's a professional investigator like me, and you can trust him completely. I vouch for him," Curtis explained hopefully.

"Okay, okay. Nikita had a... Let's say, troubled past. She used to work on the streets. She had an expensive habit to support. But you have to trust me when I say this: she turned her life around. In recent years, she barely used drugs, maybe only on occasion when we partied too hard, and even then, she wasn't as bad as some of the staff here," Frankie revealed.

"So, you mean she was a sex worker and had a drug problem?" Curtis asked.

"Yes, that's what I mean. But I don't want anyone to judge her based on that. She worked incredibly hard to get where she was. Where she is... Or was," Frankie said, getting visibly upset. "I promised I would never tell anyone. I only found out when Chloe came to the lodge looking for her."

"Of course, Frankie. Your discretion is guaranteed, as always. Do you know why Chloe was looking for Nikita?" Curtis inquired.

"Nikita didn't give me all the details, but from what I gathered, Nikita had a reputation out there. She was known as the 'momma' of the group, always looking out for the other girls, ensuring they had clean supplies and such," Frankie revealed. "Chloe mentioned that there was a new man in town who offered drugs in exchange for services, with a value much higher than what they would usually get in cash. But she was skeptical, thinking it was too good to be true."

"Thank you, Frankie. Do you have any more information about the situation?" Curtis asked.

At this point, Jeffrey's eyes widened with disbelief at the connection they had just made between the two women.

"Not specifically about Chloe, but I know that once a month, Nikita would go to a park—I think it was Crowhurst, but I'm not entirely sure. She would bring food, brush the girls' hair, take care of them, and ensure they were okay," Frankie said before pausing abruptly. Curtis looked at her encouragingly. "One of the girls mentioned that a new man had been acting inappropriately with them, and Nikita suspected it was the same man Chloe was talking about."

"I know it's a long shot, but do you happen to know the name of this man?" Curtis inquired.

"I do, actually. The girls called him Eddie, but that probably didn't mean much. Nikita told me that clients often used fake names to protect their identity and avoid being blackmailed," Frankie revealed, now sobbing. "I'm sorry, but I really need to get back to work. I only have a ten-minute break, and I've already been gone for ages."

"Thank you so much for your help, Frankie. We appreciate everything you've told us today. We'll handle this with complete discretion and hopefully get to the bottom of it," Curtis replied, feeling a sense of sadness at the impact all of this was having on so many people.

Jeffrey pondered, his voice brimming with intrigue. "Do you think Nikita suspected this 'Eddie'?"

"It's definitely possible. If she stumbled on something related to their disappearances, it would make sense for him to want to get rid of her," Curtis replied.

"This case just keeps getting stranger by the moment," Jeffrey mused.

"You're telling me! You got that right for sure!" Laughed Curtis.

"Assuming 'Eddie' isn't a commonly used alias, it's reasonable to consider the possibility that Harlow could be this Eddie character," Jeffrey suggested.

"I agree, especially since we've linked him to Chloe, Gabriella, and Sophie. But how did he know Jemma Anderson?" Curtis pondered.

"Based on what you've told me, we know Jemma was involved with a mystery married man. She had a falling out with him, and..." Jeffrey began, but Curtis interrupted.

"And one thing I almost forgot until now is that I asked Harlow for Jemma's phone records, but all he gave me was Nikita's number. She clearly wanted to tell me something, but before she could, she was killed," Curtis stated.

"That's bizarre. If Nikita had information on Harlow/Eddie, why would he give you, her number? Unless..." Jeffrey trailed off.

"Unless what?" Curtis questioned.

"Unless he had always planned to kill her and wanted you to feel responsible for it in some way," Jeffrey pondered.

"Hmm, who knows what goes through his head? He was certainly keen on me stepping back from the investigation. In fact, he explicitly told me to do so when Devonshire announced his move to Florida," Curtis recounted. "But I still wonder about Jessica Stones. She was killed fifteen years ago, yet you're convinced she's connected to these disappearances."

"I have a strong feeling, Curtis. Call it journalistic intuition if you will.

There's something that just doesn't add up there," Jeffrey asserted, his voice filled with conviction.

Later that evening, a thought struck Curtis. Although the committee meeting was no longer happening, he believed that Devonshire might be willing to share information if approached correctly.

Deciding to take a chance, Curtis dialed Devonshire's number, feeling relieved when he answered after a few rings.

"Hello, Curtis. How can I assist you? I heard the good news about Barrington's capture. Well done, old chap," Devonshire greeted warmly.

"Ah, yes, great news indeed. I was just wondering; how did you first meet Harlow?"

Curtis cautiously inquired, unsure of how far he could push. "Always curious, aren't you, Curtis? Well, when I was working on the Jessica Jones case, or rather, my Jessica, as you now know, Harlow was right by my side. Truth be told, I couldn't have gotten through it without him. We went our separate ways for a while and then reunited here a few years later, finding ourselves working together once again. But enough of the nostalgia. What's troubling you, my curious friend?" Devonshire asked, his curiosity piqued.

"Oh, I was simply curious. Harlow seems like a close friend, and I wondered if you two had known each other for long," Curtis replied, trying to maintain a casual tone.

"Is there something else, Curtis? I'm quite busy at the moment," Devonshire interjected, his tone indicating a hint of impatience.

"Yes, actually. Do you happen to know where Jessica Stones' mother lives?" Curtis asked, hoping to uncover another lead.

"I do, in fact. She still lives in the same place she did fifteen years ago. She couldn't bring herself to part with Jessica's childhood bedroom, so she stayed there all these years. You know, we tried everything to solve that case, exhausted every avenue, and pursued every lead, but... Well... We came up empty handed. To be honest, there was absolutely nothing," Devonshire revealed, his voice tinged with sadness.

"Alright, thank you for the information, my friend. I hope you're enjoying Florida. That's all for now. Goodbye," Curtis bid farewell before ending the call.

"Are you planning to do what I think you're going to do?" Katherine asked, curiosity evident on her face.

"Oh, love, I didn't realize you could hear me. Sorry, did I disturb you?" Curtis asked gently.

"Not at all. In fact, I think visiting Jessica's mother might not be a bad idea," Katherine chimed in.

"Well, well, you never cease to amaze me, Katherine Styles," Curtis playfully remarked.

Katherine laughed, "Well, Mr. Styles, I aim to please."

The sun hung high in the sky, casting its radiant light upon the frosted green pastures. Even the gloomiest place seemed to shimmer with brightness under its warm glow. Curtis stood at 31095 Glenville Drive; a place that had been haunted by sorrow for fifteen long years. He took a deep breath, preparing himself to knock on the door. Uncertain of what he would say, he knew he had to gather his courage and face the inevitable.

Though he felt a twinge of unease without Jeffrey by his side, Curtis had been on this emotional roller coaster countless times before. He had spoken with grieving families, offering them a glimmer of hope for justice. But this time was different. This time, he carried the potential to reopen old wounds, dredging up the heartache of Jessica's loss and overwhelming their minds once again.

Curtis rapped gently on the door, four soft knocks, and waited anxiously for a response. After a few moments, an elderly woman opened the door, her face weathered with age. "Hello, can I help you?" She inquired.

"Hi, I hope so. Are you Priscilla Stones, Jessica Stones' mother?" Curtis asked, his voice filled with both empathy and determination.

Priscilla eyed him suspiciously, scanning him from head to toe. "Yes, I am. Who's asking?" She replied cautiously.

"I'm Curtis Styles, an investigative journalist and a friend of Kent Devonshire. I've come here hoping to gather some information about Jessica that might help us finally understand what happened to her," Curtis explained, trying to maintain his composure.

Priscilla hesitated for a moment, then murmured, "Well, I already told Devonshire and the police everything I knew fifteen years ago. But I suppose you can come inside if you think you can help."

Stepping over the threshold, Curtis was taken aback by the interior of the house. While the exterior had an air of charm and delicacy, the inside felt frozen in time, neglected and dated. It was as if nobody had lived there for ages.

Suppressing his initial judgment, Curtis followed Priscilla inside, forcing a smile as he navigated through the cluttered hallway. "Sorry for the mess. I haven't had the energy to tidy up for quite a while," Priscilla apologized, her embarrassment evident.

"Don't worry about it. I hardly even noticed," Curtis replied, concealing the truth as he found a seat in the crowded sitting room.

"Can I ask you a few questions about Jessica?" Curtis inquired gently.

Priscilla nodded, a mix of weariness and guardedness in her eyes. "Of course, you can. Ask away. But I must warn you, my memory isn't what it used to be. And I'm certain I told the police everything I knew about Jess."

"According to the records, Jessica was meeting a friend the night she went missing. Is that correct?" Curtis began.

Priscilla sighed; her voice tinged with sadness. "Yes, she received a text and hurried outside. We don't know where she went exactly, but she was found close to home, so she couldn't have gone very far."

"Understood. And was she involved with anyone romantically at the time of her tragic death?" Curtis probed further.

"It's alright, you can say 'murdered.' I've grown accustomed to hearing it by now. But to answer your question, we don't know. Have you spoken to Kara at all?" Priscilla inquired.

"Who is Kara?" Curtis asked, intrigued.

"Kara was her best friend, her confidante. If anyone would know, it would be her. Jess and I were close, but she probably wouldn't have shared that kind of information with me. Especially after what happened when she was younger," Priscilla revealed.

Curiosity piqued; Curtis pressed for more details. "I'm sorry, what happened when she was younger?"

Priscilla took a deep breath, a mix of sorrow and strength in her voice. "We worked tirelessly with certain journalists, Devonshire and me, to ensure it never became public knowledge. But when her father, technically her stepfather, but he was always her dad, passed away, she struggled to cope. It led her down a troubled path, you might say."

Curtis felt a knot in his stomach as he broached a sensitive topic. "Priscilla, I know this is difficult, and I wouldn't ask if I didn't think it was relevant. Did Jessica ever get involved with substance abuse or drugs? And was she involved in any kind of transactional relationships?"

Priscilla met Curtis' gaze, her eyes filled with a mixture of pain and understanding. "It's okay, you can ask. Yes, she did. When she was around fifteen or sixteen, she turned to drugs as a way to escape the harsh reality of her surroundings after losing her stepfather."

"Thank you, Priscilla. You've been a tremendous help. I truly believe this information could be relevant to finally uncovering the truth. Could you provide me with Kara's address if you still, have it?" Curtis requested; his gratitude evident.

"I truly hope so too. And yes, I have her address. We still correspond occasionally. She sends me birthday and Christmas cards. Let me retrieve it for you," Priscilla said, rising slowly from her seat. Moments later, she returned with a piece of paper, placing it in Curtis' hands.

Curtis returned to his car and entered Kara's address into the navigation system. Thankfully, it was a mere three miles away. He decided that while he was in the area, he would visit her, hoping she held the key to unraveling the mysteries that haunted Jessica's untimely demise.

"A petite, plump girl swung open the door, her face lighting up with a wide grin. "Hello, can I assist you?"

"Yes, I just spoke to Priscilla Stones, and she directed me to you... I'm investigating what happened to Jessica, and she thought you might be able to provide some help. I believe you're Kara," stated Curtis.

The smile vanished from Kara's face, replaced by an angry grimace. "You police are useless. You let Jessica down when she needed you the most."

"No, no. I'm not a police officer. I'm more of an investigator, and I genuinely believe there's still hope in uncovering what happened to Jessica," reassured Curtis, starting to feel that this visit might be a waste of time.

To his surprise, Kara stepped aside and held the door open. "First door to the right." Although still angry, Kara seemed to have mellowed slightly upon learning that Curtis wasn't associated with the police. "So, what do you want to know?"

"I spoke with Priscilla, and she mentioned Jessica's history of drug use," cautiously began Curtis.

"Yes, that's how we met. We were both using together, and we managed to get clean for almost two years until Jess suddenly relapsed," Kara explained, sadness replacing her earlier scowl. "She was doing so well, but somehow, she succumbed, and her demons took control again."

"I understand, and that must have been incredibly difficult for both of you. I know this is a personal question, but do you happen to know if Jessica was involved with anyone or if she engaged in activities to obtain drugs?" Curtis asked, choosing his words carefully.

"Well, I don't think she was involved with anyone, but considering her drug use, I wouldn't be surprised if she resorted to that again. Drugs are expensive, you know," replied Kara.

"I understand that sometimes people do things that are out of character for them, but it's what they feel they have to do to get by. Do you know if she had anyone looking out for her out there?" Curtis inquired.

"As I said, I'm not sure if she was involved again, but signs were pointing in that direction," suggested Kara.

"What signs, if I may ask?" Pressed Curtis, curious to uncover more.

"Well, she always seemed to have a constant supply of drugs. I mean, it was never ending. There was no way she could afford it just by working her day job, and expensive gifts would appear without her seemingly going shopping. I did tell a police officer about all this, but he dismissed it, saying it probably wasn't relevant and that tarnishing her reputation would discourage people from coming forward with information about her. It's truly sad," Kara revealed.

"It is indeed very sad. Do you happen to remember which police officer you spoke to?" Curtis asked, his curiosity burning.

"I'm sorry, but it was a long time ago. All I remember is that he was huge, not just big, but enormous. That's all I can recall, I'm sorry," Kara apologized profusely.

Curtis, satisfied with the information, pulled out his phone and showed Kara a photograph. "Can you take a look at this?"

Kara nodded and examined the screen. After a moment, she said, "I think that might be him."

Surprised, Curtis asked, "How did you recognize him?" "How did you know that?" Said, Curtis.

"He was much younger then, but the resemblance is uncanny. I'm fairly certain it's him," Kara replied. "What does all of this mean? Why is it relevant?"

"Well, I can't guarantee that anything will come of it, but I have a suspicion that the person who harmed Jessica may have been someone she knew," said Curtis, trying not to raise her hopes too much.

"And the police officer?" Asked Kara.

"Just a hunch. It's something I need to follow up on, that's all," said Curtis, brushing off the question. "Thank you for all your help, but I really must be going now." Curtis stood up, placing his hands on his knees.

"Please keep me updated, will you?" Asked Kara kindly.

"Of course, both you and Priscilla. And by the way, I think it's great that the two of you stay in contact," said Curtis before leaving the house and heading back to his car.

Once inside the car, Curtis dialed Jeffrey's number. "Jeffrey, I think we have a lead. I believe we might have made a connection. I can't explain now, but I'll fill you in on everything when I get back," Curtis said before ending the call and embarking on the long journey back to the bed and breakfast.

A warm smile spread across Curtis' face as he looked up at his adoring wife. At that moment, he realized how incredibly fortunate he was. Katherine had not only given him two beautiful children, but she had also selflessly sacrificed her own career to take care of their family while he pursued his dreams. She had been his unwavering support throughout his career, always understanding of the risks he took and fully engaged in the details of his cases and the lives of the victims' families. She was truly one in a million.

In the afternoon, Curtis met Jeffrey at the bar of Stables Lodge. He sat with a glass of wine, observing the birds outside the window when Jeffrey joined him.

After ordering their drinks, Curtis delved into the events that occurred during his visit to Jessica Stone's mother and best friend. Jeffrey's face lit up with recognition. "Ah, Kara, now that's a blast from the past."

Surprised, Curtis asked, "You know her?"

Jeffrey hesitated for a moment before deciding to be transparent. "Well, yes. I should tell you the truth now."

Curtis nodded, appreciating the honesty. "Yes, please do."

Jeffrey took a deep breath. "Kara and I had a connection for a while. We both engaged in destructive behaviors together. While I did cross paths with Jessica Jones, it was Kara who I grew close to. But I eventually got clean and realized I couldn't be a part of that life anymore, so I had to create distance between us. When everything happened with Jessica, I got involved and tried to find out what had happened to her for Kara's sake. I always wished we could have rekindled our relationship, but I believe at the time, she had too much going on, and we would have been triggers for each other's relapses."

Curtis sipped his wine, slightly taken aback. "I didn't see that coming, I must admit. So, you knew Jessica worked as a prostitute?"

Jeffrey shook his head. "No, I had no idea until you told me. But honestly, during that time, I was often out of it and unaware of what was happening around me. It's not surprising, though. Many drug users turn to prostitution as a means to support their habits."

Curtis couldn't resist teasing. "And I haven't even told you the best part yet. When Kara mentioned she had spoken to a police officer about all this, I showed her a photograph, and she was quite certain it was him."

Suspense filled the air as Jeffrey eagerly asked, "Well, who was it?"

"Harlow!" Curtis exclaimed.

Jeffrey grinned. "We're getting closer, Curtis. I can feel it."

Curtis chuckled. "Funny, that's exactly what Katherine told me this morning, and she's never wrong." His face beamed with joy as he savored the feeling of making progress in the case.

As they basked in the moment, Curtis's phone interrupted the tranquility, startling both him and Jeffrey. Seeing an unknown caller ID, Curtis hesitantly answered the call.

"Hello?" He greeted, hearing sobbing and heavy breathing on the other end. "Are you okay? Hello?"

"Is this Curtis?" A distressed young woman asked.

"Yes, it is. Who is this?" Curtis inquired.

"It's... It's Tiana. I don't know who I can trust. I need your help!" Tiana sobbed.

"Of course. I'll do whatever I can to help you, love. Where are you?" Curtis offered his assistance.

Jeffrey listened intently, overflowing with curiosity, as he could only hear Curtis's half of the conversation.

"Okay, give me twenty minutes, and I'll be there," Curtis replied before ending the call.

"Well?" Jeffrey couldn't contain his curiosity. "Who was that?"

"It was Tiana, Gabriella Atkins' best friend. I don't know what's wrong, but she sounded distraught and in need of help. Finish your drink, my friend." Curtis finished his wine in one gulp and stood up.

Jeffrey hastily downed the rest of his drink and followed Curtis to the car. As Curtis started the engine, Jeffrey could feel the vibrations beneath him. Both of them felt a sense of unease, uncertain about the reason for Tiana's call, but they had a hunch that something significant must have happened. It unnerved them that whatever the problem was, it was now arriving at their doorstep.

"Where are we going exactly?" Jeffrey asked, his voice filled with unease.

Curtis replied, his voice tinged with anxiety, "I'm not entirely sure. Tiana gave me an address: 3 Station Farmhouse, Station Road, 786431368. We have to park nearby, turn off the lights, and wait for her. I assume she'll be there, but I must confess, I feel a bit anxious about this."

The sun had set, enveloping the countryside in darkness. Curtis and Jeffrey had been too absorbed in their conversation at the bar to notice. The narrow, eerie country roads brushed against the car as they navigated through the darkness. Finally, the car's navigation system announced their arrival at the destination.

"Are you sure this is it?" Jeffrey asked nervously.

Curtis gestured toward a small layby by the side of the road. "Seems like it. I'll park there." Curtis pulled the car into the layby and turned off the headlights.

After a few minutes, Curtis noticed a short figure approaching on the road ahead. As it drew nearer, he recognized Tiana and flashed the headlights twice to signal their presence.

Tiana walked up to the vehicle and tugged at the back door. Curtis unlocked it, and she climbed inside.

"Are you okay?" Curtis asked, concern evident in his voice. "Just drive!" Tiana pleaded.

"Where to?" Curtis inquired.

"Anywhere," Tiana replied, her voice filled with urgency, while occasionally glancing out the window to ensure they weren't being followed.

Curtis pulled out of the layby, drove up the road, and turned left at the junction. Trying to focus on both Tiana's situation and the road ahead, he said, "You sounded really upset on the phone."

"I was, I am," Tiana responded.

Curtis felt a sense of confusion intensify within him. Tiana had called him here, but she was keeping her cards close to her chest, revealing little. "What happened?"

Tiana explained, "I wasn't planning on using again, but one of the girls I live with needed drugs. I went to Crowhurst Park, and Eddie was there. He asked if I wanted any drugs, and I refused, reminding him how his drugs had nearly killed me before."

Curious, Curtis asked, "What happened next?"

Tiana continued, "Well, he wasn't pleased. He started calling me disgusting, a disgrace, and said he was glad I nearly died, regretting that it didn't work." She took a deep breath. "Then I asked him what he meant by 'didn't work' and if he had tried to kill me. He just laughed at me."

Curtis and Jeffrey were shocked by Tiana's story. They exchanged a knowing glance, both thinking the same thing. "That's terrible, Tiana. Do you think he tried to kill you?" Curtis asked, his voice filled with concern.

"I wasn't sure, but then he got out of the car and grabbed my arms, forcing me into the passenger side. He said he was arresting me for prostitution," Tiana continued, her voice quivering. "Then it got even stranger. As he drove, he went on a rant about how Gabriella and everyone else were better off now, and how he was doing good by purging the streets of evil."

Curtis couldn't hide his astonishment. Jeffrey cast a sideways glance at him, their unspoken thoughts perfectly in sync.

"That's awful, Tiana. How did you manage to escape?" Curtis asked.

"At a set of traffic lights, I had a terrible feeling about Gabriella and what he was saying. I quickly opened my door and jumped out. There were many people around, so he couldn't pursue me. He tried following me in his car, but I knew the area well. I managed to lose him down an alleyway, and that's when I thought of calling you. You're the only man I've met who hasn't wanted to use or harm me, so I didn't know what else to do," Tiana explained.

"This is all terrible. I don't believe it's safe for you to go back home. He's a retired police officer, but his connections remain. It wouldn't be difficult for him to track down your address," Curtis conveyed, his lower lip trapped between his teeth as he contemplated their next course of action.

Jeffrey chimed in, "What if...?"

"No, I don't think Katherine would approve," Curtis responded.

"What?" Tiana questioned; her curiosity piqued.

Curtis inquired with concern, "Do you truly believe this is the best choice, my dear?" He waited anxiously for a reply. "Thank you, we won't be gone for long."

Curtis glanced at Jeffrey and nodded. "Yep, she's on board."

"Well, Tiana, it seems you have a safe place to go. You'll be going back with Curtis to stay with him and his wife," Jeffrey leaned over into the back seat to address Tiana. "I do wonder, though, what was this Eddie character doing at the park? Surely, he didn't know you would be there."

"He's well-known at the park, quite popular among the girls. He provides them with what they want and, in return, makes use of their services frequently. Gabriella had a high opinion of him, but I believe her judgment was clouded by the drugs he provided. He doesn't strike me as a decent person, especially now that I'm clear-headed and can see through his facade. I suspect that's what triggered his reaction," Tiana elaborated.

"I had a feeling," Curtis chimed in. "Alright, let's get you back to my place and fill your belly with some food to warm you up."

With that, Curtis turned the car around and headed back to the bed and breakfast. Upon arrival, he introduced Tiana to his wife Katherine.

"This is Katherine, my wife," Curtis gestured towards Katherine. "And this is Tiana. She's a friend of Gabriella Atkins and is helping us out."

The two women shook hands, and Katherine pointed to the table where she had prepared a full-cooked breakfast for Tiana's arrival.

"You can't go wrong with breakfast for dinner," Katherine joked. "My daughter used to love these."

"Thank you, thank you so much," Tiana expressed her gratitude as she sat down and began devouring the cooked breakfast in front of her.

Curtis then took Katherine to one side and explained everything Tiana had told him had happened that evening and how this Eddie character had tried to abduct her under the pretense of arresting her. Curtis also mentioned Harlow's reference to Gabriella's name, though it didn't yield much information apart from Tiana's evident discomfort regarding him.

Katherine listened thoughtfully. "Hmm, it sounds like he's spiraling out of control."

"I know, but we're getting closer, so close," Curtis replied with determination.

Katherine nodded understandingly, squeezing his hand in support. "I believe in you, Curtis. Just make sure you're absolutely sure it's Harlow before you start accusing anyone."

Curtis contemplated Katherine's advice and returned to the room where Tiana was nearly finished with her meal.

"Someone had quite the appetite," Curtis remarked with a smile.

Tiana's embarrassment flashed across her face as she put her head down. "Sorry," she murmured.

"No need to apologize. You needed to eat," Curtis reassured her, wondering if he had unintentionally said something wrong. "Listen, I have a suspicion that I might know this Eddie guy. It's probably difficult right now, but do you mind if I show you a photograph?"

Tiana paused, looking up at Curtis. "Sure."

Curtis retrieved his phone from his pocket, unlocked it, and presented it to Tiana, placing it on the table in front of her.

"Yes, that's Eddie. I'm sure of it," Tiana affirmed. "How do you know him?"

"He's an old acquaintance, someone I used to know," Curtis replied, not revealing too much.

"Is he really a cop? He threatened to arrest me," Tiana questioned. "Yes, kind of. He's retired now but can't seem to stay away from police business," Curtis explained.

"Please don't let him know I'm here," Tiana pleaded, her eyes filled with worry.

"I promise, I won't," Curtis assured her. "You'll be sleeping on the couch tonight, Tiana. I hope that's okay."

"That's perfect. Thank you so much," Tiana replied gratefully.

The next morning, Curtis was awakened by the sound of his phone ringing. He reached for it on the bedside table, answering immediately when he saw Parker's name on the screen.

"Hello, Parker, how are you?" Curtis greeted his son.

"Hi, Dad, I'm great. I wanted to talk to you about some information I found," Parker responded.

"What kind of information?" Curtis inquired.

"Well, you asked me to look into Tom Haddonfield," Parker began before Curtis interrupted.

"Sorry, son, I don't need it anymore. He was found dead a few days ago," Curtis interjected.

"I know, but I had asked some ex-colleagues about him, and one of them called me yesterday to say that a Tom Haddonfield had rented an apartment from him in Montpelier a few days before," Parker explained.

"But that's not possible," Curtis replied, taken aback.

"I thought the same since I read about Haddonfield's murder. Anyway, I asked him to send me the CCTV footage from the office building they co-owned, and he sent it over," Parker continued.

"Interesting, go on," Curtis urged.

"Well, there are plenty of pictures of Haddonfield on the internet, and when I compared them to the CCTV footage, it's not him. I'm certain of it. I've attached a still image of the mystery man from the cameras and sent it to your email. I don't know if it's helpful, but it struck me as odd—someone pretending to be a dead man just to rent an office. It doesn't sit right with me," Parker speculated.

"Oh, God, you've inherited the keen eye of suspicion from your old man, haven't you, son?" Curtis playfully remarked a hint of pride in his voice. After a brief chat, they ended the call, and Curtis opened his email on his phone.

Curtis exclaimed, "Aha!" The man posing as Haddonfield in Montpelier was, in fact, Lyndon Whiteford. This revelation led Curtis to ponder why Whiteford was present and whether he could still be tied to Annie Soles' disappearance. As Curtis revisited the specifics of Annie's case, he started considering the possibility that her vanishing might be linked to this area, rather than Montpelier. Despite law enforcement solving four other missing women's cases, Annie's remained unresolved and unrelated, a fact that struck Curtis as quite unusual.

"So, let me get this straight," Jeffrey said, trying to grasp the connection. "You're saying we need to link Harlow to the Annie Soles case?"

Curtis nodded, a sense of determination in his voice. "Exactly. There has to be a hidden link we've overlooked. When I first learned about Annie Soles, I was given a pen drive that contained Lyndon's novel. Initially, I didn't think much of it, but as I read further, the novel began mentioning Annie Soles."

Curiosity piqued, Jeffrey asked, "What did it say about Annie?"

Curtis scratched his head, recalling the details. "Not much, from what I remember. It briefly mentioned her recovery from drug addiction and suggested that if she had connections to the other missing women, she might have been involved in prostitution as well. Unfortunately, I didn't finish reading that part, so I don't have more information."

An idea struck Jeffrey. "If we know where Lyndon is staying or visiting, couldn't we pay him a visit?"

Just as the two were discussing their plan, Katherine entered the room, accompanied by Tiana, their arms linked. Katherine spoke, diverting their attention. "Don't mind us. We're just going to help Edna with her gardens, aren't we, dear?" She directed the question to Tiana, who nodded weakly, offering a faint smile.

Realizing they were overheard, Curtis filled Katherine in. "Actually, we have a lead on Lyndon in Montpelier. Jeffrey thinks we should visit him."

Katherine's reply caught them off guard. "Sure, that works for me. Are you feeling alright, Tiana? You seem a bit pale."

Tiana gave a weak smile and reassured them. "I'm fine. It's just that I had a friend who moved there, and I've always wondered what happened to her."

With the matter resolved, Curtis watched as his wife and Tiana walked arm-in-arm. He admired Katherine's ability to show kindness to everyone, a trait he greatly valued.

Curtis and Jeffrey arrived at the Montpelier address provided by Curtis' son, Parker, at nearly noon. Curtis sought reassurance, asking, "Are you sure about this?"

Jeffrey, with a touch of nervousness, replied, "We're not left with many alternatives, are we?"

They reached apartment 78 and knocked on the door urgently. The door swung open, revealing a thin, exhausted-looking woman in her twenties or thirties with straggly hair and heavy bags under her eyes.

Curtis, slightly confused, introduced himself, "Hi, I'm looking for Lyndon, Lyndon Whiteford." Both Curtis and Jeffrey noticed the woman's expression change suddenly, displaying fear, panic, and uncertainty.

"It's okay, we're friends of his. Do you know where he is?" Curtis asked, trying to reassure her.

The woman hesitated before responding, "How did you find where I live? What do you want with my dad?"

Curtis and Jeffrey exchanged glances, surprised by her words. Curtis pondered, "Dad? Does this mean she's Lyndon's daughter?"

"He leased this apartment under the name of someone else, someone we're acquainted with as well, and that's how we found you. I promise we're not here to harm you in any way. We simply need to have an urgent conversation with your father," Curtis clarified, aiming to establish trust.

He continued, "By the way, may I ask for your name?"

"Um, Emily. Well, if you're friends with my dad, why didn't you just call him?" Emily asked.

"We actually lost his number, you know how he is, always changing numbers. But we really need to talk to him. Could you give him a call while we wait out here?" Jeffrey interjected.

"Sure, I guess," Emily replied, then forcefully closed the door.

Curtis and Jeffrey stood in the corridor, looking at each other. Curtis asked, noticeably shocked, "Lyndon has a daughter?"

Jeffrey responded, "I never knew that."

Both men remained in the corridor, hoping Lyndon would eventually arrive.

After waiting for half an hour, Curtis glanced at his watch and proposed, "It's evident that he's not going to show up. Perhaps we should leave."

Just as Jeffrey was about to agree, they heard heavy footsteps coming up the stairs, as if someone were running. Moments later, the door to the stairway swung open, revealing a sweaty and red-faced Lyndon Whiteford. It was clear he had rushed to his daughter's apartment, gasping for breath.

"L-Lyndon..." Curtis started.

Interrupting, Lyndon shouted angrily, "If you've laid a hand on her, I'll bury you myself!"

Confused, Curtis replied, "What? Mate, I would never hurt her, ever. I just needed to talk to you."

"You threatened me! I got the message loud and clear, and I stepped back," Lyndon declared.

Curtis looked even more perplexed. "Threatened you? I haven't, I would never."

"You handed me that envelope in the car, and your threats were unmistakably clear," Lyndon said, finally regaining his composure.

Curtis defended himself, hurt by the accusation. "That wasn't from me!

I was forced to deliver it, and I have no idea who it came from." Lyndon asked, "Then who gave it to you?"

Sensing the need for a change of subject, Jeffrey intervened. "Lyndon, why don't we go inside the apartment and talk? There's a lot we need to catch you up on."

Lyndon contemplated the offer for a moment, then knocked gently on the door. Emily promptly opened it, and Lyndon reassured her that everything was alright and that they needed to have a conversation. Despite her nerves, Emily placed her trust in her father's judgment.

"So, you're saying the envelope contained photos of Emily?" Curtis asked, seeking confirmation after Lyndon explained its contents.

Lyndon nodded gravely. "Yes, it had 'HER NEXT' written on the back. Initially, I thought it was from you, but now I understand it must be from someone else."

Jeffrey redirected the conversation. "Have you heard about Haddonfield?"

Lyndon's head lifted slightly. "Yes, regrettably. Penny informed me of everything—Barrington and the entire ordeal."

Surprised, Curtis inquired, "You spoke to Penny?"

Lyndon sighed deeply. "There's a lot of history there. Besides, she's Emily's mother."

Both Curtis and Jeffrey were taken aback, unable to break their gaze from Lyndon. They struggled to comprehend what they had just learned.

Curiosity got the better of Curtis. "But if Penny is Emily's mother, why didn't she live nearby?"

"Not that it's any of your business, but Penny went through a lot when Emily was born. It was an unexpected child, and by the time we found out about her, it was too late for other options. Penny had a breakdown, and I decided it would be better for both Emily and Penny if I moved away and took our daughter with me," Lyndon explained.

Curtis realized he might have crossed a line but still asked, "Does Penny ever see her?"

"No, she never has. It brings back painful memories for her. Sometimes she asks about Emily, how she's doing, but our relationship doesn't go beyond that," Lyndon replied sadly.

Curtis continued, "By the way, did Haddonfield know about Emily?"

"Most definitely," Lyndon confirmed. "I'm fairly certain that's why he ended up the way he did."

"You mean dead?" Curtis asked.

Lyndon nodded solemnly. "Yes."

Intrigued by Lyndon's confidence, Curtis pressed further. "What makes you so certain?"

Lyndon, looking for reassurance, inquired, "Curtis, can I place my trust in you?"

Curtis nodded, indicating his trustworthiness.

"Penny asked about Emily, and I informed her that I had received a threat regarding Emily, assuming it was from you," Lyndon explained. "Subsequently, she shared this with Haddonfield. He likely deduced it wasn't your doing and began searching for answers."

Curtis responded, "That's not good."

"Not good?" Lyndon repeated, his tone conveying the severity. "That's worse than not good. It's awful. I just want to know what he discovered that led whoever is behind this to kill him. It must have been something significant to risk eliminating someone as high-profile as him in this investigation. As for Barrington..."

"They essentially framed him, or at least that's what Penny believes,"

Curtis shared.

"I know, she told me everything. I genuinely don't believe Barrington would have killed Haddonfield. While he wasn't fond of him, he had started to warm up to him in the past few months," Lyndon said.

Curtis expressed his sadness, saying, "It's truly heartbreaking. But all this injustice only strengthens my determination to get to the bottom of it, even more than before."

"I agree, but you can't breathe a word about Emily to anyone. Not a whisper. Otherwise, I'm out. My priority is to protect her now. I want justice for these women, but Emily comes first," Lyndon stated firmly.

After absorbing Lyndon's revelations, Curtis found clarity in understanding his actions and motives. It all fell into place, as Curtis realized that Lyndon had been driven by a paternal instinct to safeguard his daughter—a sentiment Curtis could relate to if he were faced with the same circumstances.

Curtis exchanged a questioning glance with Jeffrey, tilting his head slightly, confident that they shared the same thoughts. Jeffrey reciprocated the look and nodded, affirming their synchronized thinking.

"Let me update you on everything," Curtis directed his attention toward Lyndon, eager to share the connections he had discovered among the missing girls. He delved into the revelation that Gabriella, Chloe, and Sophie were all involved in some capacity as sex workers, whether openly or in secret. Furthermore, each of them battled with substance abuse or drug addiction. Curtis proceeded to recount his visits to Priscilla Stones, Jessica's mother, and Jessica's best friend, Kara.

As Curtis continued, he unveiled Kara's belief that Jessica had a history of drug use and engaging in the trade to support her addiction. Lyndon, captivated by the revelations, listened intently.

"There's more," Curtis declared with excitement. "I read the novel you wrote, Lyndon. Or at least most of it."

Lyndon responded, prompting Curtis to ask, "Annie Soles, the character in your book, was also involved in sex work and drugs. Is that correct?"

Lyndon confirmed, "Yes, it is."

Intrigued, Curtis questioned, "How did you come to know about this?"

Lyndon glanced at his daughter, their shared thoughts evident as they simultaneously looked down, enveloping the room in silence. Both Curtis and Jeffrey wondered about the unspoken connection between Lyndon and his daughter, but neither dared to inquire.

Lyndon lovingly addressed his daughter, "Emily, why don't you go and make us all a drink?"

Emily quietly left the room, disappearing into the kitchen, while Lyndon prepared to share the full story. Curtis and Jeffrey leaned forward in their seats, ready to absorb every word.

"Emily had her own struggles with drugs and, well, other things," Lyndon began. "She was friends with Annie and knew her well. They both traveled to your area together and encountered a rather unsavory character. Emily managed to refuse when he asked them to get in his car, but Annie didn't. Emily called me, distraught, informing me that Annie had left with this man in his car and pleaded with me to come and get her."

Lyndon scanned the room, ensuring Emily had not returned yet. "Naturally, I couldn't disclose this to anyone. If the police found out, it would ruin Emily's future. She would be forever labeled as a drug addicted prostitute, preventing her from getting a decent job."

Curtis understood, drawing from his own experiences with his daughter. "I understand. But I have one question."

"Yes?" Lyndon replied.

"Do you happen to know the name of the man in the car?" Curtis asked. Just as Emily reentered the room with mugs of drinks, Lyndon skillfully redirected the conversation, engaging in small talk about the weather. Curtis took the hint and joined the discussion, both of them carefully avoiding the sensitive topic.

After savoring their drinks, Lyndon rose from his seat. "Well, it's time for us to leave, Emily."

Curtis and Jeffrey also stood up, accompanying them to the door. Emily embraced her father before shutting the door behind him. Curtis and Jeffrey lingered outside the apartment door as Lyndon began walking towards the stairs. He turned back and faced them. "His name was Eddie." With that, Lyndon resumed his descent, leaving Curtis and Jeffrey in astonishment.

Curtis's eyes widened, and he exchanged a stunned glance with Jeffrey. It was the same man they had been investigating. "Lyndon?" Curtis called out, uncertain if Lyndon had heard him. However, Lyndon didn't respond and continued down the stairs.

"Do you think it's the same man?" Jeffrey inquired as they drove away from the parking lot.

"I'm certain of it," Curtis replied with a hint of joy in his voice. "We're getting closer, Jeffrey. We're almost there!"

"Why are you so happy?" Asked Jeffrey.

"I'm happy because we are so close now, we almost have him!" Replied Curtis.

The journey back home proved lengthy but without any noteworthy incidents. They encountered smooth traffic and clear roads throughout the trip. Initially, they traveled along broad and expansive highways, which gradually gave way to slender country lanes as they neared the bed and breakfast.

"I'm home, my love!" Curtis declared as he stepped into the cottage. "Something smells delicious."

Curtis stepped into the kitchen and found Katherine by the stove, and Tiana was busy at the countertop, appearing to be baking.

"Right here, dear. We're making pie," Katherine responded, turning around. "You've been gone for ages. What happened?"

Curtis smiled, noticing Tiana's curious gaze. "I'll fill both of you in over dinner," he said. "I just need to change."

In the evening, Katherine, Curtis, and Tiana sat around the dining table, savoring the delicious pie they had prepared earlier. Curtis broached the subject delicately, being considerate of Tiana's emotions, as he began to narrate the events involving Lyndon.

He shared the secret daughter he had with Penny, her role as his "informant" connecting Annie Soles' disappearance to the local missing cases, and how Emily was certain that the last person to see Annie was a mysterious man named Eddie.

"That's awful, but in a way, it's a breakthrough," Katherine empathetically expressed. "Curtis, I'm proud of how you're handling all of this."

Curtis looked at his wife, gratitude filling his eyes. "Thank you. That means a lot, love."

Tiana, eager to contribute, asked, "What do we do now? We need a plan."

Curtis contemplated for a moment before responding, his tone cautious. "I'm not entirely sure, but whatever we decide, we must proceed with caution. We don't want the wrong people catching wind of our progress."

Curtis sat at the kitchen table, savoring a slice of toast slathered with jam when his phone abruptly began to ring.

"I think we need to talk," a voice on the other end of the line declared as soon as Curtis answered.

"Lyndon?" Curtis inquired.

"Sure, where should we meet?" Curtis asked.

"I'll send you the address. Let's meet at one o'clock," Lyndon replied before swiftly ending the call.

A few minutes later, Curtis's phone chimed with an incoming text displaying an address: 763 Brookview Avenue. He promptly dialed Jeffrey's number, providing him with details about the meeting.

Jeffrey's response was quick and affirmative, "I'm in."

With five minutes to spare, both Curtis and Jeffrey reached the designated meeting point. They revisited the information Lyndon had shared the day before while a blacked-out car silently glided to a stop behind them. Lyndon emerged from the vehicle and warmly greeted them before climbing into their car.

"I know we didn't cover everything yesterday, and I'm sure you both have many questions for me. Talking about Emily gets me emotional, so it was challenging to open up fully," Lyndon explained.

"I understand," Curtis nodded empathetically. "But I have to ask, what's the deal with the novel? Your associate handed it to me and said it would provide all the necessary information."

Lyndon chuckled and replied, "I was wondering when you'd mention that. When I started digging into the disappearances of those women, I couldn't take the risk of the culprits discovering I was onto them. There was a chance they'd figure out that Emily had tipped me off, and that could put her in harm's way. So, I needed a way to document my findings without arousing suspicion. When I found out that you and Haddonfield were already investigating, I thought my 'novel' could be a great way to share what I'd learned so far. I just wish I knew what Haddonfield had uncovered before he met his end. He must have been getting close."

"Lyndon, we know who Eddie is. We have witnesses who have identi-fied him through photos and similar situations to what happened to your daughter. She's not alone," Curtis assured him.

"I'll help you bring him down, but please, keep Emily out of this. She's trying to clean up her life and leave this chapter behind. Let's protect her," Lyndon pleaded.

"Message received loud and clear," Curtis affirmed. "What do you suggest we do? Eddie is a retired cop. We can't go to the police without solid evidence, or he'll know we're onto him and we'll be in his crosshairs. That's why I wanted to meet you today."

Wait, he's a cop?" Lyndon asked, visibly taken aback.

"That's what we've been trying to tell you," Jeffrey chimed in. "He's the one who gave Curtis Nikita's phone number before she was murdered. My guess is he's behind it."

"I wouldn't be surprised. It's always the ones closest to you," Lyndon mused.

"But we do have something he doesn't know about, or rather, someone," Curtis revealed.

"Tiana?" Jeffrey guessed.

"Exactly," Curtis confirmed.

"I hate to burst your bubble, but she isn't the most reliable witness, is she?" Lyndon questioned.

"True, maybe not in the eyes of the law. But everything she has told us aligns with our previous findings. She's just filling in the missing pieces," Curtis explained.

Suddenly, Curtis sensed a strong vibration emanating from his pocket. It was his phone signaling an incoming call. "I apologize, but I need to answer this," he said, tapping the screen to accept the call. "Hello?"

"Hi, Curtis. It's Devonshire. I think we need to talk," the voice on the other end announced.

"Hello, Devonshire. How are you?" Curtis asked.

"Let's cut the small talk. Why did you visit Priscilla? Why?" Devonshire demanded.

"Jessica's mother? I wanted to gather more details about the case. I suspected a connection between the local missing women and Jessica's murder," Curtis replied.

"Why would you think that? These women have disappeared, while Jessica was brutally murdered outside her own house," Devonshire retorted, clearly agitated.

"I know, and I understand it must be difficult for you. But I truly believe there's a connection," Curtis insisted.

Jeffrey and Lyndon exchanged curious glances, trying to decipher Devonshire's side of the conversation as Curtis grew increasingly frustrated. "Don't visit her again. Let sleeping dogs lie, okay? It won't bring her back," Devonshire grumbled.

"Did you know Jessica was involved in prostitution to support her drug addiction?" Curtis boldly asked, causing Jeffrey and Lyndon to be taken aback.

Devonshire fell silent for a moment before finally responding, "Curtis, things are more complicated than you think. You have no idea."

"Don't you want justice for your daughter?" Curtis pressed, aware of the concerned looks he was receiving from Lyndon and Jeffrey.

"Of course, I do, but I know it won't bring her back. It would devastate Priscilla if she found out..." Devonshire trailed off.

"Found out what?" Curtis inquired.

"Nothing. Just drop it, Styles," Devonshire abruptly ended the call, leaving Curtis puzzled and with a flurry of unsettling thoughts.

CHAPTER 13: UNDERCOVER SIGHTINGS

Curtis found himself while recounting his conversation with Devonshire when his attention was drawn to his phone screen flashing on the car dashboard. He hadn't noticed it vibrating since he had placed it there after the call. Glancing at the caller ID, he saw it was Katherine calling, but he decided to ignore it and continued talking. A few seconds later, the phone rang again, and it was Katherine once more.

"Sorry, it's Katherine. She's called twice. I need to take this," Curtis apologized to Lyndon and Jeffrey before answering the phone. "Hello, love, what's going on?"

"Curtis, Tiana is missing. We were talking about Eddie this morning, and when I returned from helping Edna Braithwaite with her pruning, she was gone," Katherine said, her voice filled with concern.

"Okay, calm down. Any idea where she might have gone?" Curtis asked, trying to steady his own growing worry.

"Well, that's the thing. She left a note, 'Gone to sort this mess out, going to CP.' Does that mean anything to you?" Katherine asked anxiously.

"One moment, honey." Curtis lowered the phone to his hand. "Guys, Tiana has gone missing. She left a note saying she'd gone to CP. Any idea what that means?"

Almost instantly, Jeffrey perked up. "CP? Could it be Crowhurst Park?"

"Ah, yes!" Curtis raised the phone back to his ear. "We think we know where she is, Katherine."

"Curtis, my gun is gone!" Katherine exclaimed.

"Your gun?" Curtis asked sharply, taken aback. "Why do you have a gun?"

"After everything that happened, I thought it would be best to be safe. You need to find her. I'm worried she might do something dangerous," Katherine explained urgently. "You have to find her."

"I will my love. Trust me, I will," Curtis assured her before ending the call.

"Crowhurst Park?" Questioned Jeffrey.

"Yes, let's go. I don't know if you heard, but Tiana has taken Katherine's gun," Curtis informed them.

Lyndon stayed quiet but swiftly secured his seatbelt, catching Curtis off guard. Curtis ignited the car's engine and swiftly steered toward Crowhurst Park. Typically, the drive would consume about fifteen minutes, but with Curtis's sense of urgency, they made it in just nine minutes.

"Where should we search?" Asked Jeffrey.

Curtis brought the car to a stop. "Let's get out and split up. Meet back here in ten minutes."

The trio dispersed in separate directions, each man breaking into a jog. Curtis, with a racing heart, combed through hedges and took corners in a desperate attempt to spot Tiana. A sudden realization struck him as he inspected behind a sprawling, open bandstand – Lyndon had no idea what Tiana looked like. Regrettably, there was no time to relay this information. A full ten minutes later, they regrouped at the car, their faces etched with shared disappointment.

"No luck?" Asked Curtis.

Both Lyndon and Jeffrey shook their heads, sighing deeply.

"Alright, let's get back in the car and drive around, see if we can spot her," Curtis suggested.

The three of them reentered the car, and Curtis drove around the park's circuit several times before stopping at a crossway in the center. "This is pointless. Let's park here and keep an eye out," Curtis decided.

Neither Lyndon nor Jeffrey disagreed, so Curtis parked the car and peered eagerly out of the window. With few people around, he hoped Tiana would be relatively easy to spot. Then a thought struck him.

"What if CP doesn't stand for Crowhurst Park?" Curtis wondered aloud. "This is where you met her, where she met Eddie. I can't think of any other place it could be," Jeffrey replied supportively.

"I suppose you're right. I just have a terrible feeling about this," Curtis said, continuing to survey the area.

An hour passed, and their hope was fading when suddenly Jeffrey exclaimed, "There! I think that's her!"

Curtis looked out of the window and saw what appeared to be a slender young woman matching Tiana's description. He was about to step out of the car to approach her when Jeffrey grabbed his arm.

"Wait," he urged. "Is that Eddie?" Jeffrey pointed at a small blue estate car pulling up beside her.

"I think it is. I recognize the car," Curtis confirmed, releasing the door handle. "What do we do?"

"Well, we can't just go over there. He'll know we're onto him," Lyndon reasoned.

"What do you expect me to do? Just sit and watch him take Tiana like he did with those other women? No, we must do something," Curtis protested.

"Look, they're just talking. Maybe Tiana is gathering information from him. We don't know if anything suspicious is happening. For now, let's sit back and wait. We can see her clearly, she's safe. If anything indicates she's in danger, then we can intervene. But until then, we wait," Lyndon suggested sensibly.

Curtis thought for a moment and then hesitantly agreed with Lyndon. Curtis thought for a moment, hesitating, before reluctantly agreeing with Lyndon. The three men remained in the car, watching as Tiana stood beside Eddie's car, engaged in an animated conversation. Darkness descended, and they could barely make out Tiana's silhouette illuminated by a nearby street-light.

Curtis couldn't help but feel a deep sense of responsibility for this young woman. She was only a few years younger than his own daughter, and he had developed a strong bond with her. Katherine had grown to care for her, and Curtis had found himself growing fond of her presence in the cottage.

Suddenly, the car's headlights flickered on, drawing their attention to the vehicle they were observing. Tiana walked around the back of the car, entered the passenger side, and closed the door.

Curtis panicked. "What do we do?"

"I guess all we can do is follow that car," Lyndon replied, also feeling the tension. "But let's not get too close. We don't want to spook him."

Curtis pulled out of the parking bay and began to tail the car ahead, keeping a distance of about eighty yards to avoid arousing suspicion. They drove down the main street, and then Eddie's car abruptly turned off onto a dark, winding country road with no streetlights.

Observing Eddie's car speeding up, Curtis pressed harder on the gas pedal to maintain pace. Suddenly, without warning, Eddie's car made a sharp right turn, disappearing down a side road. Curtis slammed on the brakes and reversed the car to pursue Eddie and Tiana. Curtis braked hard and reversed the car so he could follow down the turning in pursuit of Eddie and Tiana.

After managing to turn the car around, they followed the road until it led to a long driveway leading to a house. Frustration overwhelmed Curtis as he pounded his fist against the steering wheel.

"We've lost them! They must have taken a different turn!" Curtis exclaimed in frustration.

"What do we do now?" Asked Lyndon, adrenaline coursing through his veins.

"Calling the police is out of the question," Curtis replied angrily, dismissing the suggestion.

In the dimly lit environment, Curtis felt his heart quicken its pace. The sole sources of illumination came from the subtle radiance of a nearby house and the passing car headlights.

"I don't know what to do. Tiana is in danger," Curtis exclaimed, panic evident in his voice.

"But she has a gun, right?" Jeffrey asked. "At least she can defend herself."

"What? And risk being charged with murder?" Curtis retorted. "Well, technically, it would be self-defense," Jeffrey pointed out.

"Not helpful, buddy," Lyndon chimed in. "Besides, who do you think the police would believe? A drug-addicted prostitute or a respected retired cop?"

"You might have a point there," Jeffrey admitted.

"This isn't helping!" Curtis shouted, frustration rising. "We need to find her. We need a plan."

"Maybe we should return to Crowhurst Park and see if she shows up there again," Jeffrey suggested.

"Well, I guess it's better than nothing," Curtis reluctantly agreed as he turned the car around.

"Slow down!" Lyndon yelled as the car raced along the dimly lit country roads.

"No, this is a matter of life and death, Lyndon," Curtis replied, ignoring the warning and accelerating even more.

Ten minutes later, they returned to the park, now shrouded in almost complete darkness. Women strolled around, approaching vehicles, likely in search of customers. Figures with hoods lingered in the shadows, casting an unsettling atmosphere. Curtis secured the car doors, his gaze darting nervously across the surroundings. The area was bustling with people, yet Tiana and "Eddie" remained conspicuously absent.

"Maybe we should ask around?" Curtis suggested, his nerves getting the best of him.

"And say what exactly?" Jeffrey questioned pessimistically.

"I don't know, just ask if anyone has seen Tiana," Curtis replied. "I'll do it."

Exiting the vehicle, Curtis drew in a deep breath, firmly closed the car door, and walked toward a woman standing beneath the glow of a streetlight. "Excuse me," he began, "we haven't met, but I'm a friend of Tiana's. Have you happened to come across her?"

"Hello, sweetheart, looking for some action?" The woman replied, misunderstanding Curtis's intentions.

"No, nothing like that! I'm just a friend trying to find her," Curtis explained anxiously.

"Just a 'friend,' huh?" The woman remarked, raising an eyebrow. "I haven't seen her, but there are plenty of other ladies around here looking for a good time."

Feeling defeated and realizing that most conversations would likely go this way, Curtis turned around and walked back to the car. As he looked up, he noticed Jeffrey running toward him, panting heavily.

"Curtis, Curtis," Jeffrey exclaimed, catching his breath, "Tiana just called. I picked up because the phone was ringing. She insists on speaking with you, and she sounded deeply distressed."

Curtis swiftly reached for the phone and brought it to his ear. "Tiana? It's Curtis! Are you alright?"

Tiana's voice trembled as she spoke through the phone. "Something terrible happened. I need your help!"

Curtis, concern welling up in him, inquired anxiously, "Has he hurt you?"

"No, but I... You need to come. I was trying to fix everything. You have to come, Curtis," Tiana sobbed.

"Where are you?" Curtis inquired urgently.

"I'm down the road from Stratford Golf Club, I think. Follow the road past it, and you'll come across a field gate. Open it, and we're right next to Stratford Forest. Please hurry!" Tiana pleaded before hanging up, leaving Curtis with a sense of urgency.

"What did she say?" Lyndon asked eagerly, joining them outside the car.

"Get in the car. I'll explain on the way," Curtis said, hurrying back to the driver's seat.

As the car raced down the road leading to Stratford Forest, Curtis couldn't help but be troubled by a persistent thought. "It's strange that 'Eddie' would take Tiana to Stratford Forest; don't you think? Unless..."

"You don't think he took the other women there too, do you?" Jeffrey interjected.

"Well, Devonshire took me there a few weeks ago, and when I told Katherine, she had the same suspicion," Curtis revealed as they approached the gated field. "We're getting close now."

Jeffrey got out of the car and walked towards the painted metal gate, its peeling paint a testament to its age. He lifted the bolt, causing the gate to swing open, and then secured it again before returning to the backseat. Ahead of them lay the dark silhouette of a forest, unmistakably familiar despite the absence of daylight.

Curtis drove the car closer until he could discern the outline of another vehicle at the forest's edge. As they drew nearer, two figures became visible. One stood over the other, who knelt on the ground. Panic and worry coursed through Curtis's veins. What was happening? He brought the car to a halt, and he, Lyndon, and Jeffrey hurriedly got out.

Jeffrey placed a hand on Curtis's shoulder and said, "Be careful."

Ignoring the warning, Curtis quickened his pace and walked purposefully toward the two figures. As he approached, he recognized Tiana standing and Harlow, or "Eddie," kneeling before her.

"Tiana!" Curtis called out.

Tiana turned her tear-streaked face toward him, a gun clenched tightly in her hand, pointed at Harlow's head.

Harlow shifted his gaze to Curtis, wearing a look of profound shock. "What are you doing here, Curtis?"

"I could ask you the same," Curtis replied calmly.

"This isn't what it seems," Harlow protested. "This little twinkle has misunderstood. You really don't need to be here, Styles."

"How do you know Curtis?" An agitated Tiana asked, her voice trembling. "Answer me!" She shouted, waving the gun in Harlow's face.

"Okay, okay. We work together. He's a colleague. No, he's a friend," Harlow revealed.

"Is this true? Are you friends?" Tiana asked, her hand shaking as she held the gun.

"It's not what you think. I didn't know who he really was," Curtis assured her. "You can trust me, Tiana. I'm here for you. I want justice for Gabriella, for all these women, just like you do."

"Harlow, why did you bring her here, Tiana?" Curtis questioned.

"I didn't. I don't know. I have no idea why she's here," Harlow replied smugly.

"Enough with the lies, Harlow, or Eddie, or whichever alias you prefer, "Lyndon emerged from the shadows, standing just a few meters away from Harlow.

Harlow grinned. "Ah, Lyndon, Lyndon Whiteford. Didn't see you there, old chap. How's your daughter?"

Without warning, Lyndon lunged at Harlow, but Jeffrey managed to catch him in time, grabbing his arm. Curtis quickly joined, restraining Lyndon from further assaulting Harlow.

"It was you!" Lyndon shouted. "You threatened my daughter!"

Harlow looked at him and burst into laughter.

"But that means you were the one who took Katherine, the one who crashed into my car. You made me give that envelope to Lyndon," Curtis realized, his shock evident.

"I have no idea what you're talking about, mate," Harlow smirked. "But you should know by now, I have plenty of connections. Why would I dirty my own hands?"

Curtis glared at Harlow in shock. "I thought we were friends."

"You're the one who decided to get involved, Curtis. I told you to step back, but you just couldn't listen," Harlow began. "I have a great deal of respect for Katherine..."

"Keep her name out of your mouth. You're nothing more than an untrustworthy pig," Curtis spat, hoping Lyndon would attack Harlow.

Tiana interjected firmly; her voice filled with determination. "I'm sorry to interrupt your reunion, Eddie, or should I say Harlow."

Eddie approached the firearm defiantly. "Or what? What are you going to do? End up like your foolish friend Gabriella?"

A loud bang echoed through the forest, leaving Curtis stunned. Tiana had shot Harlow in the leg. Harlow writhed in pain, collapsing to the ground, blood pouring from his wound.

Tiana, still holding the gun, had a determined glint in her eye as tears streamed down her face. Curtis cautiously approached, but she turned, pointing the gun at him. "Stay back!" she shouted, resolute. "I came for answers and won't leave without them."

Curtis took a step back, observing the tense standoff. He glanced at Lyndon and Jeffrey, their eyes filled with fear and equal apprehension.

"You told me about your little sister. If you want to see her again, you better start giving me the answers," Tiana declared, her gaze fixed on Harlow.

Curtis, surprised, interjected, "I didn't know you had a sister."

Harlow groaned, clutching his leg wound. "It wasn't your business to know."

"Special needs, you said. Why? Did your mother not care enough?" Tiana taunted.

"Shut up about my sister!" Harlow shouted in anger. "No, it was my despicable mother's fault. She drank and took drugs when she was pregnant with her."

"What happened to Gabriella?" Tiana shouted, moving the gun closer to Harlow. "Tell me now, or maybe I'll pay your dear sister a visit."

"You wouldn't dare," Harlow spat defiantly.

"Try me," Tiana replied with a sinister smile. "Are you willing to take that risk?"

"She got what she deserved, a repugnant piece of trash. Someone had to remove her from the streets," Harlow muttered, his face turning pale.

"Tiana, we need to get him to a hospital," Curtis interjected, trying to maintain a sense of calm, though panic churned inside him.

"I don't care if he bleeds out. I want answers," Tiana retorted, her attention returning to Harlow. "So, you killed her?"

"I don't like to think of it as killing, more like a cleansing, a purging," Harlow replied, his voice filled with unsettling conviction.

"Where is she now?" Tiana demanded, but Harlow remained silent. "Answer her question. It's best if you cooperate," Jeffrey urged. "She's there," Harlow gestured toward the forest.

Katherine had been right all along. But why did Devonshire bring me here? Was it a coincidence? Was he involved? Curtis contemplated silently. "And what about the other women?"

Harlow looked at him and smiled. "They're in there, but you'll never find them. I made sure of that." He gestured back toward the forest.

"Alright, get up," Tiana commanded, pointing at Harlow.

"I can't stand. You shot me, remember!" Harlow exclaimed.

Tiana then directed her attention toward Lyndon, Curtis, and Jeffrey. "They can help you."

Reluctantly, Jeffrey and Curtis lifted Harlow under each arm, helping him to his feet. Lyndon stood nearby, teeth clenched, visibly on edge.

"Now, we're going for a walk," Tiana declared, her gaze fixed on the forest. "And you're going to tell me where Gabriella is, along with the other women."

Tiana led the group into the forest, with Harlow slumped against Jeffrey and Curtis, their burden heavy. They shuffled through the trees, Lyndon trailing behind, his silence raising suspicions.

"Take a left at the large oak tree," Harlow mumbled, guiding them toward a clearing. "Right around here."

Curtis reached his limit and released his hold on Harlow. He collapsed to the ground as Jeffrey struggled to bear his weight alone.

"These women... They were the scum of society," Harlow began, his voice strained.

"What? Like your mother? Is that why you hated them so much?" Lyndon interjected, his voice laced with accusation.

"Shut up about my mother. She was selfish, just like these women. They were weak. All they cared about was themselves. They only thought about their next fix—the things they would do. Selling themselves, giving away their most intimate parts for what? A brief high that would fade within hours, only to repeat the cycle the next day," Harlow explained, his condition deteriorating.

"We know about Jessica Stones," Curtis interjected, attempting to catch Harlow off guard.

"What... What do you mean?" Harlow inquired, surprised by the reference to her name.

"What I want to know is why you brutally killed her and left her outside her apartment. Why didn't you bring her here?" Curtis inquired.

"She was different. You wouldn't understand," Harlow replied cryptically.

"I don't think you're in any position to tell me what I do and don't understand, do you?" Curtis retorted. "Did he know?"

Harlow looked puzzled. "Know what?"

Curtis insisted, "You know well... Devonshire." Harlow chuckled, "What gives you that impression?"

"It's quite evident. Devonshire brought me here. It felt like he had something to reveal," Curtis explained.

"I won't say a word about Devonshire," Harlow replied defiantly.

Curtis then pulled out his phone, dialed a number, and placed the call on speakerphone. "Devonshire?"

"Hello, Curtis. How can I assist you?" Devonshire's voice sounded cheerful.

"I am with Harlow, and he said some things. I have inquiries regarding Jessica," Curtis stated firmly.

"I am unable to talk right now. Can I call you back later?" Devonshire sounded flustered.

"Harlow has been shot, and he's bleeding out. It's best if you talk to me now," Curtis insisted, holding the phone for everyone to hear.

C urtis it's a complicated situation. I don't think stirring things up is a good idea," Devonshire cautioned.

"So, you knew he killed Jessica?" Curtis inquired, surprising Devonshire.

"What?" Devonshire exclaimed, outraged. "What on earth are you suggesting? He helped her!"

Devonshire explained, "Following the disappearance of Harlow's mother, leaving him in the care of his sister, he dedicated himself to a mission of aiding working girls—those who were caught up in substance abuse. He played a pivotal role in helping them transform their lives."

Curtis looked puzzled. "What makes you think this?"

"When Jess went missing, he was devastated. It hit him hard. Then a witness came forward, saying they saw her talking to a man the night she disappeared," Devonshire replied.

Curtis pressed for more information. "And what did he tell you?"

"That he helped women like her, and on the night, she was killed, he was the one talking to her. He tried to convince her to change her life, to get clean," Devonshire revealed.

Curtis inquired with a curious tone, "What about her being killed?"

"He didn't know how she was killed. He saw someone with her, but he thought it was probably a customer. He did everything he could, but she was determined not to stop. I agreed not to reveal her lifestyle choices to her mother," Devonshire explained, his sorrow evident.

"And that's when you stopped investigating?" Curtis asked.

"Yes, I knew it wouldn't bring her back, but I could at least protect her mother from knowing what Jessica was doing," Devonshire replied.

"I'm sorry," Curtis said sincerely.

"What for?" Devonshire asked. "It was fifteen years ago now."

Curtis's tone became somber. "I'm sorry because I think I know who killed Jessica."

Devonshire's voice wavered as he asked, "What? How?"

"I believe it was Harlow, no, I'm sure of it," Curtis asserted.

"No, he was helping her, trying to protect her," Devonshire insisted. "I'm sorry, mate, but that's just not the case. I've been following leads, and it looks like Harlow killed the missing women, killed Jessica," Curtis revealed, realizing Devonshire was unaware and not involved.

The phone call fell silent, and Curtis could sense the gears turning in Devonshire's mind. "I'll kill him," Devonshire said angrily. "I'll actually kill him."

Curtis responded, "I believe someone might have already handled that, my friend. Look, I've got to run, but I wanted to make sure you were aware. I'll catch up with you another time."

Ending the call, Curtis turned to face the rest of the group. Harlow sat on the floor, head bowed down, tears streaming down his cheek. Curtis felt no remorse toward this monster, and the others seemed to share the sentiment.

Lyndon finally found his voice. He looked down at Harlow and asked, "What about Annie Soles?"

Harlow ignored the question, prompting Lyndon to push his foot against Harlow's wounded leg. "I said, what about Annie Soles?"

Harlow let out a scream of pain. "SHE'S HERE. SHE'S HERE TOO!" Lyndon removed his foot. "Why her? Why not my daughter?"

"I didn't know she was your daughter at the time. I thought she was just another working girl. I didn't know until I did some research on you," gloated Harlow.

"If she had gotten in your car that night?" Lyndon questioned.

"Then she would have met the same fate too," Harlow declared matter-of-factly.

Curtis was appalled that someone he had regarded as a friend could carry out such cruel and heinous deeds without a trace of remorse. Harlow embodied malevolence. Not only was he capable of committing such atrocious acts, but he also displayed no remorse whatsoever, devoid of any semblance of guilt or regret. He was simply, unequivocally, evil.

"Why Jemma?" Curtis inquired, attempting to rationalize the link. "I see the link between Chloe, Gabriella, Sophie, Annie, and Jessica, but

Jemma wasn't involved in that line of work," he added, puzzled.

Harlow laughed. "Jemma Anderson?"

"Jemma Anderson?" Asked Tiana.

"Yes," Curtis confirmed, surprised that Tiana finally spoke up.

"She used to bring us food, and blankets and tried to help us get out. Most of us didn't want to, but it was nice to have someone to talk to who wasn't trying to exploit us," Tiana explained.

"And you saw her as a threat?" Curtis directed his question at Harlow. "She just wouldn't leave me alone. She approached me, telling me what I was doing was immoral, assuming I was one of the perverts who wanted their services. I had to teach her a lesson," Harlow confessed.

"So, you killed her?" Asked Curtis.

"I only wanted to talk to her, but things got out of hand. I drove her here to have a peaceful conversation, but she tried to escape from the car. I tried to stop her, and she hit me. I panicked and ended up grabbing her by the neck. I didn't mean to kill her," Harlow explained, his voice tinged with remorse.

"And what about Nikita?" Curtis inquired.

"Nikita Marsh, she deserved to die," Harlow laughed coldly. "So, you killed her as well," Curtis stated.

"I saw her in Crowhurst Park. I spoke to her employer and found out she would be at The Stables Lodge, so I followed her. I waited until she came out, then I approached her just to talk. I wanted to explain that she had misunderstood me. She reckoned we were 'all the same' and that people like me were the problem. She knew too much and had information that could expose me. I couldn't let that happen, so I followed her in her car, forced her into mine, drugged her, and dumped her at the Salem River," Harlow detailed without remorse.

"You are a monster, and you don't deserve to live," Tiana declared firmly.

"I'm feeling really unwell. I've told you everything. Now, you need to call an ambulance," Harlow pleaded.

"We can't call an ambulance for him. He deserves to die!" Tiana shouted angrily.

"Tiana, I understand your anger, and we can't bring Gabriella back. But don't you want justice for her?" Curtis tried to calm the situation.

"No!" Tiana shouted. "He needs to pay for what he's done."

"I'm as angry as you are, Tiana. One day, I'll sit you down and tell you all about my daughter. But right now, we need to call an ambulance, we need to call the police, and we need to ensure justice for Gabriella and all the others," Curtis said calmly.

Tiana distanced herself from Harlow, gently lowering the firearm. She sank against the tree behind her, tears streaming down her face. "Alright."

Curtis swiftly dialed 911, urgently calling for both the police and an ambulance, marking the end of their journey and the beginning of a new chapter in their lives.

With a sense of urgency, Curtis promptly dialed 911, summoning both the police and an ambulance, marking the conclusion of their voyage and the commencement of a fresh chapter in their existence.

As they waited in solemn silence, Harlow's condition deteriorated, surrounded by a pool of blood. Jeffrey and Curtis, their own clothes stained, stood nearby, helpless. Tiana fought to hold back her tears and sobs, while Lyndon loomed over Harlow.

Time seemed to stretch endlessly until police cars, their blue lights flashing, arrived at the scene. Curtis stumbled towards them, but a chorus of shouts filled the air, and he fell to his knees as police officers aimed their weapons at him. Slowly, they moved into the forest, closing in on the group.

With guns pointed at them, everyone raised their hands, except for the barely conscious Harlow. Tiana, Lyndon, Curtis, and Jeffrey were taken into custody, their hands bound by handcuffs, while paramedics rushed to attend to Harlow's injuries. They have been led away, each placed into separate police cars.

The situation had taken a dire turn, leaving them with an uncertain future.

Katherine bailed Curtis out and embraced him tightly. "Curtis, what's going to happen now?"

"Thank you for bailing me out, Katherine. I explained everything that Harlow said, and they're searching the forest for the bodies of the young women," Curtis replied, a tear welling in his eye.

"What about Tiana?" Katherine asked with concern.

"She has been charged with attempted murder," Curtis replied, his voice heavy with sadness.

"Come on, let's get you home," Katherine said, her voice choked with tears.

Five days had passed since the events unfolded at Stratford Forest. Curtis sank into the couch, searching for the television remote. Katherine joined him, settling in beside him.

"Ah, it's good to be home. The cottage was nice, but it isn't home," Katherine remarked.

As Curtis turned on the television, press coverage of the investigation at Stratford Forest caught his attention:

"We have breaking news from Stratford Forest. Five bodies have been discovered, and the identities of these women remain unknown," the commentator announced solemnly. "The cause of death for all five victims appears to have been strangulation."

"It's so sad," Katherine said. "Any updates on Harlow?"

"Well, I have a friend who works at the hospital. It was touch and go for a while, but he's going to pull through," Curtis replied.

"Shame, really," Katherine responded.

"I think him dying would be the easy way out. He needs to face up to what he's done," Curtis said thoughtfully.

Two weeks later, as Curtis prepared for the day, he heard the familiar buzz of his phone ringing. After a lengthy conversation, he said his good-byes, and Katherine entered the room.

"Who was that? What did they want?" Katherine inquired.

"It was a... friend, Curtis replied." "Apparently, Harlow's court date is next Friday. He's facing charges related to the murders of seven women! He has confessed to everything but seems to think he's playing God with all of this," Curtis explained.

"God?" Katherine questioned.

"That's his exact statement. I'm not surprised. When he told us every-thing in the forest, he believed he was doing the world good, 'purging' it, as he said. Bloody delusional, that man," Curtis remarked. "And Tiana?"

Katherine asked. "Well, there's actually no proof who shot Harlow, so there isn't much that would have stood up in court," Curtis replied.

"Ah, yes, it was her court date this afternoon, wasn't it?"

"Yes, I'm sad we couldn't be there, but her defense said it was probably for the best if we didn't attend. Hopefully, we should hear within the next hour," Curtis said.

The next four days dragged on, and Katherine and Curtis sat beside the phone, eagerly awaiting its ring. Finally, there was a knock at the door, and Curtis leaped up, hoping it might somehow be Tiana.

"Oh, it's you," Curtis said.

"Well, that's no greeting!" Jeffrey replied. Lyndon stood next to him, chuckling.

Curtis gestured for them to come in. "Sorry, come in."

Both Jeffrey and Lyndon settled on the sofa. The atmosphere was unsettled, as everyone knew what they were waiting for. They engaged in conversation for twenty-five minutes, discussing Harlow's wickedness and sharing their thoughts on the case. They all agreed that it would be unjust if Tiana were charged and expressed their hopes for her acquittal.

Katherine asked if anyone wanted coffee when Curtis' phone started ringing. Curtis felt his palms sweat and the nerves creeping up on him.

"Well, answer it then, love," Katherine urged.

Curtis picked up the phone and raised it to his ear, listening intently. "Okay, okay, yes, thank you very much. You too," Curtis said as he ended the call.

All three of them stared at him, eagerly anticipating his explanation. Curtis took a deep breath, scanning the room. He focused on Katherine. "Love, she's free. Tiana is free. There wasn't enough evidence to prove that she shot Harlow or tried to murder him. The prosecution's case was torn apart by the defense, and she got off!"

Curtis leaped up, punching the air with ecstasy.

"That's great, friend. I'm really happy," Jeffrey said. Lyndon nodded in agreement.

"Well, this has been great, but I'm sorry, gentlemen. We need to go and get Tiana," Katherine declared, addressing Lyndon and Jeffrey.

They took the hint and made a swift exit, they bid both Katherine and

Curtis farewell and wished them luck with Harlow's upcoming court date.

Not long after Jeffrey and Lyndon departed, Curtis and Katherine embarked on their car journey to the courthouse to collect Tiana. Katherine harbored private concerns that Tiana might not be present upon their arrival, a fear silently shared by Curtis. As they parked their car beside the courthouse, Katherine noticed Tiana's mischievous smile a few meters away from the vehicle, her face glowing with happiness.

"There she is!" Katherine exclaimed.

Katherine had meticulously prepared a stack of waffles, placing them on the table alongside three empty plates and one plate piled high with toppings. The table was adorned with various accompaniments, ready to create a delectable meal.

"I'm truly glad you're here," Katherine said, directing her words to Tiana. "I'm immensely proud of everything you've endured. I know it hasn't been easy, but it's almost over, dear. You've come such a long way."

Tiana glanced up from her plate and offered a half-hearted smile. Curtis could sense that Katherine's comment, though well-intentioned, evoked bitter sweet emotions. It served as a reminder of the tragedy of losing her best friend to an abhorrent monster.

Curtis had initially pondered why Katherine had developed such a profound bond with Tiana. He had considered that perhaps it was just part of Katherine's nurturing nature, as she often extended her care to others. However, when it came to Tiana, it seemed to run even deeper. Over the past week and a half that they had spent with Tiana, Curtis couldn't help but notice remarkable parallels between her and their daughter. While their daughter hadn't experienced the tragic loss of a best friend like Tiana had, she had confronted her own set of hardships, including addiction and various challenges. Curtis didn't want to delve too deeply into Tiana's past, but he had a suspicion that Katherine held a wealth of knowledge about it that he wasn't privy to.

"It won't be much longer," Tiana whispered while enthusiastically savoring the stack of waffles.

"We will bring justice for Gabriella, and for everyone," Katherine reassured, her words filled with conviction.

"I hope so," Tiana responded, her voice carrying a glimmer of hope.

Curtis recognized that many people held high expectations for Harlow's upcoming trial, particularly the families of the victims who were desperate for answers. Discovering their loved ones had been brutally murdered and buried nearby had left them in a state of fear and longing for closure.

Despite Harlow's confession, Curtis couldn't shake his unease about the path ahead. Retirement plans had been supplanted by thoughts of Harlow's heinous acts. Curtis attempted to divert his attention but kept finding himself drawn back to the computer, relentlessly scouring the internet for updates. He felt an insatiable urge to check for any new developments, even though he knew he shouldn't. Curtis was well aware of Harlow's cunning and familiarity with the justice system, which left him skeptical about a straightforward conviction.

"Curtis?" Tiana spoke up, her voice timid and concerned.

"Yes, what's on your mind?" Curtis asked, lowering his glasses to the tip of his nose.

"I need you to take me somewhere," Tiana replied. "I could go alone, but I don't have a car, and it's quite a long walk from here."

"Alright, where do you want to go?" Curtis inquired, casting an inquisitive gaze toward Tiana.

"Please don't overreact, but I want to go to Crowhurst Park," Tiana revealed.

"Crowhurst Park? Why do you want to go there?" Curtis placed his glasses on the desk. "You're not slipping back into old habits, are you, Tiana?"

"No, nothing like that. But if there are others out there like Harlow, I want to try and help as many women as possible. Can we take them some food, talk to them, and offer our support?" Tiana requested.

Curtis couldn't refuse her. He looked at her and smiled. "Of course, we can."

After informing Katherine of their plans, she insisted on joining them. So, Curtis, Tiana, and Katherine set off that evening to Crowhurst Park, armed with sandwiches, hot meals prepared by Katherine, and flasks of warm beverages.

Arriving at the park, they observed numerous working women walking along the paths and approaching parked cars.

"Are you sure about this?" Katherine asked, her nerves apparent.

Tiana nodded, offering reassurance. Curtis knew that this was something Tiana felt compelled to do, a way for her to give back and help these vulnerable women in any way she could.

As the night wore on, they approached different women, their initial apprehension gradually giving way to confidence. Curtis could sense that Tiana struggled with the surroundings, as it brought back memories of Gabriella and her past life. Nevertheless, after approximately half an hour, Tiana regained her composure. She interacted with the women, attentively hearing their stories, providing hot meals, and offering solace during their moments of distress.

Curtis couldn't help but swell with pride for his wife. He had spent many years venturing into questionable environments to collect information and engage with sources, so this situation wasn't too far from his usual territory. However, for Katherine, it was an entirely novel experience. Remarkably, she navigated it with remarkable ease. The women regarded her as a motherly figure, readily sharing their thoughts and finding comfort in her presence. Curtis couldn't have been prouder.

Following a lengthy night at Crowhurst Park, they made their way home, sharing their thoughts about the experience during the car ride. Their consensus was clear - it had been an undeniable success. When Tiana proposed the idea of repeating it, Curtis couldn't help but feel a slight unease, mindful of possible triggers. However, any concerns he had swiftly faded as Katherine enthusiastically embraced the suggestion, her excitement evident.

It was settled then—this would become their new mission. Instead of seeking out the dark side of humanity, they would lend their support to vulnerable individuals, offering a shoulder to lean on and serving as their support network, hoping to prevent others from experiencing the same fate that had be-fallen too many unfortunate women.

CHAPTER 15: THE LAST LEG

T he atmosphere in the house had become emotionally charged over the past few days. A heated argument had erupted between Katherine and Tiana, fueled by suspicions of Tiana's relapse, leads to a tense exchange. Tiana eventually left the house, leaving Curtis and Katherine anxious about her return.

Hours later, Tiana surprised them with a respectful knock on the door, bearing flowers, and offering a sincere apology. Katherine graciously accepted the apology, acknowledging that she may have overreacted.

Tiana explained that the stress of the impending trial had driven her actions but expressed profound respect for Curtis and Katherine. Despite the earlier turbulent moments, Curtis felt that their bond had actually grown stronger with Tiana's presence.

As the looming court hearing continued to weigh heavily on them, they made concerted efforts to stay positive. Curtis noticed Tiana's increasing apprehension about the trial and struggled to find the right words to offer her comfort and support.

"How are you feeling, Tiana?" Curtis asked gently.

Tiana looked alarmed and quickly responded, "I'm fine. I promise I'm not using it again!"

"I know you're not," Curtis assured her, "but the trial starts today, and I know it's going to be hard on you. I just wanted to see how you are."

"It would be a lie if I said I'm completely confident," Tiana admitted, "but I'm trying to stay positive. They have the evidence, his confession. I hope he goes down for a very long time or life."

"Are you two ready?" Katherine interjected, entering the room. She was dressed smartly in a black velvet two-piece suit that complemented her shoulder-length curly grey hair.

"Ready, love," Curtis replied, and he and Tiana joined Katherine by the front door.

The three of them piled into the car and drove to the courthouse. After parking, they made their way to the front door of the courtroom, where they were surprised to be greeted by Lyndon, Jeffrey, and, to Curtis' surprise, Devonshire.

"Hello, old chap," Devonshire said nervously.

"Hello, pal," Curtis replied calmly.

Suddenly, it seemed like all issues had been resolved. They greeted each other as though they were old friends, setting aside any ill feelings. Jeffrey and Lyndon exchanged friendly remarks, and the six of them entered the hallway outside the courtroom.

"It must be this one," Curtis said awkwardly, pointing to a door sign that read, "Paul Harlow."

A court staff member summoned everyone to the Paul Harlow trial, and they quietly filed into the chamber. Taking their seats in the dock, waiting for the judge to speak. When the judge stood, a clergyman announced, "All rise," leading everyone to stand until the judge was seated.

Curtis knew the routine of a trial and court proceedings, but this case felt different. He was personally involved and more invested than ever before. After a quick summary, the judge called Paul Harlow to the stand. The chamber door creaked open, and Harlow climbed the stairs to the dock with a harsh thudding noise.

Harlow looked terrible—pale, unkempt, and as if he hadn't had an easy time in jail. Curtis whispered to Katherine, "Probably a lot of people he has arrested in there. Criminals don't tend to like cops, especially in jail."

"Shhh," Katherine replied, listening attentively.

The judge read the charges of false imprisonment and murder, and the prosecution presented their case. A thorough female lawyer eloquently laid out the facts, while Harlow sat in the dock with a smug look on his face, unfazed.

Finally, it was time for questioning. The prosecution called Harlow to the stand, and he shuffled up with the chains on his wrists and ankles jangling at each step. The prosecuting lawyer asked about the crimes committed against Jemma, Sophie, Chloe, and Gabriella, leaving everyone on the edge of their seats.

To everyone's surprise, Harlow didn't deny a thing. "I did what I had to do. Yes, I took them, and I killed them. They were selfish, evil vermin. I had to purge the streets of them."

The confessions and revelations shocked everyone in the courtroom, revealing Harlow's sick and twisted mind. When the prosecution summarized the evidence, Harlow simply nodded and smiled.

"Sorry, Harlow, but you need to speak up for the recording, am I correct?" The prosecution asked.

"Yes, yes, I suppose you are," Harlow replied smugly.

With a quick recess before the defense, Curtis was confident they would struggle to mount a solid defense after Harlow's admissions. Outside the courtroom, Lyndon, Harlow, Devonshire, Katherine, Curtis, and Tiana took a breath of fresh air. Tiana reached into her pocket, pulled out a cigarette, and put it to her lips.

Devonshire lit her cigarette, offering reassurance with a smile. Tiana thanked him and inhaled deeply. Devonshire then spoke to Curtis, expressing remorse for not realizing the truth earlier and starting the committee to uncover it.

"I'm truly sorry I didn't see through this earlier. I started the committee hoping to uncover the truth. If I believed for a second that Harlow was responsible, I would have reported him immediately," Devonshire stated firmly.

"I know, and I haven't had the chance to say it yet, but I'm so sorry about what happened to Jessica," Curtis empathized.

"I'm just glad we finally caught the person who did that to her. I can't believe I fell for Harlow's lies. It sickens me," Devonshire admitted.

After some brief conversation, a loud call for recess echoed through the court, signaling everyone to return for the remaining proceedings.

"Well, that was quick," Curtis commented to Katherine and Tiana as they got back into the car.

"I must admit, I'm surprised by how poor his defense is," Katherine replied.

"I feel hopeful now. I just have a good feeling," Tiana said, winding down the car window and letting the wind rush through her hair.

Curtis and Katherine initially found Tiana's behavior unusual, but they had grown accustomed to it during their recent car journeys.

On that evening, they savored a takeout dinner while relishing a timeless film, all while the Paul Harlow case dominated the headlines. Around eleven, they retired to bed, gearing up for their final day in the courtroom.

The next morning, as Curtis and Katherine were having breakfast in the kitchen, Tiana entered the room in tears.

Filled with concern, Katherine asked, "What's the matter?" Tiana, unable to find her voice, handed her phone to Katherine.

"What's on the screen?" Katherine inquired as she reached for her glasses. Before Tiana had a chance to answer, the contents became apparent to Katherine—a poorly informed article penned by a vindictive journalist who seemed oblivious to the intricacies of the case.

Katherine commented, shaking her head in disapproval as she read the headline: *"Attempted Assault on a Respected Police Officer by a Drug-Addicted Prostitute."*

After finishing reading, Katherine handed Tiana her phone and took off her glasses. "Don't pay any mind to it, dear. It's just a journalist with little credibility trying to grab attention by saying things that don't hold any truth. He's completely clueless about the real story. Just disregard him."

Tiana nodded, but both Katherine and Curtis could tell that it still upset her.

They made their way to court, where they greeted Lyndon, Jeffrey, and Devonshire as usual. Just as they were about to enter the courtroom, their surprise grew as they noticed someone unexpectedly ascending the stairs to join them—Penny, Haddonfield's former partner.

"Penny, I'm surprised to see you here," Curtis said rather bluntly.

"Well, he killed Tom, he got my brother arrested. Why wouldn't I be here?" Penny retorted sharply.

"Sorry, that's true. How is Barrington?" Curtis asked.

"He's pretty messed up. Since he was released, he's been staying with me. He drinks too much and gets into fights. But ultimately, he's torn up about Tom. He held Tom's lifeless body in his arms, knowing there was nothing he could do. So, what can you expect, really?" Explained Penny.

"That's... True. I'm glad he's out, though. I always knew he was innocent," replied Curtis, unsure of what else to say.

Much to Curtis' joy, they were called to enter the courtroom moments later. They took their seats, and the court proceedings followed their usual course. However, when Harlow was questioned about Annie Soles and Jessica Stones, everyone expected him to come up with an elaborate story. Instead, he smirked and candidly confessed to killing them both, justifying his actions as helping society by eliminating them.

His brutal honesty stunned everyone, but there was more to come. Harlow had clearly lost touch with reality. Curtis understood why his informant had referred to Harlow's "God complex." Harlow genuinely believed that everything he had done was for the greater good, showing signs of true delusion.

As the questions became more specific, Harlow provided exact details about each woman—how he killed them, where he took them, and why. Finally, only two significant questions remained.

"Tom Haddonfield..." The prosecution began.

"Yes, I killed him. He got too close; he was onto me. So, I killed him. And yes, I framed his brother-in-law, Barrington. And I enjoyed it," Harlow coldly stated.

Penny gasped loudly and began sobbing. Katherine put her arm around Penny, trying to comfort her while half-listening to the court proceedings.

"Nikita Marsh..." The prosecution continued.

Before the sentence could be completed, Harlow interrupted, "She was complicated. I never intended to kill her. In fact, I didn't even know about her past; otherwise, I might have killed her sooner. However, she had been talking to some of the other girls. She spoke to Chloe before she died. She knew who I was, she was prying too deep."

Before the sentence could be finished, Harlow interjected, "She was quite complex. My intention was never to end her life. In fact, I was completely unaware of her past; had I known, I might have taken action sooner. However, she had conversations with some of the other girls, including Chloe just before her death. She was well aware of my identity, delving far too deeply into matters."

"Did you provide Curtis Styles with her contact information and then proceeded to kill her?" inquired the prosecutor.

"I don't even need to answer that, but I might as well. Yes, I was going to kill her anyway after I found out she knew several of those dreadful women and was prying. But I wanted Curtis to think it was his fault. I wanted him to have a reason to step back from the investigation." Harlow turned to look directly at Curtis and laughed.

Curtis felt a wave of relief wash over him. Finally, he no longer blamed himself for Nikita's death. He felt a firm grip as Katherine squeezed his hand.

The prosecutor questioned, "What was your motive for killing these women? Why did you feel it was necessary to purge the streets? These women posed no threat to you."

Harlow calmly recounted his past with composure, explaining, "My mother struggled with addiction and resorted to sex work to support her habit. She left me to care for my sister alone. That's when I dedicated myself to cleaning up the streets and ridding the planet of these vermin," Harlow displaying no sign of remorse.

"Do you have any idea what it's like to be abandoned by your own mother?" Harlow inquired, his voice filled with frustration and hurt.

After a brief break, everyone reconvened in court for the final phase— the sentencing. As the charges were read, Curtis leaped into the air and exclaimed, "YES!"

Tiana sat with a proud expression on her face. Lyndon, Devonshire, Penny, Katherine, and Jeffrey all wore painted expressions of relief and contentment.

"I can't believe they got him!" Curtis exclaimed excitedly.

"I know, eight counts of murder, eight life sentences. He'll never see the light of day!" Katherine exclaimed, turning to Tiana. "How do you feel, love?"

Tiana let out a deep sigh. "Relieved."

Three months had passed since Harlow's sentencing to eight life terms. Curtis and Katherine were hosting a barbecue at their new house nestled in a tranquil corner of Stratford. The entire group was present— Penny, Emily, Lyndon, Barrington, Tiana, Jeffrey, and finally, Devonshire. Laughter and conversations filled the air as wine and beer flowed freely. Curtis, relinquishing his role as the grill master, enjoyed the company of his loved ones.

Tiana had found purpose in her life as a support worker for a charity aiding individuals battling drug and substance abuse. Although voluntary, the role carried immense responsibility and brought her a profound sense of fulfillment. She had moved into her apartment just two doors down from Curtis and Katherine but still frequented their home for dinners and gatherings. Together, they continued to lend their support to the vulnerable women trapped in Crowhurst Park.

Penny and Emily had managed to forge a strong bond, thanks in large part to Barrington, who stressed the importance of family after the tumultuous events they had endured. Devonshire had laid bare his affair with Priscilla and the tragic fate of their daughter Jessica. Through heartfelt conversations and a renewed commitment, he and his wife had rebuilt their marriage, stronger than ever before.

As for Jeffrey and Lyndon, Lyndon had finally completed his novel and, with Jeffrey's support as an esteemed journalist, had secured its publication. The book became an international bestseller, captivating readers in eighteen different countries. Inspired by their success, Jeffrey and Lyndon established a well-respected publishing company, encouraging women who had experienced trauma to share their stories with the world.

The group remained bonded in a bittersweet yet unbreakable way. Occasionally, memories would flood back, like a recurring nightmare, but they knew they had each other to lean on. They disregarded the speculations of journalists and conspiracy theorists, refusing to indulge in baseless claims that the missing women had staged their own deaths. They alone held the truth, the horrifying fate that had befallen Harlow's victims.

Curtis had reached out to Harlow's sister and was taken aback by the stark contrast between her and her malevolent brother. She possessed a heart of gold, harboring no resentment or ill feelings toward anyone. Curtis chose to maintain contact with her, visiting Montpelier monthly to nurture their newfound connection.

Though life required adjustment, everyone managed to move forward from the horrors associated with Harlow. The topic was not taboo; they openly discussed their lost loved ones, reminiscing about those they dearly missed and wished were still with them. An unspoken bond united them all, for each had experienced some form of loss. They had bid farewell to those taken too soon; their souls scarred by grief.

Despite the pain inflicted by Harlow, they made a pact—to cherish each moment, living as if it were their last. They refused to take a single second for granted, embracing life with newfound appreciation. The darkness that had clouded their existence dissipated as they collectively decided not to dwell on the past. Together, they confronted Harlow, ending the torment and anguish they had endured. Each moment of sorrow had served a purpose, and the days of struggling to face the morning were finally behind them. It was time to truly live.

Never could they have anticipated finding solace in one another, especially given the circumstances that brought them together. But one thing remained clear—they had united for a reason. They had apprehended Harlow, ensuring he could never harm anyone else. And with unwavering determination, they would make the most of their lives, for themselves and for those they had lost. They had succeeded.

ABOUT THE AUTHOR

Dr. Ally Simbert

Dr. Ally Simbert, an emerging literary voice, holds a Doctorate in Business Administration from the University of Maryland Global Campus. Despite his strong foundation in engineering and cutting-edge technologies, what sets him apart is his passion for storytelling. Dr. Simbert has lent his expertise to pioneering projects across diverse sectors and finds his true calling in weaving tales that merge technical  intrigue with human emotion. His experiences with prominent organizations in the defense sector have further honed his problem-solving skills. Now, he embarks on a journey to combine these worlds, bringing a distinctive flavor to the literary scene.